MW00462556

Where Are You, Echo Blue?

Also by Hayley Krischer

* * *

Something Happened to Ali Greenleaf
The Falling Girls

Where Are You, Echo Blue?

A NOVEL

Hayley Krischer

DUTTON

DUTTON

An imprint of Penguin Random House LLC
penguinrandomhouse.com

Copyright © 2024 by Hayley Krischer

Penguin Random House supports copyright. Copyright fuels creativity, encourages diverse voices, promotes free speech, and creates a vibrant culture. Thank you for buying an authorized edition of this book and for complying with copyright laws by not reproducing, scanning, or distributing any part of it in any form without permission. You are supporting writers and allowing Penguin Random House to continue to publish books for every reader.

DUTTON and the D colophon are registered trademarks of Penguin Random House LLC.

LIBRARY OF CONGRESS CATALOGING-IN-PUBLICATION DATA

Names: Krischer, Hayley, author.
Title: Where are you, Echo Blue? : a novel / Hayley Krischer.
Description: [New York] : Dutton, 2024.
Identifiers: LCCN 2023047002 | ISBN 9780593473511 (hardcover) |
ISBN 9780593473528 (ebook)
Subjects: LCGFT: Novels.
Classification: LCC PS3611.R5546 W47 2024 | DDC 813/.6—dc23/eng/20240105
LC record available at https://lccn.loc.gov/2023047002

Printed in the United States of America
1st Printing

Title page art: Los Angeles skyline © J Dennis / Shutterstock
BOOK DESIGN BY ALISON CNOCKAERT

This is a work of fiction. Names, characters, places, and incidents either are the product of the author's imagination or are used fictitiously, and any resemblance to actual persons, living or dead, businesses, companies, events, or locales is entirely coincidental.

To Melissa, for inspiring me.

But she never escaped my mind, and I just grew
Tangled up in blue.

—Bob Dylan, "Tangled Up in Blue"

Where Are You, Echo Blue?

Filmography

• • •

Slugger Eight, 1992
  Joey

Pollyanna, 1993
  Pollyanna

Holly and the Hound, 1994
  Holly

Stars Everywhere, 1994
  Pricilla

Holly and the Hound 2, 1996
  Holly

Emma, 1998
  Emma

Goldie

. . .

1.

In 2000, right after the turn of the millennium, I began my search for Echo Blue, who was the most famous child star of the late twentieth century.

I was obsessed. But you already know this.

I was covering the New Year's celebration at the *New York Times* because I wasn't talented enough to get a job at the *New York Times*. Instead, I was an entry-level reporter at *Manhattan Eye*. I was at *ME* because they were the only ones to give me a callback. This wasn't something I would readily admit.

I was twenty-two, and I should have felt lucky to have the job. *ME* was an institution, a respected magazine, a stepping-stone for *Times'* journalists and editors, but it was also a dinosaur sans the *Times'* subscription numbers.

I had agreed to this assignment because I didn't have any plans for that night, and I thought I could at least introduce myself to a few people. Except all the editors were drunk. There was no networking to be done.

Among the desks and offices of the *Times'* eleventh floor, a fancy dinner of filet mignon and shrimp was served by waiters wearing white gloves, while jazz from a live band floated from the brightly lit balcony.

Old white editors stood around their printers and desks in stuffy black-and-white tuxedos. It was like witnessing the sinking of the *Titanic*.

The staff writers huddled alone at their desks behind big-windowed offices, clearly too busy to participate—or at least hoping to seem like they were. I passed the office of Pulitzer Prize–winning columnist Siobhan O'Donnell three times, staring as she clacked away at her keyboard, until she threw a book at me and screamed to stop skulking around her door. I nibbled on a few shrimp, took a sip out of the engraved champagne flutes that read *01-00-00*. I snapped a photo of the incorrect date. Then a reporter who I think was on acid shouted, "Don't you dare take a picture of me," and hid behind a cubicle.

In the corner of the room there were three large televisions on a table turned to local news stations. No one seemed to be paying attention, so I inched my way over to one of the televisions and casually flipped the channel to MTV, where I expected to see Echo Blue cozily chatting with *TRL* host Carson Daly. They had promoted her appearance for weeks. Instead, a commotion had erupted, with producers on their mics, scrambling in the background.

Then Carson Daly spoke directly into the camera. "Okay, guys, it looks like Echo Blue can't make it." The studio audience groaned. "I know. Really sorry, everyone." Then he whispered to someone off camera, though the mic was still hot, "They don't know where she is *at all*?" He composed himself and faced forward. "I know everyone was looking forward to hearing from her—I certainly was—and I'm sure we'll see her soon. Echo, Happy New Year."

It was like an electric bolt jolted me back into my childhood, where I had locked up years of memories. Echo Blue hadn't shown up for her gig? What did this mean? I looked around for someone who was as alarmed as I was. There she was, her face plastered across the screen of at least one of the televisions. But these arrogant *New York Times* editors remained focused on their millennium cake and shrimp. These had been people I wanted to impress only minutes before, but now I judged them for their indifference toward what was potentially the biggest celebrity news story of the decade.

In June, Echo Blue had finished a stint in rehab for "exhaustion." Up until that point, Echo's life was a movie unto itself. Her parents were Hollywood royalty. Her mother was Mathilde Portman, who starred in the classic television show *Gold Rush*, and her father, Jamie Blue, was once one of the industry's most handsome and charismatic stars. Plus, Echo starred in six films in six years, one of them winning her an Oscar for best supporting actress when she was only fourteen.

I hate sounding like a tabloid, but for the sake of brevity, Echo went from golden child to messy ingénue practically overnight. That's when the trouble started for her, the kind of real salacious gossip that turns actors into caricatures. There was the emancipation (though she insisted it was just to get around child labor laws), the romance and breakup with the much older boyfriend. There was the threat of stalkers, many of whom—all male—she reportedly took out restraining orders against. There was the rumored shoplifting incident at Bergdorf Goodman, though I never found a police report confirming it. And that messy interview with *Vanity Fair* where she openly drank a martini at a bar as a teenager. The *New York Post* headline screamed, "ECHO: HOW LOW WILL SHE GO?" I had followed it all.

But she was about to make a comeback—at least that's what the promotions for her New Year's appearance declared. She was embarking on an independent film, *I Hate Camp*. She was clean and had cut ties with the bad-boy boyfriend. Why would someone who just got her life together not show up to one of the biggest promotional events of the *century*? Something didn't fit.

I felt numb and shaky, so I attempted to slow my breathing like my therapist had taught me years ago. It was time for me to get out of this boring party. For some reason—I blame my nerves—I did a contrived princess wave to one of my contacts and slipped out of the newsroom. I panted underneath the fluorescent lights in the elevator, trying to calm myself down, knowing answers would only come in the sour scent of the morning paper.

2.

My obsession with Echo Blue started in the summer of 1992, right before my sophomore year of high school, when she starred in her first movie, *Slugger Eight*. She played a twelve-year-old girl who joins a softball team coached by a cranky divorcé. It was supposed to be a girls version of *The Bad News Bears*.

My father, a Shakespeare professor at NYU who was always convinced everyone was screwing him over, spent the second half of the summer preparing his lectures, while my mom worked at the makeup counter at Day's Emporium, a small department store in North Jersey. My parents would drop my brother Sam and I off at an eleven o'clock matinee at the local cinema and wouldn't pick us up until five that evening. You could sit in a theater all day as a kid back then, as long as you bought popcorn and soda. We could've at least switched movies throughout the day, but I, and therefore Sam — as the younger sibling, he had no choice — opted to watch *Slugger Eight* on repeat.

This is the scene that hooked me: The practice had gone on forever, and the crotchety coach was showing no signs of letting up. Echo's character, Joey, crossed the field to the dugout with a swagger reminiscent of

Matt Dillon in *The Outsiders*, demanding they at least get a break for some Frescas. Echo, with her wild mop of blonde wispy hair and her tanned skin, her angelic cheeks contrasted with a shrewd stare. She had this habit of taking off her cap and shaking her hair out, roughly scratching her scalp, then carefully placing the cap back on. It was a move I tried to copy, but any time I did it, my mom asked me if I had lice.

Echo tapped at the dugout fence and said, "I don't care who we're playing, if you don't give us an hour to recharge, I promise you half the team is walking off."

She had a hardness to her and barely fidgeted when she spoke.

She was beautiful.

One critic called her the Norma Rae of softball.

I had never seen a girl in a movie be that dangerous or that confrontational. They always backed down to the older male figure or didn't speak up to him at all.

"You'll get back on the field like I told you to and you'll finish out this practice," the coach commanded.

She stepped out of the dugout, then whistled to the girls with her index finger and thumb. I only knew one person who could whistle with their fingers like that, and it was my father. (So he had some good qualities.) The girls dropped their mitts all at once and walked off the field, running up behind her. I wanted to swallow her whole and become her. She gave teenage girls permission to disregard society's rules, to battle patriarchal leaders. To take up space. To be bad.

There was me in the theater, barely a teenager, shy and subservient, and there was Echo on the screen taking control. That one scene took me out of my life, the one where I was powerless. Me with my fluffy curls and my deep stare that I couldn't help ("You want people to think you're weird?" my father would say), my used Doc Martens because my parents wouldn't fork over the money for new ones. I could watch Echo for as long as I wanted in that dark theater without anyone's judgey glares. If I could study Echo, learn everything about her, maybe I could be like her.

• • •

My father, and his difficult past, shaped my childhood. His mother, my grandmother, whom I never met, was a superstitious Polish immigrant. In one of my father's favorite abusive-parent stories, she tied his left hand behind his back for a week, trying to get him to use his right hand. She saw his left-handedness as a sign of weakness, he said, and never failed to remind him of this.

He tried to be different from his rigid mother, at least that was what he told us. But our presence irritated him. In the car, when we listened to old Beatles tapes, singing, humming, and snapping were forbidden. Sam and I would sit, hands folded, nodding our heads to the beat. He hated a "ruckus." He never failed to mention the way we walked up the stairs like "elephants." The way we left toothpaste in the sink like "pigs." How we folded our clothes like "slobs." At dinner, he was irritated if we were too chatty or jumped around in our seats or used too much ketchup or crunched on our pickles too loud.

He started marking up my papers when I was in the fifth grade, and I'd have anxiety attacks in my room waiting for him to return them. *Structure lazy. Examples redundant. Rewrite from the top.* My mother would tell me he was just trying to help, but writing was his love language and it felt like I was getting hate mail. "Do you want to be a good writer or a shitty writer?" my father would always say. "If I'm not honest with you, how else will you learn?"

There were no belts, no slaps. But no compassion either. I think I became a writer not because I enjoyed it, but out of spite.

My mother was a strong woman with her own opinions. But she didn't like to go against my father. "It's important to pick your battles with men," she'd tell me. Or, "Your father always comes down hard first, and then he softens." She had a lot of sayings about appeasing him, which I cringed at. "Why are you always defending him?" I'd ask. But she saw his softer side, and she wanted me to see that side too. Her father was an alcoholic who didn't say much. She never failed to remind me of how lucky we were.

And she was right. My father wasn't all bad. I don't like to admit this, because it takes away from the hard-as-nails narrative I created, but I knew he loved me. Every night, he'd stop by my room to say good night, often dropping off a book he'd brought me from his university's library. But that didn't change the pressure I felt under his gaze, the feeling that who I was wasn't enough.

• • •

In those years, the hardest of my childhood, Echo felt like a kindred spirit. I memorized her lines in *Slugger Eight*. I practiced her stance on the field in the mirror. I cut out snapshots from *Teen Beat* magazine. I bought four copies of her cover issue of *Sassy*, the one where she wore a red cropped T-shirt with big lips smacked across her flat chest. I made a collage, carefully gluing images of her together, draped it with a heart garland, and hung it up over my bed. My favorite was the photo of Echo and her also-actor dad, Jamie Blue, leaving a restaurant, his arm slung over her shoulders, protecting her, the way I wished my father did.

In the shower, alone by myself, the heat stinging me, I thought of Echo washing off after a day on the set. What shampoo did she use? Did she have those flakes in her scalp like I did? Did she have rashy skin and red bumps on her inner thighs? "Goldie! What are you doing in there so long? I have to take a shower too!" Sam would yell and pound on the door, startling me so I cut myself shaving. Echo didn't have a brother like I did; she was an only child. She probably had her own shower. A huge shower with fresh towels and bath soaps that smelled like lavender.

Echo Blue was my only friend during my early teens because the boy-crazy girls in my grade intimidated me. They talked about sex and wanting to be fingered. Meanwhile, I still played with dolls. I was an October baby, and some of the girls in my grade were almost a year older than me. They had breasts and pimples and smelled like body odor. I only had sprouts of hair under my armpits. I had fuzz for pubic hair, not a thatch like I imagined they did. I wanted to make friends and I tried to, but I just couldn't connect.

That didn't stop my mother from making me invite the girls from school for a sleepover when I turned fifteen that October, after my summer of *Slugger Eight*.

"You don't have to have a lot of friends, Goldie. You don't have to be in a group, but you should at least have a person. It's not healthy that you don't have a *person*," she insisted. "We'll just invite some of the neighborhood girls, like Emma Branfield and Ashley Manley—remember you used to walk to school with them?" I hadn't hung out with Emma or Ashley since I was six, but it was clear I had no choice.

She urged me to take down the pictures of Echo that adorned my room for the birthday party, but I wouldn't do it.

"I thought you told me friends should accept you for who you are," I said.

She stared at my collage of Echos, her face in a worried pinch. "That's true, but . . . They won't understand all this, honey."

I don't know why I refused to take her point. It was possible I wanted to punish her for forcing me to have a slumber party when, really, I just wanted to bake myself a vanilla cake. I wanted to go to a restaurant with my father like Echo did. I wanted my mom to accept that I was different; I wanted her to think I was beautiful, funny, not awkward with terrible posture and food stuck in my braces.

Though my mom set up the party in the basement—decorated with colored sodas, pink balloons, and a disco ball—the girls eventually wanted to see my room. I underestimated Ashley, the queen bee, and how cruel she could be. "The last time I was in your basement was eight years ago, and I almost had an asthma attack because it smelled like mold." She wasn't wrong. The air was thick and heavy down there, and sometimes my eyes itched. Girls like her don't care if it's your house or your birthday party. They decide what you do.

Upstairs, Ashley looked around.

"What the fuck is all this?" she said.

"That's Echo Blue," I said.

"I know who it is, idiot. Why do you have a shrine of her on your wall? Are you a lesbian or something?" This was a very big deal back then, if you were a lesbian or not.

I didn't know if I was gay, but that wasn't the point. Ashley wanted an answer and nothing I said would please her. I could see the animal in the girls' eyes. They knew the smell of blood and they craved a sacrifice. They were seasoned mean girls.

Ashley stood on my pillow and peeled the large poster of Echo I had made off the wall. She didn't stop there. She went for the *Slugger Eight* movie poster. The black-and-white signed picture from the fan club. The *People* cover of her and her dad. The *Sassy* cover. The photos of her arm draped over Belinda Summers, her co-star, from *Seventeen*. She butchered the bedazzled collage of her smiling face that I bought at the mall, then picked off the dangling heart garland like it had cooties. Ashley ripped it all down and threw it on the floor while the others silently witnessed the horror.

Suddenly, my mother knocked on the door and asked if we were ready to eat pizza. Later, after cake, they all slept in the basement while I slept in my room—I guess the mold was preferred to my "shrine." I could hear them giggling until one in the morning. I'm sure my mom heard it too. Meanwhile, I stared at the images of Echo Blue, which I had quickly restored to their rightful places.

I went to see Dr. Watts shortly after because my mother found a stack of letters that I wrote to Echo but never mailed. In my defense, it was more like a pile of journal entries. I wrote to Echo like she was a higher power. "Isn't my closeness to Echo the same as how people feel close to God?" I said to my mother, thinking it would soothe her. "People pretend to talk to God every day. That's what this is."

She thought for a second, exasperated. "Echo is not a religion, Goldie. That's the problem."

Dr. Watts was young and lovely, and she had giant leather seats that I could twist my body into, but our sessions didn't change how I felt. She said my passion was a good thing, but she wanted me to redirect it. Join the drama club. Or the newly founded feminist club. Or the movie club. That was a way I could meet friends with similar interests—and people who could talk to me about Echo in real life so it wasn't all inside my head. But Echo was my security blanket. She was the person I created an interior life with.

Eventually, I learned to hide how I felt about her, to keep these dreams to myself, and when I got to college, I asked for a single dorm so I didn't have to explain myself to anyone. Seven years later, I was still isolated, but I had come a long way since then. Echo was no longer the focus of my life. But hearing that she had disappeared struck a chord, awoke something that had been dormant. And there was no going back.

3.

I managed to contain myself for a full week before going to the office of my editor, Dana Bradlee. Since Echo's New Year's no-show, there had been no legitimate news on her whereabouts. Some early reports speculated she was dead or back in rehab after a wild night. But if any of those scenarios were true, she wouldn't have vanished. She would have been found. I imagined someone discovering her body, like poor Natalie Wood off the coast of Catalina back in 1981.

But no. Echo never showed up anywhere, dead or alive. Seven whole days. One source said her father, Jamie Blue, was terrified for his daughter's life and he just wanted her home safe. Another source quoted her agent, saying, "Not to worry, Echo's totally fine." But I knew enough to know she was probably just saying this to calm the rumors. Echo was *missing* missing, and as each day passed, I convinced myself that I was going to be the one to find her.

I knew I was going to get pushback from Dana because Echo wasn't my beat. I wasn't a celebrity reporter (yet), and I didn't have a list of agents, managers, and PR contacts at my fingertips. But I was a hard worker. I took the assignments that no one wanted, like how the Fifth Avenue neighborhood was pushing for a Washington Arch renovation.

Or the demolition order by that fascist, Mayor Giuliani, of the elevated tracks covered in wild grass above Tenth Avenue, and how a group of locals was trying to save it. My biggest article to date was an interview with Jimmy Glenn, who owned the Times Square Boxing Club, on what it was like to work in the middle of a newly renovated Times Square (oddly, this was my father's favorite).

Echo's disappearance was finally a story I was invested in. One I was born to write. I just needed to do some convincing.

Dana was a young features editor and got the job at *ME* because of a series of blog posts she wrote about her life as an assistant at a big publishing house, earning minimum wage and living in a studio apartment on the Lower East Side. She accused publishing giants of nepotism (ironic, since she was Ben Bradlee's granddaughter) and said that all the editors were drunk. This wasn't such a secret—in the '90s, liquid lunches and expense accounts for upper-echelon editors still existed. But she was begging to get fired.

Her human resources department sat down with her, warning her that she would be seen as a "whistleblower," which Dana thought was hysterical, and so the next day she wrote about the HR sit-down. A few days later, she did a blind item on a certain editor behind at least three bestsellers who often fell asleep at her desk. Next, she called out a book exec who touched her ass in the elevator. The *New York Post* called her the "gossip maven" of the publishing world. Shortly after, Dana got a call from *ME* because they were looking for some younger editors on the masthead, writers who would cause a ruckus and sell more copies. Dana said it was all timing, but I thought she was a total badass. If anyone would understand my ambition, it would be her.

I knocked on her office door and she waved me in.

"I got another call just this morning about the *Times* millennium piece—not an email, a call—asking me for a retraction on the bit about the printing fuckup on the champagne flute. Something to do with this being a historical event. A whole week later," she said and smiled. She was far too polished to be an editor at a small magazine, with her severe bangs, her tight ponytail, and her thick black glasses. "Great job with that, Goldie. No one else got that detail but you."

She smacked the bottom of a pack of Marlboro Lights with the heel of her hand and told me to sit down.

"So what's up? What's next? Are you going to take down *Vogue*? Give me some good scoop on Anna Wintour?"

I took a deep breath. Dana was blunt, so I knew I had to get right to the point. "Actually, I want to write about Echo Blue's disappearance."

Dana looked perplexed.

"Echo Blue? She probably overdosed or something. Isn't this what happens to all child stars?" she said nonchalantly. "I saw her at Max Fish once. People were doing heroin in the bathroom. What a disaster."

I had seen a blip in the paper that she was canoodling with someone at Max Fish, but nothing to do with heroin.

"Don't you think it would have been reported if she'd OD'd?"

"Look, Goldie, even if something mysterious *did* happen to her, it won't be that easy for me to assign it to you. I have other entertainment reporters who are going to want this if it turns into something. For one, I'd have riots in the newsroom if I just gave it to you. Plus, celebrity isn't really my area. I'd have to pull strings to get you a feature like this."

I felt a stabbing in my throat. Every journalist needs a break. And after nearly a year at *ME*, I was tired of writing stories I didn't care about. Plus, wasn't Dana interested in more female voices? We were a week into the new millennium, and it was still mostly men in journalism interviewing actresses. Who could forget that Winona Ryder interview by Stephan Brody in *Rolling Stone* back in 1994? She wore beat-up overalls with no T-shirt underneath on the cover.

This was the lede: *Winona Ryder walks into the café thirty minutes late but I don't care, because this is the woman of my dreams. She's the woman of all of our dreams.*

Here we were, barely into 2000, and the news surrounding Echo's disappearance was weighed down by misogynist accusations like she was hiding a pregnancy, or that she had killed herself over a bad romance. Only one outlet went with the theory that she was kidnapped, and I'm sure, eventually, they'd find a way to blame her for that too.

If I got the chance to write a story about Echo, it would come from the heart. One of my old fantasies of walking down a quaint SoHo street with her, arm in arm, replayed in my head. I'd ask her about those times she and her father would play Frisbee across the Venice canals, and she'd say, "How did you know about that?" And I'd tell her, "Oh, I've done my research," because I didn't just research her; I *inhaled* her. Her childhood history was my childhood history. We'd get back to her house and she'd make me dinner with old pots she picked up at the Rose Bowl Flea Market (someone took a picture of her there once). She'd show me some old stills from the *Slugger Eight* set. I'd ask her about her acting philosophy, about her life, about who she truly was. I would not fawn over her looks.

Yes, it would take a true journalist, someone who respected her, who *understood* her, who didn't want to make fun of her, who was careful and compassionate, to get this story. Someone who knew her inside and out. That person had to be me.

"What if I told you I knew where she was?" I suddenly blurted.

"Oh? And where is she?"

"Look, I've been—how shall I put this?—following her for years, since I was a teenager. I have some good leads. But nothing I'm ready to share yet," I said. It was all a lie. I had nothing. My hands shook, and because I was afraid they'd give me away, I shoved them under my thighs. *Keep it together, Goldie.* "Like you always say, a journalist must protect their sources."

"So you're telling me you got all these leads in a week?" she said, eyebrows raised.

"You have no idea how badly I want this story, Dana."

She took a cigarette out of her pack and waddled it between her fingers. She sighed. "Here's my real issue, and I would say this to any of our staff writers. Echo Blue is a recovering addict, right? Let's say she OD'd, which is most likely. What makes that a *story*? This isn't *People* magazine, for Christ's sake. Yes, she was very famous and people cared about her and nostalgia, blah, blah, blah, and now she's missing. But is there anything else here? That, I would like to know."

"Okay, here's a question for you," I said. "Why does Robert Downey Jr. have so many people on his side, but someone like Echo Blue gets fed to the wolves? He has Sean Penn sitting in the courtroom of his jail trial, and Echo has people writing articles about how her career is over at nineteen. They only do that to women. They only do that to child stars. Men get a million and one chances."

Dana seemed to like this. She stared at me and nodded. She rolled the cigarette to the end of the desk, tore open a pack of Nicorette, clawing at the foil, then shoved a piece of gum in her mouth, furiously chewing. I wasn't a smoker, but I knew I had at least three minutes until her Nicorette wore off and she escaped to the curb where the tobacco fiends blocked the entrance to the building. The minute you stepped outside, you were encapsulated by a tunnel of smoke, and it would be difficult to talk in private. At least the old smoking rooms kept them separated.

I continued. "Echo Blue deserves to have a profile written by someone who cares about her, who understands her. Someone who wants her real story, from *her* perspective. You don't want to put someone on this story who is going to have to watch all of her movies in one afternoon. I've watched those movies already, Dana. I've digested them. They're part of my psyche. I have tons of archival material." (I left out that this "archive" was a box under my bed at my parents' house.) "I've essentially been preparing for this story since *Slugger Eight* came out."

"I never saw *Slugger Eight*," she said, expressionless.

"What? How is that possible? In every other movie before *Slugger Eight*, the girls were side pieces or slasher victims, or chasing guys named Jake Ryan on their sixteenth birthday. Look at the movies that came after *Slugger Eight*, movies where the girls had agency: *Clueless, 10 Things I Hate about You, Slums of Beverly Hills*. I know every line from *Slugger Eight*—"

She cocked her head and lowered her glasses, staring at me over them.

"You're not going to pull a *Misery* on me and lock Echo Blue up in a cabin and break her ankles with a sledgehammer, are you?"

I barked a laugh. I had to tread lightly. My fixation on Echo would make me seem deranged, like I wanted the story just to meet her. And while I *was* excited to meet her, I was also sincerely interested in writing a profile piece that would change the direction of my career. My dream was to write the kind of story that would push me onto a "twenty-three under twenty-three" list. Yes, I know that sounded shallow. I know that's not what you're supposed to be striving for when you're a writer. But Echo was incidentally the subject I knew best.

"Please, Dana. Let me have this story. I'm the only one who can write it. I'm begging you."

"I might never hear the end of this, but someone gave me a chance once, and so, Goldie," she said and slapped her hand on the desk, "today's your lucky day. If you find her and get a real sit-down with her, and I'm talking more than fifteen minutes, because calling her up and listening to her dole out some bullshit spiel about how she needed a 'break from life' does not make a celebrity interview. I'm talking the real deal here. A good celebrity story isn't just about the celebrity, or you being a *star fucker*. It's about the writer's ability to make the story interesting. So if you can make this a deep dive, if you can find her and talk to her, and then also write a cultural commentary on the world around her, then, and only then, I'll make sure this story gets good placement."

A white-hot bolt rushed through my arms up to my shoulders and neck. The blood sped to my head so fast that I thought I would faint from excitement. Had she just assigned me the story? *And* promised me she'd pay attention to it? Did she also call me a *star fucker*? *Easy, take it easy*, I told myself. I didn't want to pass out and rock Dana's confidence in me before I even had a chance to write anything. Thankfully, her head was in her drawer as she ravaged her desk, so she didn't notice my fuchsia-hued face. "Where the fuck is my lighter?" she mumbled a few times, talking to herself. Then to me, "You don't have a lighter, do you?" I shook my head.

"Do I get a travel budget?" I said cautiously.

She snorted. "Yeah, we'll make sure the company limo takes you to the airport."

"What about expenses?"

"Do you have a credit card?"

I nodded. My credit card had a $2,000 limit, and I had already used most of it.

"Good," she said. "I need a cigarette or I'm going to kill someone. See what you can come up with." And then she was already out her office door before I could thank her.

Echo

1980–1991

. . .

4.

Both of my parents are actors. My mother was a child star. She was in the biggest television show of the 1970s, *Gold Rush*, which was based on a series of pioneer books about a girl who lived in California with her family. She was one of those adorable creatures with the freckles and the long straight hair in braids and the little lisp. Big brown eyes. There were dolls made of her. Halloween costumes. She was the highest-paid television star at the time.

I was about nine when she started telling me the truth about her career. We'd be curled up in her king-size bed, where we spent most evenings wrapped in the mauve, silky sheets with the lights off and the shades drawn, watching movies like *What Ever Happened to Baby Jane?* My mother was always on one of her many medicines, pills she took for a variety of ailments from back and belly aches to "just life."

My mother smoked in the bed regularly and sometimes a hole would blister the sheet, or a burning ember would sink into the carpet. I learned to catch her cigarette just as it was slipping out of her fingers or her mouth and prop it in the little divot of the thick glass ashtray filled with butts next to her bed. She'd ramble on with cautionary tales of fame, how she never had normal friendships, how people were constantly asking her what was next after *Gold Rush*.

"Did I tell you someone tried to kidnap me once?"

"Yes, Mama."

"I was just a little kid," she'd lament.

"You were special, Mama." This was something I said a lot. I often thought about her famed appearance on *Johnny Carson*. She was so young, only about ten. She pretended to go to sleep on the chair she was sitting on, a joke about spending the whole night filming. The poor thing, exhausted from making everyone's favorite television show. She wanted someone to notice. But when she ran off the stage, thinking that she had done so well because the audience laughed during her bit, my grandmother smacked her on the behind for being fresh. "You don't pretend to fall asleep with Johnny Carson! You don't pretend to fall asleep on national television." My grandmother never failed to remind my mother that there were hundreds of thousands of girls who wanted her job on *Gold Rush*, and there she was, being disrespectful.

I felt so sorry for my mother, all of the pain that she experienced, all of the mistrust she had in the system and even in her own overbearing mother. Like Rose from *Gypsy*. She swore that she would never let that kind of thing happen to me. That I would live as normal a life as possible.

When NBC bought all of the rights to *Gold Rush*, my mom was given a killer back-end deal (Nana had signed my mother with a very good agent; she wasn't about to let her little girl get screwed). It's unheard of how much money she continues to make in residuals. *Gold Rush* was, and still is, shown in US history classes all over the country as a teaching instrument about the children who mined for gold with their parents on the Northwest Passage and the Oregon Trail. My mother is the poster child of *Gold Rush*, that famous picture of her character, Lottie, holding her blind sister's hand as they walk behind a wagon. People can watch it on TV Land, TBS, and Nick at Nite, or get it through mail order on Netflix DVDs. Every time they license it, my mother makes a cut.

That's how I managed to watch it, despite it being forbidden. She'd drift off and then I'd sneak downstairs to turn on the reruns. How could I not? Other kids had their parents' photo albums, but my mother's youth was right there, captured on my television screen. Her bright eyes stared back at me, and they were my eyes too, our age about the same. Lottie looked remarkably like me. I wanted to hate *Gold Rush*, but I fell in love with it. This energetic, charming version of my mother, a version of her I never got to meet. I was desperate to remind my mother who she truly was. Tell her how much the show meant to me.

One time, after I watched the episode when she got lost in the wilds of Wyoming, I couldn't hold it in anymore. I turned the TV set off and tiptoed into my mother's room. She wasn't quite asleep yet. She took the cigarette from her mouth and rested it in that thick glass ashtray, outstretching her arms. She was in a good mood. I took advantage.

"You were so beautiful, Mama, so talented," I said, my head to her chest; the odor from her armpits snaked between us because who knows the last time she bathed, and I didn't care. Because I loved her and it felt good in her arms. I wasn't sure what her reaction would be, but I wanted her to know I was proud of her. I wanted her to see how much she had to offer the world. This should not have been the job of a ten-year-old, but I wanted her to be okay. She petted my head, smoke from the cigarette lingering between us. "Sometimes I don't know where Lottie from *Gold Rush* ends and Mathilde begins" was her only response.

It became clear that my attempts to praise her wouldn't get her out of her smoky bed. You can't *will* someone out of depression. She sunk back into that mattress like she had for years. And while I wanted to support her, wanted to help her feel better, I also thought nonstop about my dad, wishing he would rescue me. Rescue us.

• • •

My dad, Jamie Blue, was nothing like his ex-wife. He lived for the limelight. He was born James Stewart Blumenthal in Passaic, New Jersey. His parents were a famous singing-and-acting duo in the Catskills, and his grandmother was Bertha Kalich, one of the most famous Yiddish actors in the early 1900s. When he got to Hollywood, my dad cut the last part of his name off in one fell swoop like many other actors did, erasing decades of Jewish identity.

My parents met at a birthday party for Max Shine, who had produced *Gold Rush*. It was my mother's last year working on the show. She was nineteen. My dad was twenty-one, fresh off his success in his first role in *Sunshine through the Forest*. Directed by Donnie Champlain, it was one of those huge breakthrough independent films that cost $2 million to make and earned $200 million at the box office. He saw my mother across the pool and was struck by how innocent and out of place she looked. I've heard the story countless times.

"You don't look happy," he said to her, handing her a drink.

"Why should I be happy?" she said. "I'm at a boring party with people who only talk about themselves, and the shrimp tastes like it belongs back in the ocean."

My dad apparently laughed his head off. He had only been in Hollywood for a few years, but he had gotten used to people pretending to be content and eager, with their fake smiles and ass-kissing. He found my mother's bluntness refreshing. "I hate this Hollywood shit too," he said to her that first night. "I want to make real movies like Newman. Take on gritty characters like Brando. I don't want to compromise. I want to find characters who are authentic. Characters who haven't gotten all the life sucked out of them yet." She believed in his speeches back then. All he had to do was mention Brando and Newman, and how the core of acting was about "finding the truth," and she was lovestruck.

They eloped a few days later. I tend to think they both used each other for something in getting married. Whether she wanted to admit it or not, she wasn't ready to give up Hollywood, the comforts of fame. And with my dad, she got to stay in the background. To be Hollywood adjacent instead of the star. To be free of the pressure for a while.

For him, she was an entryway into legitimate Hollywood royalty. People wanted her to transition into movies, her beauty only growing as she got older, but she refused, making her even more interesting. She was an enigma, which held its own kind of allure. As long as you're a mystery, you'll stay famous.

From what I heard, their years together consisted of passionate love and equally passionate fighting. And predictably, they crashed and burned. You can't expect a child to understand the nuances of her parents, but they weren't suited to have children, being children themselves, I will tell you that.

5.

My dad moved out when I was two years old and devoted his full attention to his career—and sleeping with every beautiful woman in Hollywood. And my mother retreated, pulling as far back from the limelight as she could manage. One of my earliest memories of my dad was seeing him on the cover of a magazine in the supermarket checkout line. It was a paparazzi shot of him holding hands with his recent co-star, Alexandra Moore. Their wild sex scene in a white Ford Thunderbird convertible to the tune of Roxy Music's pulsating "Love Is the Drug" became their love affair's theme song. But when I flipped through the issue, I noticed one pap shot of just him staring into the camera, like he was looking directly at me. He wore a white V-neck T-shirt, and the sunlight brushed through his messy hair. My mother grabbed the flimsy magazine and turned it over, muttering, "Trash," under her breath. I wanted to pick it up and squeeze it against my chest and never let it go.

Most of my visits with him between the ages of five and seven were on film sets to accommodate his busy schedule. In the summer of 1985, he made *Frannie and Frankie*, a takeoff on Truffaut's *Jules and Jim*. It was his second picture with Donnie Champlain, and they had a bigger budget now. My mother would drop me off at the studio lot and warn me to stay with either the makeup department or wardrobe because she was para-noid about anyone touching me or hurting me, or worse—"Trying to get you to act." I made friends with Crystal, a twenty-one-year-old makeup assistant who thought I was adorable. "Like a little adult," she'd say, and we'd crouch on the floor to watch my dad work.

I'd sit there for days. I loved watching him back then. He was funny and didn't mind being goofy, which wasn't typical for such a good-looking man. He was loud too, boisterous with a lot of suggestions. "I have an idea!" he'd say. Everyone would stop talking because he com-manded the set. I didn't understand the nuance of what was happening, that his "ideas" often came up when someone else, like Donnie Cham-plain, or his co-star, Talia Bryson, was talking. It confused me when Donnie would roll his eyes or when Talia would sigh, because wasn't his creativity inspiring?

I'm not sure why, I guess for attention, but I started doing an impres-sion of him saying it: "I have an idea!" Crystal thought this was charm-ing, so she'd prompt me to do it for other crew members like the assistant mic guy, the boom handler, and the assistant grip—all at the bottom of the food chain, the ones who needed the most comedic relief. My heart-beat quickened when I performed it for them. I liked making them laugh and seeing their faces light up.

One day, my dad and I were in his trailer between takes, him running lines and me playing with my doll, repeating my little impression over and over—"I have an idea"—louder and louder, just like he would say it, with that raspy voice of his. "Hey, Daddy," I finally said. "You like this delivery? *I have an idea!*" I wanted him to hear me and hoped he'd share the same reaction as the crew members did; I imagined he'd shine with pride.

"Echo, give it a rest," he said sharply after a minute or two. "I'm try-ing to learn my lines here."

"But I'm doing you, Daddy."

"What does that mean, you're doing me?"

"You know, how you always say, 'I have an idea!'"

The script supervisor (I can't remember her name now) slipped out of the trailer, saying she needed a cup of coffee.

I could see the embarrassment in my dad's face, then something else—a sneer of anger. "Echo, just take your dolls and play outside, okay? You can 'do me' all you want when I'm driving you home. Some of us need to actually act."

I ambled out of the trailer with my doll under my arm, and he slammed the door behind me. Later that week there was a blind item: *Which rising male hunk is so pompous (even for Tinseltown standards) that he dismissed his young daughter in front of the crew?*

I got home that day from the set feeling rejected. I had thought I was his little sidekick. My mother held me in her arms, smothering me in her large bed, and I cried about making him mad, all the while feeling like I was betraying him. "Daddy has a temper, Echo. That's why it's better if you just stay here with me."

"He's not always mad," I whispered. I hated when she talked about him like that, even if it was true. She didn't see him on the set and how funny he was. She didn't see how the makeup girls fawned over him. I learned many years later that he was sleeping with Crystal.

I thought my dad was never going to spend time with me again after that incident, but then a week later, I was relieved when he picked me up for an unexpected beach day. He held my hand at the edge of the ocean and we ran in, hitting a hard wave together, screaming from the cold. He twirled me into the horizon, sweeping me over the whitecaps. My dad had forgiven me, and I was elated. I wanted it to stay that way forever.

6.

When I was in the fifth grade during career day, while other kids talked about their parents being entertainment lawyers or costume designers or therapists, I said, "My mom stays in bed." I thought it was funny. "It's just a joke," I quickly clarified, when my teacher's mouth dropped open with alarm. It was one of my first acting lessons: self-deprecation. But it was too late to backtrack. The school therapist contacted my parents, and it was decided that my dad needed to be more present in my life.

My mother was also becoming aware that her issues were affecting me. I'd heard her begging him to take me more, complaining that she could hardly get out of bed, that she was paranoid about my safety, and it wasn't the way for a kid to live. I wanted that too. I hated admitting this, but she had started to repulse me, the way she collapsed in her bed, sometimes with her breasts hanging out of her silky gray robe. I couldn't even complain about a teacher or one of my friends, because her way of consoling me was suffocating. I didn't want her to touch me, out of fear she'd rub off on me, but I couldn't tell her to get away from me either, because that would send her into hysterics. I didn't want to give her an excuse to moan about how I thought she was a failure like everyone else did.

My best friend Kat Bergen's mom (her aunt was Candice Bergen) was kind and warm. She was the type of woman who wore matching white-and-blue-striped pajamas to bed. She kept her hair pulled back in a tight bun to reveal her glowing face. She smelled like lavender. Why couldn't my own mother be more like her? I loved my mother, I was *part* of her, but I also yearned to escape.

At the time, my dad was making two back-to-back local movies after a long stretch working on location out of town—*Revolutions* and *West Side Witches*—which worked out perfectly. He began taking me once a week to dinner, then for an overnight at his house. Dan Tana's was his go-to spot because it was a low-key celebrity hangout, which sounds like an oxymoron, but for L.A., it was down-to-earth. The two of us squeezed into a little red leatherette booth with a red-and-white-checkered table-cloth neatly spread across the table. Old Chianti bottles wrapped in straw hung from the ceiling. Sometimes Bruce Springsteen would be there, sometimes Geena Davis, sometimes Jack Nicholson. I'd hold my dad's big hand while we waited for our food, feeling safer than I had for months with my mother. I'd drink a Shirley Temple, and he'd have a martini with extra olives. He'd let me slurp the vodka off the olives, and I'd get a little buzzed. I took it as that warm feeling you get when you're with someone you love. I didn't know any better.

The waitresses always flirted with him, which put him in a good mood. I noticed early on that he liked when women were paying atten-tion to him. I could see him calm down when a co-star, especially one he was dating, touched his back or laughed at his jokes. The way the women in wardrobe teased him about how cute his boxers were and how he'd moon them, making me squirm with discomfort. How when he was up-set over a squabble with a director, which was often in those days, a woman on set, like the script supervisor or a producer, or even the second assistant director, would whisper in his ear, enough to relax my dad, to boost his confidence again. I liked to dream that I was one of those women too—not like *that*, nothing sexual, but that I was as important to him as they were.

"You think you'll ever get married again, Daddy?" I said one night at dinner.

"What makes you ask that?"

"I see you in the magazines with a lot of ladies."

"Who showed you the pictures of me in magazines with all those ladies?" he said, smiling.

"They're in the supermarket," I said. "I see pictures of you all over. I read Madonna was the only woman whose heart you haven't broken yet."

He almost spit out his food he was laughing so hard. "Madonna? Is that right?" He reached over and kissed my head. It warmed my stomach to make him laugh like that.

"Echo, you're the only woman I have time for right now. It's good for both of us to have each other."

"Does that mean I'm going to live with you?"

He took his arm off the edge of the booth, where it had been resting around my shoulders, and sidled away a touch.

"Me? No, no. You can't live with me."

"Why not? The last time I slept over, you said you bought the house next door. You said you were gonna make a compound like Dennis Hopper. Isn't that what you told me? That I'd have a whole room in your house, or a whole wing?"

"Listen, honey," he said. "I'm not set up long term for a little girl—you have to understand. You're just a kid. And you need your mom. She's gonna get better, trust me. Just give her some time."

"But aren't I yours just as much as I'm hers?" I asked.

And he seemed to care—he really did. "You're staying over tonight, aren't you?" He kissed my head again and ruffled my hair. I wanted to clutch at him, convince him that I wouldn't make a mess, that I would be good, but I knew even then that I couldn't overdo it. I had already said enough.

He called over the waitress and asked for the check. I heard him whisper, "Tell the paps in the back we'll be coming out in five."

While we exited through the alleyway, he shielded my eyes from the photographers with one hand, putting the other up in front of him as though he didn't want to be photographed. That's the game in Hollywood. Look at me, look at me, but don't catch me looking at you. Don't let it be known that I want you to look.

In his Porsche, the pink glow of the sunset ahead of us as we drove toward Venice Beach, I wished this was how it always was. That I lived in his lofty house. With its Persian rugs and white couches, its kayaks we launched into the canal, and a pool out back. It felt like the perfect future for the two of us. And it felt alive, unlike my mom's small house with the shades always drawn, the orange fireplace, the heavy leather chairs, antiques bought in the 1970s right after *Gold Rush*. I suddenly knew what I had to do. I had to make it so my dad would *want* to be with me all the time. Otherwise, he was going to find someone steady to drape on his arm, and I'd have lost my chance. It was now or never.

"I want to act, Daddy," I announced.

He looked over at me and swerved slightly, surprise on his face.

"Look at the road. Don't get us in an accident," I said.

He chuckled. "Does your mother know about this?"

"No one knows about this," I said. "But I've been thinking about it for a long time." (I hadn't. Which shows you that I was a natural at giving a performance.)

He revved up the engine and continued down Venice Boulevard, into the setting sun.

"Daddy?"

He pulled into the driveway and turned to me. "I think you would be a phenomenal actor, Echo Blue. But you know it would take a lot of work."

I nodded my head.

"You're going to have to work hard to memorize your lines, do photo shoots and press constantly. Do you get that, Echo? You're going to have to do things you don't want to do. That's part of this business. You'd have to stand there for hours while someone paints your face and makes you look the right way into the camera. This is boring stuff for an eleven-year-old."

He didn't know that I had become my mother's roommate. That I could make my own omelets for breakfast. That I had single-handedly prevented my mother's house from catching on fire by plucking her lit cigarettes from her mouth as she slept. I understood responsibility. But I also wanted him to believe I was innocent, untouched, that I needed him. Isn't that what all fathers want to believe, that their eleven-year-old daughters haven't been scalded by life yet? That we're their babies still? (Mothers knew different. I learned that from her.)

"Yes, Daddy. I get that."

"It would also mean taking off time from school with your friends."

"I hate my friends," I shot back. If he had known anything about my life, he would have known that wasn't true. I loved Kat Bergen, and I probably loved Kat's mom more. Then there was Ayana Devlin, who made short films with her dad's sixteen-millimeter camera, and Zoe Tyler, who was the prettiest girl in our grade and who everyone said was going to be a model. We had all whispered together countless times when Mrs. Brillstein, the music teacher, wasn't looking, and in the confines of Kat's massive bedroom, huddling together with secrets deep and ugly, vows made to each other, to our friendship. These were girls I'd known since kindergarten. We talked about going into middle school together, as a foursome, that we'd never separate.

"They only want to talk about boys and play video games," I continued, ignoring the doubt scratching at me.

"And you would rather act?"

Did I really want to? I was eleven years old. I had no idea what I wanted to do. I loved my friends—that was easy. But I craved my dad's love more. I wanted him to like me and wanted him to be around me like their fathers were. What kid wouldn't want that?

"Yes, Daddy."

And that's how my acting career started.

It's also how my life started to end.

31

Goldie

. . .

7.

Monday at work, my first official day on the story, Ethan Pench stopped me in the hallway in front of his office. Pench's big claim to fame was his exclusive of Edgar Cross, the twenty-eight-year-old novelist who had been deemed by critics as the author who would "save fiction."

Edgar Cross was a Berkeley dropout—in fact, he roomed with Pench there; hence, the exclusive—who wrote a very long, boring book called *Our Way* about a Gen Xer whose obsession with reality television leads to his demise. You can read between the lines. *Our Way* went to the top of the bestseller list. A year later, Edgar Cross was a tenured professor at Stanford and was married to a model. Pench had his own office and a BlackBerry of new connections. This resulted in most of the writers, including those who were decades older with lesser status, hating him. And his proclivity toward Phish T-shirts did not help things.

I ignored Pench as I usually did, but he jumped in front of me, waving his arms out like a goalie.

"I'm not playing with you today, Pench," I said and elbowed him into the wall. He was slightly built, but I had grown up with a brother. It wasn't difficult for me to be physical. He followed me to my cubicle anyway. I was filled with nervous energy—Echo had been missing for ten days now; I was trying to stop my eye from violently twitching.

I was carrying a stack of tabloids I'd picked up from the newsstand. At the top was one particularly unfair shot of Echo walking down the street last year, her hair in her face, no shoes on, and hunched over. The headline read: "ECHO AT ROCK BOTTOM AGAIN?" I'd scrawled a sticky note: *DON'T BELIEVE IT.* I didn't want Pench to see. He wouldn't understand. He'd look at me like he was my mentor and say something condescending like, *The key, Goldie, is to remain objective.* "What do you want?" I finally acquiesced.

"Heard you landed the Echo Blue story. That's a big get. How did that happen?"

"Oh, *thanks.*"

"You know what I mean. Obviously you're super qualified, but, you know, it's not exactly your usual type of story. All the Dorothy Parker wannabes in the office are talking about it."

He slung his arm over my cubicle wall.

"I didn't say you could do that," I said, looking at his arm.

He smirked and lifted his elbow. "Can I at least stand here?" he said softly.

I shouldn't have felt attracted to him in that moment, but I did. I guess I've neglected to mention that Pench and I had been sleeping together for the past six months, but it was more of a transactional relationship than a romance. He wasn't handsome in that way you'd ogle over someone. He had a large nose and dark, greasy hair. Plus, there were those Phish T-shirts he'd wear and, sometimes worse, the lingering smell of patchouli. He liked to jump in front of me in the hallway or launch spitballs at me. But I was attracted to men who gave me attention—it didn't matter what kind. I didn't know why he wanted so badly to please me, but it worked for me. Generally, my feelings toward Pench vacillated between disgust and envy. I hated that his career came so easily to him and that he had an office all to himself. But I liked that he wasn't scared off by me. I also begrudgingly liked how smart he was. How nice, but I would never let him know that.

The first time we had sex, I kicked him in the back afterward and told him he should sleep on the floor. "I don't feel comfortable sleeping next to people," I told him. I gave him a blanket I hadn't washed in weeks, and he curled up at my bedside and slept through the night.

He reminded me of my brother when we were little, always wanting to be next to me even if I threatened to pierce his ears or tear up his baseball cards. I was a mean child because my life felt out of control, and when you feel out of control, you want to dominate the few people who are beneath you.

"You have sixty seconds to speak," I said to Pench.

"Here's Hazel Cahn's number," he said and dangled a small piece of paper in front of me.

I snatched it out of his hand.

Hazel Cahn was Echo's shrewd Hollywood superagent. My mother and I once watched a *60 Minutes* profile on her. Hazel Cahn smoked cigarettes while taking phone calls. She wore big glasses and a lavender caftan. My mother made a comment that she must have been the most powerful woman in Hollywood. When I asked her how she knew, she said, "Women don't wear caftans to work unless they're in charge." My mother met at least fifty women a day at the makeup counter at Day's Emporium. She had a knack for spotting important people.

This was a huge deal. I had planned to just call Hazel Cahn's agency to harass her assistant. Now here I was, with her direct number. Presented to me by Pench.

He shoved his hands in his pockets. I had this urge to force him back into his office and make him undress, to write Hazel Cahn's phone number on his belly so I could step on his chest while I dialed her number.

I was a terrible person, I know. But the idea of dominating Pench, right as he was offering me a key to my story, gave me some pleasure. I was getting turned on.

"Thank you," I said. But I didn't want to seem too grateful. Too desperate. "You can leave now."

He stood there meekly in front of me, like a snail.

"Okay, Goldie, let me know if you need any help," he said. He tapped on the top of the cubicle wall and slinked back to his office.

8.

After a long and awkward conversation with Hazel Cahn's assistant (she abruptly hung up on me first, and then on the second try, I miraculously managed to get enough words out to convince her I was doing a story on women in Hollywood), I booked a meeting with the superagent herself.

I was going to meet her in four days.

In L.A.

The more it sunk in that I was going to meet *the* Hazel Cahn, the more I felt alive. This was really happening.

My mother's best friend from high school, Dolly, a costume designer, lived in L.A.'s Laurel Canyon near the Chateau Marmont. But if I wanted to stay with her—which was necessary if I was going to be able to afford a plane ticket—that meant I had to tell my parents. I knew, because of my history, they would be worried. I called them that night over a take-out container of fried rice at my kitchen counter.

"So, I got a big story at work," I began. They were both on different landlines, him sitting in his office, her at the kitchen table. I had to spit it out before they got excited thinking about me covering a new gentrification story.

"It's about Echo Blue."

There were a few seconds of silence on the other end. Then I heard my mother click her tongue.

"I saw Larry King mention her when I was watching CNN," my father said. "Seems like some kind of publicity stunt for her new movie."

"No, this is a national story, Dad. A big, *big* story."

"I thought you were doing local stories. What happened to those?" my father said. "Your story on the boxing gym was wonderful."

"Here we go with the boxing story," I said.

"Patty, was it not a great story?"

"It was a great story," my mother said.

"Those stories are boring to me, Dad. That's not what I want to write about. I'm interested in the world of celebrity."

"The last great boxing ring in the city surviving in Manhattan is boring to you? What are you going to write about some Hollywood brat who's run off? Where's the vulnerability in that? Where's the moral compass?" he said.

That boxing piece was my father's pride and joy. He had it professionally framed and hung it up on his office wall next to his autographed photo of Muhammad Ali. He bragged about it to his colleagues. He wrote a group email about it to our entire family, even second cousins we hadn't seen in years. You wouldn't think a Shakespeare professor would love boxing the way my father did, but he was attracted to the machismo of brutal sports, Roman war tragedies, and sword fights.

I, on the other hand, hated boxing. I hated when he watched it on Saturday nights, hovering over the television and barking at the screen as men pummeled each other. But at *ME*, I took what I could get, and knowing that my father would be all over the story when it came out, I had accepted his eager invitation to his uptown office to borrow his copy of Joyce Carol Oates's book *On Boxing*. At the very least, I could get ahead of his critique and cull a little of his knowledge. I hadn't been to his office in years, and being there brought me back to childhood afternoons when I'd act out scenes from *Romeo and Juliet*, pretending my father was a mean old Montague, because there was no one else to look after me. It smelled like musty, decaying paper, and books were scattered around the floor in messy piles.

"Did you know Oates fell in love with boxing because of her father?" he asked, giddy. I had to admit his enthusiasm was a bit contagious. Maybe this wouldn't be so bad after all.

He read his favorite passages out loud to me. "'The boxers will bring to the fight everything that is themselves, and everything will be exposed—including secrets about themselves they cannot fully realize.' Do you understand what she's saying, Goldie? That boxing is a psychological exercise."

For the first time, I saw his point. It did seem kind of artful when you put it that way. I perked up.

"This is what you should think about when you're interviewing the guys at the gym," he continued. "But I know you always hated boxing, so you should bring it to me before you submit it to your editor. I'll help you get it right."

My blood boiled. I should have been more wary. Of course he could never give me advice without trying to micromanage me. Of course he couldn't have faith that I'd do a good job on my own.

"Don't tell me how to write an article," I said icily. "You're a professor, not a journalist. It's condescending."

He looked at me, confused, like a sad little boy. He was wounded now. Fuck. I had to look away. If he had offered his help instead of forcing it on me, maybe I would have said yes. Why did it always have to be a power struggle with him? I grabbed the book out of his hands and told him I had a meeting to get to. I went in there with fractured sincerity and walked out feeling like my fifth-grade self, once again held hostage by his red scribble on my schoolwork. Outside, I tossed the book in the trash. Two minutes later, I returned to fish it out from under a coffee cup, and the first few pages were stained brown. Don't tell Joyce Carol Oates.

Now on the phone, I thought about the advice Dr. Watts had given me about dealing with my father's criticism.

"Did you notice what an accomplishment this is?" I said, my teeth gritting as I spoke. This was called a shift to the positive.

They didn't respond.

"Does your editor know how much you liked Echo Blue as a child?" my mother said. She was speaking slowly, choosing her words carefully.

"*Liked* is not the word I would use, Patty," my father said gruffly. "We had to get her a therapist about this obsession." My mother coughed and started mumbling about a fly in the kitchen, her favorite way to change the subject.

"Taking comfort in a celebrity is not an abnormal thing to do, as Dr. Watts told me the *four times* I saw her. I just had a hard time making friends like every other middle schooler in the country. Plus, fandom didn't just appear in the nineteen nineties with Echo Blue. Do you two understand that?"

"No one ever said—"

"What about the Beatles? Would you rather I was like one of those girls who passed out on the floor because John Lennon was singing 'Shake it up, baby'? What about *NSYNC?"

I was talking so quickly by this point that my words were falling over each other. "Do you know how many girls were crying and fantasizing about changing their last name to Timberlake? I have the opportunity to write a story that's interested me for a lifetime. What's so wrong about that?"

That got them to shut up for a minute, but I knew what they were thinking. That girls across the world *shared* in their hysteria over boy bands and that it was practically a group activity. My devotion to Echo Blue, on the other hand, was lonely and isolating.

"I'm the youngest reporter on staff to be assigned a big feature like this. It's a national story; it's not just my little obsession. This is a big deal. They're giving me a huge expense account." I know, I know, but the detail would put them at ease. "I got this story *because* of my knowledge of her, because of my persistence, because I worked hard on the other stories that no one else wanted. Can't you be proud of me?"

"We're always proud of you, Goldie," my father relented. It felt like there was a *but* missing from the sentence. *We're proud of you, but we're disappointed that you've changed trajectories. We're proud of you, but we're concerned about your mental health.*

I'd have to prove them wrong, that's all. And prove to my father, finally, that I was good at something.

9.

With the call to my parents out of the way, I made my final preparations for the trip. At my apartment, I packed my books about child stars like Judy Garland, Tatum O'Neal, and Drew Barrymore. I would have to cram on the plane to make my story to Hazel Cahn plausible. I also brought a behind-the-scenes tell-all about *Gold Rush*, the TV show that Echo's mother starred in as a child. Pench left *Jamie Blue: The Unauthorized Biography* on my desk and stuck a Post-it Note on the cover: *For background*.

Then I made a sloppy call list of other people in Echo's life I'd try to interview in L.A. I threw everything at the wall and managed to get a few meetings, the biggest of which was with Olivia Breakers, one of the softball players from *Slugger Eight* who had since done a few bit parts on sitcoms and was still trying to make it in Hollywood. She told me over the phone that she had "insight," whatever that meant. I could tell she was thrilled to have someone in media interested in her.

But most importantly, before I left for L.A., I needed to talk to someone at MTV, someone who was there on New Year's Eve. When I called the studios for *Total Request Live*, MTV's popular daily show, various people from the production team assured me that someone would be in touch, but they never were. To speak to someone at MTV, you either had to be a journalist at *Rolling Stone* or Britney Spears. I'd have to try in person.

I grabbed my bag and raced uptown to their massive Times Square offices, completely forgetting about the swarm of kids who flocked to their studios on a daily basis hoping to catch a glimpse of their favorite boy band. Broadway opened its mouth and vomited teenagers. I fought my way through them until I caught the eye of a security guard, then flashed an old press badge (it gave me clearance for city hall, but he barely glanced at it), and he waved me in.

I took the elevator to the second floor, entering an all-black narrow hallway with neon signs stretched across the walls. I'd walk around until I found someone approachable. A distracted guy donning a headset atop an Eminem bleached-blond buzz cut passed me and gave me a once-over. Panicking, I ducked into the women's room. I'd have to operate from here. I just needed the right person to walk in so I could strike up a conversation; otherwise, I'd have to come up with a plan B. I was already regretting this terrible idea.

About two minutes later, a frazzled woman with a beat-up flannel and a lanyard around her neck that read "Heather O'Rourke, production assistant, *TRL*" burst into the bathroom.

I stared in the mirror, applying lip gloss while she went to the bathroom and then stood at the sink next to me to wash her hands.

"Kind of a crazy night the other night, huh?" I said as I smeared on my fifth layer of gloss.

"Absolute chaos," she said, then paused and looked at me funny. "Wait—you work on *TRL*?"

"Uh, yes. I'm new," I said, swallowing so loud I could have sworn she heard me.

She glanced down at the old press pass hanging down from my neck and so I flipped it over. "I wasn't working that night, but I heard she was a no-show," I continued. It was clear which *she* I was referring to.

"So, any inkling of what happened?" I said. It was a bold approach, but I decided to act like I was on a crime procedural. Those people got to the point.

Heather looked around to make sure no one was in the bathroom and leaned in. "Echo was here earlier that night. Then she was just gone." Heather O'Rourke gestured with her hands like *poof.*

She had shown up and then left. So she had been intending to do the appearance.

"What time did you see her here?" I tried.

"I guess around seven thirty, in the makeup chair."

"What about the people she was with? Were they surprised that she disappeared? I'm sure there were a lot of loudmouths with something to say." I rolled my eyes conspiratorially.

"Don't I know it. But no. She wasn't with anybody. She was alone."

This stopped me in my tracks. "Echo Blue was *alone* on New Year's Eve? Doesn't that seem odd to you?"

"Yeah, it was. I'm used to talent coming with a posse. But she had, like, no one. Not even a makeup artist. In-house makeup worked on her." She paused and lowered her voice to a whisper. "As I'm sure you heard, there was a lot of champagne floating around that night. A lot of coke."

"Oh yeah. I heard," I said.

"I know Echo was supposedly clean, but I can't see how she would have avoided all that." Heather furrowed her brow and looked down, recalling something. "She *did* get a phone call right before she disappeared. Maybe it was a call from her dealer or her sponsor. Who knows?"

Just then, someone else drifted into the bathroom, and Heather O'Rourke quickly turned and grabbed a paper towel from the wall. I flashed her a peace sign and slipped out.

· · ·

I got a cup of coffee at the cart on the corner to try to get my brain straight. I wasn't sure what to make of what I had learned, but it was at least clear I was on to something. The circumstances of her disappearance were not normal. Being alone on New Year's Eve when you're one of the most famous people in the country is not normal.

The double ribbon ticker scrolling continuously on the new ABC news building read *Echo Blue still missing.* People bumped into my arms as I worked my way to the middle of the street, reading it with a combination of dread and curiosity.

I thought about Heather's suggestion that the caller was her sponsor. (Echo had a sponsor, right? Of course she did. Or a sober coach. *Someone.*) Maybe she saw the champagne, saw the coke, and knew she had to get out of there. Yes, I liked this. It meant that she was taking care of herself.

But would her sponsor tell her to leave MTV? Would her sponsor want her to shirk her business commitments? Wait—that meant that Hazel Cahn couldn't have been the caller either. Hazel Cahn would never have told her to break her contract and leave. If anything, Hazel Cahn would have convinced her to stay. So who the hell called her and what did they say?

The news ticker read something different now: *We scooped you, Goldie! We found Echo Blue and she's flying back to ABC studios for an exclusive. Hahahaha.*

I threw my coffee cup at the taunting news ticker, but it barely reached the front door.

"No littering, bitch!" a woman with too much lipstick screamed at me, bringing me back to reality. When I looked back, the ticker returned to normal. I was pitiful. What was wrong with me? *Focus, Goldie.* I needed to get going to catch my flight. Los Angeles would have the answers. It was a town of promise, after all. Yes, it was also a place that swallowed up countless wannabe starlets, women who traveled from all parts of this country with high hopes only to end up as some cocktail waitress, pregnant by a producer who'd vowed to cast them in lead parts in their movies . . . But I wasn't a wannabe starlet. I was a goddamn journalist.

I swiped the rose-tinted lip gloss my mom got me from Day's across my cracked lips. Out west, the dry air, the blue skies—that's where I'd find everything.

10.

Los Angeles. That morning, after my early flight, with the haze high up in the canyon, I squinted as my driver climbed the snaking roads. The hills were green because it rained that winter, the houses on stilts, nestled together like lovers.

Could I see her house from here? Was she in a window, staring back at me?

Dolly wasn't there when I arrived. *Hot yoga*, she'd scribbled on a note, along with the code to the lockbox so I could let myself in.

Her house was a midcentury modern tucked under a row of eucalyptus trees. Spikes of rosemary jutted out against a well of meticulously trimmed bright green hedges. I strolled back to where I'd be staying: the casita behind the pool, which had not one single leaf in it. Four lounge chairs, perfectly spaced out with unstained white cushions, lined the edge. Dolly had done well for herself.

Inside, there was a queen-size bed with white sheets, and a large beveled mirror. One of those high-backed midcentury modern lounge chairs sat in the corner, and I'm sure it was an original. Potted plants lined the periphery. The sun shone through the windows, wicked, like it had something to prove. This was January in Southern California. No seasonal affective disorder here.

I immediately dragged a giant palm into the middle of the room to reveal an empty stretch of wall. Before I left New York, I had collected at least twenty pictures of Echo. Images of her on shopping trips down Melrose and Robertson, linked arm in arm with her former best friend, Belinda Summers. Splashes of her in teenybopper magazines. Then there was that full spread of her and the "hot" teen stars of 1996 in *Hollywood Daily*. The one of her smoking when she was about twelve. I smacked up the blurry printouts and the sloppily torn magazine pages. When my task was complete, I took a deep breath. I felt grounded. I marveled at all of it there on Dolly's wall, my curated vision of Echo Blue. Even though it was eerily similar to my childhood bedroom, at least this time I was on assignment. I had an *excuse* to be obsessed with her.

I was particularly drawn to a recent photo of Echo, taken by a famous photographer whose name I don't remember. She was on a Vespa in a black taffeta dress and no shoes. She had a long gold locket around her neck, and her hands were in her messy, bleached-blonde shaggy hair. Echo, so free, like she was under a magic spell. Shouldn't it always be like that for her—for everyone?

There was another one. An airport shot of Echo and Jamie Blue. They both looked gorgeous as always, with their golden hair and bright blue eyes. She was about twelve. His arm was wrapped around her, her shoulder tucked into his armpit, her rib cage against his torso, like they were fused together.

Dolly knocked on the door, startling me. She was holding her yoga mat under her arm and had a sweaty glow to her face. Her cheeks were full and flush, maybe from shoulder stands, and her skin was bronzed and clear—no hyperpigmentation, something my mom was always pointing to as the worst part of aging. Dolly probably used high-quality sunscreen or got laser treatments. She was only a few years younger than my mom, but they seemed light-years apart.

"Goldie!" Dolly said, coming in and throwing her arms around me. "I haven't seen you since you were a snotty teenager!"

Then her thin eyebrows—a leftover look from the '90s that I wished would go out of style because I didn't have the discipline to tweeze mine—rose as she took in the rest of the room.

"I'm sorry for the mess," I said, a string of more *sorrys* following as I stared at the clumps of soil on the floor. "I couldn't find the vacuum. I hope this is okay?" I'd actually been planning to move the plant back in front of the wall when I was done so that Dolly wouldn't report back to my parents and give them ammo to call and harass me. But the cat was out of the bag now.

She stared, horrified, at the wall with my collage of photos. "Wow, I wish I knew you were using Scotch tape," she said. "I hope it won't tear the paint off the wall."

"Shoot, I should have asked you first. I guess that jet lag really messed me up," I said, but I'm sure she wondered what else I would wreck.

She nodded, her hand placed carefully on her toned waist. Dolly had kindness in her eyes, but she was looking me up and down, clearly reconsidering her decision to let me stay here. It then occurred to me that her expression was also about my outfit. My long black wool coat was covered in pilling. My scuffed-up black cowboy boots stood out starkly against her gleaming wood floors, when I should have safely assumed she was a no-shoes-indoors kind of person. My dark, wavy bangs were too long and in my face. I wanted to defend myself, explain that I was a messy New York journalist, not some high-paid, slick costume designer living in Laurel Canyon, but what was the point? Dolly was doing a mitzvah by letting me stay here. I needed to shut up.

"So your mother mentioned you're here to work on an Echo Blue story?" Dolly said. "That poor girl. I never worked with her, but I've always felt so bad for her. Her parents seemed like such a disaster. Maybe she's finally found some peace and quiet."

I could see my mother instructing Dolly on what to ask me. *Make sure this is a real assignment. She told us that she had a huge budget. If they're giving her so much money, why does she have to stay at your place? Wouldn't a well-respected magazine put their journalists up in a hotel?*

"It's a good, solid assignment," I said. "Tough too. Filled with moral ambiguity."

I didn't know what I was talking about.

"Look, your mom is worried about you chasing this story. She told me about how . . . *complicated* your relationship with Echo Blue was."

"I don't have a relationship with Echo Blue. She's the subject of my article, nothing more."

Dolly looked back at me skeptically. Even I could admit that it might be hard to believe me while my collage hovered behind us. I had to backtrack and convince her I was composed and professional.

"This is a huge break for me, Dolly. I had to fight for it, and you must know from your work how important it is for passionate journalists to write these celebrity stories so they don't come off as hack jobs," I said. "Please tell that to my mom. You know she worries about everything."

"Well, that's true," Dolly said, softening. Then she looked over at the black blazer and jeans I had tossed on the bed. "Is that what you're going to wear on your first interview?"

"I don't have anything else."

"I'll let you borrow something," she said, patting my arm. "Stop by the main house once you've had some time to get centered."

Centered was such an L.A. word.

Once Dolly left the casita, I called my brother.

"I can't believe you made it out to L.A.," Sam said. "What's it like?"

"It's already kind of awkward with Dolly. I put some photos of Echo on the wall for inspiration, and she freaked out. Something about the paint ripping off."

"Wait—you pasted up pictures of Echo Blue? On Dolly's wall? Someone we've met, like, a handful of times? That sounds over-the-top, Goldie."

"First of all, Dolly is one of Mom's dear friends. She's known us since before we were born. Second, I'm doing a story, Sam. I have to *embody* her. You should know this as an artist. And it's not *all* about Echo. I'm also trying to understand how women in Hollywood are portrayed, how they're put on pedestals and demonized by the media. Don't you understand?"

"You really think you're going to find her?"

"I have to. There's no story if I don't," I said.

"But you just said the story wasn't only about her—that it was also about women in Hollywood."

"Well, I just mean that in a more, you know, all-encompassing way, like it would be really good for the story if I found her." I didn't even believe myself now.

"Serious question. What do you think you're going to get from her?"

I've thought about this question since the first time I saw Echo in *Slugger Eight*. What *did* I think I was going to get from her? The only thing I was certain of was that once we met, I'd feel less lonely. That I'd have someone who finally understood me. Yes. That's what I hoped to get from her. Friendship.

"This conversation is giving me agita, Sam. I'm on a job; everyone should be proud! What the hell is wrong with you people? Anyway, can you call Mom and Dad for me? Tell them not to worry?"

"Okay, okay. I'll back off. And I'll see what I can do, but I can't change generational Jewish anxiety," he snorted, and we hung up.

11.

I borrowed a better-fitting black blazer from Dolly, and she polished up my boots, despite my protests. ("That's the *look*," I said. "Grunge is dead," she countered.) Hazel Cahn's office was on Wilshire Boulevard, a section of town that felt more like a city, and I felt briefly homesick for New York. I waltzed into the tall building like I was supposed to be there (and yes, obviously, I *was* supposed to be there, because I had an appointment, but I was very insecure in those days). Inside was like a museum. Light reflected off of ten-foot-tall mirrored columns, creating dizzying rainbows across the lobby. I shivered thinking how I was walking the very same steps Echo must have walked countless times. On a marble table in the lobby, there was a copy of the newest *People*, with a despondent Jamie Blue staring out at the Pacific Ocean stretched across the cover. The headline read:

JAMIE BLUE:
SEARCHING FOR HIS DAUGHTER
*Crushed by Echo Blue's disappearance, this former
ladies' man wants his "baby girl" home.*

I shoved it in my bag, got a pass from a disinterested security guard, and hopped in the elevator. When I got to Hazel's floor, the receptionist told me to have a seat. And then about a minute later, Hazel Cahn herself came sashaying into the lobby, and even the receptionist seemed surprised, immediately standing up. Hazel had a sleek blonde bob and oversize rose-tinted glasses. She wore a long black caftan with a paisley pattern, three-inch platforms, and both wrists jingled with silver bangles. Just as my mom had said, only a powerful woman could walk around a business office dressed like Elizabeth Taylor. Despite my makeover from Dolly, I was embarrassed by my jeans and blazer. I looked like a student.

"Sit, sit," Hazel said to the receptionist. "I'm not the fucking queen." And then she turned to me and said with a gravelly voice, "Though I love it when they're scared shitless of me. You can print that!"

I followed her into a large corner office with a huge shag rug in the center, tall gold table lamps, and a pink velvet couch. The couch was deeper and softer than I would have liked, and I had to sit up on the edge of the cushion so that I wouldn't sink back into it. The point of the couch was obvious: she wanted you comfortable so she could slit your throat. I opened my bag and took out my little Olympus tape recorder and asked her if I could prop it on her desk. She nodded and I slid it toward her.

"First I want to say thank you—" But she cut me off immediately.

"I don't do small talk, love. So tell me. Why are we here?"

I nervously shuffled through my notes, feeling her watching me. Even though I'd rehearsed this over and over again in my head, I was acting like an amateur. Someone who got on a "twenty-three under twenty-three" list wouldn't even need notes. They'd have the smarts to talk to her off the cuff. I took a deep breath and collected myself. Since I had gotten this meeting under the pretense of a story on women in Hollywood, I had to start there.

"In the past ten years, there've only been a handful of movies in Hollywood about strong women, and they mostly haven't caught on. *G.I. Jane* was a box office flop. There was *Out of Sight* with Jennifer Lopez, which, in my opinion, was the best movie of nineteen ninety-eight—"

"I loved *Out of Sight*," she said, her eyes wide. I was taken aback. Did Hazel Cahn and I just have a . . . connection? My body tingled.

"Right?! My favorite scene was when Jennifer Lopez and George Clooney are in the hotel drinking bourbon. She's pretending not to be the ass-kicking federal agent, and he's pretending that he's not some suave bank robber. The snow falling in the distance . . ." I said breathlessly, intoxicated with excitement. Her eyes were locked on mine.

"Now that was a great love scene," she said. "Breakout roles for both of them."

Could I safely segue myself into asking about Echo without her feeling threatened?

"You want to know the problem with *Out of Sight*?" Hazel continued, surprising me. "*Armageddon* opened a week later. And *G.I. Jane*? Ahead of its time." And just then, the big black phone on her desk buzzed. She picked it up and threw her head back with a hearty laugh. She motioned at me and then at the recorder with her nails, so I shut it off. Damn it.

"Darling, would I steer you wrong? I'm *wiiiilllld* about it. When I get this reporter out of my office, I'll tell you what I really think!" and she cackled. Something shifted in her face, like I was running out of time. "Yes. Yes. My love to Tallulah," she said and hung up.

I reached forward without asking and resumed the recording. Hazel Cahn had the attention span of a five-year-old. I'd have to move quickly.

"Now, where were we?" she said.

"Do you think *Thelma and Louise* would have been as successful if it had been directed by a woman?"

"I think it *had* to be directed by a man, or else they would have called it a man-hating movie, which happened anyway."

"It's not news that there are more men than women in power in Hollywood," I said, because I had to make it sound like I was casually thinking about this. "Do you think the entertainment industry is making strides to change this imbalance?"

She looked around her office with animated gestures. "Am I on *Candid Camera* or something? Are you telling me you came all the way from

New York to ask me about the lack of female representation in the entertainment industry?"

Hadn't her assistant told her that's why I was here? Our connection fizzled. The phone rang again, and this time she twisted her chair toward the wall of windows to answer. I had to stop futzing around and force myself to be direct. After another quick and exaggerated phone conversation, Hazel ran her nails through her blonde hair and turned back to me.

"Please cut to the chase," she said with irritation. "Tell me why you're here again?"

"Strong women in the industry. Strong female leads," I said. "Would any of your clients be interested in going on the record about how hard it is for women in Hollywood?"

"Not for an article like this," she said, laughing. "You think they want to lose any opportunities in this town? They'd be deemed difficult or ungrateful. And you can't quote me on that. You can use the quote, but don't attach it to me. Understood?"

I nodded.

"What about women who have a lot of power? They can't speak out either?"

"My dear, actresses with power in this industry make up *point one* percent of Hollywood." She held up her index finger, emphasizing *one*. Her nails were so long it was like she had a ruler for a finger. "There's one actress in this town, Julia Roberts, who got paid twenty million dollars for *Erin Brockovich*. The *first* time for a woman to get paid that amount! An unheard-of deal. Why would she want to ruin her clout just to sound ungrateful? You have to be careful with the power you wield, darling. Believe me—this I know."

She glanced at her watch. A gold Rolex with diamonds around the face. "I have one more minute."

It was now or never. I couldn't leave Hazel Cahn's office without mentioning Echo. I took a deep breath in, and the question rolled out like an army tank, combative and dangerous.

"What about Echo Blue? Do you think she has that kind of power?"

Her face went from bored to annoyed to stunned. She jutted forward, and I swear I thought she was going to slap me, but instead she snatched my tape recorder. I heard the click of the record button pop back up as she pressed it.

"This interview is over," she said.

"I'm sorry. I-I don't understand," I stammered.

"Oh, I think you do. Who do you think you are coming into my office pretending to talk to me about feminist representation, then blindsiding me with a topic that was completely off-limits?" she said, her voice rising. "My life coach said I should help people beneath me, and this is what I get for listening to her." Hazel Cahn had so much power. I could lose the story.

Compose yourself, Goldie, I told myself. *You worked hard to bullshit your way into this office. You've already pissed her off; now you have to dig your feet in.* I needed to change tack. To appeal to Hazel Cahn by making it clear I was a true fan. I wasn't going to screw Echo or write an exploitive story. I had to come clean.

"In an interview once, you said that *Myra Breckinridge* by Gore Vidal was your favorite book. You quoted the first line: 'I am Myra Breckinridge whom no man will ever possess.' I always admired you for that."

She still looked irritated, but it seemed like I had bought myself some time. She leaned back in her chair, listening.

"I promise you I'm not here to write anything slanderous. I've been following Echo my whole life. I want nothing more than to make her look like a thriving star in the public eye. And I respect her privacy—I do. Obviously, *Manhattan Eye* is an institution; we're not the *New York Times*, but we're not the *Post* either. We care about our subjects. We're the magazine that's historically protected celebrities."

I could have named four different celebrities who were notoriously on drugs when they were interviewed by *ME*, but their blatant addictions didn't make the pages. Anyway, I didn't need to. Hazel Cahn had to have known this about us. A few of those addicts were probably her clients.

"And I want you to know how grateful I am to be in your office and how seriously I take Echo's disappearance, how I'm sure it has affected you."

I sat there waiting for her response. But she just kept staring at me. She didn't say anything, but she wasn't kicking me out of her office either. Did she want me to keep going? Did she expect me to be like her and go in for the kill? So fine, I did.

"Talking to me about Echo would also paint you in a better light because, you know, the public has questions about how her team, her *management*, have treated her." I pulled out the *People* magazine from my bag of Jamie Blue and his pout, gazing out at the Pacific. The one I snagged from the lobby.

"How about this?" I said. "Her father seems to be upset about the whole thing. What about her agent?"

"Put that away," she growled. "My public perception has nothing to do with what that useless Jamie Blue has to say. If you weren't a rookie, you would know this." Then she muttered, "The only reason I took this interview is because I was relieved to talk about something *other* than Echo."

I couldn't let her dissuade me.

"Why was Echo alone that night she disappeared when she was clearly still vulnerable? She had gotten out of rehab only a few months earlier. Shouldn't someone have protected her?"

With this, I sensed a shift in Hazel. She rose from her chair, her nostrils flaring, and slowly stepped out from behind her desk. She leaned against it, her legs spread apart in a modified power position, and clutched my tape recorder.

"Did Echo send you here?"

Did Echo send me here? Holy shit. There it was. Hazel Cahn, the biggest agent in Hollywood, had no idea where her client was. I *knew* her sound bites about Echo being "totally fine" were bullshit. Now here she was, asking *me*, of all people, if I was some spy for Echo. I was having a hard time processing this.

There was a collection of silver-framed pictures nestled among Hazel's collection of scripts. I zeroed in on a photo of her and Echo. I had imagined it so many times, me and Echo conspiring against the world. How bad would it be if I told her yes?

"You're right," I said and sat up straighter. "Echo sent me here."

For a split second, it felt like she was relieved.

"Did she—" And she paused, tightly smacking her lips. "Did she tell you where she is?"

It surprised me to hear the great Hazel Cahn falter.

"I don't have that information just yet," I said coolly.

I felt crazy. Where would I go from here? Maybe it was the frightened look on my face that gave me away. I wasn't some award-winning actress like her client.

Her eyes narrowed at me, and she tapped one nail on the desk like a military instrument. "You almost had me," she said witheringly. "Echo didn't send you here."

"I can explain—"

"I'm calling the police," she said and picked up her phone. I had to scramble, to say something to stop her. She'd accuse me of kidnapping or conspiracy, and I had just gotten there!

"What are you going to tell the police?" I said. "That you have no idea where your most valuable client, America's sweetheart, is? Because you've assured the public that everything is 'fine.' Are you going to risk having this leaked to the rest of the world? Do you know how many L.A. police officers sell stories to the *National Enquirer*? Oh, I'm sure I don't have to tell you. I know you know."

"Listen, Ms. *Manhattan Eye*, or whoever you are. I've known Echo since she was born. She's a complicated girl, a complicated *woman*, who doesn't always know what she needs. So that's where I come in. But if she's not going to listen to me, my hands are tied. I'm getting really fed up with the diva behavior. Now, it's time for you to get the hell out of my office."

She hit a buzzer and her assistant hustled in. "Show this grifter the door," she said. "And, darling, if you say a word to anyone about this conversation, this joke of an interview, if you print any part of what I said, I'll deny every fucking thing and ruin your career."

She tossed my tape recorder in my lap and turned her back to me.

● ● ●

I shuffled down the hallway past all of the other agents corralled behind their glass doors, their ears glued to their phones, their assistants scrambling around their desks like rats. I got into the elevator, and since another woman was in there, a very tall, super skinny brunette with no makeup, I held in my jubilation. I had gotten Hazel Cahn to admit that this wasn't a PR stunt, and more—that she knew as much about Echo's location as the rest of the world. Now the question lingered about what happened at the last minute before her *TRL* appearance.

I had something. The sky was blue and bright, and I had a beginning.

Echo

1991

. . .

12.

When you're the daughter of one of Hollywood's most famous actors, you can tell him that you want to be in a movie, and after just a few calls, you're signed with his shark of an agent and starring in a movie.

The biggest hurdle was breaking the news to my mom.

She was at the kitchen table reading *Variety* (something I never understood—if she wanted to remove herself from Hollywood, why continue the self-torture?) when she got the call from Hazel.

"Why are you calling me, Hazel?" my mother snapped. "I'm not interested in a Lifetime movie. I already told you that last year."

I put down my toast and watched her talk. I wished I could hide under the table. Suddenly, she turned and stared at me.

"Echo?" she said in the phone. "What do you want with Echo?"

My mom listened for another second, her face turning red, then she threw the phone across the room. It crashed on the floor near the oven. "He's a monster! Your father is a monster," she screamed. She started ranting about Dana Plato, a former child actor from the eighties sitcom *Diff'rent Strokes*. How she, at age twenty-six, had just robbed a video store in Las Vegas with a pellet gun. "The guy who called the police said, 'I got robbed by the girl who played Kimberly on *Diff'rent Strokes*.' Is that the kind of legacy you want to leave in this life, Echo?" I didn't even know who Dana Plato was.

I stared down at my toast, which was now cold, frozen in my chair until she locked herself in the bathroom.

I immediately called my dad, which I never did, and begged him to pick me up. I told him Mom was acting scary and that I felt unsafe. It was only somewhat true. I wasn't afraid she would hurt me (if anything, I thought she was going to hurt herself). I was afraid she wouldn't let me act and my plan to get closer to my dad would be ruined.

It would have been a lot easier if I'd backtracked, promised my mother I wouldn't act after all. But would that have really made her happy?

My dad had his girlfriend at the time, Deborah Morris, come and get me because he was on set making *Time's Up* with Barbara Deblasi—my dad was very good at getting women to do uncomfortable errands for him. I had never met Deborah, and all I knew was that she was an acting teacher who had gotten her degree at Yale. I never understood the connection between her and my dad until, years later, I read in an article that Deborah saw my dad as her one nihilistic relationship. She had been curious about what it was like to be with an ubermasculine "Apollo." "I was insanely attracted to him," she said. When Deborah arrived at my mother's, poised, stable, and friendly, I practically threw myself at her, backpack and pillow in hand. I didn't know what it would mean to leave with this woman. I also didn't care; my body was making the decision for me. This wasn't the last time I acted on impulse and lived to regret it. Directors would tell me for years that my instincts for my characters were always right, but my instincts for myself were lacking.

"Hi, honey, are you okay?" Deborah asked. She was a beautiful Black woman with long braids and a cute hat.

"My mom is having a breakdown," I said quietly. I was shaken, but I tried my best to hold it in. It wasn't that I didn't have any emotion, but when you live with a mentally ill parent, you learn to compartmentalize; you learn to put the hard feelings in a pocket and zip it up tight. "I can't do this anymore."

We could both hear my mother screaming and crying from inside the house.

"It's going to be all right," Deborah said, enveloping me in a hug.

I had no reason to believe her, but strangely I did.

• • •

Back at my dad's house in Venice, it was like another world. An omnipresent housekeeper and an assistant and a clean kitchen. His house wasn't cloaked in sadness. The dishes weren't piled up in the sink.

My mother called later that night when my dad got home from the set. I heard him yelling at her. "What the fuck are you doing? You're going to kill yourself? Because your daughter wants to be in a movie? I don't even know what you're saying, Mathilde. You need help, Mathilde. You need some serious fucking help."

I thought of the time my mother and I went to the beach at Santa Barbara when I was about eight. I could still lie on top of her then, my whole body stretched over hers, listening to her heartbeat, her inhale and exhale. My cheek pressed to her breast. It was a rare outing—she hated risking being noticed in public—but she had a big black hat on, so no one recognized her. The waves lapped against the sand, and I told her I wanted to stay like that forever. I felt so safe. She promised we'd get out of the house more and do more trips, just the two of us, as long as she had her big black hat. We never did, though. I knew she wanted to take me places; she just couldn't.

I hardly slept that night. I remember feeling like I was about to lose my mother for good, and one way or the other, I was.

13.

My first day as an actor, a table reading for *Slugger Eight*, my dad was on location in Mexico, so Valeria, a South American model my dad was now dating, drove me to the Paramount lot. It had only lasted two more months with Deborah, but it had been a great summer, despite my lingering guilt about my mother. The three of us acting like we were a family, my dad doing a picture in Burbank while Deborah and I read Chekhov plays at home, dinner together every night at seven. But then my dad met Valeria and stopped coming home after work. Shortly after, Deborah moved to New York.

My dad was pumped about me working on the Paramount lot. "This is the studio that brought us *The Godfather. The* fucking *Godfather!*" he said before he went to Mexico. He wasn't wrong. There was a mystery around it, like a castle, walled off to the public with the security at the front gate and the palm trees like soldiers. One guard, an older man with a gray beard, leaned in and gave me a warm smile when Valeria told him my name. "Tell your pop that Mel from Queens said hello."

We drove in through the majestic arches that glowed in the bright California sunshine; all of the people shuffled quickly past the car looking serious and important. The Hollywood sign hovered in the mountains. But as we got closer, you could see it for what it was. The yellowing buildings with the massive painted stage numbers, the shabby trailers, the golf carts, the assistants rushing around in headsets and with sweat dripping down their cheeks. It made me uneasy, like someone was going to take me prisoner or throw me in a dungeon.

Valeria signed me in with a young PA outside of soundstage eight (that's right—the same place they filmed *Breakfast at Tiffany's* and *Rosemary's Baby*) and said she'd be back in an hour.

"You're just going to leave me here?" I said.

"I told your father that I had an appointment in West Hollywood. He didn't tell you?"

I shook my head.

The PA rolled his eyes. "I have to report it to the union rep if a guardian is gone longer than an hour. But he doesn't get here until one o'clock so you should be fine."

Valeria turned to me. "Echo. You're gonna be a movie star. It's going to be a new adventure for you. Think of it like the first day of school."

But this was nothing like school—I knew what I was supposed to do in school. I had friends there. I had finished fourth grade before officially withdrawing, so the summer, spent with Kat, Ayana, and Zoe, felt normal. Now it was September and my friends were back to their usual routine—school followed by soccer or chorus or any other of the endless after-school activities available to L.A. kids, and I hardly saw them. I would take classes on set with a studio teacher the production company hired for all of the kids. I assumed I'd go back to real school by January. But my dad and I didn't have a plan. *"Let's see what your schedule looks like,"* he kept saying when I asked.

Once Valeria zoomed off into the distance, I almost caved and called my dad, which he explicitly told me not to do. *"No calls unless there's blood, get it? I can't be disturbed."* So instead, I wandered into the dark soundstage with some direction from the PA. Dwarfed by its cavernous ceilings engulfed in intricate lighting tracks like the trenches of the Death Star, the crew were building what I guessed would be one of the interior locations, like my character's house, or the school the kids went to. Hazel had already told me that we'd shoot the exterior neighborhood on the Paramount lot, a fake outdoor urban/suburban street.

Off to the side, a circle of adults armed with clipboards clustered around a person who was clearly in charge. I hoped someone might turn around and notice me. *Don't cry, don't cry, don't cry.*

Then I felt a hand on my shoulder. I was surprised to recognize that it belonged to a skinny woman with stringy blonde hair, wearing no makeup (clearly, she wasn't an actor). It was Sandy Summers, a costume designer I remembered meeting when my dad was doing *Frannie and Frankie.*

"Echo? Is that you?" she asked, giving me a big hug. I must have sighed with relief. "Where's your dad?"

"His girlfriend dropped me off. She's coming back." At least, I hoped she was.

She rolled her eyes. "Oh, typical Jamie. He can't bring his daughter to set the first day?"

Sandy took my hand and walked me toward a table of breakfast foods where her daughter, Belinda, who I learned was playing my teammate Mallory, was standing. I was relieved I wasn't the only one here because of my parent's job.

Belinda had a short brown bob with little bangs, and she wore a wrist full of thin gold chains, some friendship knots fraying on the edges, and one chunky bracelet with small beads that spelled out her name. She was eating a chocolate donut. "Want one?" she said, with her mouth full. I nodded, picking one up and taking a bite. I hadn't remembered to eat that morning.

"Belinda, chew before you speak," Sandy tsked, but not in a mean way. Belinda shrugged and Sandy hip-checked her playfully. They were cute. Sandy turned to talk to a line producer holding another ubiquitous clipboard, and I shoved the rest of the donut in my mouth.

"I think our parents had sex once," Belinda said flatly.

I almost choked on my donut. Belinda had to smack me on the back. She laughed and shushed me so that her mom wouldn't hear.

"Your dad was coming out of the bathroom in the middle of the night, and I saw his tush. His hair was the dead giveaway. My mom tries to hide men from me, but sometimes I end up bumping into someone when they think I'm asleep." Belinda was funny. I wanted to be her friend from that moment.

I wished my dad were a little more discreet with the women who came into our lives. I had only been living with him for three months, and he'd already had two girlfriends and three "sleepovers" with women whose names I don't remember.

"Come with us, sweetie," Sandy said, returning to the table and taking Belinda's hand, then mine. "We'll go into the read through together." I was relieved but also felt a surge of jealousy. Yes, I was slightly suspicious of Sandy now that I knew she had slept with my dad, but at least she was right by her daughter's side. It would've been impossible for my mother to be here like this, supporting me. She had at least called the night before to wish me good luck, though I had to listen to a long diatribe about how children shouldn't be allowed in the entertainment industry.

"What about Judy Garland?" I had said. "You can't erase her from Hollywood history, Mom."

"You want to be like Judy Garland, Echo?"

"Okay, fine. Judy Garland *without* the pills," I countered. I knew my stuff by now.

"Just be careful, Echo," she said, sniffing before hanging up the phone.

We followed Sandy into a large room with oversize windows and big curtains to block out the light. Desks were arranged into a square, and everyone's name and role were written in large letters on white cards. I would be playing the fearless captain of the team and shortstop, Joey, and I was supposed to be sitting between Olivia Breakers and Cassandra Ellen Burdock, who played Steph and Lizzie, but since neither of them were there yet, I switched the cards so I could sit next to Belinda.

A read through is supposed to be just that—a chance for the whole cast to read through the script in its entirety so everyone in the same room can get a feel for what the story sounds like. There's no blocking. It's not even a rehearsal, at least according to my dad, who explained it to me the night before in a short phone call from some beach in Mexico. *"As long as you can read, you've got this in the bag, Echo."*

But that's not how Theo, our director, wanted it. He bounced between cast members, unable to sit still. Theo didn't like how I delivered my lines. "A little flat, Echo," came the first critique. Then I was speaking too softly. Then, during a quick pause, he squatted down next to me and explained how I should work on my "inflections." Every time he gave a direction, I saw other adults in the room jotting notes. Was I that bad? I was convinced they were writing down lists of girls they wanted to replace me with and thinking that casting me had been a huge mistake.

My dad and Hazel promised me that this was just a practice movie. *"A small kids' movie with no budget,"* Hazel said. *"Zero expectations,"* she said. Yet here I was, completely unprepared for the first day.

* * *

We took a lunch break, and the other girls and I huddled in a circle. Not only did I screw up the read through, but it quickly became clear I was an outsider among my peers. They exchanged war stories from theater camp, and many seemed to know each other from years of acting. It was impossible for me to contribute to the conversation because I had never acted. I'd never even been to camp. My mother made sure of that.

Olivia Breakers, who was fifteen, had gotten into LaGuardia High School in New York City, which, I learned, was a performing arts public school. According to her, it was "very hard to get into." She told us this a few times within the span of five minutes. "It's the most prestigious acting high school in New York City, maybe the country," she said. When Olivia turned her back, Belinda rolled her eyes, and I almost squealed in laughter.

The other girls—Delilah Cooper, Sidney Pierce, Cassandra Ellen Burdock—were middle schoolers who had moved to L.A. from across the country because their parents had big dreams of them getting Disney contracts or booking a show like *Full House*. Sidney Pierce's mother made her wear a tight sports bra because she was too developed. "Boobs make you look old," she said knowingly. "I can't look sexy when I'm up for a show where I have to play a thirteen-year-old."

"But you *are* thirteen," I said.

"It doesn't matter."

That was the acting world my mother was afraid of. Actresses all over the place being judged for their own flesh.

Delilah Cooper, who was originally from Atlanta, had done a small part on a Disney show and then it got abruptly canceled. She kept saying she was *so close* to getting another series and squeezed her thumb and index finger together. Apparently, this movie was also going to get us *so close*. It took me a few minutes to realize she was talking about fame.

Cassandra Ellen did community theater where she lived in Westchester, New York. She and her mother and sister moved to L.A. so she could audition while her father stayed back east to work. "He misses us," she said. "Sometimes I wonder if it's worth it."

"As long as this movie doesn't go straight to video, it'll be worth it," Sidney said.

"What's your experience, Echo?" Delilah said. "How did you get the lead?"

"That's a question," Olivia snorted.

"Well, she got the lead because her father is Jamie Blue," Cassandra Ellen said.

I didn't respond. I could feel my face turn hot.

"It's fine, Echo. Nothing to be embarrassed about. My father says that nepotism accounts for eighty percent of Hollywood jobs. It's just a fact of life," Cassandra Ellen said.

It all sunk in at that moment. These were kids who worked hard to be here, who were striving to get the best agent, determined to book a Disney show or at least book a *one-liner* on a Disney show. I had no acting experience. My agent was Hazel Cahn. I was Jamie Blue and Mathilde Portman's daughter. I was supposed to belong here, but with these girls,

I felt like a phony. My family didn't have to move to L.A., and no one was left behind. I didn't have to starve myself. I didn't even have to audition for this role. What could I tell them? That acting was in my blood? That this is what I was born to do? They'd see me as a fraud.

"I had some private auditions," I said. "Like, they called me back ten different times. They tortured me."

I told them Theo didn't even know I was Jamie Blue's daughter when I first went in. That I had taken years of acting classes. That I had called the producer of the movie myself and then called the director and begged them for a shot at the part.

I found it so easy to lie. I'd had to do it my whole life with my mother. And maybe that's what made me a natural actor. (*"Never call yourself an actress,"* my dad told me. *"It makes you sound cheap."*) I had an imagination, and when I needed to turn it on, I could sink into a character. That day when those girls interrogated me in the circle, I was playing the part of Echo Blue the actor. Not Echo Blue the person.

This stopped them from asking any more questions.

"I think Breakers is Olivia's stage name," Belinda whispered later at the table. "I think her real last name is something like Brukowski." I squeezed her hand and smiled. I didn't tell Belinda in that moment that my dad's last name, Blue, was also a stage name. "By the way," she continued, "I don't care if you got the role because of your dad. You're here now, and that's all that matters. All these girls would die to have a dad in the business." It was nice to have someone there who didn't view me as competition.

"I like your bracelet," I said, wanting to reciprocate her kindness.

Her face lifted with pride. "I made it from a bead kit left over from when I was, like, five. I was bored the other day. I can make you one . . ."

"I'd really like that," I said, feeling like maybe things would be okay. That being an actor was in my DNA. That I belonged here.

14.

The next month consisted of a softball training camp. I had never picked up a baseball or softball in my life, nor had most of the girls, but those days were a dream. Outside in the sun, sweating and covered in baseball dirt. I went to bed at nine every night and woke up at six. My shoulders and thighs ached from practice, but it was a good ache. It filled that need for structure since I wasn't in school anymore.

My dad got back from his shoot the last week of training and came to the field with *Entertainment Tonight* in tow. *ET* wanted behind-the-scenes footage of the wholesome girls playing softball, the kind of scene that sold well to television advertisers.

Hazel had a T-shirt made for my dad that read in big letters ECHO'S DAD. Everyone thought it was so cute, and the trainers told me how lucky I was. I heard the production team discussing how the picture of Jamie in that T-shirt should be part of the early marketing campaign. The on-set photographer got a shot of him and Hazel with her giant sunglasses in the stands watching us. Paps lined the fence around the field, despite the *ET* crew yelling at them to step back.

Once everyone got bored and the *ET* crew took off, my dad started packing up his stuff to leave too. "Can we go to Dan Tana's tonight,

Daddy?" I asked him as he started tramping through the dusty parking lot.

"Look, Echo, I have baseball dust up my nose. I have to go home and shower."

"We can shower and then go?" I said eagerly.

I could see him getting irritated. A cloud of dust kicked up around us as other people pulled out of the parking lot. He rubbed his eyes aggressively.

"Hazel's going to take you home, and I'm going to catch up with you later, okay?" he said tersely, then kissed me on the head and left.

I knew better than to chase him or to beg him in front of anyone. The paps were gone, but some of the crew and a few parents were still lingering. *What will people think?* I scanned the field and saw Hazel wobbling toward me in her wedges and oversize round sunglasses, her big caftan blowing behind her in the wind. I wanted to run from her, but I was stuck.

I didn't cry much in those days, but Belinda must have noticed that I was upset. She read me well early on. She came over next to me, not saying a word, then twisted the BELINDA bracelet off her wrist and looped it around her finger. With her other hand, she gently stretched the bracelet over my wrist. I remembered Belinda saying she'd make me one, but it was more special to have hers. My eyes filled with tears, and I wiped them away with my dirty forearm.

I was never going to take it off.

Goldie

. . .

15.

Outside Hazel Cahn's office building, the first person I called was Pench. It sounded like he was on a boat, his words chopped up.

"Goldie? Can you hear me now? Can you hear me now? I'm moving to the lobby; maybe I'll have better reception. Can you hear me now?"

I looked around at the looming palm trees while he searched for a better spot. People actually *lived* here in Southern California, with the sunny weather all the time, the wind blowing gently. I was going on three hours of sleep and I wasn't even mad. I was invigorated.

"So what happened?" he said.

"Hazel Cahn doesn't know where her client is—that's what happened. Echo showed up for the New Year's Eve gig and then she left, and not even her agent knows where she is. Boom. No trace."

"You're kidding. That's huge. How did you get that out of her?"

I considered making up some elaborate story on how I convinced her to talk to me, but I also worried Hazel would call Pench and I'd be outed. Worse, that she'd track down Dana. Or even higher, our publisher.

"She was more open than I anticipated. Let's just put it that way. But this adds another element to the story. It tells us Echo's not in rehab, and this isn't just some orchestrated publicity stunt to get attention for her new movie. Something is seriously up."

"So basically, you think she's being held hostage in some lakeside cabin? Like in *Fargo*?" Pench said, then, in Frances McDormand's character's Minnesota accent, "*I guess that was your accomplice in the woodchipper.*"

I couldn't listen to Pench's dad jokes.

"No, obviously not. This is real life. Anyway," I said, irritated. I refused to imagine Echo suffering an indignity like that. "If you get a phone call from Hazel Cahn, beware. She was very . . . on edge."

"What does 'on edge' mean?"

"She kicked me out of her office, Pench."

I could hear him sighing over the phone, his breath heavy.

"Well, I guess I should toss Hazel Cahn out of my BlackBerry," he said. "But it sounds like you're onto something. You're gonna need a research person on this to help you. I can fly out there first thing in the morning if you want and, you know, just help you organize your notes."

"You don't have your own deadline?" I said.

"I could take a day or two off. Just a quick trip."

It was a sweet gesture—he wasn't even angry I'd jeopardized his relationship with Hazel Cahn—but it was also questionable. On the one hand, it was comforting to know I'd have help. It's not like I would snuggle in bed with him at the end of a hard day (I'd never let him see me that vulnerable), but he could listen to my ramblings and help me brainstorm. Then we could fuck and he could make me come to disperse some of my anxiety. On the other hand, I didn't want him taking over my story. I told him I'd call him later.

My next appointment was with Olivia Breakers, who was one of the softball players in *Slugger Eight*. We were supposed to meet at one. I walked over to the Beverly Hilton and stood in front of a large palm, flagging down a taxi that was pulling out of the hotel.

"Can you take me to Canter's Deli?" I asked the driver as I got in. I had tried to get the owners to talk to me because I read Echo hung out at the Kibitz Room, a little bar next to the deli. But they wouldn't go on the record. Meeting Olivia Breakers there would at least put me close to them, and maybe I could get them to talk on the fly.

I looked at the license that was stuck behind the window. The driver's name was Shane Dellabata.

"Sure, we can take Santa Monica to Beverly, or take Sunset," he said.

"Either is fine."

"So what are you doing in L.A.?" he said as he drove, making eye contact with me in the rearview mirror.

"How do you know I don't live here?"

"Because everyone in L.A. has a car. And if you're taking a cab, it means that you're not local. Also, you would have an opinion about which way to go."

"I'm a journalist here on a story assignment." I sat up straight in the back seat, proud of myself. Me. A celebrity journalist.

"Oh, cool," he said, because that's what non-writers say. *Cool.* They think that writing is an ethereal career where the words shine down from the clouds and effortlessly pour onto your paper.

I watched him in the rearview mirror. He had a sweet smile, but his eyes looked a little dead. I liked the way he rubbed the steering wheel with his right hand. He had nice fingernails. Not ragged or too short. Blond hair fell down to his shoulders. I liked men with long hair; there was something feminine and soft about them. Safer. Maybe I was fooling myself about this theory; it was entirely possible that he was just a psychopath. Or worse, a surfer.

"Gonna eat a pastrami sandwich at Canter's?" he asked.

"I'm a vegetarian," I said.

"Too bad, because they have great pastrami sandwiches. Super sour pickles too," he said. "So what's your story about?"

I was tempted to make up something, that I was on a story about Jewish delis as celebrity hot spots in L.A. That would have been easy enough. But then, about a block from where we were, I noticed the corner of the street was packed with cars and photographers.

"What's going on there?" I said.

"Oh, that's North Robertson," he said. "Paparazzi central. The Ivy's over there. An absolute madhouse."

I thought about a photo I had of Echo just after her Oscar win. She was in the passenger seat of a big silver Mercedes, shielding her face from the cameras.

"So have you driven a lot of famous people?"

"Some."

"Name one famous person you've driven."

"Celebrities have their own drivers, but on the off chance I have to pick someone up at a seedy bar, it's Al Pacino. Great tipper. Gave me a hundred bucks." I liked the way Shane spoke. Like an old-timer in a surfer's body.

He pulled up in front of Canter's. The big yellow-and-green art deco neon sign hung in the front of the building like a movie marquee. It must have looked like a painting at night.

I leaned forward in the seat. "Any chance you can come back for me in, like, an hour?"

He spun around so I could see his face. He was very pretty. Strong jaw. It took my breath away a little bit. I wondered what it would be like to bring him back to my casita and get into bed with him. He'd run those soft fingers all over me.

"I could be anywhere by then. It's not like I stay in one area. You want to keep the meter running and I'll wait?"

"I'm kind of on a budget. I don't have an expense account," I said and gave him my best flirtatious smile. "But how about I bring you a pastrami sandwich?"

Grinning back, he agreed.

•   •   •

Inside it looked exactly the way it did in pictures, with the terra-cotta booths, another giant Canter's sign in cursive above the round bar, the yellow walls. The waiter brought me a plate of giant pickles, and Shane was right—they were sour and crunchy. My mouth puckered. When Olivia arrived, a few minutes late, I could see her frantically scanning the room for me. Even though the last time I saw her was in a movie over seven years ago, I recognized her right away. I waved to her, and she speed walked over.

"I'm so sorry. I've been getting so many phone calls since Echo disappeared, and then suddenly, I got three back-to-back auditions, so I'm running from a callback, and oh my god, are those pickles?" She didn't take a breath.

I pushed the plate toward her. "Please, help yourself," I said.

"Yeah, it's been crazy," she said, chomping on a pickle and signaling the waiter. I hoped Olivia wouldn't order anything too expensive, and I was relieved when she got a diet cream soda. Without preamble, she launched into a diatribe about her life, how hard it was to transition from child actor to adult roles, how her agent dumped her after she broke out in cystic acne when she was seventeen. "She could have just sent me to the dermatologist."

After fifteen minutes of this, I had to break in. "So you said over the phone that you had some insight?"

"Well, I have a couple of thoughts. For one, I think Echo's entire career was a sham. She rode on Daddy's coattails. And don't even get me started on him."

It made me edgy. Clearly, she was envious. Echo and her dad had a solid relationship. "What do you mean?"

"Their picture-perfect relationship?" She took a big munch of her pickle. "*Fake*."

There was a smugness about Olivia that felt like a front. I remembered reading somewhere that she briefly tried to have a singing career to reinvent herself and failed miserably. She too was a child star, and it couldn't have been easy, especially if she compared herself to Echo all those years. I tried to take her seriously.

"Why do you think their relationship was fake?"

"When we were doing *Slugger*, Jamie Blue came to the set *once*. We made that movie for four months. My mom was there every day. Everyone's mother was. Then he shows up when *ET* was there? And acts all lovey-dovey? It was bullshit. There's honestly something sinister about him. I don't know why everyone's afraid to admit it."

I thought of the iconic photo of Jamie Blue wearing that ECHO'S DAD T-shirt on the *Slugger Eight* set. He looked like he was going to jump in and coach the team. There was a snapshot of him playing catch with her in the outfield too, wasn't there? I'd have to look through my box of images.

I often wished my father, the hunched-over, cranky professor, was more like Jamie Blue, the handsome, all-American star with the blond hair, so supportive of his daughter's life. I remembered the days when I'd try to avoid my father's attacks on my English papers, or his droning lectures about Hamlet's soliloquy, and I'd fantasize that we could be like Jamie Blue and Echo. I'd picture the two of them palling around on set, out to dinner at their favorite spot, Dan Tana's (which reminded me — I had to try to make a reservation there), on walks at the beach. What Olivia was saying made no sense.

"What about this new article in *People*?" I said, pulling the copy I had from my bag. I thumbed to the article. Inside, the pull quote read, "We haven't always had a perfect relationship, but I'm determined to find my daughter. Whatever it takes."

Olivia squinted at it and shrugged. "It was all an act. It's still an act. Look at the emancipation," Olivia said. "Does that not tell you enough?"

"But Echo was open about the emancipation. It was to get around child labor laws so she could work longer hours," I said. "Did you ever see the two of them fighting?"

"No, but—"

"Did she confide in you about her father?"

"Not exactly," she said. "But I know what's real. And I know what's not. And I bet if you follow the Jamie Blue trail, you might have more insight into where Echo is. If you ask me, he did something to her. He was jealous of her. How could he not be?"

"He could be a normal parent and be proud of his daughter."

"Actors aren't *normal*," she said and gave me a wide smile, a bit of pickle between her two front teeth. "Anyway, let me tell you more about this new project I've got a part in. It's called *Coyote Ugly*, and it's about a struggling songwriter who has to work at this seedy bar in Manhattan."

"Sounds fascinating." I wrapped up the conversation, promising her I would write all about the movie, asked the waitress for a pastrami sandwich to go, and thanked Olivia for meeting me.

"Can I take the rest of these pickles?" she said. "They were delicious."

16.

Outside, Shane was waiting in his cab. I handed him his pastrami sandwich when I got in the back seat. "Do you mind if I sit here and eat it for a second? You know, so I don't get Russian dressing all over my shirt?"

"Go right ahead," I said, resting my head back. Jet lag was catching up to me, and that conversation with Olivia Breakers gave me a lot to think about. I'd have to look back at my old teenybopper magazine clippings from that time, but I recall a remarkably canned interview where Echo was asked if she still talked to the girls in *Slugger Eight*. Her response: "I love all those girls like sisters, but our lives have gotten so busy. Belinda's the only one I keep in touch with—obviously!" It's true that Echo was only ever seen with Belinda. That is until their mysterious separation that no one knew the cause of.

If Jamie and Echo were estranged, if their relationship was an act, how would Olivia Breakers even know? She wouldn't know. That was the point. Plus, it was clear that Jamie was worried sick about Echo. I felt compelled to go to Venice, where I knew Jamie lived. Who knows? Maybe I'd get a peek of him outside his house, kayaking on the canal or something. At least it would give me a sense of where they had lived together.

"Hey, so how far is Venice from here?"

"With traffic, about a half hour," he said.

"Any interest in going with me? Like walking the beach or the canals or something. Since I'm from out of town, I would be completely lost." He eyed me with a little apprehension, so I gazed at him as seductively as I could manage in the mirror. It felt risky to ask a complete stranger to walk around with me, but not as risky as wandering the notoriously sketchy Venice Beach alone.

"Sure, why not?" he said, looking hopeful. "But I still have to charge you for the cab ride. Sorry. They count the gas mileage."

• • •

We parked the car, cut through an alley, and there it was, the Pacific gleaming in the sunlight. Music floated through the air, and we walked down the sand path into a crowded area where hundreds of people filled up a long walkway between the shops and the beach. I wanted to ask Shane if he knew anyone famous—Hollywood was a small town; you never know—but he was too busy spewing factoids about the big community push to save the graffiti that covered the walls and create new murals in Venice. It was the kind of story I would have done if I lived here in Los Angeles, the kind my father would have been proud of. Instead, I tuned out Shane's blathering.

Shane stopped in front of a mural of a female drummer, where a crowd of real-life drummers, bongo players, and smelly white guys with dreads and tambourines gathered. A photo of Belinda and Echo riding their bikes past a mural flashed in my mind. It had to be the same one. I dodged a very tall man wearing a ROCK STEADY, BABY T-shirt who aggressively tried to give me a tambourine.

"Where are the canals?" I yelled to Shane over the music. He took my hand and led me through a path between the houses, leaving the beach and the music behind. I had never held a stranger's hand so quickly before, but I was never almost assaulted by a man with a tambourine either. It was awkward, so I let go as we crossed the street.

"What do you do when you're not driving your cab?" I said.

79

"Oh, I'm an actor, like everyone else in this town."

"Do you like acting?" I asked him.

"I love it. But the rejection is tough. I thought I was going to come out to L.A. and make some real connections. I have a good acting class that supports me, but the industry is cutthroat. It can be a little lonely."

He combed his hair out of his face with his fingers, movie-star style. You'd think he'd have been a big deal just off his great teeth, or at least a soap opera star. I wondered if he went to the dentist to get them that white or if they looked that way naturally.

"So, you didn't answer me earlier when I first asked you," Shane said. "What's your story about?"

"It's about women in Hollywood, but also about Echo Blue, the actress. You've probably heard that she's gone missing."

"Interesting," he said. Did I see his eye twitch?

"I know this might sound outrageous, but I heard her father lives in Venice. Any idea where?" Yes, I knew he lived on the canals, but I didn't want to sound obsessed. "Just, you know, out of curiosity."

We walked about five minutes, past the smaller houses all piled on top of each other, until we hit the canals. It felt completely different from the rest of the city. Quaint bungalows and larger homes lined both sides of the waterway with wooden pedestrian bridges to the left and right. A group of ducks floated past. Shane and I strolled down a walkway, and as we crossed a bridge, he pointed to a big gray metal building. "There it is," he said.

"How do you know?"

"Everyone around here knows," he said, shrugging.

We came to a dead halt, and I held my breath. I wanted to run over and knock on his door, but of course that would have ruined everything. *Don't act like a maniac, Goldie*, I told myself. *You're playing the long game here.*

"You should pick me up tomorrow," I said. Never mind that that's when I was supposed to fly back to New York. This story was going somewhere. I had to ask Dolly if I could stay longer and change my flight.

Maybe Dana would chip in when I filled her in on what I'd gotten out of Hazel.

"I'll pay for the taxi for the whole day. I'll pay for lunch. It'll be fun."

I don't think I had used the word *fun* in any sentence ever. But I needed to seem upbeat and open. Shane Dellabata would be my perfect unofficial tour guide of L.A. Who better than a struggling actor? Someone who wanted to get close to Hollywood royalty as much as I did? Was I using the poor guy? Yes. But I was there for the most important story of my life. I was there to find Echo Blue.

● ● ●

When I got back to the casita, I listened to my messages. There was one from my mother and then another from my father, both calling separately to ask how things were going. I'd deal with them later. The third message was from Dana. "What the hell happened with Hazel Cahn? Wow, she's a terror. She threatened to talk to our publisher, that she'd blacklist every single *ME* reporter and cut off access to all of her clients." My heart lurched. Then she laughed. "Oh, I love it when agents get their panties in a bunch. Whatever went down, good work."

Echo

1992–1993

. . .

17.

Slugger Eight turned out to be a huge sleeper, defying expectations. Shot for $10 million, it made $205 million at the box office, alongside *Aladdin* ($504.1 million), *Home Alone 2* ($359 million), *Beethoven* ($147.2 million), and *The Mighty Ducks* ($50.8 million).

"Three pictures about boys and one picture about a giant dog," Hazel said in an interview with the *New York Times* about the film's surprise success. "*Slugger Eight* was up there with all those movies, and you know what? It had what they don't, which is eight teen girls. Here's a lesson for you all out there. Never forget about the teenage girls."

Conversely, my dad's latest film, *Good Night, Awake*, had underperformed. It was a huge picture with a wide release starring him and Oscar nominee Sandra Davies. In retrospect, the whole premise of the movie was doomed: my dad's character and Sandra's character fight for most of the movie until she finally leaves him for a dorky accountant. The reviews were terrible.

Jamie Blue's charm has fizzled.

If I were Davies's character, I would have dumped Blue too.

And the dumbest one: Good Night, Awake *put me to sleep*.

Still, my dad wanted to go to New York City and celebrate all our hard work. "Let 'em say what they want about our movies. We're gonna go have a good time." I didn't correct him—that it was only *his* movie they were saying bad things about. I already knew better.

We stayed at the Carlyle Hotel on the Upper East Side in a two-floor suite. It was fancy, super art deco versus modern, the way my dad's house was back in Venice. It overlooked Central Park, had New York–themed paintings hanging on the walls, and our initials were monogrammed into the white pillowcases, but I felt lonely in this big suite by myself while my dad and Greta, a model who was his flavor of the week, went out dancing. When they'd come back drunk and stoned (I knew they were on something because they smelled of sweat and were slurring), I'd curl up at the foot of their king-size bed because I didn't want to be in the other room all by myself.

After a few nights of this, I begged him not to leave me behind the next time they went out.

"You're right, Echo," my dad said. "If you're old enough to be in a blockbuster movie, you're old enough for a night out."

Greta protested. "This is no way to raise a girl; she hasn't even gotten her period yet, Jamie." I was twelve, but she was right. I was still flat and looked like a little kid while Belinda was already wearing actual bras.

But my dad and I won the argument. I know it became something the press focused on, that I "partied" with my dad, but it wasn't like that. That first time, we went down to Bemelmans Bar, the famous Carlyle haunt with the walls intricately painted by Ludwig Bemelmans, who drew all of the *Madeline* books. We sat in a leather booth with the backdrop of a mouse in a suit smoking a cigar. A jazz band played Ella Fitzgerald. They ordered me a Shirley Temple with a splash of prosecco because, as Greta said, "In Switzerland, I had my first glass of champagne at six." (Greta had lots of conflicting rules.)

Someone took a photo of the three of us that night with me sucking on a cherry from my drink, and it ended up in one of the tabloids. "LIT-TLE LOLITA," the headline read. My cheeks were round and flushed in that picture. This became our routine for the rest of the week. I loved those nights at Bemelmans. When we'd go out for the day, for lunches at Isabella's on the West Side, just on the other side of the park, a visit to the Met, or feeding the turtles in Central Park, Greta liked holding hands with me while my dad trailed just a little behind us — "For protective reasons," he would say with a wink. My handsome dad, so strong and secure as the paps snapped pictures, looking like he would kick your ass if you came near me. Greta thought the pictures in Page Six were enchanting. "We're like a little family. Daddy looks like a big papa bear," she'd say and stroke his cheek. I heard him speaking to Hazel about me only once during that time. She must have told him to stop bringing me to Bemelmans because it was going to endanger the Disney contract she had been trying to nail down since my success in *Slugger Eight*. "She's drinking a fucking Shirley Temple, Hazel," I heard him say.

Then one night he told me to put on party clothes because we were going dancing at the Limelight, a club that was built inside a massive Gothic-style church in Chelsea. Greta bought me a daisy-covered empire-cut minidress and a tube of sticky lip gloss. I knew not to ask about Disney. I was convinced my father knew best when it came to my career.

We breezed past the line of people, my dad holding on to my hand. One woman screamed when she saw me. "My daughter loves you!" Her eyes were wide and bloodshot, her lipstick smeared. It was the first time a fan scared me. I gripped my dad's hand tighter.

Inside, a large man with a piercing in his lip escorted us through the crowds, past two women dancing in cages on platforms, to the VIP section. There was a huge gargoyle hanging from the ceiling and green and pink lights reflecting off the bar.

We had been there for about a half hour when Grace Jones came over and introduced herself. She was wearing dark glasses and a bra and thigh-high boots with black shorts. Her bulging cheekbones glittered in fuchsia. "You're an icon, sweetheart," she said and kissed me on the head. I asked her for her autograph, and she signed my arm with purple lipstick.

Greta turned to my dad and teased, "Grace Jones never came up to you, Jamie. She only approaches us when Echo is here." A muscle in my dad's brow jumped. "I need another drink," he grumbled and stormed off. Greta told me to stay put and chased after him. I snuck a sip of Greta's champagne, and it felt good, the bubbly feeling in my mouth and that fuzziness in my head. Then I gulped the whole thing, and I was no longer worried about them disappearing or fighting, or whatever they were doing, and I got up and danced around the table by myself. A day later, there was a photo of me in Page Six dancing with the champagne flute in my hand.

My mother called me and left a frantic message after she saw it.

"I thought your dad was going to act like a dad. I didn't know he was going to act like Drew Barrymore's mother and start dragging you to clubs. Are you addicted to cocaine too? Please be careful, Echo. This isn't good for you." I didn't call her back.

● ● ●

Two days later, my dad sent me back to L.A. to stay with Alma, our house manager, while he stayed in New York to "wrap things up." Things were tense between him and Greta, and he suddenly couldn't stand the photographers who had been chasing us down since my Limelight appearance. Plus, I was going to start shooting my next movie, a *Pollyanna* remake, soon. "Miraculously," according to Hazel, the contract with Disney had gone through, but not without a stipulation that they only wanted to see me in "family-centric" situations in the press. My dad scoffed at this. "Oh, me taking my daughter out at night isn't family-centric? What would they rather me do, leave her with a nanny all day? Give me a fucking break!"

I felt so lonely back at the house without him after our week by his side at the Carlyle. To be lonely as a child isn't something you understand until you're an adult. You ache, but you don't understand why. You rock yourself back and forth to get to sleep, holding the covers tight, embarrassed to say what you feel. To be close to my dad had been all I had ever dreamed of. For once it was me by his side in the tabloids (and Greta too, but that was okay). And now I was back home by myself.

No one my age was around to hang out with either. Belinda was in a school play, so when she wasn't in class, she was constantly busy with rehearsals, and my social group had whittled down to just her. I'd never quite hit it off with the other *Slugger Eight* girls, and I'd hung out with my old friends a couple of times since getting my role, but it felt different now. They'd ask me about my "new life," as they put it, and when I told them about craft services, or how I had to once do eleven takes to get a line right, they'd just look at me with blank stares. I didn't like to think about how little we had in common now. My only company was my tutor, whom I had been seeing at home three hours a day since *Slugger* wrapped, and Alma. Plus once-a-week visits with my mom.

After several days without my leaving the house much, Alma suggested taking me to Disneyland. "I'm not a baby," I shot back in an angry tone I didn't fully recognize. We could have ridden Space Mountain, and part of me even wanted to go on "it's a small world" like I did when Kat Bergen's mother took us once. But if I wanted to hang out with my dad, I had to grow up. Instead, I had Alma take me shopping at an outdoor vintage market in Santa Monica because I missed those days in New York, being surrounded by people. I wore a baseball cap and sunglasses as a disguise, which probably just made me more conspicuous because it was foggy that afternoon. The market was jammed with kids who looked like high schoolers, giggling as they tried on floppy hats, their arms linked together as they walked through the crowd. I felt lonelier than ever. After only half an hour, Alma and I drove back to the house in silence as the fog lifted.

That night, I took a Klonopin out of my dad's pillbox. (I'd seen him take one when he'd get off the phone with Hazel. Or when he was talking to a director he didn't like. Or when he was breaking up with someone.) I never saw him take a whole one, just halves, so I did the same. About ten minutes later I was asleep in bed, not worried about a thing.

Life.

Shut.

Off.

18.

Pollyanna would be my first solo role after being part of an ensemble in *Slugger Eight*. The iteration of *Pollyanna* starring Hayley Mills was set in the early 1900s, but this remake would be set in the present with a stubbornly optimistic Pollyanna, now a kid in foster care, who goes to live with her rich, miserable aunt. Pollyanna was irritatingly happy. When her father couldn't afford to buy her a doll, she played with the crutches from the nearby medical center. The soup kitchen she volunteered at with the rich aunt had no money for art, so she crafted flowers out of paper cups.

I was in almost every scene, a problem because I was only twelve, almost thirteen, and there were rules about how many hours a minor could be on set. Kids from ages nine to fifteen were allowed on set for nine hours but could only work for five hours of that day (three hours were set aside for class instruction, and one hour for rest). Once you turned sixteen, you could work for six hours. "Can you turn sixteen already, kid?" my director would joke. (No one laughed.)

My dad paid someone to be my on-set guardian, an earnest young woman named Irene Papa, who doubled as my studio teacher. I ran lines while learning about the Revolutionary War. I was the only kid on the

Pollyanna set except Tyler James Masterson, the little boy who played Jimmy Bean, the other foster kid Pollyanna hangs around with. But his part wrapped in just three weeks. So most of my free time was spent with Irene or alone.

My dad wasn't around at all during that time. He was shooting a movie in Wales, a "masterpiece," he said, *Matthew, Matthew.* He came home maybe twice in six months. It was all for the chance to work with Samuel Tobin, an experimental director famous for demanding an unheard-of number of takes and, according to rumors, even once causing an actor to have a nervous breakdown. My dad didn't care. He said he'd do a hundred takes if that's what Samuel wanted, because this was the role for him. He wasn't going to take *Philadelphia*, because he wasn't going to play a gay guy with AIDS — "No way in hell." And he wasn't going to do *Forrest Gump*, because he didn't understand the character. "If I act that way for a whole movie, you know, 'special,' are people going to think I'm like that?" My dad was ready for his Oscar, and he was banking on *Matthew, Matthew* to deliver it to him. The director of *Pollyanna* was older. Very gentle. Hazel told me he'd be patient and would take great care of me. He acted like it was fine when I flubbed a line, which had been happening a lot. Unlike the cool, brash Joey from *Slugger Eight*, Pollyanna was passive and sunny. I hated her. And I hated myself even more when I got things wrong, regardless of the director's kindness. Being prepared was important to me — no, it was expected of me. I worked on set with adults, I sat in my trailer with an adult, I went back to my house with Alma, an adult. I was supposed to be a responsible adult.

Around that time, I started sneaking cigarettes. I'd lock myself in the bathroom, window open, away from Alma. Every time I inhaled, I could feel myself calming down. I told Alma I needed more privacy in my bedroom and my bathroom, not to clean it every day. "I'm practically a grown-up with a full-time job," I protested. "I need privacy, Alma." She left me alone. I hid the cigarettes inside a toilet paper roll and would flush the butts, which I know was awful.

Two weeks into filming, Irene started to worry about me. I was exhausted and couldn't remember the branches of government. I had more important things to remember, like my lines.

"Echo, you look so tired, honey. Are you okay?"

"Don't worry, Irene. It's nothing that makeup can't fix."

"I'm not worried about the makeup. I'm worried about you."

"Worried about me? Why?" But I knew why. I was a kid on a set without parents.

I heard from my dad soon after. "Irene tells me you're depressed. That true?"

"I don't know what she's talking about, Daddy. She thinks she's my therapist."

"How about a visit from Belinda?"

"Belinda can't come. She's doing a school play," I told him. I'd have to wait until she was on break to spend real time with her.

"How about Deborah? She called to ask about you."

Deborah was the only one of my dad's girlfriends whom I stayed in touch with, and she usually called me once a month. Sometimes it felt awkward talking to her because I wanted her to come back into my life, stay by my side like she did that summer after she got me from my mother's house. There were times I wanted to tell Deborah I felt abandoned by her when she moved to New York, but I also knew she was rooting for me to succeed. Deborah had a beautiful quality. Her voice was calming and silky when she called me "sweetheart." (Deborah was an acting coach now, but she had voice-over gigs too. With that voice, how could she not?) On the phone, my dad was saying he could look into flying her out here. Of course I wanted Deborah to visit. But it wasn't her I wanted to see. It was *him*. I wanted to watch movies with him, have him drive me to set, have him take me to dinner at Dan Tana's.

"Can't *you* take a break for a few days?"

"Echo . . ." I could hear irritation in his voice, and I immediately regretted my ask. I knew he was under so much pressure to make a good movie. *Matthew, Matthew* had to blow critics away. We couldn't have a repeat performance of *Good Night, Awake.*

"Okay, Daddy. I'd love to see Deborah."

"You got it, kiddo."

• • •

Deborah came right from the airport to my trailer and did one of those *Look how big you've gotten* shticks that people do to kids when they haven't seen them in a while.

"How's the movie going?" she said.

"Pollyanna is so frigging happy all the time. It makes me want to puke."

What I liked about acting was you could play someone different from you.

But how could anyone be this happy? There were long days when I imagined Hayley Mills's Pollyanna, her curly blonde bangs and the big gingham bow in her hair, with her sailor-style drop-waist dress. She'd be judging me from the corner of the set, saying, in her sweet English accent, *Echo, you have to find something to be glad about.* It was torture.

Deborah opened up the script to the scene that I had to shoot later that day. She stroked the page like it was a living thing.

"Let's go over some lines," she said and pointed to the part where Pollyanna first arrives at her aunt's house. "I'll be Aunt Polly. You start."

                POLLYANNA
    I'm sorry about the T-shirt, Aunt Polly.
    I know it's too big on me.

                AUNT POLLY
    Looks like you got it at the Salvation
    Army.

                    POLLYANNA
Goodwill, actually. But my dad used to
say, sure it's secondhand, but I should
be happy it's not a potato sack.

                    AUNT POLLY
That isn't something to be glad about,
dear.

                    POLLYANNA
My dad used to say—

                    AUNT POLLY
Don't worry about what your dad used
to say.

"Aunt Polly is a bitch," I said, instead of my next line.

"Yes, she is," Deborah said, laughing. "But let's talk about Pollyanna. What is her *action*?"

"I want her to scream at Aunt Polly. I want her to defend her father. I want her to take charge."

"Oh, sure. She could play it annoyed," Deborah said. "She could snap at Aunt Polly, right? But what good would that do her? Deep down, Pollyanna knows she'll be going to foster care if she's difficult. She has no other family. Cheerful and polite is her defense mechanism. It's Pollyanna in survival mode."

"So this is a survival story? What's the moral—that you have to pretend like you're happy or else you'll go to foster care? It's backward."

"Her whole life has been dictated to her, Echo. She's making the change with this positive attitude. That gives her some control."

How had I not realized that Pollyanna was so similar to me? She was suffering too, while trying to make all these adults around her smile. Deborah and I went through a few different scenes, breaking them down, concentrating on how Pollyanna pushes the other characters to get a specific response from them. It was the Stella Adler method, Deborah explained.

After that, everyone ended up loving my take on Pollyanna—and I had grown to love my character. I just wished my dad were there to see it. "I'm hearing good things," he said in a quick call one night. "Turns out you've created a complicated little Pollyanna. Good for you, Echo."

19.

Thankfully there wasn't much downtime between Deborah leaving and Belinda's school break. I was elated at the prospect of having her with me.

"You don't mind hanging out while I work for the week?" I asked when she called to tell me she was free to come.

"Are you kidding? I wish I could be on set every day."

"You'll be on your own set soon enough. What's your next project?"

"My mom is worried about how much stress another job would put on me. She wants me to take a break. Focus on school. But I want to act again. Nothing good has come along anyway, though."

Imagine that. My "team"—which consisted of Hazel and my dad— didn't think about my stress levels. They were signing contracts for me left and right.

"I'm going to make sure Hazel gets you in all of my movies," I said.

"That's the best idea I ever heard," Belinda said.

Within an hour of Belinda being around, I practically turned into Pollyanna, skipping around that set all sunshine and lollipops. Belinda and I would bike around the studio lot, me in my preppy costume with the plaid Victorian, long-sleeved ruffled blouse (harkening back to the original film) and matching skirt, Belinda in her jeans and flannel shirt around her waist. Some pap got a good long-lens shot of us, and I had Hazel buy a copy and send it to me. I hung it up in my trailer.

The night before my thirteenth birthday, we snuck into my dad's liquor cabinet in his office and made ourselves vodka sodas. This was new for both of us. The room smelled like him.

"Everyone at school thinks that because I was in a movie I've had all this experience," Belinda said. "But all these kids are drinking and making out at parties, and I wouldn't even know what to do. We're so much more sheltered than real kids. Except for you dancing on tables at the Limelight," she said slyly.

"That was only once," I said, rolling my eyes and laughing.

"Did you ever notice we have more power at work than we do in real life?"

"What do you mean 'power'?"

"Look at how everyone listens to you on set, Echo. You think that happens at school? I sit in class for forty-five minutes listening to a teacher drone on about algebra."

I thought about my studies with Irene. If anyone needed me during those three-hour sessions, they made this lame joke — "*Study hall is over*" — and pulled me back to the set. I didn't exactly have authority in that way, but on the other hand, if I needed a soda, someone ran and got it for me. If I had a comment about how Pollyanna's line should be delivered, my director listened. I was number one on the call sheet. The adult actors knew me. They introduced themselves to me. The crew asked me how I was feeling. I'd be lying if I said I didn't feel a sense of importance on set.

"Anyway, happy birthday, Echo," Belinda said. "Here's to getting shit-faced."

We clinked the glasses, and I took a big swig of my vodka soda. It burned the back of my throat and felt like an explosion in my stomach. Much different than champagne. I let out a huge burp, and we started hysterically laughing. We drank more, eating M&M'S between sips. My skin buzzed and my fingers tingled, like I lost touch with my body. To stay this way with Belinda eternally, it seemed so appealing.

"Did I tell you about what happened with Tiffany Schaeffer, that popular girl at school?" Belinda said, her eyes glassy.

"No. What?"

"She said I was too ugly to be in a movie, which is why I wasn't in any more of them."

Belinda had her own beautiful quality—the brightest hazel eyes, full lips, her long face. She was awkward, the way she stood with her hands holding her shirt instead of placing them on her hips or something, but never ugly. "Anyone can look like a Barbie doll, Belinda," I said. "But you're the prettiest person I know because you *don't* look like one of them."

I stood up, full of confidence from the vodka. I pretended to be a big shot ready to beat Tiffany Schaeffer up, walking with a swagger through the hallways of her school, looking for her. "Tiffany . . . where are you, Tiffannnyyyy?" I shrieked. We drank more and laughed more. It got easier and easier, even though the burning in the back of my throat never settled. We fell asleep together on my dad's office floor.

Thank God the next day was a Sunday because I woke up with the worst headache I'd ever had in my life. Like someone was stepping on my head. It was the first time I got wasted. Thirteen with my best friend.

Alma made us French toast, but we were so hungover we could barely touch it. I told her it was food poisoning from the Chinese delivery the night before, and she believed me. My dad sent me two dozen pink roses that afternoon. "Happy birthday, kiddo," the generic card read. That's all I heard from him.

•   •   •

When Belinda had to return to school, I felt lonely and depressed both on set and at home. No matter how I tried to channel Pollyanna's power to create the outcomes she wanted, nothing changed how much I missed Belinda. Whenever I could, full makeup or not, I would crawl into the little bed in the back of my trailer, which felt like a dark cave.

When I started missing scenes, Irene called my dad again, and he called Hazel, who immediately came down to the set. You know there's trouble when your agent shows up.

"Echo, darling, what's going on? Did you get your period? Do you have cramps? You probably just have PMS. I always wanted to kill myself when I had PMS at your age. We can get you on birth control to regulate the hormones. It'll fix you right up."

I pulled the covers over my head. "Oh my god, *no*, and if I did, why does everything in my life have to be public knowledge? That's not why I'm upset."

"Echo, I need to know everything that goes on with you. Do you understand? I'm not the public. I'm your agent. So tell me, darling," she said and tried to get under the blanket to stroke my hair. I could tell she hated me in that moment; I could hear the strain in her voice. "You were doing so well . . . What's going on?"

"I don't want to work. That's what's going on."

"That's not exactly very Pollyanna of you, is it?" she squeaked out. "Listen to me: a bad reputation ruins a child actor's career because they can get another cute kid to fill your space. You start not getting out of bed at thirteen years old, then people are going to wave red flags. Even Judy Garland wasn't a drug addict until she was seventeen."

"So I have to wait to be an addict until I turn seventeen?" I said. "Noted."

Hazel rolled her eyes.

"We've got another two movies to do with Disney, and your dad has already gotten a reputation for being the difficult Blue. We don't need a *second* one."

"I'm not trying to be difficult," I said. But I was lonely, and no amount of coaching or advice could change that. In the bedroom, you could hear the hum of the air conditioner from the back of the trailer. I closed my eyes, wanting to sink into the sound of the whirring motor.

"You know what? How about I give you a coffee? Have you had coffee before? It'll wake you up, and it's also a diuretic and will make you feel less bloated too. I'm sure you're depressed because you feel bloated."

"Yes, of course I've had coffee. What do you think I am, five?"

So she called Michelle the PA to get me an espresso and told me to "drink it like a shot." That, plus my desire to get away from Hazel, got me right out of bed and onto the set. They even had to tell me to slow down because I was delivering my lines too fast.

That night, back at home, I called my dad in Wales. "Dad, aren't you going to come home for a break? I hate filming *Pollyanna*. It's so boring."

"Listen to me, Echo. You wanted to work. This is what work is. Sometimes it's boring."

"Is it true that people think we're difficult?" I said.

He laughed. "If anyone thinks we're difficult, they can go to hell. You and I have a name for ourselves to protect, you hear me?" I liked when he talked about us as a unit. He didn't just feel like my dad; he felt like my protector. My savior. He took me out of my mother's house when she was sinking into the depths, and he brought me to a place that felt alive. I'd always be grateful for that.

After we hung up, I took another half Klonopin from his stash to fall asleep. Couldn't have them complaining again that I looked too tired.

• • •

When the principal filming for *Pollyanna* was finally over, I knew something had to change. Alma was doing errands, so I went out to my front porch to call Hazel over a cigarette. Geese glided on the canal. The evening air was crisp, and I wrapped myself in a sweater.

"I want you to get me a script that I can do with Belinda," I said.

"Oh, you *want* me to get you a script, do you?" Hazel said. "Looky how far we've come."

"You know what I mean, Hazel," I said. "I think it would be good for me to, you know, be around more kids. Be around people my own age. And Belinda is my best friend."

"You're not wrong," she said. Then she paused. "Actually, I just read a script for another Disney movie called *Holly and the Hound*, which is very much the kind of script that could be made into a series. The amount of money you'll make off of marketing alone will be outrageous. The main character—Holly, of course, who you would play—has a best friend that works as a detective with her." The idea made me giddy. Belinda would have to convince Sandy to let her work again, but I knew we could talk her into it, especially if the story leaned into female empowerment.

"The more I think of it, this is actually a fabulous idea. I have to tell you, Echo, I'm very impressed with how you and Belinda have been handling the paparazzi. Really shows media savvy."

"What media savvy?"

"You and Belinda, in the papers. Riding your bikes all over Venice Beach. Giving the homeless guy a one-hundred-dollar bill. It was genius. Just what we needed after the Limelight situation. I know that was months and months ago, but people don't forget."

She was right—I had done that on one of our recent outings. But it wasn't premeditated; I just thought he looked hungry.

"Wait—that was in the paper?"

"Oh, come on. You had to have seen the photographers there. There's nowhere to hide on the beach."

"I didn't, Hazel. I happened to have money in my wallet because my dad . . . well, he left me a lot of one-hundreds when he went to Wales. I didn't have anything smaller."

Hazel laughed and sighed. I could hear her nails clicking the desk in delight on the other end of the phone.

"Oh, Echo, darling. We might not even need to get a publicist for you. You're doing perfectly on your own."

Goldie

. . .

20.

Dana approved me staying for three more days. How long had I even been in L.A.? Two and a half days? Was that possible? Today was Sunday, and I had barely slept. I only got to L.A. on Friday, the day of my meetings with Hazel and Olivia, and I had been nonstop ever since.

Yesterday, I had two interviews. First, I went into West Hollywood to speak to Irene Papa, Echo's teacher on *Pollyanna*. "I hate to say anything bad about her because she was a kid, and a sweet kid, but I never thought she liked acting. I think they forced her into it." What was she talking about? Of course Echo liked acting. She did four more movies after that. Plus, she got rave reviews for the *Pollyanna* remake. How could someone who hated acting have been that good?

The second was a call with a semi-famous former film critic. "Yeah, she's got some trouble under her belt, but hopefully they didn't rehab the talent out of her yet," he said. "If she can make a great movie after disappearing like this, it'll be a perfect comeback. Everyone knows Hollywood loves a comeback story."

In between those, I scoured the news. Echo had now been gone for sixteen days. Where was she? Could she have gone into hiding? There were a few exceptions, like Brando and Garbo, but generally actors liked attention. It was their job! Plus she was only nineteen. Do nineteen-year-olds become recluses? I was grateful Shane and I had planned to go to the library this afternoon—I needed to clear my head.

Right before he picked me up, my father called.

"I've been thinking about your new assignment," he said. "Listen, not everything can be your boxing story. You should have won some kind of award for that—"

Again with the boxing story!

"Dad, I have a frien—I mean, a co-worker picking me up soon. I have a big lead on the story. I don't have time for your criticisms."

"That's not why I called you, Goldie. And by the way, I know you take my words as criticisms, but it's always been me trying to help you."

"I've taken your words as criticisms because they're critical."

I knew he was trying to be nice, but late apologies took time to sink in. I spent years trying to convince him my interests were worthy. I slumped over my knees; the blood rushed to my face.

"What is this about, Dad?"

"I know I've been hard on you. I know I've been controlling sometimes. I know I could have had more tact."

I paused, speechless. My father doubling down on his apology was foreign to me. He had never actually acknowledged his own part in our complicated relationship. Sometimes I look back on this conversation and wonder if I remember it accurately. Not all my memories are reliable. Sam liked to say, *"There's reality, and then there's Goldie's reality."*

"Well, thanks, Dad. I mean, that's what I've been saying this whole time, but still, thanks," I said, then thought about it. "Where is this coming from?"

"I don't know if you remember our neighbors, the Balickis?"

"Yes, they had a son and daughter. They were about ten years older than me and Sam?"

"Right. Well, the daughter, Rebecca, just died of breast cancer. She had been fighting it for a few years, apparently. It's very sad, and your mother and I were thinking of paying a shiva call."

"That's awful," I said and thought about the Balickis and how devastated they must be. Rebecca babysat for me once, and we watched *The Exorcist* together. It was one of the most exhilarating nights I'd ever had, even though I had nightmares for three days. "But, Dad, I promise you I don't have breast cancer."

"I know, Goldie, I know. You're so far away . . . and I know your mother and I upset you by not being more on board with your story. And I wanted to make sure we were good."

You know how in a movie the music swells when the scene gets emotional? That's how I felt. Swelling. My coldhearted father was checking in on me. It was surprising but genuine. Death warms people that way.

"We're good," I said.

He kept talking. "So, how's the weather out there?"

"Sunny. Beautiful. Seventy-five degrees. Absolute torture. You'd hate it."

"You know it's not normal for weather to be the same every day. Depressive rainy days are crucial. What normal person can stand blue skies every day of the week?" His grouchy weather opinions made me miss him a little. "Sometimes you need to get in bed with a Woody Allen movie and sulk."

"Except for *Manhattan*," I said.

"*Manhattan* has a stunning opening of the city under Gershwin's 'Rhapsody in Blue.' And I tell this to my students all the time—if we can forgive the men in Shakespearean tragedies because they're led by free will, we can forgive Woody Allen."

"He has an affair with a seventeen-year-old girl in the movie, Dad. You're saying he's exhibiting free will by falling in love with a teenager, and that's acceptable?" I didn't even mention Mia Farrow's daughter or the molestation allegations.

"I think he meant it as a joke, or a critical look at how men act."

My father was so boringly obvious. I had to admit we had had a moment, but it only took two minutes to fundamentally disagree again. It was hard to make sense of, and part of me wanted to avoid trying. Then, just in the nick of time, like they say in the movies, I could see Shane's cab pulling up out the window.

"Listen, Dad, my ride's here."

His voice was filled with disappointment when I told him I had to go. I sighed. "I know you meant for this to be a nice phone call, Dad. I promise not to die of breast cancer, okay? But I have to go. I love you." And I hung up.

21.

The library was an art deco masterpiece, a building rising into the blue sky smack in the middle of downtown L.A., busts of Plato and Shakespeare towering above us. In New York, everyone knows where the big library on Fifth Avenue is. It is an institution with the steps, the pillars, and the lion statues at the entrance. But Shane admitted when he got there that he had never been to the library in L.A. before. My father would have been appalled.

Inside, the librarian pointed me to the bound magazines while Shane strolled around. I went through a stack of old *Rolling Stone*s and found an interview between Echo and her dad. The title of it was "Blue Unleashed."

There was a picture of Jamie Blue in the desert with his legs kicked up on an old wooden table, wearing a big cowboy hat and with a cigarette hanging out of his mouth. They were trying to make him look like James Dean in *Giant*, and it worked. Echo sat by his side, her arm draped over his thigh, her hair windblown in loose curls, with very little makeup and no shoes. She squinted in the sun, staring right at the camera.

RS: You and Echo seem to have a great relationship, Jamie. Can you talk about that?

Jamie: We do. We like to keep to ourselves, though, because Ms. Big Shot here has become a pretty big star. I'm so proud of her.

RS: That's true, she has become a pretty big star. People want to know how you and she are dealing with that—

Jamie: What do people wanna know? I support her 100 percent, teach her everything I know. In fact, I'm about to do a picture with her. You'll see it when they start marketing us to the vultures. I'm proud to bring her into one of my gigs.

RS: How do you feel about that? It's about a father and daughter, right? Echo, are you excited to work with your dad?

Echo: Oh, yes. I can't wait. My dad and I have a pretty solid relationship. I think that if we didn't, it wouldn't work out. He protects me like a dad should, but we also work together. It's really magical. I know I'm lucky to learn from an actor of my father's caliber.

Jamie: Well, thank you, love. [winks]

I can't imagine someone interviewing me and my father at that age. How did she have the maturity to answer those questions? "My dad helps me stay grounded," Echo had said. Meanwhile, my father was extolling the virtues of Woody Allen. Despite my father's attempt in that phone call to play nice, how can I forget our history? In the summer I was fourteen, Echo's age in this interview, I was crying about the way my father circled all of my serial commas and how he noted that *Vogue* was not a "legitimate source." (*"They have a staff of fact-checkers!"* I debated. *"Anna Wintour said that in a magazine!"* It didn't matter.) God, I wish my father had been someone I could have learned from instead of someone I feared. Now, it felt like it might be too late.

I tossed the magazine aside. The real reason I was at the Los Angeles Public Library was to visit the database of scripts donated by crew members and housed in a separate room. A huge sign hung on the door.

WELCOME TO THE SCRIPT LIBRARY.
THE CONTENTS OF THIS ROOM ARE FOR REFERENCE ONLY.

I flipped through the *S* section until I got to *Stars Everywhere*, the film Jamie had been referencing in the interview.

I scanned through the pages, doodles and notes scattered across the margins with handwriting that belonged to—

It was Echo's writing in this script. Oh my god.

I recalled the autographed picture stashed away back in my parents' house and how Echo drew her *E*. Rounded, in cursive, that big, flourished tail up above the first hump. She practiced that *E*, you could tell, because it was perfect, like calligraphy, almost. My whole face got hot, and I glanced around to see if anyone noticed my warped excitement. I almost peed in my pants—I really did. I could feel her close to me. I inhaled the pages. This had to be her copy.

I flipped through until I got to the pool scene, with Echo as Pricilla and Jamie as Malcolm, which was undoubtedly the most famous interaction between them in *Stars Everywhere*. I started reading.

EXT. THE CHATEAU MARMONT POOL—DAY

PRICILLA GAINES, 13, sitting on a cushioned lounge chair, has a serious look on her face. Not aloof. Not shy. Serious. Like she has business to attend to, and she does. She stares ahead at a couple splashing around in the pool. It's a round pool, lush and surrounded by ferns and palms, as if it were a private residence, in someone's garden. Pricilla pretends to read her book, *The Virgin Suicides* by Jeffrey Eugenides. By her choice of literature, it's clear this teen is wise beyond her years.

She looks up from her book, over at her father, MALCOLM, who is in the lounge chair next to her.

Across the pool she watches models and beautiful people drinking cocktails and smoking cigarettes.

                    PRICILLA
          Come swimming with me, Daddy.

An ACTRESS, 25, across the pool with platinum blonde hair wearing a bright yellow bathing suit smiles at Malcolm. Malcolm smiles back.

                    MALCOLM
          Not now, honey.

                    PRICILLA
          We could have a tea party underwater.

Malcolm doesn't answer her. He places the script over his face. Folds his hands across his chest.

The actress across the pool pulls her oversize white sunglasses from her mess of blonde hair to the rim of her nose. Then she crosses her long, tanned legs.

Pricilla copies her. She crosses her skinny legs, one over the other. Slips on her father's aviator sunglasses from the table.

Malcolm doesn't notice much, but he notices this.

> MALCOLM
>
> Take those off. You're going to break them.

> PRICILLA
>
> How can you even see what I'm doing with a script over your face?

POOL WAITER comes by with an order. Double bourbon for Malcolm and a milkshake.

> PRICILLA
>
> I told you I don't want a milkshake.

> MALCOLM
>
> I ordered you a milkshake, so you're going to drink it.

PRICILLA takes a long swig, staring daggers at Malcolm. She drinks half, then gets up and jumps in the pool. Under the water, life is clearer.

When she comes up for air, the actress is sitting in her lounge chair, talking to Malcolm. He's smiling, talking animatedly.

Pricilla gets out and stands between the two of

them, her body dripping wet all over the script on the lounge chair.

                    MALCOLM
     Jesus, Pricilla, you're ruining the
     fucking script.

                    ACTRESS
     I should go back to my friends.

                    MALCOLM
     No, stay, stay.

But Malcolm is slurring, trying to dry off the script with a towel.

Malcolm nudges Pricilla to the side. He's a little too rough and she trips over herself.

                    MALCOLM
     Are you okay, honey?
          (to the actress)
     She's always in the middle of everything.
          (to Pricilla)
     Why don't you go back in the pool
     and play?

                    ACTRESS
     I didn't realize you had a kid.

                    MALCOLM
     She's not really my kid; she's more like
     my protégé.

Pricilla fumes.

MALCOLM

What's gotten into you?

PRICILLA

You. Will you *ever* be a man?

That was odd. In the movie, she threw the milkshake. Broken glass everywhere. And the line she recited, that she won the Oscar for, that brought tears to your eyes in the theater, that made the audience want to strangle Jamie Blue (his character, not him, of course) was "Will you ever be a father?"

So why did the script read, "Will you *ever* be a man?"

I looked up on the page. Next to Malcolm's line, where he says, "She's not really my kid," there's an arrow, then handwriting: *Does he mean this?* I could see her sitting by the pool at the Chateau Marmont, the castle hovering and the lush gardens like a curtain behind her, as she trailed her finger across her lines, carefully reading and concentrating, trying to digest the words, questioning, sinking herself into the character. Then in the bottom corner of that page in tiny letters: *Rejection, rejection, rejection.*

What was the rejection? She must have been getting in character. No one could've played this part like Echo . . . unless maybe she wasn't acting.

My stomach growled, taking me out of the moment. I didn't know the last time I ate. I felt crazed.

I couldn't let go of this script. I couldn't put it back into the library for everyone to see how vulnerable this creature (she was just a child!) was.

I slid the script in my bag and sat there for a few minutes humming softly to make sure no one saw me. Only one other person was in the room with me, a tall guy with a beard wearing a green winter cap and hoarding the Tarantino scripts. We exchanged a look of tacit agreement

111

that we would ignore each other. As I walked out of the room, I passed a shelf of Danielle Steels and grabbed two as a distraction.

I dropped them by the librarian's desk and told her I'd be right back for them. She said it was no problem, smiling warmly.

For a split second, I wondered if the scripts had some security tag on them—the whole script library seemed so loosey-goosey, running under the honor system. Back in New York, you couldn't get out of any reference room without a guard checking your bag.

I found Shane in the architecture section. He was kneeling on the floor, books spread out all over the puke-green carpet.

"Who knew this place was so great?" he said in a quiet library voice.

I grabbed his arm and pulled him up.

"We have to go."

"Can I at least check out? Or put the books back?"

"No, you can't put the books back. Don't you know that librarians hate that? They hate when people put the books back because they always put them in the wrong place."

"That can't be right."

I took his hand; my palm was so sweaty, but it didn't matter, because my excitement was boiling over. When I reached my hand inside the bag and touched the script, I could feel a whole-body shiver ride up my belly, not unlike an orgasm, and I couldn't wait to get back to Dolly's casita to flip through it for more small notes and stains. I can't explain what it meant for me to find something I wanted so badly, how immediate it now felt. It had Echo's essence. She was all over it. Outside, I turned to Shane, my adrenaline pumping, and I kissed him passionately, with tongue, right there on the sidewalk.

I grabbed his hand, marched past the eucalyptus trees and back to his cab, which was parked next to Maguire Gardens. The purple flowers from the jacarandas hung down around the taxicab like some trippy psychedelic movie. I scrambled in the back, pulling my jeans off, then Shane climbed in and I dragged him on top of me. *Hurry, hurry,* I was whispering, sounding possessed, but I didn't care. I unzipped his jeans and pulled out his penis, it was hard, and Jesus, Shane was physically beautiful. I wondered again how he was not famous yet for that hair and jaw alone. "If you don't put your cock inside me, I'm going to die," I said.

I had fucked in a car before, but this was different. Shane was trying too hard. I didn't want to insult him, but his sincerity and all of his questions ("Does this feel good? Is this nice?") were turnoffs. Who makes love in a cab? You fuck in a cab. So I faked an orgasm, which was fine. I didn't need to come; I just needed to feel his heavy body on top of me, crushing me. I needed to feel filled up, and I needed it to be over. My fake orgasm got him to come pretty quickly, and he nestled his blond hair into my neck. One day he'd be a movie star, and I'd tell people proudly, *Hey, I fucked that guy!*

"I really like you," he whispered into my ear. Gross. I wriggled away.

"Yeah . . . I wish I weren't leaving L.A. soon. What a bummer."

"What if I could help with your story? Would your boss let you stay longer?"

My ears perked up. "I'm sure she would. But it would have to be something really good." I waited.

His face turned red. "Okay, so, I didn't want to tell you this, because it seemed like an invasion-of-privacy kind of thing, but I actually know Jamie Blue."

I shot up in the seat, wiping my hair from my sweaty face.

"Is this a joke? I mean, we already had sex. Are you trying to get anal out of me or something? This is not funny if that's the case. I take my job very seriously—"

"No, really. I worked with him on a project about six months ago."

"Jesus Christ," I said and touched his cheek. "You know him?"

"Well, we did a dog food commercial. I was supposed to play his brother or something. Me, him. Beach. Golden retriever," he said. "I'm sorry for keeping it from you. Confidentiality and all. But I know I can trust you now." His whole face lit up. He was excited to tell me. I could see it.

It made me think of all the times I used Echo as a positive sign. If I

was having a hard day, and I flipped on the television to one of her movies randomly playing, I'd know things would turn around. Or the time
after a brutal deadline that I passed her billboard for *Emma* on the West
Side Highway. Yes, she was one of the most famous actors of the decade
and her face was ubiquitous, but that was beside the point. When I
needed her, she was there, staring back at me. Now I, of all people, had
gotten into a cab with someone who actually knew her father. I'd found
her own script with her handwriting. All of it kismet, leading me toward
her. Confirmation that I was the one for this story. A tickle went up
my whole spine, like someone had injected me with stardust. I almost
shrieked. Jamie was someone I never expected to get even close to in my
search. Production assistants, has-been co-stars, yes, but Jamie? He was
an icon—even if he was now doing dog food commercials. As Echo's father, he *had* to be the key to her story. Granted, he very publicly claimed
not to know where she was, but maybe there was a secret pact between
them. At the very least, I needed to follow up on Olivia Breakers's allega-
tion, even if I didn't buy it.

"So," I said, slowing down. "What do we do now?"

"What do you mean?" His hands were cupping my ass. He didn't
want to leave.

"I know he's going through a lot right now, but I'd love to meet him,"
I said breathlessly. The demand seemed to explode out of my mouth. I
grabbed Shane by the shirt. I was desperate. I didn't care. "I need to
meet him."

"Let me see what I can do," he said and shook his hair with his big
hands. Little crystals of sand, or maybe it was dandruff, tumbled out of
it. *Attaboy*, I wanted to say, slightly disgusted with myself. *Now, take me
to meet Jamie Blue.*

Echo

1993–1994

. . .

22.

Pollyanna was another huge box office hit, taking in $11 million in the first weekend. During the press tour, people kept asking me if it felt great to have a number one movie, and I kept giving the same answer — "It's amazing" or "It's so exciting" — with that sickening drop in my stomach. I had learned to be a very good performer. I played the part of a child star, grateful for her abundance of successes.

"I owe it all to my dad," I would sometimes say, hoping he would get a glimpse of me on *ET* and swell with pride, or that it would make him happy, how grateful I was for him. If he saw, he didn't say a thing. I had seen my father drunk more often than I saw him sober over the past year. *Matthew, Matthew,* the movie he had been working on for a year, the movie that he told everyone was going to be his "masterpiece," the movie he bet his career on, the movie he put his life on hold for, was a flop.

One reviewer wrote:

The film is shot beautifully, but Jamie Blue is a wreck and looks distracted and annoyed toward the end of the film; you can sense he's not thinking about his war-hero character, Matthew Cosgrove, and is instead wondering how he got suckered into this long, masturbatory project.

Do I need to go on? My dad was devastated. Now we were both between movies, and I felt uneasy around him. The air in our house felt heavy, tense. Belinda tried to get me out to do "normal" kid stuff with her, but it was such a stupid concept. Everything we did, whether it was going to the mall, a movie, or a football game at her school, was the furthest thing from normal because paparazzi followed me wherever I went. I had to hide my new cigarette habit, which was up to about a pack and a half a day, because you can't smoke when you're Echo Blue, Disney's little princess.

My real escape was at night, when a few of the crew I stayed in touch with from the *Pollyanna* art department took me to Sin-a-matic on Santa Monica. I would wear a sleeveless silk pink slip, a black bobbed wig, and multicolored paste-on eyelashes. Kids were lined up outside, waiting to get their IDs checked, while I slid by them, unnoticed. Inside, after downing several glasses of Dom, I danced like an animal, sweat saturating the silk.

I smoked so many cigarettes those nights that I'd wake up in the morning with my throat scratchy and coughing up phlegm. Behind me flashed images of naked men sucking on each other's toes. A tall guy with blond hair and big shoulders who told me he was a model said it was an installation by Tom of Finland. I didn't know what he was talking about, but it didn't matter. Except for Desire, a very sweet drag queen who recognized me, escape *was* attainable.

At least I thought so until my picture showed up with me, no bra, my drenched silk dress, see-through in the photographer's light, the wig halfway off my head, right there in the *L.A. Times* dancing side by side with Desire.

"Did you not notice people taking pictures of you?" Hazel demanded.

"Um, no. I thought it was part of the laser light show."

Hazel threatened everyone I had been with, giving each of their agents a legendary "They'll never work in this town again" speech.

Around that time, an old picture of Debbie Harry from the '70s inspired me to get a messy platinum bob with two-toned black chunky strands showing underneath. I wanted it to look reckless, like I was just a regular kid and had come home one day and done it myself. But another thing about my life was that I couldn't just go to the hairdresser. I had to get permission from Hazel, who had to get permission from the director of *Holly and the Hound*, who had to get permission from Marty Lyons, the studio exec.

Two weeks later, Tracey Fields, the head of hair and makeup for *Holly*, got the go-ahead to cut my hair in a shag, slightly below my ears. She dyed it a few shades lighter than my natural blonde, with dark brown hair peeking out underneath. Hazel kept reminding me that she was the one who made this happen. Hazel knew how to get me what I wanted, but it was her way of controlling me. Now I had to give her what she wanted, so I agreed to let *E! News* take pictures of me in the salon getting my new look. When the segment aired, the very forgettable host squawked into the camera, "Not so little anymore, *Echo Blue chops off her blonde locks!*" Hazel sat behind me in the mirror, a big grin on her face as Tracey carefully lobbed off my hair. In a moment I was expecting to feel empowered, I was consumed with resentment. It felt like nothing was ever just mine and that it never would be again.

23.

One night when Belinda was at her winter school dance (only enrolled students of her school were allowed to attend), I found my dad on the couch alone watching *One Flew over the Cuckoo's Nest*. He wasn't usually by himself on a Friday night. An open bottle of vodka sat on the coffee table. "Now this is the kind of role I should be getting," he said, slurring. "All the good parts disappeared after the seventies."

"You're going to get a great role, Daddy. They're still out there—I know it," I said, trying to comfort him.

He sat straight up and glared at me. "Like you know everything now, Echo? Because people ate up that saccharine crap *Pollyanna*? Get real."

He reached for the bottle of vodka, and it spilled over the table. "God-dammit," he groaned. He took a big swig and didn't even bother to wipe it up. I crept to my room to stay out of his way.

As I walked in my bedroom, I heard the sound of breaking glass. I hid in my closet, listening to him bang walls and slam kitchen cabinets, ranting about his failed career. As much as I wanted to call someone to ask for help, I also didn't want to get him in trouble. So I took a full Klonopin that I had stashed away and fell asleep on my closet floor.

The next morning, he knocked on the door solemnly. "Sorry if I scared you," he said. "Going through a rough time, honey." He had huge bags under his eyes.

"You just need some rest, Daddy. You need a facial. You need a celery juice. Should I go ride my bike down to the store to get it?" This wasn't something I was eager to do because that winter in L.A. was cold and rainy. But I wanted him to be happy.

He touched my face gently.

"Kiddo, I need a good movie. That's what I need."

I thought maybe things would change, because every time this happened, he was so apologetic, his eyes always bursting with love the morning after an episode. But it went on like this for weeks with him getting drunk and screaming on the phone to Hazel, calling her horrible names. The one adult who had helped me manage this was Alma, and she recently had to go back to Argentina to take care of her sick mother. I couldn't risk my mother asking for sole custody if I told her. Our once-a-week visits were fine but I couldn't live with her. I couldn't abandon my dad. Not now.

The final straw came when the smear article in *Hollywood Hills Magazine* facetiously titled "The Prince of Venice Beach" came out. It was supposed to be a glossy home tour, some harmless good publicity that would show my dad at his best. But there was a damning section that went like this:

> *There's a portrait of Jamie Blue hanging in the dining room that looks like a Warhol painting.*
>
> *"Is this a real Warhol?" I ask him.*
>
> *"I had always wanted a Warhol painting, you know, of myself, the way a lot of iconic actors and celebrities had in the 1970s and 1980s. Jagger, Kareem Abdul-Jabbar, Muhammad Ali," Blue says.*

Warhol also painted Mao, I think. And Lenin.

"Does this mean it's a Warhol?" I ask.

"Yeah, it's a Warhol," Blue says, and ushers me out of the dining room to the bedroom, where he points to a king-size bed draped in black linen sheets. "I'm supposed to say this is where all the magic happens, right?" Blue laughs.

Except I wonder how funny this is since his teenage daughter's bedroom is the one right next to his.

And as if that weren't bad enough, a week later the editor-in-chief called Hazel to tell her they were going to issue a correction in their next publication. The reporter, doing some simple fact-checking, got in touch with the Andy Warhol Foundation, who told him they had no record of Warhol painting Jamie Blue.

My dad went on a tirade. He drank three shots of tequila, then almost an entire bottle of wine, stumbling around the house with the magazine, ranting.

"How was I supposed to know it wasn't a Warhol? I gave some guy a picture of myself, and they told me Warhol would paint it. It was a friend of your mother's. She had all these connections back then. How the hell was I supposed to know?"

"Daddy," I said, and I hugged him. His body was practically limp, and he didn't hug me back. "I don't care what they say about you. You're the greatest actor in my eyes."

He pushed me away and I tumbled into the couch. I was scared and shielded my body with a pillow, a weird reflex. My dad had never hit me before.

He mumbled about how I'd have to pay the bills now, and then he picked up a black leather Milo Baughman chair (I knew this because he screamed, "A real fucking Milo Baughman. Signed! How do you like that, motherfuckers?"), commanding me to open the sliding glass doors, so I did, panicking. He stomped out to the deck and to the edge of the canal and hurled it in. It made a huge splash, and he stood there watching it sink.

I called Hazel, and the police came around the same time she did.

They didn't want to press charges, because he was Jamie Blue and they loved him—one even asked for a picture with him—but he was too drunk to stand. I had seen my father angry before, but never like this.

They told Hazel that they couldn't look the other way because I was a minor. If I hadn't been there, they could have written him off as another actor getting drunk and throwing his shit into the Venice canals. Dennis Hopper lived around the corner—you think they weren't used to that? But there was a kid in the house, even if I felt like anything but a kid.

They arrested him and brought him in on charges of disturbing the peace and disorderly conduct.

24.

That night, Hazel did a very un-Hazel thing. She mothered me. Well, maybe not *mothered*. A mother would cradle you and comfort you. But she parented me. She ordered us a pizza after the police left with my dad, while someone tried to fish the Milo Baughman from the canal. Hazel told them if they could get it out, they could have it.

"Do you want to sleep at my house tonight?" she said.

I shook my head. I couldn't imagine Hazel's house feeling at all comforting. I imagined it to be clinical and cold, and she probably had her housekeeper vacuuming up behind you wherever you walked with a little dustbuster. She didn't want me there. She just felt complled to offer because I was her highest-profile client and had nowhere to go. What I really wanted in that moment was to go back to my mom's. I had been so hard on her, so angry and resentful toward her for sleeping her life away, for being stuck in her house worrying about the paparazzi. But my mother didn't destroy furniture. She wasn't violent. Or drunk. And she didn't belittle me, didn't take my success as an insult.

"This is going to look very bad," Hazel said. "Your father is going to have to go to rehab after this. He's got to clean up his reputation."

"What does his reputation matter at this point? This is about him getting better, isn't it?"

"Normally you can be a bad boy and nothing will stop them from forking over their money at the box office if the movie is good. A handsome male movie star with talent can usually get away with anything. But this is different. He's a dad, and he lost control while his daughter was in the house. That's the issue."

He also hadn't been in any good movies for a long time.

"The other issue is that Jamie is not the only movie star in the house. See where I'm going with this, darling? You have *Holly and the Hound* coming out in the summer. We don't want this problem continuing, because we don't want it to overshadow you."

• • •

Holly and the Hound began filming in January, while my dad was at rehab, which was a great distraction. I felt like I was a part of something from the start. Before we began shooting, Belinda (who was playing Holly's best friend, Roxy—her mother had come around) and I got to meet with Christine Camper, our director. We told her we didn't want Holly and Roxy to be cutesy and sweet. We wanted them to be artsy and edgy. I showed her some of my Debbie Harry inspiration photos, how she often wore a T-shirt and jeans while performing at CBGB. She was cool and gritty but still approachable. That's what I wanted Holly to be like.

"Oh, so you don't want to make another *Pollyanna*?" Christine said, laughing.

"Hell no," I said. "I hate that bitch."

At that stage of my life, I was feeling bold. I had opened two movies that were number one at the box office, and I knew my worth. I knew I had bankability. I knew I was, as they say in the industry, "viable."

Christine Camper was this small woman who wore leather jackets and bright red lipstick. She had made an independent film and also directed a number of television shows. She was an anomaly back then because either you were a TV director or you were an independent filmmaker—you weren't both. She told us that she didn't expect her first studio feature to be a Disney movie, but she took the gig for the money. She was determined to bring originality to it, to create a film that wasn't condescending to teenagers. Disney, shockingly, liked her ideas. It was a perfect match.

Entertainment Tonight came while we were shooting at an outdoor school location to get behind-the-scenes footage.

"Do something fun. Do cartwheels across the field or something," the *ET* producer said.

Instead, Belinda and I sprung off the metal bleachers, stole pom-poms from wardrobe, and taunted the extras in cheerleader uniforms. Then I persuaded the old guy who was using the striping machine on the baseball field to let me run it, and I made zigzags from third to home base.

I could sink into Holly because she was someone I wanted to be. Holly was messy. She took chances; she didn't exactly fit in or try to make anyone happy. She wasn't a people pleaser like Pollyanna—she didn't need to be, because her parents supported her no matter what. And she got to gallivant around her small seaside town with her best friend and her hound dog. I envied Holly's life.

Those days, I stayed between my dad's house with Alma and my mom's. My mom had been working with a life coach and, with no one else to take care of, had a fully scheduled life. Yoga at eight in the morning. Chai tea at ten. Meditation at two o'clock. Painting at four o'clock. Martini at five. Toast and eggs at ten before bed. She had alarms set for everything. The yoga, the martini, the meditation, and when she could take her anxiety pills.

Something about staying with her felt awkward. She was always watching me, which was different from when I lived there when I was little. It was more subtle than how she used to smother me in her dark bedroom. Now, she was trying this whole newfound "love and light" approach. Everything was a suggestion.

"You should really meditate, Echo. It would be good for you to calm your brain."

"Did you always sleep this much? Or is this something new?"

"Maybe you need to take a pottery class. Using your hands might recalibrate your energy."

I wanted her to say what she was thinking—ask me if I was taking drugs. (At this point, I was averaging at least a Klonopin a day, mostly at night.) I needed to know that someone cared. That was the wrong word. She *cared*, but wouldn't it have been nice if someone had taken me by the hand and said, *Here, we're in this together. Here, let's get this mess cleaned up.* But she didn't; she couldn't. And despite her positive self-work, I was just as alone as I'd always been.

• • •

By the time *Holly* wrapped in the beginning of March (with all signs pointing to another success), my dad was scheduled to get out of rehab. Hazel wanted to discuss a few things before the press got all over it.

"The first question I have for you is about your mom. Can we get Mathilde to show up at the premiere? Coming out of hiding to support her daughter would be a huge story and overshadow your father's release from rehab."

"She would never," I said flatly. "Also, about him. Why do we have to be on the defense? Aren't we past that?"

Hazel pursed her lips and lowered her sunglasses to the bridge of her nose. I could see what she was thinking.

I continued. "He's sad, Hazel. That's why he acted like that. He committed a year of prep and a year of filming to that picture. And the article—"

"Echo, darling. I have advice for you. Do not make excuses for destructive men or you won't be able to quit. Do you understand me?" She lit a cigarette. "No one loves your father more than me, darling. No one has put herself on the line for him more than I have, but he should not act that way for the sake of his fans or, more importantly, for you. You were hiding in the closet that day, afraid for your safety."

"It wasn't like it was a tiny closet, Hazel," I said. "I have a pretty big walk-in."

But she was right. I kept doing this. Defending both of my parents. My response was always the same when people asked. "My mom's great. She paints. She's very happy staying out of the spotlight." And "My dad? Oh, my dad—he's good. *Matthew, Matthew* was an artistic project for him, and he knew not everyone was going to get it. It's not about the box office. It's about the craft."

Isn't that what you did for emotionally broken parents? You made excuses for them. And he was out there, in the spotlight, taking chances. You had to give him some credit. Not every movie star was doing that. Most of these leading men took safe roles; they didn't move to Wales for a year to work with an experimental director. I only wanted to make things better for my dad.

They all told me to act like an adult when it suited them, because I had a job. Because I had fame. Because the paparazzi followed me. Couldn't I act like an adult when it mattered the most—to help my dad?

"What if Dad and I did a movie together?" I said to Hazel. I was fourteen. She puffed on her cigarette for a minute and then lifted her glasses. She wiped her eyes, just under her long mascara-heavy lashes. Women like Hazel never really let you know what they're thinking until they decide to be blunt and slice you in half. Her success depended on keeping those cutthroat convictions coming but packaged in a bow.

"I thought about this and haven't broached it to your father yet."

"Why not?"

She took a whopping drag of her cigarette and exhaled, the smoke rings looking like little angels flying into the clouds.

"Can I have one?"

She laughed as if I entertained her by asking.

"Since when do you smoke?" I generally tried to keep my habit pretty low-key, but it was hard to believe Hazel had no idea. I just figured it had never been convenient for her to mention it. I played along.

"Didn't all the glamorous movie stars smoke?" I said. "Lauren Bacall. Marlene Dietrich. Bette Davis." I despised the briefly concerned look that crossed her face. I was beyond childhood, and she knew this.

"You have me there," she said, amused, before sliding her lighter and a cigarette across the table, which I then lit, blowing jagged smoke rings at her. She raised her eyebrows, impressed.

"Be straight with me, Hazel," I said. "Don't coddle me."

"People will come to see your dad, yes, but they want to see your dad *with you*. Which is very different than your dad being the main billing at the box office. You are in prime-time mode, and Disney wants more teen vehicles for you. They want to extend your contract. *You* don't need to do a movie with your dad."

This wasn't about what I needed. She should have known that.

"What, am I going to do Disney movies forever? I don't know if I want that."

"I'm not going to respond to that comment." I didn't have to ask what she meant. If I stuck with Disney long enough, I was set for life, even once the public stopped thinking I was cute, and even if I got ugly (which Hazel often reminded me happened to child actors all the time).

"The truth is, your father will see it as a big blow to his ego, darling."

"Getting bad reviews for a movie he worked on for a year isn't a big enough blow?" I said. "How much worse can it be?"

"Having your teenage daughter pull you out of the ditch is not how a man like your father operates. You have to understand, Echo, and maybe you already do, but women and their appreciation of him are a big part of his makeup. He likes to have his ego stroked. Not buried."

"I'm not one of his girlfriends," I said uncomfortably.

"Still, you are a girl, my dear. And your daddy, who looks like a confident, debonair guy, is a very fragile man."

She crushed the cigarette out in the crystal ashtray already overflowing with lipstick-covered cigarette butts. I did the same.

"I understand that. But I have an idea. We have to make it like *I* need *him*, like he's doing me a favor. Like he's adding to my career," I said to her. "Or better, like I miss him after his long stretch away making *Matthew,*

Matthew and want to spend time with him." I leaned forward, pushing my elbows into the table, giving her my best sell. I had a painful feeling that this had to happen and that I couldn't do it without her. "You can do it, Hazel. You can find something that brings out the teen aspect, but that's about the savior/father aspect too. It has to be very specific."

"It would have to be artsy. Highbrow," Hazel replied after a long pause. She was coming around.

"Right," I said, surprisingly excited. Sure, this movie was going to be about me saving my dad's career, but it really would be good for me to branch out. Despite the long-term benefits, being a Disney girl was already getting weird. I didn't like how much responsibility I had with the kids who followed me and who wrote me fan letters and who spilled their life stories. You're supposed to love your fans, but I couldn't help but think that mine were delusional. Did they really think they were friends with me? And why did they scream when they saw me? Why did they have to be so awkward and tearful and make everything so uncomfortable?

"We'd have to find something quirky. Because you know the Academy doesn't ever nominate teen movies."

"Forget the Academy, Hazel. We want good reviews," I said. "This is to pump up his ego."

"Right, darling. Of course—you're right. Let me see what I can do."

25.

And that's how Hazel found *Stars Everywhere*, about a young girl who goes to live with her single dad at the Chateau Marmont, high up in the Hollywood Hills. He's a successful stage actor who's in town for a movie, and his daughter wants to get to know him better. They bond and hang out with the oddballs staying at the hotel like they are. She gets a new perspective on life and a renewed vision of her dad.

I willed myself into believing it would be a perfect transition for my dad (and why wouldn't it?), who had gotten back from rehab happier than I'd ever seen him. The three months did him good. "I promise you, Echo—things are going to be different," he said that first night. "My priorities are all gonna change. It's going to be me and you. I've been feeling sorry for myself, self-medicating, being destructive. That's not going to happen anymore." He squeezed me tight, and I could smell a patchouli scent on him that he said a guy from rehab gave him to "center" himself. I felt so proud of him, so hopeful. He was back to his old self, and I felt like his daughter again. I didn't know anything about addicts then. I didn't know moments like these were impermanent. That this fleeting good behavior, that magical time when he put me on a pedestal, was something I'd always be attracted to when it came to men.

Hazel and his publicist got him a cover story in one of the tabloids focusing on his relationship with me. "I JUST WANT TO GET BETTER FOR ECHO," the headline read. Hearts melted across the country.

We went for these nightly sunset bike rides through Venice Beach—earnest father-daughter moments were part of his redemption tour. One night, I told him that I was worried about my career. He signaled me to pull over. The two of us sat on the beach together, looking out at the waves crashing into the sand. Surfers bobbed on the horizon. The skaters clanged on metal railings behind us.

"Talk to me, Echo."

"I hate the Disney movies," I said, which wasn't entirely true. (I hated *Pollyanna*, as I've made very clear. But I loved *Holly and the Hound*.) "I want them to give me something that actual teenagers will watch. Something everyone else will take seriously."

"Okay. Did you talk to Hazel? She can start looking at new directors."

"It's not that," I said. "I want to do an adult movie. I need another star to back me up. You know what I mean? Someone who could be the anchor of the movie and really come in strong. Someone that people love—"

A smile tugged at his mouth. "I see where you're going with this."

"You do?"

"You want me to be in a movie with you."

I was trying to be sly here. I didn't want to seem like I felt sorry for him or show how excited I was that he was biting. I turned it on.

"I don't want it to seem like I'm using you," I said. "I know you're a huge star. I know you don't exactly have time for something stupid like this."

"I'll consider it. No promises," he said.

"I understand, Daddy."

"You really want me to be in a movie with you, huh, kid?"

"I missed you when you were doing *Matthew, Matthew*. I missed you when you were in . . ." He didn't like the word *rehab*. "Mom is all over the place. You're the person I want to spend time with. You're the person I want to be with."

"Please don't talk about *Matthew, Matthew,*" he said, running his hands through his hair. He hadn't cut it the whole time he was in rehab, and he looked like one of those wild surfers. He slung his arm around me and gave me a kiss on the head. He told me he'd talk to Hazel and see if she could find us something.

There were no paparazzi photos of that moment, and that was just fine with me.

Goldie

. . .

26.

I woke up Monday morning to a barrage of voice mails from Hazel Cahn's assistant telling me that they would file a lawsuit if I published the interview. I deleted all of them and spent the day studying the borrowed *Stars Everywhere* script. (I didn't want to call it *stolen*, exactly, because maybe I'd return it. I could put it on the library steps, wear a hoodie and sunglasses like I was dropping a baby off at a firehouse.) I turned on the local morning news show, *Good Day L.A.* After an update from the "meteorologist," a thin blonde woman with tight jeans and a halter top, one of the anchors announced that the NYPD was doing an investigation into Echo's disappearance. The rest of the segment devolved into a spirited debate about whether she had joined a cult.

Tuesday, I met with Charlotte Pierson, the actress who was in the pool scene in *Stars Everywhere* with Jamie and Echo. "All I remember was a loving relationship between them," Charlotte said. "Yes, Jamie was a womanizer, which I'd rather not get into, but he was with that kid all the time." It was a direct conflict with what Olivia Breakers had told me at Canter's. I chose to believe Charlotte's version of things.

Later that afternoon, I did a phone interview with a UCLA professor. "This town doesn't have room for complicated women," she said. "That's why they put female child stars on a pedestal, give them iconic status, and when they show threatening behavior, like dabbling in drugs or anxiety or messy love affairs, they're shunned in the media for it."

By Wednesday night, nineteen days after Echo disappeared, through some sheer miracle, I was on my way to Jamie Blue's "compound," as Shane called it. I'd see for myself what I could glean from him in person. The property, made up of three houses, was between the canals and the beach. The entrance, which was flanked by two stout palms, looked like a giant metal box with misshaped windows. Some guy with shaggy long hair answered the door. Shane had told me to expect this. Everyone with money in Hollywood has house staff who take care of them.

"They do all the little things that you don't want to do around your house, you know? Like your dishes, or your laundry, or mail something, or get a new tire. These people do everything for them," Shane said.

"Isn't that a personal assistant?"

"No. A personal assistant is one more rung up the ladder, but they're still low—believe me. I tried to be a personal assistant once, and it lasted a day. Nothing like getting screamed at by some asshole executive because his latte was lukewarm. I'd rather drive a taxi."

"Hey," the guy said, greeting us. He introduced himself as Keith.

"Hey, I'm Shane. Jamie knows I'm coming."

"Who's she?" Keith said, pointing at me.

"This is my friend Goldie. She's an artist. Like from New York." Keith seemed to be pleased by that. He said, "Cool." Then he offered me a cookie. I took the cookie and shoved it in my mouth. It was warm and gooey, like it had just come out of the oven.

Jamie's main house was massive, with unfinished ceilings and exposed beams. The floors were all concrete, with Persian rugs complemented by white couches. The second floor was completely open to the first floor, like we were in an old building that had been carefully and very expensively restored.

Shane and I talked for about ten minutes until Jamie Blue walked down the metal stairs in a pair of baggy jeans, a gray T-shirt, and striped socks. He was probably ten years younger than my dad. His skin glowed and his still-thick blond hair rested behind his ears. He was extremely handsome.

"Now, who do we have here?" he said. His eyes were red, and he talked with a Southern drawl even though it was common knowledge that he was from New Jersey. He seemed incredibly stoned.

The most recent picture I had seen of Jamie was on that *People* cover, him staring despondently out at the Pacific, presumably wondering where his daughter was. Now he had this shit-eating grin on his face.

"This is my friend Goldie, the artist I was telling you about."

Shane had told me that was all you needed to say in Hollywood, that you were an artist. I could have been working on paint-by-numbers and it wouldn't have mattered. Jamie wasn't going to ask me any follow-up questions. Shane also made me promise to be discreet. This was an important connection to him.

Living in New York, I'd seen my share of people who were just as famous as Jamie Blue, if not more. But this was Echo's father. Someone I knew so much about, someone who had been real in my mind for so long. Not to mention I had been poring over the six-hundred-page unauthorized biography on him whenever I could find a minute. It should have been called *The List*, since the book mostly detailed Jamie Blue's famous sex life—the models, the actresses, the waitresses, the costume designers. I couldn't help but imagine what it would be like to have sex with him, and the night before, I masturbated thinking about him. I didn't know why, but something about it felt incestuous, and I had to talk myself into the orgasm. He was Echo's father, not mine, and it was perfectly fine to fantasize about him going down on me on a beach.

Anyway, it felt like Jamie Blue and I had a shared history, and now he was here in front of me. I wanted to say something witty, something to impress him, or even something compassionate, like, *I know this is such a hard time for you, with Echo missing*, but I just stood there, as I assumed most people did when they first met him, gawking. It was hard not to stare. He had so much of Echo in him. They could have been twins with their fluffy lips that always seemed chapped and their round blue eyes. I held back all of the compliments on the tip of my tongue, like that *Matthew, Matthew* was underrated. I didn't want to sound desperate. I was here to observe Jamie Blue so he could possibly lead me to Echo. I couldn't come off like a fan.

"Pleased to meet you," he said, breaking the silence. "So tell me, what kind of artist are you?"

I stared at Shane. I was screwed. I had walked into this meeting so confident, and now here I was, having to come up with a fake backstory. The first thing that came to my mind was a papier-mâché elephant that I had made in middle school.

"Landscapes," I said instead.

"Oh?" And he smiled again. That smile had charmed the pants off of women in Hollywood for the past twenty years. "What kind of land-scapes?"

"Uh . . ." And I looked at Shane, who wasn't any help at all. "Deserts. Yeah, I paint a lot of desert landscapes."

"Oh, like Joshua Tree?" he said. "I love going out there. It's like the one thing that gets me super inspired about Southern California, that you can drive out to Joshua Tree and it can make you feel . . . free, you know?" He looked up at the sky and pointed at the stars. "It's like you can see the whole galaxy out there." Was this a joke? Olivia Breakers's theory that Jamie did something to Echo was laughable. Had she met this guy?

I remembered him talking about his travails in Joshua Tree in the splashy redemption article that came out in *GQ* after Echo emancipated herself. He had a big intervention from life. He asked the desert for for-giveness and said he was a devout Kabbalah follower, though I didn't see a red string around his wrist.

I nodded my head, even though I had never been to Joshua Tree.

"I'm more into deserts like the Sahara," I said. I didn't know what I was saying. I felt tingly and soft, like jelly. "You know, or the Negev. The Negev is cool."

I burped quietly, just a little undercover burp, so neither of them noticed. It was more like a hiccup. But it was sour. Instead of the sweet aftertaste of a chocolate chip cookie, it had a medicinal quality. Then a stronger tingle came over my body, starting from my feet and spreading out to my fingers, like a wave. I exhaled loudly. Too loudly.

"Feeling it?" Jamie said and smiled slyly.

"Feeling what?" I said.

"The cookie. Did you have one of the cookies?"

"Cookies," I said, stunned.

"Kevin made a fresh batch. Right out of the oven. California's finest homegrown."

"I thought his name was Keith," Shane said.

"Yeah, Keith. I get mixed up with *K* names," Jamie said and slapped Shane on the back, laughing.

"Wait—those were pot cookies?" I said. I turned to Shane, and he shrugged. I was a little scared. The problem with pot cookies is you don't know how strong they can be. The last one I had sent me under the covers for six hours. "I thought you were sober," I said to Jamie, and he gave me a look. "I mean, I thought I read that somewhere."

"I am sober. I just get high," he said with a straight face.

A big gong echoed from another room. Or maybe it was in my head.

Jamie Blue rubbed his palms together. "That's my signal—my soaking gong. Do you like to soak?"

"Soak, like, in a bathtub?" I said.

"I have a special hot tub that's kind of like the natural hot springs in the desert. I have this guy come once a month to replace the salt and flush out the tubes. I should live up in Montecito where they have natural hot springs, but I guess I'm a creature of habit living in Venice. You two want to join?"

I had hoped to be sober—actually *sober* sober—while talking to Jamie Blue, but that moment had passed. I had no reason to say no to the soak now. My biggest fear was getting too uninhibited, because I didn't want to give away the real reason I was there. He'd kick us out—I was sure of it. I didn't trust myself.

I thought of my mother warning me about how pot could be laced with absolutely anything, and I considered vomiting up the cookie, but it had been a while since I'd eaten it and I wouldn't be able to get it up. I didn't want to go through my whole life thinking everything was dangerous. No, I had to embrace this moment. It was going to be a ticket for my new life. I was going to find Echo. I would charm Jamie Blue. I was going to be on one of those "twenty-three under twenty-three" lists. I was going to go in a hot tub, and I was going to casually interview Jamie Blue just to prove my mother wrong. Spite was a powerful intoxicant.

Out in the triangle-shaped courtyard, two other metal houses stood facing the one we were in. They were similar in structure but a bit smaller. There was a labyrinthine path around the center of the yard, which led to the hot tub. Then off to the side there was a lap pool. Bougainvillea climbed up the walls of one house and white roses climbed on the other.

Jamie pointed to a glass door of the one with the roses where he said there would be a bathing suit that would fit me. He told Shane he could get changed inside another door.

"You're also welcome to go in your birthday suit. That's how I do it. Like the real natural way, you know?" Jamie leered at me.

"Oh," I said, and when I looked over at Shane for help, he was already walking away.

27.

I stumbled in the door, so high that I could hardly walk. I squatted to catch my breath. Every time I burped, I got higher. My digestive tract was punishing me for eating that cookie. After a few minutes, or maybe it was a half hour, I stood up and looked around.

I was in a round room, and along the walls were at least fifty photos of Jamie Blue. Jamie Blue in *Cowpokes*, *The Angel*, *Through the Trail*, and *Matthew, Matthew*. Photos of him with Carson and Letterman and Marlon Brando and Paul Newman. With other men and women I didn't recognize. I spun around, searching for Echo's face, but I swear I went through all of them and there was not one picture of her. Not one of his own daughter. Could Olivia Breakers have been on to something after all?

I wanted to think that Echo and Jamie were special. That their relationship was solid. They were Jamie and Echo Blue! Hollywood's father-daughter darlings! Yes, he'd had some addiction problems, but hadn't they gotten through those together? And the emancipation was just a career move—Echo had said so dozens of times. Still, I couldn't shake it. What kind of parent doesn't have a picture of his famous daughter in a room filled with photos? Even my father had my stupid boxing story framed in his office. It was possible my father saw me as an appendage of himself and that's why he liked to draw attention to my byline, but that wasn't the point. I was *represented.* If you didn't know anything about Jamie Blue, you wouldn't even know he had a child if you walked into his house.

A photo caught my eye of Jamie without a shirt, standing by a pool with what appeared to be the Chateau Marmont hovering behind him. I squinted at the picture, and I realized half of it had been ripped off. His arm had been hanging over someone's shoulder. And now it wasn't there. My god, this must have been a photo from the set of *Stars Everywhere,* and he had cut her out of the picture. His own daughter.

Suddenly, I was sober. At least I felt sober, like I had been slapped. Outside the circular room there were rows of hooks with white towels and white bathing suits. Bikinis and one-pieces. Only for women. Jesus, where the hell was I and what was I doing there? Just ten minutes ago, I was determined and unwilling to back down. I had convinced myself his let's-get-naked request was friendly chitchat, hadn't I? But how would I broach the subject of Echo when he didn't have a trace of her in his house? Jamie Blue had no connection to his daughter. This was a mess. I regretted coming here. I regretted eating that stupid cookie. The *People* magazine cover with him and that sad-as-fuck face—was it even real? For so many years I had convinced myself that Jamie Blue was the father I wanted, but I only wanted him in his public role of "cool dad," not for who he really was.

There was a small table with a little phone, so I dialed Dana. I hoped she'd tell me what to do.

When Dana hired me in April 1999, she told me she was taking a chance on me. I was twenty-one, had graduated six months early from college, and was living with my parents, writing obits for the local paper. She liked the way I asked the families questions, tackling the obits like real news stories instead of like press releases, which was why she hired me as the local beat reporter at *ME.* An editor hadn't ever trusted me the way Dana had, and I owed so much to her. And after nine months of doing the job I was hired to do, she was letting me chase after Echo (or I guess write a story on women in Hollywood—same thing), taking a chance on me again. I wanted to make her proud. But I was also high at Jamie Blue's house. I had become a parody of a reporter. An absolute joke. I was stumped on what to do next.

"Dana Bradlee," she answered, her voice gruff.

"Dana, it's Goldie. I . . . It's an emergency. I wouldn't have called you after hours otherwise."

"Don't worry. You know me, a real night owl. I'm actually up reading that Edgar Cross book. You know, the guy Pench is friends with?"

"Yeah, I know it."

"I figured I'd finally give it a go. I can't believe it's still a bestseller. What a shit book," she said. "Anyway, what's up? Everything okay?"

I cupped my mouth and whispered. "I'm in Jamie Blue's house, and I'm very stoned."

"What do you mean you're stoned? Did he agree to an interview?"

"I ate a cookie at the door, and I didn't know it was a pot cookie."

"Are you kidding me, Goldie? Don't you know not to eat cookies at a stranger's house without asking what's in them?"

I didn't answer. I could barely put two words together.

"Did he agree to an interview?" she asked me again.

"See, he has this saltwater hot tub—"

"Jesus, Goldie, did you sleep with him?"

"What? No! I'm with this actor, Shane, who brought me here."

"Did you tell Jamie Blue you're a journalist?"

"I told him I was a painter. I mean an artist. But this isn't the reason I called you."

"I'd *love* to hear the reason you called me."

I carefully looked around, making sure no one was in earshot.

"He doesn't have a relationship with Echo. There's, like, a trophy room, like the one Elvis had in his house in Graceland. Have you ever been there? Jamie's is filled with pictures of himself, but not one single photo of his daughter. His only daughter! His daughter who no one has seen in nineteen days. Don't you find that strange?"

"Maybe there's another room dedicated to her?"

"I thought that too, but it doesn't make sense." I lowered my voice. "Look, Dana, my instinct is to get the hell out of here. But I'm supposed to put on a bathing suit and get into the hot tub with him. I think he's going to be naked."

I had convinced myself that Jamie Blue was going to be key to unlocking my Echo story. Now, every minute I spent in this man's house, I felt like I was betraying Echo.

She groaned loudly.

"We're going to have all sorts of issues with management if you don't disclose you're a reporter. I mean, it's not technically illegal, but it's not ethical. We're not a gotcha publication," she said. "I think you should suck it up and get in the tub."

This was not the answer I wanted to hear.

"Really? You want me to get in the tub? He's not going to help me find Echo—I can tell you that."

"It doesn't matter if he'll help you find Echo. What matters is you have exclusive access to him, and you should take advantage of it. Get in the tub *and* tell him you're a reporter. And make sure to sit far away from him. You can call me right back if things get weird—or weirder than they already are. I'll send police over there. By the way, it sounds like you should stay in L.A. It's clear you're getting some great stuff."

Before I hung up with Dana, I gave her the address, then I sifted through the bathing suit options, hoping and praying that one of his house boys or housekeepers washed the suits before new guests wore them. I plucked out a one-piece. There was no obvious evidence of wear— yes, I looked in the crotch. I know that's disgusting, but I had to check. I put it on and hoped I wouldn't get crabs.

Dana was right. Jamie Blue might not know where Echo was, but there must be something helpful I could get from him. I was a journalist. Talking to Dana reminded me of that. No story was perfect, but here I was in the childhood home of the girl I'd idolized since I was fourteen.

That raw desire that I had for Echo when I was younger bubbled inside of me now.

• • •

Outside, Shane and Jamie were in the hot tub, laughing and sharing a joint. Jamie pointed to a basket of chips and guacamole. I needed to eat something to soak up the pot cookie.

"Anything in the guac I should know about?" I asked. "Angel dust? Heroin?"

Jamie Blue laughed like it was the funniest thing he had ever heard. I gobbled up most of the chips until I felt full and stretched out on a lounge chair, running my hands over the silky suit. My confidence from a few minutes earlier had quickly dissipated. I thought about Hedda Hopper and how she would never have gotten a story this way. She had power in Hollywood. She could ruin a career. I was just a low-level journalist in a middle-aged man's backyard. At the very least, after all this, I was going to keep the suit. I wasn't going to give it back to that prick.

Jamie Blue and Shane called for me to come in the hot tub. I got up, and all of a sudden, I was high again. My legs felt thick and heavy, so I gingerly climbed in. I didn't want to fall in face-first. Jamie Blue was right about it feeling natural. There was no chemical smell like the chlorine that usually overpowers a hot tub. The water felt silky, and I sat back into the wall and took a deep breath. I had promised Dana, but I didn't know how I was going to tell him I was a reporter.

Jamie Blue turned to me and nudged close to my ear, his hair wet. "I've been collecting art for years. I almost did a deal with Julian Schnabel. What a guy. You must have seen his exhibit at the Pace Gallery in New York?"

"Oh yes. Of course. Brilliant," I said. I forgot for a second I was supposed to be an artist. I had never seen the exhibit and had never heard of Julian Schnabel. My stomach started turning from the guacamole. I was flustered and kept drifting into paranoia. Merely twenty minutes ago, I was sure that Jamie wasn't dangerous, but I wasn't sure now. *Was* it possible he did something to Echo?

I shook my head. This was nuts. I felt nuts. It was the pot cookie. It was just the cookie.

"You don't have a turret here or anything, do you?" I said.

"Huh?"

"Like"—and I whispered this—"a secret turret? Like from 'Rapunzel'?" I imagined Echo locked up and banging on a window.

"Yeah . . . a turret," he said, looking at me strangely. Then in the most caring voice, "How about you take a break from the hot tub?"

So I climbed up on the side of the tub and the cool air helped. What was wrong with me?

"Better now?" he said and laughed. "The heat can really get to you, make you imagine things. I had some profound hallucinations in Joshua Tree . . ." As he rambled on, I relaxed, and Shane crawled out of the tub too, then lay back, resting his head on the concrete and mumbling about the stars.

All of a sudden, I felt a hand on my thigh. It was Jamie Blue's big hand, and he was rubbing it back and forth, not even glancing at me. I had just gotten over thinking he was a kidnapper and now he was hitting on me. Me, only three years older than his daughter. I wanted to shove him off, but I sat there, frozen.

"Wanna do mushrooms? I have some in the house," he said.

"Like, now?" His hand was still on my thigh.

"Yeah. My friend picked them from his organic field in Oregon. He's a farmer. It's important to live inside your own private Idaho and understand who you are in the world. Actors aren't just a vessel, you know? We're real people. With hearts and feelings." His speech sounded a lot like a practiced version of his big interview that he gave a few years ago. I tried not to openly cringe. He paused for a second and squinted his eyes at me the way I'd seen him do in plenty of movies when he was about to kiss his leading lady. "It's kind of amazing how well you fit into that suit."

144

All right, I was done. I didn't care that I promised Dana I'd get something.

Jamie Blue was disgusting. Here he was, trying to drug me up, take advantage of me. Little did he know I was trying to take advantage of him! Ah-ha, Jamie Blue, how would you feel if you knew the grift was on you?

It didn't matter how good-looking he was; Jamie Blue was dirty from the inside. The kind of guy who would tie you up and ignore safe words. I thought of the women he'd slept with over the years. All of the articles about him being a playboy. Enough conquests to fill a six-hundred-page book. How he became more famous in Hollywood for his womanizing than he did for his movies. No, Jamie Blue didn't do anything to his daughter. That would mean that he'd have to take the spotlight off himself, and I don't think Jamie Blue was capable of anything that wasn't transactional.

"Let's do the 'shrooms," I said, probably a little too energetically, but I knew he had to go back to the house to get them. "I'm ready to do the 'shrooms."

"Me too," Shane said.

"Cool," Jamie said. "I'll be right back." He got out of the tub with a slightly erect penis. He lifted his muscular arms above his head and stretched, and I swear I never saw a man with a better body. I didn't typically like men's naked bodies, because they're weird and hairy with things sticking out, but Jamie Blue's body was tight and muscular, and his ass didn't have one single pimple on it. And he knew it.

As soon as he was out of sight, I stood up and turned to Shane.

"We have to leave. As in right now."

"Right now? I thought you were into this. I thought we were doing 'shrooms."

"I'm not into this, and we have to go."

"What if he sees me getting dressed? What'll I tell him?"

"Tell him I'm nauseous or something. That I got my period. Tell him anything."

Shane stood up, turned in a circle, staring at all three doorways. "How the hell do I know where my clothes are? All of the houses look the same."

He wasn't wrong. I felt like Jack Nicholson in *The Shining*, dizzy and lost in a maze, searching for the exit. I was almost positive that I had the house with the roses and Shane was in the house with the bougainvillea. We separated and agreed to meet outside.

•   •   •

Inside, my clothes were hanging up in the hallway where I'd left them. I was never more grateful to see them. I reached to grab my clothes from the hook, but because I was still wet, I slipped on the concrete floor and fell on my backside so hard that it knocked the wind out of me.

"Hello?" a woman called out in a Spanish accent. I scooted onto my hands and knees, gasping for air, when she approached me. She was small with what looked like a uniform on (Jamie Blue *would* require his staff to dress the part). "Are you okay?" She leaned over and rubbed my back until that gasping sensation went away. I was about to cry. Her touch felt like my mother's.

"I'm so sorry; it was wet and I slipped." She took my arm and helped me up. I introduced myself, and then she wrapped a towel around me.

"Who are you?" I asked, forgetting that I was the guest.

"I'm the house manager," she said and looked at me strangely.

"I thought Keith was the house manager."

"Keith is Jamie's assistant. I'm Alma."

"Ah, of course. Alma," I said. *Alma, Alma.* I racked my brain trying to recall her name and how she fit into Echo's life.

"I'm a friend of Echo's," I said, and she stared at me blankly. "I've been worried about her."

"Echo?" she said, hesitating. "Friend from where?"

"A friend from the . . . movie set," I said. I sounded like a broken robot.

She looked me up and down, but I could tell from her face she didn't buy it.

"You don't know Echo," she said coldly. "Friends of Echo's don't show up at her daddy's house. I can tell you that much. Not looking like this." She was talking about the white bathing suit.

I could only imagine the women Alma had seen in this same suit with dazed looks on their faces, trying to figure out how they wound up at the home of this middle-aged man who wanted nothing but to fuck them and steal their youth.

I could feel her getting wary of me in the way she shifted her weight from one side of her hip to the other and lowered her chin.

It didn't bother me that I hadn't identified myself to Jamie Blue, but for some reason, I felt guilty about not identifying myself to Alma.

"My name is Goldie Klein. I'm a writer for a magazine in New York," I confessed.

"Does Mr. Blue know this?"

"I didn't exactly get a chance to tell him," I said. "I came here with a friend. I'm sorry. I was concerned about Echo. I shouldn't be here." I collected my things.

She gave me a pained smile and led me to a big wooden door that exited out to the street. "Thank you for the towel and helping me up," I said.

Alma looked at me searchingly, before reluctantly whispering, "If there's one person who could help you find Echo, it's Belinda."

Huh? I never even thought to look for Belinda, because their mysterious friendship breakup seemed so permanent. Echo hadn't been seen with Belinda in years.

"I hope you can find her." Alma gently closed the door.

* * *

With my clothes and my boots under my arm, I sprinted down to the end of the street in my bare feet to find Shane—my hero!—waiting in his taxi for me. I collapsed into the front seat and started pulling up my jeans but couldn't get them over the wet bathing suit, so I sat there, breathing heavily with my jeans around my thighs. I couldn't believe this night.

"You have to get me home. Immediately," I said. I'd sit like this with my jeans halfway up until we hit Laurel Canyon. I didn't care.

"Goldie, I feel really bad about what happened back there. I didn't know he was gonna get naked. I didn't know you didn't realize the cookies were full of weed. Are you sure you're okay?"

"Shane. *Drive*," I said. I needed the urgency of someone from the East Coast. There was too much lingering in California. Too much checking in. Suddenly, a wave of heat rolled up my body, and my stomach loudly gurgled. "Actually, don't drive." I threw open the cab door and projectile vomited all over the curb.

Using my arms as leverage, I propped myself back into the seat while Shane stared at me in horror. But it didn't matter. As I slammed the cab door shut, I had a clue. I knew what was next. I could see her face in the lights as we drove through Venice. It was Belinda Summers. I was going to find Belinda Summers.

28.

Shane dropped me off, and I promised to call him tomorrow, knowing full well I would not. He knew it too, his face sorrowful like he wanted me to stay and talk it out or reassure him. But why would Shane need my reassurance? He had his good looks and his smile and his easy personality. Shane would be fine.

In the casita, I sprinted to the bathroom, smearing toothpaste across my teeth, and then put fresh underwear on. If I was going to be the one to find Echo, to *save* Echo, I had to be the one to talk to Belinda Summers. All those years and I had convinced myself that she and Echo had no connection anymore, but what did I know about the intricacies of friendship, its peaks and valleys? Wasn't that what my mother told me once? Anyway, this lead was like seeing a bright new world in front of me.

I went straight to a *Holly and the Hound* fan database I had scrolled through a few times called Pig Sandwich. The name was a joke between Belinda's and Echo's characters in *Holly and the Hound 2*. Pig Sandwich was a messy black hole stuffed with fan fiction about how Belinda and Echo were lesbian lovers, scripts for *Holly and the Hound 3*, petitions for Belinda to make more movies, and theories about Belinda and Echo's relationship, all of which were old news to me. There was a long, populated thread about what happened to Echo. Sure enough, one suspicion was that Jamie kidnapped her. I wanted to write back, *If you only knew.* Another was about how Echo was on Bill Clinton's payroll to distract from all the problems of his presidency, and she had to go into hiding because there was a CIA hit on her. None of the theories were remotely plausible. The story was still mine.

I scrolled down a long list, past more Echo Blue disappearance conspiracy theories, and found a thread about Belinda's acting career. I clicked.

> **SluggerChick28:** Sometimes I think that Belinda was a better actress than Echo and I hope she didn't give up acting. Belinda has the "it" factor. Why do you think she went from being this sidekick in HH1 to a lead player in HH2?

> **TwistedSister:** Belinda was the only good thing in that movie IMHO.

I kept scrolling, looking for something—anything—to jump out, and then . . .

> **ChellyBelly:** I heard from a friend whose sister lives in L.A. that Belinda is still in acting classes.

A shock hit my body. I finally felt no longer alone in this. I always thought of myself above fan groups, but of course, these were *my people.* Not exactly my people, because they were Belinda's people and I was clearly Team Echo, but nevertheless, these were the people who theorized and discussed all of the ideas, or at least some of the ideas, that had tugged at me for years.

I immediately registered for the group as "Mallory," Belinda's character in *Slugger Eight*, but it was already taken. Fuck! I tried again as "WriterGirl12"—the 12 a nod to Belinda's softball number—and posted a question.

WriterGirl12: *@ChellyBelly* I've always wanted to be an actor. I'd love to take acting classes too. Any idea where she's studying?

JoannaNails: *@WriterGirl12* We don't allow stalkers or trolls in this thread.

Really? There was zero self-awareness in this fan group. "You're all stalkers!" I yelled at the computer. I had to rethink my approach. I stared at my question, feeling dumb about it. I came on too strong. I would have red-flagged me too. I could change my name and reenter as someone else, but I liked the WriterGirl12 handle. I decided to explain myself.

WriterGirl12: I'm sorry, everyone. I've loved Belinda since S8 and even tried to get the Mallory handle but it looks like that was already taken. Real *respectful* fan here. :) I'm interested in acting and since I like Belinda's style, I thought it would make sense to go to an acting studio she was involved with.

I waited a few minutes, refreshed what felt like twenty times, and nothing. Message boards were notoriously slow. I had to walk away from my computer so that I wouldn't throw it against the wall. Someone would answer me because it was late, and that's when fan sites were most active, right? Because people like me, people like them, were lonely, bored, and couldn't sleep, so they'd turn to their laptops.

The next time I refreshed, four replies came up.

JoannaNails: *@WriterGirl12* Understood. I've learned to give new members the benefit of the doubt. Everyone's a little excited at first.

ChellyBelly: *@WriterGirl12* Thanks for explaining. I don't know the exact place, but pretty sure it's run by someone legit.

TwistedSister: @ChellyBelly Ha, if you can call anyone who
has been with Echo's dad (I can't even say his name) legit.

An acting class run by an ex-girlfriend of Echo's dad? It looked like
that brick of a biography would be good for something, but it was going
to take some serious digging.

I closed my laptop and ripped out a lined sheet of paper from my
notebook, opening up my *Jamie Blue: The Unauthorized Biography*, searching for one of Jamie's girlfriends who was an acting coach. Why didn't
this book have a fucking index? I started jotting down names of women
mentioned in the book. There were so many actresses, but who was serious enough to open her own studio?

I was completely hopped up on adrenaline. My skin was itchy from
that saltwater tub. I should have washed off in the shower, but I wanted
to talk to someone to get the energy out. I called Pench and he didn't
answer, then I called Sam and he wasn't home either. Why did everyone
have plans all the time? Why did people have so many friends? I called
my mom. She would calm me down. She would ground me.

My father answered groggily. "What time is it?" he said. "Mom's
asleep." Oh, that's why no one had been answering—it was the middle
of the night back east. But since we were on the phone anyway, I opted
to vent.

"I have a huge lead that I can't talk about, exactly, but all the signs are
pointing in my direction. I've never felt surer of something in my life." I
was talking quickly, faster than I normally spoke. I had to wipe the spit
from my mouth. My hands shook like I was on speed. "I'm going to find
her, Dad. I feel so close to her. So connected."

"You sound agitated. Is everything okay?"

"Everything is great!" I yelled, practically shrieking. "Can't I be happy?
I called to share this huge news with you. Maybe excitement is supposed
to sound agitated! Have you ever thought about that?"

"Calm down, Goldie."

But telling someone to calm down when they're in a heightened state always fails. It makes you feel judged and disconnected, like there's something wrong with you. And I already had enough of that from him.

"I'm calm! I feel electrified. I didn't realize it was the middle of the night. I'm sorry." I hung up. I was gruff, and I was irrational, but what he said stung. Calling me "agitated." He never failed to knock the wind out of my sails.

• • •

I finally fell asleep and woke up in the morning to my list of Jamie's conquests crinkled up underneath my arm. I got up to pee and stared in the mirror. If my father had been worried by how I sounded, he would have been appalled at the sight of me. My black eyeliner made rings around my eyes, my brown hair too thick and wild, like I hadn't brushed it in days. My curly bangs, hanging in my eyes.

I took my list to my computer. Time to see what Yahoo! would reveal. What did that poster, ChellyBelly, mean by "legit"? Did legit mean an actress not a model? Or did it mean formal training? Yes, that had to be it. Only three women I had jotted down had been connected to an acting program: Stacey Strasberg, who started the Coastal Playhouse community theater in Malibu; Robbie Trager, a Juilliard graduate who met Jamie at a duke's house on the coast of Wales, where he was shooting *Matthew, Matthew*; and Deborah Morris, who went to Yale School of Drama and who lived with him and Echo right before Echo filmed *Slugger Eight*.

Strasberg, whose aunt Paula Strasberg was famously Marilyn Monroe's acting coach, was the first one to jump out at me, but when I looked up the Coastal Playhouse, they were taking a yearlong hiatus while Stacey was on a sabbatical in Barcelona. She was out. Robbie Trager was now married to some royal and lived in Carmarthenshire, Wales. She was out. When I looked up Deborah Morris, I scrolled through her endless résumé of small acting jobs, from Broadway to the Westport Country Playhouse to *Law & Order*.

Next, I typed in *Deborah Morris acting lessons Los Angeles*.

Then right there in front of me, a classified Yahoo! ad: *Private acting lessons in Los Angeles with Deborah Morris*. I clicked on it, holding my breath.

It read, *Private or group acting lessons with actors serious about their craft run by a Yale School of Drama graduate*.

That was her. It had to be the same Deborah Morris.

I collapsed on the floor, underneath where I had hung pictures of Echo's world. The one of Echo and Belinda wearing matching white tank tops and engineered jeans rolled up at the bottom called to me. They had walked out of Fred Segal in Santa Monica (the name was printed on their bags in red-and-blue cartoon letters), deep in conversation. I was so happy, ecstasy blanketing me. I wanted to feel something. Pull my hair out. Scream her name out the back door.

I turned over so that my pelvis flattened to the floor. I was so turned on that I humped the rug. My thighs rubbed together and tightly squeezed until I made myself come. The orgasm pulsed out of me.

I didn't see Dolly's car in the driveway, and I assumed she was at yoga or getting her chakras read. So I went outside and waded into the pool in my underwear. It was like silk, and like Jamie's, had no overpowering smell of chlorine. And it was warm, almost too warm, but floating in it was delicious, and I wanted the water to eat me up. I wanted to drown inside of it. I know floating in a fancy pool in Los Angeles sounds cliché. My father would have had a problem with that much beauty. "Where's the truth in it?" he'd say. Have you tried losing yourself in water that doesn't sting your eyes? Dunk your face in and you don't even need goggles to see? It's all right there, a little blurry, sure, but it's right there in front of you.

Echo

1994–1995

· · ·

29.

Turns out when you make a movie about a relationship between a messed-up father and his daughter with your own messed-up father, people become mesmerized. That famous scene that people would talk about forever was by the pool at the Chateau Marmont. It was what would get me the nomination. I had a cold that day. We kept having to redo the shot where I jumped in the pool because my dad was forgetting his lines. I was freezing, and the milkshake I was forced to drink—part of my dad's character's attempts to shut me up—made me phlegmy. Every time I took a sip, I wanted to throw up.

I was only supposed to be filming for five hours total per day, but the studio teacher was super lenient about schoolwork, so it ended up being more. "Independent films have a little more flexibility," I heard her say to the line producer. And my dad didn't seem to care. I was completely run-down.

"Someone give her some more fucking cold medicine; she's sniffling and it's messing up the takes," my dad said.

"How are you doing, Echo?" one of the producers asked me. Every night during that shoot, I took an Ativan to sleep. That's how I was doing. "Okay to keep going?"

"Echo can keep going. She's a workhorse; she's fine," I heard my dad say.

"Oh yes. I'm fine," I said, wiping boogers away. I didn't want to upset him.

Aside from a brief glimpse of light right after rehab, my dad had been worse than ever. Yes, I had seen him angry before—the whole world knew that—but what I hadn't seen before was this anger directed at *me*. I guess it made sense; I was his co-star now, and this was how he treated the people he worked with. Also, he was worried about his career, but it still had taken me by complete surprise.

Our director, Tony Markowski, sent a PA to get me some cold medicine, but it didn't do much for my ears, which were clogged and pounded against my skull each time I had to go underwater. (After the shoot was over that day, the set doctor told me I had a double ear infection and put me on a Z-Pak. It was my second Z-Pak in three weeks.) "We'll get you to a real doctor when the shoot is over," my dad kept saying. It was only Tony's second movie. He didn't know how to deal with a guy like my dad. He submitted to him more than he should have.

"Okay, let's go again," Tony said. "Echo, your character is feeling rejected by Dad, so let's see you get angry. Throw a tantrum."

"She doesn't have to pretend," my dad quipped. "Tantrums are her favorite thing."

I wanted to throw the milkshake in his face for saying that. We both knew that I never threw tantrums; he just hoped to get a laugh from the crew. I had been so worried about him, so concerned about his health and about his ego. And here he was, humiliating me in front of everyone on the set.

For the first time, I was simply furious at him. Not feeling sorry for him, not making excuses for him, just angry. He said his line to Charlotte Pierson—"She's not really my kid; she's more like my protégé"—and it felt too honest, like he meant it. My dad wasn't that good of an actor. I finally lost it. I threw the milkshake to the ground, which they didn't expect. I barely remembered doing it. It splashed on Charlotte Pierson's yellow bathing suit. "What's gotten into you?" my dad said.

Then I said the line.

I said it real sickly and low, that scrag in my voice coming out, the opposite of how the voice coach taught me to speak, which was from my diaphragm.

I was supposed to say, "Will you ever be a man?"

Instead, I said, "Will you ever be a father?"

"Goddammit, Echo, that's not the line," my dad said after Tony yelled, "Cut."

Tony stared at me. They all did. They knew I delivered that line from a place of pain. I couldn't hide it. No matter how talented of an actress I was, my dad's behavior on that set had exposed our relationship, full of neglect. Broken. Something had been done that I couldn't take back, and I didn't want to. There was glass all over the concrete. The wardrobe assistant told me to sit on the lounge chair so they could get me flip-flops.

"Jesus, we have to go again. It's not the fucking line." My dad got up and kicked my lounge chair. "You can't throw a milkshake at me. I'm your goddamn father," he growled. Later, my dad told Tony that he'd sue him if he used that take. Hazel threatened to get him blacklisted. But Tony didn't care, because he knew that line, along with my unbridled despair, would pull people into the theater.

For the rest of my life, I'd try to capture that moment again. Yes, I did it out of humiliation, out of pain. But I couldn't do that kind of acting ever again without him. I dreamed of it plenty of times, going to that place where I let go of myself and sink into the character, where I'd blend the two, so that the character would become me and I would meld into her. I'd never sound that innocent, yet so enraged, again. I'd always sound older and damaged.

But that was the take that catapulted my career.

30.

With all the buzz around *Stars Everywhere*, the studio opted for an extremely limited Christmas release in 1994 so that it could be eligible for an Oscar nomination. (It played at the Angelika in New York for a week.) Reviews were incredible, and we were an instant hit on the indie circuit, giving the film a ton of momentum once it came out in February. *Stars Everywhere* did $9 million at the box office on its opening weekend, even beating out a big action picture that was made for three times the amount and was playing at twice as many theaters. During the press tour, every journalist asked my dad if he'd work with me again. He always gave this dry response: "Let's see if she can fit me in for lunch first." He always got a laugh.

I was as surprised as anyone when the production company behind *Stars* took out a full-page Oscar ad in *Variety*, saying, "For your consideration, Echo Blue for best supporting actress."

They took one out for my dad too, but he insisted that the effort was fruitless. Too many other good performances. Tom Hanks for *Forrest Gump* and John Travolta for *Pulp Fiction*.

"How am I gonna compete with a guy who plays an accidental hero, the kind of all-American guy everyone loves? Goddammit, I should have taken that part," he said. "Not to mention it's a lot easier to get a nomination in the supporting role when you're really the star of the picture."

"But we were both stars of the movie, Dad."

"I was the leading man, Echo. And what a leading man I am," he said, his whole face sullen. "I got upstaged by my own fucking daughter."

Because Hollywood is Hollywood, I was expected to film myself watching the Oscar nomination announcements. This is a stupid tradition that is used to promote the movie. Belinda came to watch with me—I'd officially moved into another house on my dad's compound. He said he needed space. Belinda was the only one I told that I didn't want the award.

"What actor doesn't want an Oscar?" she said. "I'm sorry to say it, but your dad is a piece of shit. I know you don't want to admit that, but whatever complicated feelings he has, he should suck them up. You can't let him stop you from enjoying this moment, Echo."

Hazel walked in with bagels before I could respond. She had an unbelievable amount of energy for five in the morning. "One day of calorie intake right here, girls. Let's get fat!"

We dug in, because if an adult like Hazel gave you permission to eat, you ate.

"Nothing to be worried about, darling," Hazel said. "Simply being *considered* makes you a bona fide star."

"That's what everyone says, Hazel."

"Yes, and there's a reason everyone says it. Because it's true. And you know I wouldn't lie to you."

I tried not to guffaw.

As Belinda and I ate, I could see Hazel staring out the window toward the main house. "Is he really not going to come over?" she mumbled, but I pretended not to hear. I didn't want to feel hopeful for something that wasn't going to happen.

At five thirty in the morning, Pacific time, Hazel turned on the live broadcast. They started with the best picture nominees first, then they dragged you through the animation and documentary before it was time for best actor, to trap the audience. Everything was for ratings, even those stupid announcements.

When they finally got to best performance by an actor in a leading role, first they called Tom Hanks for *Forrest Gump.* Then came Paul Newman for *Nobody's Fool* .

"Fuck," Hazel yelled. "Fuck fuck fuck."

She was cursing because the only way my dad could have gotten on that list was if Newman hadn't been nominated. *Nobody's Fool* was an unmemorable movie. But this was Paul Newman, and the last time he won an Oscar was in 1987. This was one of those you're-overdue-for-a-recognition kind of nomination.

And now my dad was going to be shut out.

The other nominations didn't even matter because they were expected: Morgan Freeman for *The Shawshank Redemption.* Nigel Hawthorne for *The Madness of King George.* John Travolta for *Pulp Fiction.*

"Will you call him?" I said to Hazel.

"Coddling your father is going to have to wait," she said and looked over at Belinda. "Get that video camera out. Make yourself useful."

Belinda gave Hazel the finger to her back.

The bile in my stomach was now in my throat. I could taste it and wanted to spit it out but didn't have a tissue, and I knew Hazel wouldn't let me leave this spot. This was a performance. I had to pretend to be a teenage girl who was excited about possibly getting an Oscar nomination. I had to pretend I was nervous because I wanted it, not because I was worried about, even devastated for, my dad.

So I did my silent rapid-fire clapping exercise that Deborah taught me last year in a quick trip she made to the *Holly* set. (She had been so helpful during *Pollyanna* that we kept working together.) It was a trick for when you needed to get back in the moment.

When I was done, Belinda turned the camera on and pointed it to me. Hazel, of course, needed her moment too and squished against me on the couch, clasping my hand. "Whether you get it or not, you've already won, darling," she said. How many times would she repeat that?

It was such crap.

The names were slowly announced. Rosemary Harris for *Tom and Viv*. Helen Mirren for *The Madness of King George*. Uma Thurman for *Pulp Fiction*. Dianne Wiest for *Bullets over Broadway*.

Hazel squeezed my hand tighter. "Holy shit, Echo. Holy shit." Rosemary Harris was a surprise nomination, which meant that this could go a few different ways. Hazel had already warned me that they might choose Jennifer Tilly over me, and she was the only other name not called.

And then, there it was. My name. On the television set.

Echo Blue for *Stars Everywhere*.

My ears went numb and Hazel started screaming, and she vaulted me up from the couch with her, flailing around, her voice in a deep cry like she was drowning, and I had no other choice but to hop up and down too because she had me in such a lock.

Belinda caught the whole thing on tape. Hazel's exuberant celebration blocked my face for a lot of it, which was good, because if the camera had been on me, it would have caught my big smile, my big *Oh my god, yes*, quickly descending into horror. Into the paralyzing realization that I got nominated for an Oscar and my dad didn't.

31.

The Oscar wasn't the only nomination and award I received—I won a Golden Globe and was up for a BAFTA, a SAG, and an Independent Spirit, while my dad won an MTV Movie Award, which he tossed in the trash—but it was the most important. Hazel had sent the Oscar nomination reaction video to *Live with Regis and Kathie Lee*. And though there were many other videos of actors reacting to being nominated, mine stood out. Something to do with my hair bouncing off my pajamas and how sweet it was that I was only fourteen. It was authentic, they said.

After watching it, my dad stormed into "my" house. I was sitting at the dining room table by myself doing algebra homework. (I know everyone says this, but it did seem like a waste of time for a professional actor to be doing algebra. I once mentioned this to my homeschool tutor, trying to make her laugh, and she said, "Don't be one of those kids who thinks they're going to be an actor forever." That shut me right up.)

My dad walked up to my chair, and I turned to him like any daughter would if she hadn't seen her father in a few days.

"Hey, Daddy," I said, nonchalant even though I could see he was angry. And maybe that's what made it worse. My delivery was so unenthused. Like his presence was a burden. (And wasn't it?)

That's when he slapped me in the face. He'd never touched me physically like that before. But the rage in his jaw—I'll never forget it. He was big and strong, hulkish, and it scared me. The slap knocked my head back, and I felt my neck twist, pain radiating from my cheek. For the first time, I worried that maybe he was going to really try to hurt me, and in that moment, it occurred to me that he absolutely could. I lowered my head into my elbow and cowered away from him.

He fell to the floor, crawled over to the other side of the room, hovering over his knees, ashamed for what he had done.

I was speechless at first. My mouth flapped open and shut, open and shut. Then he scurried into the kitchen, came back, and shoved a bag of frozen peas in my lap.

"Here, put that on your face," he said.

His stance softened, and he held his head in his hands. The moment happened so fast—one minute I was contemplating the usefulness of algebra; the next minute I was getting smacked.

"What did you do that for?" I spoke but I didn't comprehend what I said. I held my hand to my cheek, but it was a numb limb. There was no sensation, as if I had watched someone else's daughter get slapped. Not me.

He stood very still for a few moments, pulled up an ottoman in front of me, and sat down, then mumbled to himself like he was deep in conversation with his future, and it was looking dour. I scooted away from him. I didn't need to help him through this. A well of tears came up into my chest, emanating from my belly and up to my neck, creeping into my nose and tear ducts, and then released like a wave. I think I was in shock.

"Shit, Echo. I didn't mean to do that. But that video this morning. On the talk show. With Regis. You do not go on television bragging about your Oscar nomination. It makes you look immature and childish," he said, gritting his teeth.

"Hazel videotaped me getting the nomination. I didn't even know she was going to do it. Talk to her."

But it was a lie. I watched her take out the camera, instruct Belinda to tape us. I was totally complicit. I felt for him that he hadn't gotten the nomination, but I did nothing to stop Hazel from capitalizing on my success.

"Bullshit," he said to me. "You and Hazel had a plan to humiliate me."

"I don't want this nomination, Dad. It's not like I'm actually going to win. I'm going to sit there for the whole night bored. Isn't that what you said always happens there anyway?" I tried to steady my voice, but it all came out at once. I couldn't hold it in anymore. At least I was telling him the truth now.

I got up from the dining room table with the bag of peas attached to my face, collapsed into the couch, buried my face in a pillow, and let the bag drop to the floor. He hovered over me. I could feel his rage behind me.

"You wouldn't have even gotten that nomination if it weren't for me. Because I'm the one who decided to put you in movies. I'm the one who decided to do *that* movie with you. The only reason you even have any talent is because of me. Not your paranoid, agoraphobic mother, whose career shriveled up. You should at least be grateful. Turn over and look at me!"

I slowly turned my face to him. He was disgusted. Half my face was still buried in the pillow, the only thing protecting me from him. He outstretched his finger at me. "You keep acting like this, like an entitled brat, and your career is going to be as long as hers. Which means it'll be over very soon."

The more I cried, the angrier he got, pacing back and forth heavily and muttering about what bullshit all of this was. He was right about me having talent because of him, and one could argue that he taught me how to cry on cue. All those times he was cruel, and my tears would fall. Usually that would soften him. But right now, he was unrecognizable. I had no choice but to attempt to pacify him. I told him everything I had was because of him. I promised him that I understood that. "I don't mean to sound ungrateful, Daddy. But I hate what this award is doing to us."

He growled at the ceiling, let out a few *fuck*s, and left.

I couldn't tell anyone what had happened, not even Belinda. I already knew she felt sorry for me and the sad state of my relationship with my parents, and I couldn't stand more pity. Plus, she'd try to suggest solutions—calling the police, leaking what happened to a gossip rag, moving out of my house—but I couldn't do any of them. I didn't want to risk ruining him. Despite what powerful men in Hollywood got away with, he had now hurt someone Hollywood cared for even more than him. I couldn't be responsible for his demise.

He wasn't just my dad.

He was Jamie Blue.

Jamie Blue, the handsome, rugged movie star. Jamie Blue, the super-dad who brought me to Dan Tana's and let me slurp the vodka off the olives. Jamie Blue and his cowboy allure even though he was just a Jewish kid from New Jersey.

I loved him. I loved him. I loved him.

He'd been working his whole life to get a nomination—he was a de-scendant of Bertha Kalich, a legend of Yiddish theater!—and I was a lit-tle nothing, a *pisher*. Except now, I would always be Echo Blue, Oscar nominee.

• • •

I asked my mother if I could spend the weekend with her. Not only did she not know about the incident, but I hadn't shared anything about how bad it had been in recent months. She didn't know that my dad wasn't talking to me. She didn't know I was living in a separate house on the compound. If I had told my mom about what really happened, she'd see me as a terrible daughter. I'd left her house—"abandoned her," as she said—to move in with this womanizing monster who wasn't just jealous of my career but who also slapped me across the face. How could I admit that I loved him despite all that and still wanted to protect him?

Instead, I told her I had a sore throat and my dad was working. I wanted her to take care of me, tuck me in bed, and make me matzoh ball soup. With the new her, this was actually a possibility.

She wrapped me in a blanket, and I asked her if we could watch *What Ever Happened to Baby Jane?* like we used to because I liked to torture myself.

"I shouldn't have shown you that movie, Echo. I wasn't in a good place back then."

"Why not, Mom? It's our life, isn't it?"

She stroked my hair, lightly pulsing her fingers through the back of my scalp.

"What's going on, Echo? Talk to me."

"That's what's going to happen to me, isn't it? I'm going to go mad like Baby Jane. Aren't I?"

"God forbid, honey." But isn't that what she had been predicting all along? Now that she was "healthy," she tried to convince me otherwise. "You're a talented actress making art movies, Disney movies. You've got a whole life ahead of you. You're going to have experiences that have nothing to do with this town. Nothing to do with your career. I promise you, Echo."

I folded into her lap, begged her to go to the Oscars with me. The ceremony was coming up, and obviously, my dad wouldn't be attending. But I had to go—Hazel made that much clear: *"Imagine you win and you're not there to accept it. We can't have that, can we, darling?"* But my mother said she couldn't. She said she couldn't handle the attention. She was the antithesis of Baby Jane. She didn't want her old life back at all. She wanted to separate herself and hide from it as much as possible. All this meditation had helped center her, she said. She had to drown that old life out to maintain this new version of herself.

"I've been doing so much better, baby, but I still feel fragile. They'd hound me, ask me questions . . . I'm not ready for that. I'm not sure I ever will be."

I couldn't blame her.

I brought Klonopin with me that night and I took two, but dreams banged around inside my head, and I must have screamed in the middle of the night. My mother came running, and I cried and cried that they were coming to get me. "They all hate me. They hate me. He hates me," I cried.

"Who hates you, honey? Everyone loves you. You're a wonderful person, Echo. You just had a bad dream—that's all, honey," she kept saying, but none of it made sense. I scratched at my scalp, trying to free myself from the dark images of my dream, my dad coming at me, his face raging. She shushed me like she did when I was little, rocking me back and forth.

"It's all fear about the award, honey. Just anxiety. That's all. Totally normal. Everything is okay. I promise you it will all work out."

I wish I could have taken away the nomination and given it to him. I wish that *Stars Everywhere* didn't even exist. God help me if I actually won.

32.

The Oscar statue sat on my bathroom sink, usually with a roll of toilet paper around its head. Around the base, engraved, it read:

ACADEMY AWARD

TO

ECHO BLUE

BEST PERFORMANCE BY AN

ACTRESS IN A SUPPORTING ROLE

"STARS EVERYWHERE"

1994

Goldie

...

33.

After an intense shower to wash off all memory of Jamie Blue's house the night before, I called Deborah Morris's studio, not exactly knowing what to expect. But I had high hopes that she'd at least want some free publicity. I wasn't going to mention Echo, obviously. I had thought about pretending I was an actor, but I didn't have that in me. Not after last night's fiasco. This time I was going to say I was a journalist, see if it would give me some clout.

"Hi, I'm calling to speak to Deborah Morris."

"This is her."

I didn't expect her to answer the phone; I don't know what I expected—maybe some young intern. My cheeks were flush.

"Hi. My name is Goldie Klein. I'm calling from *Manhattan Eye*. Do you have a minute to talk?"

"I have a class in an hour, but sure. Depending on what you want to talk about," she said.

"I'm writing a feature about why former actors make the best acting teachers. There's a long list of acting coaches who've been incredibly influential to their students, like Uta Hagen and Stella Adler—"

"They can also be the most dangerous acting teachers," she said.

"What do you mean?"

"The relationship between the acting coach and the student can very much be co-dependent in nature. Actors are so specifically vulnerable. We're often opening wounds to get at emotions. We're famously insecure. Wildly in need of reassurance. It's an easy relationship to take advantage of," she said. "I've seen actors teach for the wrong reasons, because they want power."

This was not at all the story I was intending to write, but I'd put it next on my list to pitch to Dana. Cultlike acting coaches. Check.

"Fascinating," I said.

"How can I help you, Goldie?"

"I'd love to ideally come into one of your classes and observe how you work, interview you. Write about your process. That kind of thing."

"The *Manhattan Eye*? That's a New York publication."

"Right. I'm speaking to acting coaches on both coasts."

My legs trembled under me. I had to sit down. If I could pull this off, it would be a miracle.

"I have a trusting, protected relationship with my actors. People like to maintain their privacy."

"Of course. I understand. I wouldn't use anyone's names in the article. Except for yours."

"You'd use my whole studio's name?" She finally sounded intrigued.

"Oh yes. Absolutely," I said. Everyone wanted publicity, no matter how protective they claimed to be. I could feel the tingle of success up my spine, an urgency that I was getting closer to Echo.

Deborah Morris agreed to let me sit in on a few classes in exchange for the lede and a photo shoot. I felt bad about lying to her. Sure, when I found Echo, I'd make sure to plug her studio, but my guilt turned into a maddening headache so piercing that I had to cover my face with a pillow. Finally, the headache subsided, and I turned to my email. Dana had been calling and writing, asking for a Jamie Blue update. I told her I had a new angle and would fill her in when I could, but I was going to take her up on her offer and stay in L.A. a little while longer. Deborah's class was on Monday. Now I just had to get prepared.

• • •

News of my little middle-of-the-night confrontation with my father spread fast, as the next thing I knew, Sam had booked a quick weekend trip because he'd never been to L.A. It wasn't the ideal time to come. I hoped to use the weekend to transcribe the lower-stakes interviews I'd been doing. I had only been there for seven days, but I knew my parents asked Sam to check on me.

"It had nothing to do with them," Sam promised me once he got to Dolly's, but he couldn't afford a plane ticket without them paying for it. He was a college student, and it wasn't a cheap fare.

With the pool occupied by Dolly and her friends for an ayurvedic water ritual, Sam and I decided to spend the day of his arrival sightseeing. First, we went to the Viper Room because Sam wanted to lay roses down at the spot where River Phoenix died. The sidewalk was urine stained, and someone had written *RIP River* on the curb. Two girls were taking "sad" pictures nearby. We were in the artery of celebrity worship, smack in the middle of Hollywood on the Sunset Strip. I righted a Jesus candle tipped over on the concrete.

"So how's your Echo project going?" Sam said.

"Is that a trick question?"

"What?" He smirked. "Not at all."

"I have a real job, and I'm on assignment, Sam. I'm interviewing people. I met with a semi-famous former film critic last Saturday and a few days ago, a UCLA professor. Did you know only nine percent of directors in Hollywood are women?"

"Oh my god, what are you—a movie encyclopedia?"

"I want you to see that I'm focused on the big picture of the story."

"Okay, okay," he said. "I'm sorry. It's just—there was a history."

We headed toward the Walk of Fame, slowly walking down the

stretch of glossy charcoal sidewalk, past the shitty gift shops, the smell of urine, the run-down buildings.

"Listen, Sam, I was a lonely kid. I was awkward. I transferred my interests into a celebrity. This is not an uncommon thing."

I wanted to say, *Look around us. Look beneath us. Celebrities are gods in our world. They're put on pedestals. Their names are engraved on the sidewalks of Hollywood, with plaques. Even the drug addicts and rapists get plaques! I was hooked on celebrity culture just like the rest of the country, like the rest of the world.* I kicked some cigarette butts off of Darryl F. Zanuck's name, though after reading a book on how he forced himself on most of the studio actresses, I should have left them. In fact, those cigarette butts, and the Diet Coke cans littered along the Avenue of the Stars, were the realest representation of Hollywood, weren't they? An amalgamation of all the glamour and all the filth? Anyway, as a lonely kid, I couldn't avoid celebrity worship. I had clutched onto it tightly and still hadn't let it go.

"I'm just saying it wouldn't be a terrible idea if you got in touch with Dr. Watts," Sam said. "You know, to check in."

"How do you even remember Dr. Watts? I was a sophomore in high school when I saw her and you were only in middle school."

He sighed and gave in. "Mom told me to mention it."

"Oh? I thought you coming here had nothing to do with them."

"Maybe it had a little to do with them."

"Everyone in this family acts like it's so unheard of to stalk a celebrity! Mom forgets that she had a subscription to *People* magazine and that no one could speak to her when she was starting a new issue. Sacred, fucking *People*!"

No one named my mom's fixation with celebrity culture, but that's what it was. The way she devoured magazines, speaking about Goldie Hawn and Kurt Russell as if they were American royalty, how she cried for days when Princess Diana died, how she talked about Susan Lucci from *All My Children* like she was some Greek goddess. They used to love to say I was "obsessed" with Echo, but wasn't I just another product of that world, just like she was? I was no more obsessed than my mother, or the millions across the globe who relished the lifestyles of the rich and famous. I truly believed that.

"So Mom taught you how to be a stalker? That's what you're saying?" He laughed.

I turned to him. "Ha ha. Look, I promise you I'm not a stalker."

"As long as you promise to tell me if you *become* a stalker. Deal?" he said. I was lucky to have a brother like him.

"Deal," I said, winking.

He wrapped his arm through mine. "All right, let's go find Bette Davis."

.   .   .

On Sunday, before Sam's evening flight home, we hiked up to the Hollywood sign. The sky was cloudless, and the steep path leading up to it was dusty and rocky. Sam only had Converse on, so he was slipping all over the place. We had to stop under a lone tree for shade. "I hate hiking so much. I could never live here," Sam said. We kept going, over the brush, staring out above the vastness of the city, the houses crowded into the valley and the hills, until we came up behind the sign. Someone had graffitied *THIS IS NOT REAL* on the back of the *W.*

"All the writers in this town, and they couldn't have come up with something more original?" Sam said.

But I related to the sentiment. Nothing that was happening to me right now *felt* real. I focused on the horizon over the two *O*s where you could see the San Gabriel Mountains. Tomorrow I was going to Deborah Morris's class. I walked to the edge of the cliff and looked out at the dusty valley, and I fantasized about meeting Belinda. We'd like each other—of course we'd like each other—and I'd gently slip it in that I was a reporter. A *concerned* reporter, not like one of those vultures. We'd talk like old girlfriends who hadn't seen each other in years. I knew so much about her—how could I not as an Echo fan? It was impossible we wouldn't connect.

"Look at all the beauty, Sam. The landscape. Like, this is all so breathtaking. It doesn't look real, does it? Maybe that's what they meant."

"You're saying 'like' a lot."

"I know. It's annoying." I hugged him tightly. "I'm so glad you came, Sam."

I *was* glad he'd come. I was actually feeling more grounded than I had in a while, but I wanted this day to end so that tomorrow could begin. Tomorrow would be my breakthrough.

That night, it was cold in the casita, and I trembled in bed. All those good feelings turned to worry. Here's what I was most afraid of. More than coming up with nothing. What if I found Echo and she hated me? That would have been the worst thing.

34.

The acting class was in a warehouse in the Valley, where it was twenty degrees hotter and the air was thick.

I walked into the studio and made a left into Deborah's office, where she was sitting behind her desk. She had long locs and smoky eyes that lacked enthusiasm—eyes that were jaded and had seen too much. Above the couch next to her desk was an oversize movie poster of *Daughters of the Dust*, an independent film by the Black filmmaker Julie Dash. I knew this because I had researched it for the "serious" part of my article about women in cinema. She saw me staring at it.

"I had a small part in that movie," she said. "It changed my life. It made me realize what was possible. And also what was impossible."

Then she reached her hand out to mine and shook it firmly. "Deborah Morris. Nice to meet you."

"Goldie Klein," I said. "Thank you for allowing me to sit in on your class." I was calm and polite, but my brain felt like it was on fire. I had to seem like a controlled East Coast journalist. You know, dead on the inside.

We talked briefly about the lack of representation of women in cinema, and she led me into a large room with a small stage and old theater chairs where I could hear people laughing and talking loudly—"projecting," as an actor might say.

Deborah asked me to take a seat in the back, so I did. The theater was stifling, and my face boiled over with heat as I watched people continue to saunter into the studio with their confident strides, their shoulders back. These were ac-*tors*, here for "the craft." I'd seen enough episodes of *Inside the Actors Studio* with James Lipton to know about *the craft*. I was a journalist. My craft was observation. So I sat. I watched closely for Belinda, my anticipation building as each person, excuse me, each *actor*, walked in the door, but one person after another, and she didn't show.

"Are we all here?" Deborah said.

Everyone laughed.

"Are we all settled?"

Everyone yessed her.

"I have one announcement to make. The journalist Goldie Klein is here to observe. She cleared this with me already, but if anyone has an issue with this, we can ask her to leave. She's sitting in the back."

My heart thumped, waiting to hear if anyone would take issue, but they didn't. Most of them turned around to wave to me. I waved back.

"Great, then let's get to work," she said. I hoped Belinda would make a late entrance once they got started. Maybe that's the way movie stars did it. She'd sweep in late so there wouldn't be any clamoring to be around her. But I waited and waited, and nothing.

•   •   •

Watching actors do their "exercises" was like watching a yoga class. Slow, boring, and tedious. After the first class ended, I couldn't believe I had to come back again. Deborah had given me her class schedule. There was another craft class tomorrow, then Wednesday, the monologue class, and Thursday and Friday's "improv"—each three hours.

The second class was even worse than the first. They made themselves cry, threw their bodies on the floor, projected their voice across the room. Acting took a physicality that I didn't ever understand—they performed the same scenes over and over, tweaking simple intonations and expressions. Belinda never came.

Deborah had warned me that the monologues on Wednesday would be long and that they all needed work. "What I'm saying is you might want to skip that day," she said. But I had to stick it out for another marathon drama class in case Belinda showed up.

I was on a stakeout, I told myself as I went over to the studio on that third day. Sometimes stakeouts could be boring. That's why detectives in movies are always falling asleep.

The monologues started, and after half an hour of agony (for me), still no Belinda. I'd been guzzling coffee to get through these classes, and I had to pee, so I got up, thinking I'd sneak out afterward, but that's when I saw her.

Her hair was like I imagined it—shiny, long, and brown down her back. She wore a black T-shirt and a flowered skirt with boots and came roaring through the back of the studio door like a real movie star. I plopped down in my seat and surrendered into the thrill of it, tapping my feet underneath me. Belinda Summers. Wow. Here she was.

It's difficult to explain how swept away you can feel when you see one of your favorite celebrities. I was trained—we, as an entertainment-focused society, have *all* been trained by Hollywood marketing departments—to believe Belinda could be my best friend. That was her role. "The best friend."

The image I always had of Echo and me walking down a SoHo side street together suddenly included Belinda, hooked on my other arm. I had the impulse to make eye contact, to stand and wave to her. Then I had to remind myself that though I *felt* like we knew each other, she didn't know me. I sat on my hands to compose myself. It was one of the last times from that point forward that I made a rational decision.

Since Belinda was late, she sat down right in front of me in the back of the small theater. I could hear her panting in her seat. I had to be professional, but then she lifted her hair up and I couldn't stop staring at the nape of her neck, with wispy, dark hairs curling softly like petals. I wondered about her morning before she got here. Did she take a shower? Or did she just slip on some new underpants and a fresh bra? Did she powder her body so she wouldn't sweat? (How was she not sweating like I was?) Was she thinking about Echo? Was she consumed with worry?

All of a sudden it was Belinda's turn. She dashed down the aisle and stood next to Deborah uncomfortably, fidgeting. "This is a monologue I've been working on. It's an original," she said. Her voice was much lower in person than it sounded on the screen.

She took a few beats, then spoke.

"You come to me at night, confused and rattled. You like to squeeze my hand when you're confessing your fears. 'You're cutting off my circulation,' I say to you. 'How can I cut off your circulation? Our blood flows through the same veins,' you laugh. 'I am you and you are me.' You promised that I'd never die, unless we died together. You made me feel safe. You made me feel protected. Then you ruined me."

Belinda turned away from the audience and wrapped her arm over her face, shielding herself from us.

"You never told me it was over. There wasn't a discussion or a breakup. If we were lovers, would you have given me that respect? I stared out the window for days. The birds ate red berries off the trees. I wanted to feel full. I wanted to feel stuffed like the birds. But I would always feel empty."

She stepped in closer to the front of the stage, then wiped tears away from her face.

"I will always feel empty," she said again, and shrugged. "End scene. That's it."

Everyone in the class applauded, slowly at first, then the clapping erupted into something more boisterous, like they needed a minute for it to sink in. I didn't think it was very good. I've only seen Belinda Summers in over-the-top roles, and I did like her subdued delivery here. But the words were cliché; that whole part about the birds and feeling full was borderline embarrassing. Of course I stood up and clapped my ass off anyway, mainly because it clearly was about Echo. *Empty*. I wondered about Belinda feeling empty. Who else can make you feel emptier than a best friend who leaves you? I studied her as she held her face in her hands, so vulnerable. She had played the loyal, cheerful sidekick to Echo's tough characters. Here, she stripped herself of that persona; here, she was melancholy and raw.

Belinda sat back down in the chair in front of me. I fought the urge to talk to her for a few seconds but couldn't contain it anymore. This was my moment and I had to take it, so I tapped her on the shoulder.

She turned around so that I was practically face-to-face with her. Her hand grasped the back of the chair. I could feel a terror rise through my lungs that I was coming on too strong too soon, that I was giving myself away.

"That was fantastic," I said, leaning in.

"Thanks," she said and grimaced. She had the face of an uninterested celebrity, as if I had asked her for her autograph. I slithered back into my seat, aggravated at myself for ruining my opportunity with her. Now she'd avoid me. Fuck. In the minutes that followed, I racked my brain for more ways to talk to her. But to my surprise, when the next person came up on stage to read *Hamlet*, I knew what I had to say.

"No offense against the Hamlet soliloquies, but my father's a Shakespeare professor, and I've heard so many of them. Very overused, in my opinion."

She spun around, squinted her eyes. This got her attention.

"That's why I wrote my own thing," she said.

"Totally," I responded, elated. *Hamlet* was unwillingly my territory! *Thank you, Dad.* "Hamlet's real problem was that he wasn't allowed to publicly mourn. He's living with grief. It's not about wanting to have sex with his mother. It's that he was forced to swallow his grief and not accept his loss. My father calls it his anti-Freudian *Hamlet* theory."

"That's brilliant," she said. "Your dad is a Shakespeare professor?"

I nodded, as if it was no big deal. It was the only time in my life up to that point that my father's career benefited me. He would have been pleased that I had listened to his theories. Though I'm sure he'd tell me that I botched it somehow.

After seven more excruciating monologues followed by Deborah's comments on how everyone needed to *activate* their interior characters, the class was over. At that point, Belinda stood up and stuck her hand out to shake mine.

"Sorry I didn't formally introduce myself earlier. We're not supposed to talk during the monologues, you know. Unless it's about Hamlet," she said and winked. "I'm Belinda."

I know you are, I wanted to say, but I shook her hand instead. It took everything I had not to gush. I wanted to tell her how I practically grew up with her. How she and Echo were the only people in the world I could relate to. No, no. I couldn't act like a fan. I couldn't scare her away. I pinched my thigh to distract myself.

"I'm Goldie; it's nice to meet you,"

"Sorry I missed your monologue," she said. Belinda was late and missed Deborah's announcement about me being a journalist. It was going so well between us. A genuine connection. I'd tell her that I was a journalist at some point, but it didn't have to be *that* moment, did it? Everyone else here knew, so it really wasn't a lie.

"Hmm. Me too."

"A few of us are going to the bar next door," she said. "Any interest in coming? I want to hear more about your father's Shakespearean theories."

"I'm supposed to meet a friend," I said, trying to sound as uninterested as possible, "but sure, I would love to come."

35.

Away from Belinda so she couldn't hear me, I thanked Deborah for letting me sit in on her class, and I promised to be in touch. Then I followed Belinda and her acting buddies to a bar where seven of us crammed in a big booth. There was Jennifer from Cleveland, Ohio, who worried that her tallness was going to stop her from getting good roles because most leading men were only five foot eight. Cheever from Scarsdale, New York, who was dedicated to theater but was out here taking bit parts in sitcoms. Stephanie from Lancaster, Pennsylvania, with her blonde curls, who wanted to be the next Goldie Hawn. Cal from a small town in North Dakota that, according to him, no one would know. I'm sure he was right. Cal was determined to "keep it real," to make it "about the work."

"We have something to toast to," Jennifer squealed. "I booked a national commercial!"

Everyone clapped and clinked their glasses. "Here's to national residual checks," Cal said. "It's about time that money rolled in for you."

A national commercial paid excellent residual checks, I guessed. Jennifer had the face of a news anchor—angled jaw, cheery smile. She'd go far in national commercials as long as the men were her height.

"My agent wants me to go out for a McDonald's commercial, but I refuse to promote a product I don't use myself," Cal said. "You have to draw the line."

"You never eat McDonald's French fries?" I asked.

"Never," Cal said. "I'm not putting that garbage in my body."

"For twenty grand, I'll eat whatever product you want me to," Jennifer said.

"Wait—you're getting twenty grand?" Cal said.

"In residuals, maybe thirty grand," she said. "If they play it in Canada, maybe forty."

Belinda was quiet during this conversation because Belinda had *Holly and the Hound* money. She had *Slugger Eight* money. She was the most famous person at the table, in the whole bar. I watched how she sipped on her drink, nodding along to the conversation but never interjecting.

"How did your audition go, Belinda?" Jennifer asked.

"Eh," she said. "I can't tell. It was really dark. Maybe too dark for me."

"What was the role?" I said.

"Oh, it was a Steven Soderbergh movie about drug dealers. I went out for the heroin-addicted daughter. It was a long shot."

"Why was it a long shot?" I asked, and then an excitement bubbled up inside me, an energy I couldn't control, so I unleashed it. I was in a bar with Belinda Summers. If I lost my chance to talk to her about Echo, I'd never forgive myself. I didn't want to make her uncomfortable, but I was here to do a job. So I spit it out. "Why was it a long shot? Because you were a child star?"

There was a pause at the table. My question had sucked the air out of the room. It was clear that I had crossed a line—I could see it in their faces. I had breached an unwritten rule: don't ask Belinda Summers about her former life as a child star.

"Bingo," she said and sipped on her beer. She seemed to be the only person not annoyed by the question.

"Belinda has the right to redefine herself," Jennifer said and leaned across the table to hold Belinda's hand and comfort her.

"I couldn't agree more," I said. "You just turned twenty, right? You have your whole life ahead of you. You don't have to be stuck in the mold created for you as a teenager." I paused, before quickly remembering to add, "None of us do."

For all of the lies I had told up to that point, for how disingenuous I might have been, I really meant this. It seemed to soften the mood.

"How do you know how old I am?" she said and looked at me curiously. Oops. I looked at her blankly, not knowing how to answer. I told her it was just a guess. Thankfully she brushed it off. "But yeah, I'm interested in finding out what this version of me wants. Because when I go in front of casting agents, I'm not the same girl they're used to seeing. I'm just like everyone else here. Except, in a way, it's more complicated for me because everyone here is starting with a blank slate. I have a history. I have to prove to them that I'm not that girl anymore. That's why I'm thinking of going to school."

"A different acting school?" Jennifer said.

"No, college. I need to redefine myself."

Jennifer clapped her hands together tightly, tears springing from her eyes. "I love how true to yourself you are, Belinda. So authentic. You deserve to be the adult you want to be."

"Right," I said, gaining confidence. "You're not earnest little Belinda Summers anymore, Echo Blue's sidekick."

When I said Echo's name, everyone gasped.

I said another forbidden thing.

I broke the fourth wall.

But it gave me an incredible rush saying her name out loud, and I wanted to scream it wildly. *Echo, Echo, Echo.* These actors had given Belinda a safe place to rebuild so she didn't have to think about the old life, and there I was, reminding her, waving the Echo flag in her face. Do you want me to lie to you now and tell you I regretted it? That I should have given Belinda her privacy? Because I didn't. I needed to cut to the chase. I had a story to write.

Belinda frowned and excused herself to the bathroom.

I jumped up to follow her, but Jennifer from Ohio snatched my hand, stopping me. "Maybe give her a little space?" she said aggressively.

"I have to pee," I said. "Is a person not allowed to pee?"

I wrestled my hand away from hers and sprinted from the table.

Belinda was standing in the hallway outside of the bathroom. Another woman was ahead of her. When Belinda saw me, she smiled, but it wasn't a welcoming smile. It was forced, the smile of disgust.

"I didn't mean to upset you back there," I said, trying to make my own smile appear gentle. I wanted her to like me. It wasn't just so that I could ask her questions about Echo either. I wanted her to trust me.

"I'm just not used to talking about that part of my life." Her eyes darted around my face. I could see she was trying to figure out my intentions as she wedged herself in this tiny hallway with me. The other woman went into the bathroom; now there was no one ahead of us. My time was running out; I had to get to the question.

"It's hard for me to look at you without thinking of her. You worked together for a long time," I said. "Plus, a lot of people are discussing her disappearance right now."

"I couldn't tell you a thing about it." There was a sadness in her voice and body language—the way she looked down at the floor and shuffled her foot.

Despicably, I pushed the conversation.

"Kind of awful, right? That she's just gone? I have a theory about it. I think she was tired of being in the spotlight. Hopefully that's all it is and not something worse, or dangerous."

Belinda sighed deeply and knocked gently on the bathroom door. The woman inside yelled, "Hold on!"

"It just seems odd to me to leave like that and not talk to anyone. I'm sure you have an opinion about it," I said. "Do you . . . have an opinion about it?"

Belinda raised one eyebrow the way she did a million times in *Holly and the Hound* (parts one and two). I could feel my hand shaking.

"Are you a reporter or something?" she said. "Because I thought you were an actor."

I fidgeted with my hair. I licked my lips. I had words prepared for this moment, but I clammed up. She stepped one foot closer to me, got right in my face. I stood there, shocked, like a terrified lamb.

"Who the fuck are you?"

She turned away from me and rapped on the bathroom door again with a closed fist.

The woman yelled from inside the bathroom, "I have my period! I need a minute."

Belinda gave me a death stare and stormed away. I chased her back to where the other actors were sitting. She grabbed her stuff, jerking everything across the booth.

My big interview—if you could call it that—with Belinda Summers was slipping through my fingers, and I didn't know how to save it.

"Please," I said, begging her. I wasn't calm. I clenched my hands together in a prayerlike position. The other actors watched us carefully from the booth. It was a performance. I was fighting for my life.

"Please don't walk away, Belinda. Please let me explain." I grabbed her wrist.

"Don't touch me," she said and shook me off. "I know this is about—" Belinda almost said her name, but people were starting to stare. Belinda wasn't completely recognizable yet, but if we kept making a scene, someone would place her. Someone would tell Page Six. She held her stuff against her chest. "I'm out of here."

"Yes, I'm a journalist, okay? I'm sorry I lied to you. I'm writing a story about Echo. I'm really trying to write a good story, not an exploitive story," I said, panicking. "I just need to know where she is."

The color drained out of her face.

"I have no idea where she is. Why would I know?"

"What's going on here?" Jennifer from Ohio said, towering over me. She wasn't kidding about how tall she was. "Is there a problem?"

"This person duped Deborah. She's an interloper, asking me about my past."

Jennifer bit her lip. I could see this was Jennifer's time to shine. Her big performance as protector. "I think it's time for you to go." She crossed her arms in front of her chest and stood in front of Belinda, who didn't seem to mind.

It was hard to believe I had put myself in this situation. That this was me. Here I was, like in a fever dream, confronting Belinda Summers in a bar. In the Valley. "I'm sorry," I said, but it was an insincere apology. I wasn't sorry. I was sorry for *myself*, that I hadn't gotten any information from Belinda. They stared me down, and I felt ridiculous. So I left.

Outside, the bright light blinded me. Why was the sun always shining here?! I shielded my eyes with my hand. Too bad I had blown off Shane, because I could really use a ride right now.

No one walks in L.A. for good reason. The streets are horrid, not at all pedestrian friendly. Someone flipped me off for crossing the street. With the light! I went into a shitty strip mall, one of those places with a stacked sign that read LIQUOR, KARATE, LAUNDRY, and TACOS. I got myself a taco with extra hot sauce, sat on the curb, and ate it.

It was hopeless. It had been twenty-six days since Echo went missing, and it was only a matter of time until some fancy reporter beat me to finding her. They were going to write a great feature about her, solve the mystery of where she went, do the news rounds, go on all the talk shows, bragging about how they had gotten the exclusive. They'd write articles for Condé Nast, get a big book deal, and become famous.

The hot sauce burned the back of my throat and scorched my tongue. The story was over. I knew I wouldn't find Echo. All my leads brought me to a taco shop in Encino. I deserved it, didn't I? I lied to Belinda about my intentions. Lied to Deborah. Journalists don't do that. Not the good ones.

I called a cab to pick me up. The ride was going to be a fortune, and it would be the final thing to max out my credit card. I cried as we left the flat, lifeless earth of the Valley and climbed back up to the cascading hills of Laurel Canyon.

• • •

When I got to the casita, I called Dana to explain what happened.

"I'm drowning. I'm in over my head. I don't have it. Belinda thinks I'm a psychotic liar. Deborah Morris is going to be devastated that I infiltrated her tight group of actors."

"What do you think this is, Goldie? A friendship-making class?"

"Huh?"

"The relationship between a journalist and their subject is inherently antagonistic. You are there to write a story about them. You are there to observe them. You are there to get them to open up to you. It's not a reciprocal situation. Do you understand? You are correct that some people aren't going to want to talk to you, but it's not a fucking job interview, Goldie. You need to talk to Belinda Summers again. This is *Manhattan Eye*, goddammit. We're not some rag."

"I've done enough damage, don't you think, Dana?" I'd really started to feel this way. As much as I said I was doing this for Echo, Belinda's disgust had penetrated my psyche. I didn't like myself. Was there any nobility in what I was doing?

"You're too in your head, Goldie. What did you do—ask her some questions? Follow her around a little? Disguise who you were?" she said. "Have you not seen *All the President's Men*?"

"I've seen parts of it."

"Watch the scene where Dustin Hoffman edges his way into the bookkeeper's house, until he gets her to talk. He's very calm. He's very focused. She's afraid to relinquish the information. But it's a matter of national security, and he has to ask her about the disbursement of the money because it's tied to the Watergate break-in. Do you understand what I'm getting at?"

I wasn't sure who was more delusional in that moment—me or Dana. She was comparing me getting an interview with Belinda Summers to

Watergate. Maybe it had something to do with her being Ben Bradlee's granddaughter.

"You don't walk away from a story because a source doesn't want to talk to you. You find a way to make them talk to you. Joan Didion wrote about a child on acid, okay?" she said calmly. "She didn't call Child Protective Services. She wrote the story."

I liked that Dana was forcing me to look at myself. She was the kind of editor I wanted to be like. She could compartmentalize a story. She could be polite and cunning. These were the kinds of qualities usually reserved for men. I wasn't used to seeing them in a woman. I paid attention.

"Look, you learned a lot from this story. And I think you're on to something. But take the rest of the week to regroup. I know you feel like you have to get this in quickly, but let it simmer. Then get yourself back to New York, and we'll figure out what you have."

I could hear the wind whip up outside, a whistle in the trees. What did they call it? The Santa Ana winds? Dana was right. I wanted to try again with Belinda. If I could just explain myself to her . . . The story was so close. Belinda's passionate reaction made that clear.

As soon as I hung up with Dana, my phone rang again. It was my mother. She sounded froggy and slow when I answered. Like she'd been crying.

"Mom?" I said. "What's wrong?"

"It's Dad," she said. "There was a car accident, Goldie." Her voice cracked and she sobbed, trying to get the words out. "He's gone."

36.

Every family has some story like this. About a person who died long before their time. I didn't think that this kind of thing would happen to us, because no one believes it will happen to them. My father was in Cambridge giving a talk on poetic structure at Harvard. He was driving home, back to New Jersey, on the Mass Pike.

My mother had been waiting for him to call her. He liked to check in with her. He liked to hear her voice. It had been hours, which she said was unlike him. Then finally the phone rang, and she answered eagerly.

It was the Worcester Police Department.

"Is this a family member of Ray Klein?"

"Yes. I'm his wife."

"Ma'am, we're sorry to inform you that there was a car accident and your husband passed away. We're so sorry."

"Passed away. What are you talking about? You must have the wrong Ray Klein. Do you know how many Ray Kleins there are? Do you understand that? If you look in the phone book, there are at least twenty other Ray Kleins. My husband is on his way home. He should be here any minute."

"Ma'am," they said to her. "We have his license. It has his address on it."

After that, she called Sam in hysterics. She told Sam he had to call the Worcester Police Department because they were saying crazy things about his father that couldn't be true. Worcester has to be a made-up name of a town, my mom said. They must have been playing some sort of joke. He needed to tell them that my father wasn't dead.

I was the next call.

Sam, who had come right over, took the phone from my mom. "Come home, Goldie. You have to come home."

Echo

1995–1996

· · ·

37.

After the Oscars, after everything that happened with my dad, I went to my lawyer and asked her to start emancipation proceedings. I was fourteen. My mother thought it was for movie logistics like I told her, that I needed more creative freedom, and I couldn't do that if I was chained to the union rules. She didn't try to talk me out of it. She never took it personally or accused me of making a statement about her parenting. She'd had to reckon with my independence since that day I left her house with Deborah all those years ago.

"You're still my baby," she said. "But you've been practically an adult since the day you were born, and I'm sorry for that. I really am." She looked so beautiful when she said that, even though part of me, somewhere deep down, resented her for not rescuing me a long time ago. But it was too late for that. It wasn't true that I was still her baby—I hadn't been for a long time, and now I wouldn't be legally either.

There were a lot of reasons I wanted to be a legal adult. It's true I did it to avoid SAG-AFTRA child labor law restrictions. Pre-production had already started for *Holly and the Hound 2*, but I wanted other movies, more adult movies that would require longer work hours.

I also did it for financial reasons. I had access to some of my money: 15 percent of my gross earnings went into a Coogan Account, a safeguard named after the child actor Jackie Coogan, who learned at twenty-one that his mother and stepfather wouldn't give him any of the millions he earned from *The Kid* alongside Charlie Chaplin at six years old. But the rest of my earnings were in an account run by my dad and his accountant, which meant he had access to it. Sure, I could have gotten his permission and moved it to a trust, then hired my own accountant to manage it, but I was angry.

Which brings me to reason number three, the most important one: I wanted to stick it to my dad. The bubble had finally burst, and I no longer saw him as the wonderful yet troubled Jamie Blue. I saw him as the man who had hit me. Who had put me down when I had done nothing but try to support him. I kept going back to the moment he moved me out of the primary house — his house — on the compound. That's when it should have all become clear. He was treating me like one of his girlfriends. He had dumped me like one of them. Now I was dumping him.

I bought a small 1920s bungalow in Beverly Hills near where Belinda lived with her mother. I hired a gardener to plant roses and moss in the back so it would look cottagey and overgrown, nothing like my dad's modern compound. I didn't even get a moving truck. Belinda and I packed my clothes and a few of my other things in a few hours. What did I need, anyway? I could replace it all. With full control over my bank accounts, I had plenty of money to buy whatever I wanted.

My dad was home the day I left, and I hoped that he'd try to convince me to stay. I wanted to see his hurt face. I wanted him to tell me how sorry he was.

"Everything's going to work out," he said instead. He hardly looked at me.

38.

I had thought finally being free of my dad's wrath would make me feel better. But I found myself feeling worse than ever. I was depressed all through the filming of *Holly and the Hound 2*, and I figured out just the right schedule to take my daily Klonopins, which I now had a prescription for, so that I wouldn't seem too off on set.

Christine Camper, who directed the last *Holly*, signed on again. Since it was now a franchise for Disney, we didn't have as much creative freedom as we did on the first one. The studio wanted Belinda and I to wear sexy schoolgirl outfits since they were popular at the time, and even Christine couldn't change their minds. You could be fifteen in Hollywood and have your own house, but unless you had your own production company or an agent who had your back (Hazel's only input was "*I can certainly speak with them, darling, but I worry you'll be perceived as difficult*"), it was impossible to win an argument against the studio. It didn't matter that Belinda was there with me—I was miserable on that set. At the same time, I selfishly wanted filming to go on forever because then I didn't have to go home alone.

Things only got worse when the movie came out over a year later.

Right before *Holly and the Hound 2* premiered, Hazel invited me to lunch at the Ivy. She wanted to discuss the Disney deal and my future.

"The Ivy? Why? It's a paparazzi breeding ground," I said.

"We go to the Ivy all spruced up, and they'll talk about how fresh-faced you look instead of focusing on the bad press. Oscar winner Echo Blue! We need to separate you from all of this drama with your father. Make sure people go to see *Holly and the Hound 2* for the right reasons."

Crowds hovered outside as we pulled up in Hazel's new Mercedes SL-class convertible, taking pictures of me like I was an animal at a zoo. One after another, grown men stuck their massive camera lenses to the passenger-side car window, screaming my name. A maître d' ushered me to a front patio table behind the white picket fence. You don't go to the Ivy to sit inside. You might think I would have gotten used to it by now, but I hadn't, and I didn't think I ever would. People hollering my name and clamoring around me like maniacs. Usually, they could only get near me for a few seconds, but those seconds were terrifying, the clicking cameras in my ear, the way they reached out to touch me. They used to be so sweet and just yell out things like "Smile, Echo!" but now they grabbed at my clothes, demanded answers. "Do you hate your father, Echo? Is he jealous of your award, Echo?" I felt trapped.

"Look happy, Echo. Just ignore them," Hazel said once we sat down.

"Really?" I said to her. "Tell that to Princess Diana. She ignores them all the time and they still harass her. One day something horrible is going to happen."

"That's not something to joke about."

"People should know that if you chase a petrified woman through the streets, something horrible could happen."

"Echo," Hazel hissed.

Someone next to us turned around. A woman with one of those Gucci by Tom Ford blue silk shirts, tight black leather pants, and blonde extensions. Everyone wanted to look hypermodern, like robots, even though it was eighty degrees out.

"I agree, they've absolutely tried to ruin her life. They're out for blood," the woman said conspiratorially, and I softened a little. Not everyone was out to get me. There were sincere fans too. But then in her next breath: "Can I ask you a favor? Can I take a photo with you?" Her voice cracked, and I realized that she already had the camera in her hand.

I was at the Ivy. I was there to be a product. To sell myself. The paps were one thing, but I couldn't say no to an "innocent" fan.

"Take the picture, Echo," Hazel said with a pained smile.

•   •   •

After lunch, which included signing six other autographs, Hazel and I pushed our way through the photographers to her car.

"Never again," I said to her once we were inside. "It makes me look desperate, like I'm dying for someone to take my picture. And I'm not dying for anyone to take my picture."

Hazel sighed as she drove us away. "Look, I'm going to be straight up with you. They need other material and photos to look at rather than early reviews of *Holly and the Hound 2*."

"Huh? I thought we were here on an anti-Jamie campaign—"

"Darling, listen to me. This is no longer about your father. If you do too many movies with Belinda upstaging you, you're going to lose your roles to her."

"What are you talking about?"

She rummaged around in her purse and handed me a sheet of paper. "I got this from a source at the *L.A. Times*." It was an early version of a review that Frankie James, the prominent local critic with the big mustache, wrote. It was coming out tomorrow.

> *If it weren't for Ms. Blue's sidekick, Belinda Summers,*
> Holly and the Hound 2 *might have turned out like the*
> *stinky droppings at the bottom of a canine cage. The*
> *story is nothing but one cliché after another, and unfortu-*
> *nately, the usually effervescent yet understated Ms. Blue,*
> *just off her Oscar win, seems to have phoned in her per-*

formance. Ms. Summers, on the other hand, gives a charming, white-hot showing, stealing every scene she's in. Otherwise, Holly and the Hound 2 *is for the dogs.*

"Since when do they review kids' movies?"

"They do it when an Oscar winner is starring in it. We'll get through this," Hazel said. "But look, Belinda is becoming a player, and you need to understand that. And what it means for you."

"Belinda isn't a player. She's an actress, and she wants to do well like anyone else."

At a light, Hazel turned to me and lowered her sunglasses to the bridge of her nose. Her eyes were like fire. "Really, darling? Is that what you want? For Belinda to do so well that she eclipses you?" Hazel drove down Robertson, trying to fight the traffic as the paparazzi continued to follow us on the street. Belinda taking my spot? She *had* been getting more serious about acting, but she wanted to be on Broadway. She had her own dreams. Of course she did. No one would want to be my sidekick forever. And she shouldn't have to be! But I was on my own now. I had to support myself. Belinda had Sandy, a mother who showed up to pick her up after rehearsals, who took her to the dermatologist when she complained about one stupid pimple, who made her dinner every night. I had given up *everything* for this career. I couldn't lose it. I looked into the passenger-side mirror. What was that, a wrinkle between my eyes?

Two days later, right after the horrific *L.A. Times* review came out, one of the tabloids posted the pictures of me in Hazel's car, staring straight ahead, blank-eyed like a zombie. The headline read, "ECHO BLUE POST *HH2* BOMB: WHAT'S SHE THINKING?"

• • •

"It was bullshit, that article about how I stole the show, if that's what you're asking me about," Belinda said when I called her about the tabloid photo.

I didn't want to listen to her, the way she propped me up even when I

196

didn't deserve it. I drifted off, hungover from the night before. I had been at a party in the Hollywood Hills for an eighteen-year-old singer named Fiona Apple, whose album hadn't come out yet. She played at a baby grand, her haunting voice filling the room. *"Your gaze is dangerous / And you fill your space so sweet."* I wanted to feel that way about someone, completely enraptured, like someone's gaze could destroy me. I drank a martini and swayed back and forth.

"You were amazing in the movie, Echo," Belinda said, pulling me back into the present. She didn't come with me to the party. Sandy wouldn't allow it. "It's not easy to play Holly, Echo. You're like the serious, complicated one, and I'm the trusty sidekick. But you're the main draw. Don't you see that?"

"I see that you might end up being a more talented actor than me. That's what I see," I said.

"Don't let them put this wedge between us, Echo."

But it was already done.

Goldie

. . .

39.

I didn't cry at the funeral. I don't know why. At my parents' house, the rabbi told me that I was having a delayed reaction. He said not to worry, that I would cry soon. "What would you like to tell me about your father?" he asked. I wondered how many of these he did in a week. I knew this was part of his job, but it felt so robotic.

"The last time I spoke with my father, I yelled at him."

"Usually we say positive things. Something that you would want others to know." He smiled politely.

I didn't know what else to say. I felt dead inside. I tried not to think of how my dad looked at me when I went into his office to get that stupid boxing book last year and how I acted like a baby. How he had recently called me to try to make amends and how I refused to budge. How I hurt him.

Mourners skulked into the funeral home, repeating themselves: "*I'm so sorry. I'm so sorry.*" That's all they could say. Two of my father's co-workers told me they thought he was the most brilliant man they had ever met. His former assistant, Paloma, who hadn't worked for him for years, approached me, her frizzy gray hair down to her protruding collarbones.

"Goldie," she said, taking my hands. "Your father thought you were a wonderful writer. I did too. He showed me the letter you wrote him when you were maybe in middle school. I don't remember it word for word, but two lines are burned in my mind: *Dear Dad, your expectations are unrealistic. My trajectory as a writer will be fruitless if you continue to penalize me for minuscule errors.* Your language was remarkable, even back then."

I was shocked. "My father saved that letter?"

"Oh yes," she said. "He thought it was adorable."

I didn't know if I wanted to strangle her or hug her. Truly, this was the essence of my father. I wrote him a letter from my broken twelve-year-old soul, begging him to not be so hard on me, and that's what he brought in to work to show his fucking weird assistant. That's the thing he chose to brag about.

Oddly, I was tickled. Yes, my father's warped sense of pride tickled me. What could I say? I was his daughter.

Later, at the graveside, my mother was possessed. She shoveled the dirt onto my father's casket, grunting each time she dug into the earth. I had never seen her like that before. Usually, family members and friends took turns shoveling—you'd dredge into the dirt one or two times, then hand the shovel to the next person. But she seemed to want to do the whole thing, her mouth open wide and her eyes practically swollen shut from crying. She went on like that for what felt like ten minutes, shoveling and grunting. The thud of the dirt. "Someone take the shovel from her, for god's sake," my uncle Arty eventually said, and Sam pried it out of her hands.

He held the shovel out to me, and I shook my head. I didn't want to shovel dirt onto my father's casket. It was grotesque.

The rabbi turned to me with his coffee breath.

"It's symbolic of leaving nothing undone," he said to me. "If you shovel, then you'll have closure. You'll be able to say you did everything. That you put your father to rest. It allows the healing to begin."

What could I tell him? That I didn't even understand where my father was right now? One minute he was here, next minute the Worcester

Police Department was calling my mother, and now here I was, watching people shovel dirt on his casket.

If my father had managed to stay alive a little longer, I could have gotten him to say to me what he told his assistant when he was alive. *You're a wonderful writer.* He was just getting there! I didn't even get the chance to tell him that I impressed Belinda Summers with his anti-Freudian *Hamlet* theory about grief. He had been flawed, but he loved me in his own warped way. Now that I found myself in this position, it felt like that was all that mattered the whole time.

I stared at the casket, the thud of dirt hitting the wood as each of the mourners took their turns. I almost expected him to lift it open and say, *Hey, kid, I was hard on you. I'm so proud of you.*

Thud. Thud. Thud. It's a sound I would never forget no matter how hard I tried to block it out.

. . .

I spent a few days at my mother's sitting shiva with her starting right after the funeral, but I wasn't any help. I lurked around the kitchen for those three days, while Sam refilled the platters of cold cuts and covered the mirrors. People picked at the food with their fingers even though there were forks. They were hungry to fill themselves up with anything to escape the sadness.

One day, in an attempt to be of some use, I took over washing dishes from my neighbor up the street, Evelyn Strickland, a real estate agent whose signs with a photo of her smiling broadly were all over the front lawns in town. I hoped she'd walk away and let me wash dishes in peace, but Evelyn wasn't just a yenta; she was a saleswoman.

"Your mother tells me you're very busy. That you were out in California on a big story. The real estate market in Los Angeles is the highest it's ever been. I don't know how anyone affords a home out there. All those movie stars buying up property."

"Oh, you know how it is. Greta Garbo and Monroe. Dietrich and DiMaggio."

Evelyn looked at me blankly. It amused me that she didn't realize I was quoting lyrics from Madonna's "Vogue."

"I always wanted to get one of those star maps—you know, take a tour of famous people's homes." She leaned her shoulder into mine and low-ered her voice as if we were having some covert conversation. "So, Goldie, did you happen to see a celebrity's house while you were out there? Inter-view anyone big? Did you get a look at how the other half lives?"

I thought of myself in that white, skimpy bathing suit in Jamie Blue's hot tub. His compound in Venice. The wall-to-wall pictures of himself and not one of Echo. My father was only fifty-two, not that much older than Jamie Blue, and that asshole was still very much alive. Why couldn't it have been Jamie Blue in a freak accident? Why did it have to be my fa-ther? If I were missing, my father wouldn't have entertained some young woman whose name he barely knew. He would have been searching high and low for me. He would've been devastated. Jamie Blue's daughter had disappeared, and despite what he said publicly, I saw firsthand it didn't seem to have any effect on him. He disgusted me.

That's what finally brought me to tears. The dishwater and Evelyn Strickland's opportunism and how Jamie Blue, the father I always idol-ized, was nothing compared to the father I had. Evelyn placed her hand on my elbow, and I stood there helpless with my yellow gloves.

"Goldie, are you okay?"

I sniffled all of the junk in my nose. "Do I look okay, Evelyn?"

She hugged me and I allowed it. After about sixty seconds, which, by the way, is a long hug with someone you aren't particularly fond of, she stuck her card in the front pocket of my sweater. "Your mother's going to need this."

40.

When I got back to my apartment after a late-night bus ride from my parents'—or my mom's now, I guess—I finally returned the missed calls I got from Pench over the past five days. I wasn't trying to avoid him. I was numb. He had said he was going to pay a shiva call to my mom, but I told him not to. Now he asked me how I was holding up, if I was "processing" the grief, yada, yada, yada. I told him to stop talking and to come over.

When Pench got to my door, he gave me a hug, the kind of hug that wasn't really a hug. It was more of a hug that you would give someone if you were nervous to touch them. He was awkward like that. He poured me a glass of wine from the bottle he brought. He didn't pour himself one, because he said that wine gave him reflux. These were the kinds of details I didn't need to hear.

He took off his sneakers to reveal socks with little foxes printed all over them.

"Those socks are ridiculous," I said, laughing. It felt nice to laugh. "They're cute, I mean. They're sweet." I was surprised by my own impulse to compliment him, since usually I wanted to strangle him.

"They're from my mom. She likes to buy me funny socks."

His face went red from his neck to his forehead. Even his ears turned pink.

"I want you to undress me," I said. "Treat me like a baby." I didn't care if it sounded creepy. I wanted someone to take care of me.

He unbuttoned my cardigan and kissed my shoulder. "This? Are you sure?" he said, and I nodded, letting him take off my pants and then my underwear.

"Do it all," I said. I didn't want to think.

"Is this okay?" he said when he kissed my bare inner thighs.

I floated, detached and sad. "Yes," I told him. He was gentle, even though his stubble poked at me, and he took my clit in his mouth with care. I came so hard, all of that rage and deep upset and embarrassment about Shane and Jamie Blue and Belinda and the story. Flashes of my mother and Sam shoveling dirt onto my father's grave. All of it poured out of me like hot water, and I cried as it happened. It hurt, that orgasm, and I held on to his hair like he was suctioned to my pussy, and I wouldn't let him go. He didn't try to get away either. He might have suffocated right there and been okay with it. He lifted his head up and saw me crying, so he placed my cardigan back over me and held me.

"Why are you so nice to me?" I asked.

"Because I like you. I think you're smart. I like how hard you work. You're not afraid of anything."

A little later, once Pench had fallen asleep on my couch, I thought about a future with him. He was being nice in that moment, but would that change if he got to know the real me? Would that change if we both wanted the same story? Would he agree to share a byline with me and then leave me off it? Yet he was also the only person I would trust to send a first draft to. I might not like what he'd have to say, but at least he'd be honest with me.

I opened my old Echo box, which I had grabbed from under my bed before leaving home. Inside were form letters from the fan club plus art that came once a month in a packet with stickers. There was the ticket for the meet and greet at Macy's in New York when she made her one and only appearance to promote her perfume. The signed headshots and the leaflets, too many to count. The letters I wrote to her that I never sent, with the words scribbled, minuscule and manic. A black-and-white image of her staring off camera, her open smile showing a tiny crook in her teeth.

I tacked all of the letters and the fan club flyers and the photos to the wall. Yes, I was aware it was the second time in weeks I'd done this. It was my way of processing. It took about forty-five minutes to get everything up. I would say it was twice the size of the collage I made at Dolly's house, which I had dismantled in a hurry before leaving. But now, I repaired those photos with tape and added them to the collection. I stretched out on the floor just below it all, those photos of Echo rising above me.

I went to the bathroom to put on a robe and splash my face with water, and when I came back, Pench was awake and staring at my haphazard gallery wall. I should have waited until he left, but part of me wanted him to see this side of me. My obsession, my grief.

"This is . . . something."

"It's from my house when I was a teenager. I had a box filled with this stuff under my bed. I idolized Echo back then. She was everything to me." There it was, out.

"So you're actually obsessed with her? Like a stalker?"

I wrapped my robe tightly around me. I was so stupid to think I could be this vulnerable with Pench.

"Okay, it's time for you to leave. It's almost one thirty in the morning. I'm exhausted."

"I wasn't trying to make fun of you, Goldie," he said. "I was just teasing."

"You called me a stalker," I said. I thought about the sleepover in high school when the girls were horrified by my homemade Echo poster. Pench had the same look.

"Hey, I'm sorry," he said gently, his expression changing. "I'm just not a visual person. I see something like this and I . . . I don't know what to think. I'm so linear. For me, writing a story is like a template. It's formulaic. For you, it's clearly different." He glanced at the wall of Echos again. "And you obviously have a vested interest. A personal connection. That's not a bad thing."

Pench seemed sincere. He'd given me Hazel Cahn's number. He checked in on me when my father died. He wore socks with foxes on them from his mom. He ate my pussy an hour ago with great fervor. I should forgive him.

I told him to sit on the couch, and I opened up about all of it. Not having friends in high school, my sessions with Dr. Watts, my parents' fear about my fixation with Echo, the fan club letters, the autographed pictures.

"We all have stuff from our past, Goldie," he said.

"That's it? So you're not running away?"

"I'm not running away." There was a pause, and I hoped he wasn't going to ask me to be his girlfriend or something awkward. But he pointed to the wall. "Has this collage helped you figure out anything about the story?"

"I don't know," I said, my mind full, the images spinning. All of Echo's expressions staring back at me, questioning. *What, Goldie? What do you want from me?*

I want everything, I thought.

What was it that Belinda had said to me at the bar after her acting class? "*I have no idea where she is. Why would I know?*" I wondered if that was true. I racked my brain, recalling her monologue. Something about betrayal. What kind of betrayal would end their friendship? It didn't have to do with a man—I knew that much. Echo was only famously involved with one guy, and that was after Belinda was ostensibly out of her life.

I scribbled down the years of their friendship on different pieces of paper, starting in 1991, when they met on the *Slugger Eight* set—and spread them across the wall. I needed a timeline of their friendship to zero in on the last time Belinda and Echo were seen together. I carefully arranged each of my Belinda and Echo photos underneath the year each photo was taken.

"How can you be so sure these dates are right?" Pench said. But I ignored him because he didn't know my thick, bursting encyclopedic brain when it came to Echo.

I focused on one of the pictures of Belinda and Echo in New York. They were wearing the same jeans, the same big white T-shirt, both with cowboy hats and flip-flops. A very nineties look. Echo had her arms wrapped around a paper bag of food, and Belinda was holding her own purse. Tucked under Belinda's other arm was a book. It went into the 1997 column.

After that, nothing of the two of them.

I looked at the messy collage on the wall, the teeming magazine tear outs. If there was a picture of Belinda and Echo in 1998, I would have had it. I went on to Yahoo! and searched *Belinda Summers + Echo Blue + 1998.* Nothing.

I zeroed back in on the last known photo. The one of the two of them in the white T-shirts and cowboy hats. The one where Belinda's holding a book.

"Can you read what that says? The book Belinda's carrying?" I said.

We tried to make out the letters, but they were too tiny. One of my father's idiotic professorial colleagues had given me a magnifying glass for my college graduation (he claimed it was perfect for taking out splinters, or to sit atop a pile of books). I tore through my desk to see if I still had it, finally unearthing it from underneath a busted stapler.

I held it up to the photo. There had to be some identifying element on the book. The author's name was impossible to read, but the first letter of the book was an *E*.

An *E*.

And that's when I realized it. Without even having to see the rest of the title. It came to me, hitting me so hard, a gut punch, that I had to sit back down on the couch, all of the wind knocked out of me.

Belinda Summers had been reading Jane Austen's *Emma.*

Echo
1996

. . .

41.

To do damage control after the emancipation, my dad fired Hazel, got a new publicist, and did a colossal mea culpa in *GQ*. According to the article, he was "finding himself" out in the desert. The interview took place at a house he was renting in Joshua Tree. He said he was into Kabbalah and that he was sober. It was a big new life for him, he told the author. "I'm thinking of working from the ground up, you know? Like a rebirth." He mentioned me once. "Echo is a raw talent, and I hope to see her happy and healthy as she grows." Neither of us had reached out to the other in months. He also talked a lot about his upbringing in New Jersey, that not everyone got an easy shot at life and he was doing the best he could, trying to figure out where he felt at home. "What about your compound in Venice?" the writer asked him. "Isn't that your home?"

"Look, man," he said. "I spend my days now walking these desert roads, sometimes for miles, reflecting. I might have been a good actor, but I wasn't necessarily a good husband or a good boyfriend or, heck, even a good father. Sometimes you need more room than the canals of Venice." I had never heard my dad say the word *heck* or call anyone "man" in my entire life.

My dad and his new life in the desert felt far away from mine, which was clearly what he wanted. And what did I expect? I gave him a big eff you. And with that, he got a sober coach, fired everyone, and escaped to the desert. Maybe he'd get his career back, maybe women would still lust after him (who am I kidding? Definitely), maybe he would have lots of little kids with a young new wife. It didn't matter. I still sometimes flashed back to that morning he slapped me. He seared his rage into me, and I couldn't escape it. Most of the time I felt numb. Shutting off, taking an extra half of Klonopin when I thought about him—that's what got me through it. I didn't need to wonder about him anymore. I didn't want to. I shoved him deep into a place where I could hide from him forever.

My mom thought I should make up with him. She didn't know everything, but it was clear he and I no longer had a relationship. "You're too young for so much negativity, Echo."

"Well, I guess I better find some positive things to think about, then."

● ● ●

A few weeks after his article came out, Hazel and I met in her office. "I want to do something different," I said.

"We have the perfume deal. That's something different."

I hated the perfume deal. Four men in lab coats asked me two questions: What smell do you like? What color do you like? Lavender and lavender, I told them. Now my name was on a woodsy yet sickly sweet lavender perfume in a purple bottle with one of those old-fashioned puffers sticking out of it. It looked like an Easter egg.

"No, I mean a different type of movie."

She ignored me. "Darling. I have a ton of scripts—"

"I don't want those. I don't want a *Breakfast Club Two* or a *Teen Angst Whatever*. I want to do something away from L.A. Get me out of the country."

"So you want to do an accent?" she asked, her nose wrinkling.

"I want to do something literary and filmic. Something that feels like it could last forever. That people could watch twenty years from now and say, 'Wow, that's a great performance.'"

"In twenty years, they'll do a remake."

"Hazel, you know what I mean."

"Let's avoid foreign language because that, my darling, would be a huge mistake. The French directors will try to get you to take your top off, and you're only sixteen and I couldn't live with myself."

So we agreed. It would be something more adult, but it would have to be English.

"Oh! Here's an idea. Daniel Chambers is talking about doing a remake of *Emma*," she said. "They want it to be big and splashy."

My heart sank.

• • •

There it was, just a few weeks ago, the *Emma* screenplay, tucked under a book of Ibsen plays on a large Moroccan pouf in Belinda's room. We had always discussed what scripts we were reading, so it was surprising to see it hidden like that, as if it was a secret, its bold, black letters written across the spine of the script, a blaring siren. Why was Belinda reading *Emma*, and why wouldn't she tell me about it?

"*Emma*?" I asked her and tugged at it. "You're reading this script?"

It was obvious that she had read it. There were dog-eared pages already.

"You know I always loved the book," she said, blushing. Belinda never blushed. "And my mom is in talks to do wardrobe. It would be a big deal for her to do a period piece."

"Oh, because I thought you were reading it for yourself or something and you didn't tell me."

She paused and pressed her lips together.

"What if I was?" she said.

I suddenly felt a tightness creeping up into my chest. "Should I, like, feel insecure about this? Is there a reason you're keeping it from me?"

I flashed back to my conversation with Hazel at the Ivy. "*If you do too many movies with Belinda upstaging you, you're going to lose your roles to her.*" Hazel. Deluded Hazel. I had to get her out of my head.

"We've never kept scripts from each other," I continued. "I don't really get it, that's all."

"Echo, I love you. You're my best friend. I'm reading it because I'm curious. I don't think I'd even be considered for something like this."

"So you *are* thinking about it for yourself—"

"Not in a realistic way—"

"But you *are* thinking about it," I said. "Are you thinking about the main role?"

"You sound like you're interrogating me, Echo."

"Only because you're being so elusive."

"Fine, yes. I've thought about playing Emma. She'd be a good role for me. She's sweet and funny, not too serious. Kind of like Roxy. But I feel a little insecure about it. It's a big part," she said and shoved the script back under the Ibsen book. "I don't even think I'll get it. It's not a big deal. That's why I didn't mention it."

What was wrong with me? Why couldn't I be the best friend she needed in that moment and embrace her? Why couldn't I say, *This is amazing; tell me all about it? If you want to play Emma, you should go for it?* Or, *Of course you'll get it?* Why couldn't I encourage her? Belinda had spent so many years as an appendage of me, and so now it was completely clear she wanted to do something outside my shadow. Who could blame her?

I could see the headlines. *Belinda Summers, an Enchanting Emma.* I was flooded with pride for my best friend but also contemptuous envy.

Fame is a sickness that torments you, like a compulsion that refuses to shut off. Fame isn't real; it's a fixation. It's a need for acceptance and empty love. It's a weakness, a hole that you can't stop filling.

• • •

Predictably, Hazel's eyes ignited once I told her Belinda had the script for *Emma.*

"Oh, someone is quite ambitious, isn't she? Our devious little sidekick." Then in the next breath, "There's no harm in you reading it too, Echo."

Hazel knew this wasn't true in the least. Once you asked for a script, that gave the studio a chance to leak your involvement in the production. To create buzz for the movie, they could send a tip to *Variety* that Echo Blue was being considered for *Emma*. Then what? If Belinda also went for it, it would turn into a media circus that we were fighting for the role. Hazel would turn me into a monster if she had the chance.

"No. I'm not doing it," I said. I crossed my arms over my chest, and even though I said it, I could already tell I didn't mean it. There was something inside me clamoring to hurt Belinda for hiding the script from me in the first place. To prove I was the better actress.

"She's not a lead yet. She's only done supporting roles. You're going to stop yourself from reading a role that would be perfect for you because your best friend has a pipe dream?"

"That's called loyalty, Hazel."

"That's not loyalty. That's stupidity. She has no chance of getting that role, and you know it."

But with her good reviews for *Holly and the Hound 2*, Belinda would have a lot going for her. She had great comedic timing. Emma Woodhouse was a silly character, but she was also the queen bee of the neighborhood and, in the end, wanted the best for the people around her. Belinda would be endearing and charming. A natural Emma.

"Belinda is better suited as Emma's friend, the one she tries to help," Hazel said. "What's that character's name? Penelope? Henrietta? Harriet something or other. And *you* would be a great Emma. Because you know how to carry a picture. Period. End of conversation."

"I can't keep asking Belinda to be my co-star. She wants to break out on her own."

But what if it *was* a better role for me? I would get a chance to go to London or the English countryside and wear costumes and get away from the paparazzi here in L.A. I could get away from the loneliness that was my little house. From my father and his vapid public apologies. I felt like a thief already, and I hadn't even done anything.

Hazel took me by the hand, like any good agent without a conscience would do. "Let me talk to Daniel Chambers. That's all. Just a quick look at the script to see if it's any good."

For a moment, I could convince myself that's all Hazel was doing. *We're investigating. We're just talking to Daniel Chambers.* I'd explain to Belinda, if she found out about it somehow, that these were just conversations—she knew how Hazel was. Of course I wasn't going anywhere near *Emma.* I didn't know what I was feeling, but it was something like floating above myself, watching bad decisions being made and not knowing how to stop them.

Goldie

. . .

42.

The first day back in the office after my dad died, the first of February, it flurried, enveloping me in white powder just before I got into the building. I had to shake the snowflakes out of my hair in the lobby, and my face was burning. I had been in L.A. too long. I forgot how the sting of cold could energize you. I walked right to Dana's office without taking my coat off, and she waved me in, chomping on what I assumed was her Nicorette.

"How are you doing?" she said. "You know you don't have to be here. You can take a few more days. I mean, your father just passed . . ." *Father. Passed.* The words didn't sink in. I didn't want them to. People giving me their condolences or mentioning him felt like someone was stabbing me through the heart. I would have preferred it if everyone had pretended like it hadn't happened.

"Thank you for the fruit basket," I said.

"Really, Goldie. Whatever you need. I feel partially responsible for you since I gave you this story. You're sure you can handle it? Because I know you have a lot on your plate."

"Actually, I have a lead, not about where Echo is, but about her friendship breakup with Belinda Summers. I think Echo stole the *Emma* role from her."

I didn't tell Dana that I was thinking of giving up on finding Echo altogether. I couldn't say that out loud yet.

Echo had been gone for a full month.

"That's heartless—wow," she said. "Amazing. Can you confirm?"

"Getting close."

"What do you need? Do you need someone else to work on this story with you?"

"No!" I said, but I was too defensive, so I turned my voice down. "I mean, no. I have a story map. I know where I'm going with this. I know exactly what I'm going to write. And I think I figured out a way to approach Belinda Summers like you suggested." *Lie. All you do is lie.*

I awkwardly adjusted my shirt and tried not to twitch, but Dana raised her eyebrows.

"In that case, I want to have a draft pretty soon. You think you're up for that?"

"Oh, absolutely. I'm so close. Gotta get to work," I said and raised up my arm like I was some color guard performer. Then I practically stumbled out her door to my cubicle.

I sat down at my desk. Now I just had to figure out how I was going to get said confirmation.

Belinda had gotten such good reviews from *Holly and the Hound 2*. *Emma* would have been a sure next step. A silly, meddling character like Emma Woodhouse would show off how charismatic she was. *Clueless*, an *Emma* adaptation by Amy Heckerling, had just come out a few years earlier, and everyone was already familiar with the story. It was a natural progression.

(My mind briefly swayed to Amy Heckerling. If I failed the task of finding Echo and *did* end up writing a story about women in film, Heckerling, who also directed *Fast Times at Ridgemont High*, with her black shag and her signature heavy black eyeliner, would be a great interview. But I had a young Oscar winner to find.)

Here's what didn't make sense: Why would Echo want this role? Emma Woodhouse was too easy, the kind of part Echo could do with her eyes closed, and she was in a breakout moment. Was it possible that she took the role because of Belinda's rave reviews for *HH2*? I felt a spark of recognition. Echo took *Emma* to hurt Belinda. But what could have provoked her to do it? I opened my laptop and typed in the web address for Pig Sandwich, that *Holly and the Hound* fan database, clicking through every thread dedicated just to Belinda. There were hundreds and hundreds of comments that read like they were personal notes being passed along to her:

> **JoannaNails:** You're the kind of best friend that everyone needs to have

> **LadyOfTheCity:** I loved you in the Holly movies

> **Patty212:** You should get your own series

> **Helloitsme:** You were the only teen actor that anyone cared about

> **Angie3210:** Where did you get the t-shirt you wore with the tiger on it

> **Belindamaven:** I feel so lost sometimes I think you're the only person who can understand me

I started to notice that on several comments, a user with the name *TheRealBelinda* responded.

> **TheRealBelinda:** Love you too

> **TheRealBelinda:** Hang in there. It'll get better

217

TheRealBelinda was so supportive, so genuinely kind. Could it really be Belinda answering these messages? I hadn't seen them last time. They must have been new.

I kept scrolling deeper until something caught my eye, a link that read simply *Team Belinda, No Side Characters.*

No side characters. This was how her fans saw her. The star of the show. I underestimated how important she was to people. Belinda had always been a side character in my mind, but here she was with her own corner of the internet. It made me ask myself why I hadn't thought more about Belinda when I was younger — why my focus was so pointed on Echo.

I clicked on the link, but it was password protected. That was weird — wasn't the whole point of a fan site to shout your fandom from the rooftops? I tried *Roxy*, her character's name from *Holly and the Hound*, but that wasn't it. Tried *Twelve*, her number in *Slugger Eight*, but no. What could the password possibly be? I scoured the internet until I hit a wall.

I knew Pench would be at his desk, so I swung by his office.

"God forgive me, I've crawled down a Belinda Summers rabbit hole," I said and slumped down in the chair in front of him, rubbing my eyes. I hadn't looked in a mirror all day.

"Backstabber," he said dramatically and grinned. "How could you do this to Echo?"

"I'm trying to get into this encrypted message board about her. There's, like, some firewall. You need a password."

"Did you look through any old interviews to see if there was a clue?"

"Is that a real question?" I snapped.

"Okay, sorry, but you're more of an Echo encyclopedia than a Belinda one," he said. He was right, and that was the problem. I needed to get into the minds of Belinda fans.

No side characters.

Belinda was never the star of her own movie. The link read *Team Belinda, No Side Characters.* Could that have something to do with the password? I scooted back to my desk and tried a few different iterations, treating it like I would a crossword puzzle.

Protagonist, I typed, but it bounced back with a red *X*. Too literary. It had to be more filmspeak. So I tried *Leadinglady*. Red *X*. I tried *Title-character*. Red *X*.

What did they want? They didn't want side characters, which was what Belinda played. They wanted a movie starring Belinda Summers. So that's what I punched in: *StarringBelindaSummers*.

My chest heaved. Fuck, please, I needed this to be it. An image slowly loaded. I gasped and screamed. The three interns at the news desk turned their heads all at once, staring at me, alarmed. There was a rush down to my toes like I had broken into a bank or something. It took at least a minute to fully appear, but the image was of Belinda wearing a striped blue-and-white long-sleeved shirt, like the kind Jean Seberg wore, and black eyeliner. It was a recent photo. She looked radiant.

Then my eyes jutted to the profile introduction:

> Welcome. This is a safe space for Belinda fans, created by two friends who have loved Belinda forever. We're a go-to source for everything Belinda. And sometimes, she'll even read our notes and answer them.
>
> From Belinda herself!
>
> "Yes, this is a fan page for me, but I'm a fan of yours too.
> Xx Belinda"

Of course she was a fan of theirs. They gave her the thing that Echo, if I was correct, robbed her of: the starring role. I could feel Belinda's longing in my bones. I knew what it was to want.

I scrolled to the bottom of the page, and an announcement for a local NYC meetup popped up.

Local Belinda Summers Fan Meetup Tomorrow!
Soho Grand Hotel / 310 West Broadway / 2 p.m.

I quickly checked the date stamp. It had been posted late last night, around ten o'clock. Holy shit, this was happening today. It felt like serendipity. I needed to speak to these superfans to see if they could spotlight anything about Belinda that I missed. If they were at all like me with Echo, they'd know details about Belinda no one else did.

I could use a nap before this. I heard back in the 1980s some reporters took naps in a closet near the bathrooms after drinking martinis at lunch. Those were the days. I settled for pouring myself a cup of coffee in the break room and tried to imagine the kinds of conversations I'd have with the Belinda fans. I needed to brush up on my Belinda trivia. I needed to get them to trust me.

43.

The bar at the Soho Grand was dark and smoky; a heavy air lingered under the dim lights. Between the dark planks on the floor and the velvet curtains, I felt even more out of my element than I did in L.A. I was practically a hermit, but if I went out, it was usually to dive bars on the Lower East Side, where the music was too loud and there was a happy-hour special—nothing this fancy.

At two in the afternoon, the bar was mostly empty except for about ten women huddling around large red leather chairs. There they were: the meetup.

I casually made my way over and introduced myself.

"I'm Deidre," a woman around my age with long brown hair responded first, smiling sweetly. She was wearing a T-shirt with a sketch of Belinda in a baseball cap from *Slugger Eight*. "I've never seen you at one of these before. What brings you here?"

"I'm Goldie. Longtime lurker, first time at a meetup."

"A newbie!" someone said.

"Joanna over there and I started the fan page and the meetup about two years ago," Deidre said. She pointed to a woman who had long purple nails. (Purple! Belinda's favorite color. It had to be the same Joanna-Nails from the online fan group.)

Joanna waved to me and bopped into the conversation. "Deidre and I wanted a place to talk about how we felt about Belinda because everything was always about *the other one.* When we discovered this group of true fans, we knew we had found our people."

"Right, the other one," I said. She was talking about Echo.

"Now with her missing, it's even more about her. Any girl raised like that, with an egomaniac father and a shut-in mother, is a slam-dunk narcissist," Deidre said. A few of the other women nodded.

I felt compelled to defend Echo. Even if she had been a shitty friend to Belinda. She deserved empathy. I could have used a little empathy when I was a teenager.

"That whole relationship was co-dependent. Once *you know who* got a boyfriend, she dumped Belinda. She's a user," Joanna with the nails said.

They were talking about Paul Reed. Even though I had my own theory, I wanted to hear more. "Oh, so the boyfriend was the reason they haven't been seen together in years?"

Joanna and Deidre looked at each other knowingly. "The boyfriend was the catalyst. I'm sure of it," Joanna said. "It's a classic story. Echo needed Belinda until she found someone she liked to spend time with even more."

"Teenage girls are trying to figure themselves out. Don't you think it's hard to do that when your whole life is happening in public?" I said.

"You don't have to dump your best friend for your boyfriend," Joanna said. "It's a classic asshole move."

"Team Belinda," someone said. As if I didn't know.

"Yes, of course. Team Belinda," I repeated.

"We might as well tell her," Deidre said, looking back at the others. Then she lowered her voice and got close to me. "*She's* supposed to meet us here."

"Who?" I paused. "Wait . . . you don't mean Belinda? She's coming here?" I went stiff as the realization hit me. I couldn't swallow.

They all squealed and clapped their hands.

"Our fan site is secure because you never know with these crazies. So it's super hush-hush. Only for our group. She just flew in from L.A., but she loves us so much that she wanted to see us."

"That's so sweet of her," I said, clutching the armchair next to me.

There was a sickening feeling in my stomach, though maybe it should have been relief. I had already been scheming out ways and coming up with nothing to talk to her again—the last time I saw her was about a week ago—and now my journalistic instincts had led me right to her. I was here with a group of women who would step in front of a train for her. Belinda's carefully selected fan gang. Joanna had nails like purple daggers! They'd be protective once they saw that Belinda hated me. They'd turn on me.

Suddenly, the energy of the group heightened. Deidre and another woman grabbed each other's hands, their necks craning, and squealed, "Oh my god, oh my god, she's here."

My heart raced, and I scanned the room, searching for a place to hide behind the heavy curtains. And I almost did scoot away, just disappear, but I was here for a reason. And there she was, her head down, her shoulders hunched, going unrecognized. She could call the police on me. It could cost me my whole story.

Every part of me, from my toes up to my shoulders, felt buzzy, and my hands were shaking like they always did when I got nervous. I had to calm down, ground myself so that I could speak to her and confront her with my theory about *Emma*. See if I could get some kind of confirmation. It had to be true.

The women all quietly wiggled over to Belinda so they wouldn't make a scene. Belinda opened her arms and tried to hug all of them at once, bringing them in and then scanning the circle around her, in complete joy and wonderment until she locked eyes with me.

Her face deflated.

"You?" she said and stepped toward me. "What are you doing here?"

"It was a coincidence . . ." I said, words erupting from my mouth. "I swear to god I didn't know you were going to be here, Belinda."

"Belinda, what's going on?" Deidre said.

"She's a journalist—that's what's going on," Belinda said and backed me up into the bar, her index finger poking my shoulder. "I'll ask you one more time. What the fuck are you doing here, you stalker?"

I was uncomfortable with the word *stalker*. Consummate fan, yes. Was there a better descriptor for me? An Echo historian? A longtime observer? An Echo encyclopedia, like Pench said. No—all of these characterizations made me sound nuts.

"I knew she seemed like an outlier!" Deidre said.

"I'm going to call the police and tell them that you're harassing me. Do you understand? There are *laws* about stalking."

I whispered, my breath staggered, "I know what happened with *Emma*. I know she stole it from you. I want you to be able to tell your side of the story." In discovering Echo's ambition, and how she put it ahead of all else, I somehow felt even closer to her. Wasn't that what I was doing too? I was putting my ambition above all else. "*Do you want to be a good writer or a shitty writer?*" my father used to say. I wanted to be a good writer. And if it meant being a shitty person, so be it.

The fan gang was closing in on me, their faces twisted and angry, hurt that I had disrupted their meet and greet.

"Yes, it's true; I am a *journalist*," I said, pointing at each of them, as if that carried any weight. "I'm trying to get to the truth here, and with the flick of a pen"—*Flick of a pen?* God, I was cheesy—"I could make you all sound like lovestruck teenyboppers. So, everyone, back off."

Belinda instructed her minions to sit down and enjoy their drinks. This was something she had to take care of, she explained, and she would be right back. They obeyed.

"We're right here if she starts any shit, Belinda!" Joanna with the nails said.

During this short time, a half dozen women, all boisterous, as if they worked together and someone had quit, rammed their way into the bar and immediately recognized Belinda as we were walking out. They screeched, avowing their love for her, breathless, and begged her for a photo. "Later. I'll be back," she promised and zoomed past them.

• • •

"I am trying not to make a scene in front of these people. Do you understand?" Belinda said, the two of us out on the street, her hair blowing in her face. She was more beautiful in New York than she was in L.A. She was wearing a black leather motorcycle jacket with jeans and a white T-shirt, her brown hair swept up in a ponytail and her dark eyelashes like velvet strands.

"I need to know about *Emma*, and then I'll leave you alone," I said, but we both knew that wasn't true. I was so deep down this hole. How could I let her go for good?

"You're not tape-recording this, are you?" she said.

"No," I hedged. "But you have nothing to lose by telling me your story, Belinda. You deserve to be heard. This should be on the record." What she actually probably deserved was privacy, but like I said, I only had one goal in mind. She turned her face away, her eyes closed.

"Belinda, the book. I saw a picture of it in your hands. The last picture of you two together."

She swung her head to me, sniffled back tears, her face open, her eyes wide. "Fine. On the record it is. What do you want to know?"

It took me aback that she wasn't bolting. I should have felt shame for cornering her like this, but I guess my longing to get close to Echo superseded any humility I had left.

"Did she know that you wanted to do *Emma*?" I said.

"*Did she know*? Yes, she fucking knew. We had gotten to a point where it was time for me to break off a little. I was getting good reviews for *Holly and the Hound 2*, and they weren't saying as much about her. My agent said Hazel Cahn was bad-mouthing me around town. I couldn't confront

Echo about it. She had no stable adults in her life. I was her family. Do you understand? So, yes. It was all part of the grand plan. Because once the studio found out she wanted *Emma*, Echo got *Emma*. Because she's Echo Blue, and I'm not."

Belinda looked back at her fan gang peering through the window and gave them an uneasy smile that would hold them off for a while.

"How did you find out?"

She let out a grunt. "I found out in *Variety*."

"Oh my god."

"Yeah."

I had that aching pain in the back of my throat when you're going to cry but you can't. Hearing it firsthand, I couldn't believe Echo—the Echo I thought I knew so well, the Echo whom I daydreamed about being my loyal best friend—crushed Belinda so publicly. I wanted to believe she was above this. That she couldn't have been as duplicitous as I was. I wanted to believe her friendship with Belinda was good and true. She was the one who was supposed to teach me to be a friend! I still loved her, but I felt a sense of betrayal. She was not who I thought she was.

"Did you two speak after?"

"I tried to forgive her. I told her if she needed the role that badly that she should take it without guilt. Maybe that's what bothered her the most. That I pitied her. You can't truly be friends with someone if you know they pity you. And I did. I felt sorry for her. She had resorted to screwing over her best friend."

"You loved her, though. She was like a sister to you, wasn't she?"

"Sure, she was. But after the whole *Emma* thing, I was crushed for six months, back and forth between thinking about her nonstop and wanting to kill her, like there was a hole that would never be filled again." She wrapped a strand of hair around her finger like a little kid and seemed genuinely bewildered. "I don't know why I'm telling you this. I try not to think about it now. It's behind me. So yeah, thanks for the in-your-face reminder."

My mind raced ahead of me. Jamie wasn't the nice guy he claimed to be. Echo wasn't the nice girl. Both of them actors. I didn't know what was real anymore.

"I'm sorry," I whispered and gave her a chance to breathe before I went back into questioning her. "So, what about Echo? She must have been destroyed by it too, even though she caused it. Even now."

"Echo? I don't know what to say about her. She's had a fucked-up life."

"And you have no desire to help her?"

"Did it ever occur to you that she doesn't want to be found?"

There it was. The question I had been desperately trying to avoid. Part of me wanted to spill everything to Belinda, to justify my search, to tell her that I felt *compelled* to find Echo. That I felt a secret connection to her. That I had spent much of my life invested in Echo, about those lonely days that I spent as a teenager and how Echo was my only friend.

"I don't think you're going to find what you're looking for," she said.

"You mean Echo?"

"It seems like you're looking for something else other than Echo."

"Yeah, this is what people tell me," I said. "I'm sorry I've acted so strange. My father just died. I've been emotional." In a million years, I never thought I'd be revealing something so personal to Belinda Summers. This should have been a pinnacle for me, but I felt no joy from this conversation. I stared back at the bar. At least Belinda had her fans inside waiting for her. I had no one. Okay, fine—I kind of had Pench. I had my brother. Still, I must have looked distraught, because Belinda gently touched my hand.

"I'm very sorry to hear that." She looked at me gravely, then shook her head. "It's not worth looking for her, Goldie. It's really not." *Worth.* How do you value someone's worth? Belinda was speaking from a place of hurt, but to me, Echo was still worth everything. The fan gang knocked on the window from the inside. They were eager for her to return. She wiped away her tears, then gave them a "one minute" gesture. What a pro.

"I can show you the research I've done," I said to her, pleading. "I can show you how serious I am about this. It's not just a story for me. I want to expose how that patriarchal system turned two best friends against each other. How they took advantage of your age and ambition," I said. "I know you might take me for a deranged fan, but I feel like I have something more to offer than the other people who are looking for her."

"Oh? What's that?" she said coldly, and I could see that any hope I might have had with her was gone. But I said the next statement anyway. I believed in that moment it was true.

"I care," I said.

"Don't you get it? Don't you understand how many fans I've met? They all say the same exact thing. 'I care so much. I love you.' But it's never actually true. You're a cheap groupie."

"Belinda, I—"

"You're like an addict, you know that? Echo is your addiction. You'll never stop. You'll never get enough. I hope you're pleased with yourself that you infiltrated this group and harassed me. Good job."

She looked at me with disgust, shook her arms out like she was getting ready for a role, then breezed back into the lobby. I could see from the street that the women were there, waiting with open arms. That was the allure. It was unconditional. It was a safety net. She had a gang dedicated to her. Who wouldn't want that?

44.

Belinda was right. I was a cheap groupie. That was the problem. I wasn't getting *close* enough to Echo and who she was in her soul. If you were really a fan, you had to take on that person. You had to *be* that person. Didn't you? Wasn't that what method acting was about — diving deep into who the character was, living like the character?

I ran into a drugstore about two blocks away and bought hair dye. Bleached-blonde dye to match the color of Echo's hair when she was last seen. I swiped a sharp pair of scissors too. Those I didn't pay for. I shoved them in my bag and walked out with them. Doing so gave me a small rush.

I got home and went into the bathroom and stared at myself in the mirror for a while. I thought about what Belinda had said. Did I care about Echo? Was that why I wanted to find her? Or was this story about me?

I stuck my head under the faucet and squeezed the blonde dye all over my hair and scalp. The chemicals burned through my fingertips, but I didn't care. I wanted to feel pain. I sat on the toilet and watched my hair bleach out.

Oh, I'd done it now. There was no hiding this. My hair was blonde. Just like Echo's.

Next, I took the scissor to the front of my hair and pulled it all forward, then chopped off the ends. When I let it go, it swirled around my face, all of the long layers now short and fluffy. I went back at it again, and I cut some blunt, short bangs like hers, that rush coming over me and my skin tingling—I couldn't tell if it was the excitement of butchering my hair or my chemically processed scalp. Cut locks scattered across my bathroom floor.

I had been sick of looking at myself, my mousy-brown hair and the unkempt curls that had framed my face. Someone told me once that I reminded them of a tortured French actress from the 1970s, with a woman-child face and my big bohemian eyes, but I felt boring and plain. I didn't realize it until I saw this woman in front of me. She was me, but she wasn't me. I dyed my hair because I thought I wanted to be closer to Echo. That if I inhabited her, I would be part of her. Except now I felt more disconnected than ever, like the woman in the mirror was someone else I was unable to recognize.

I had been lying to myself about why I wanted to find Echo. It was all for me. It was always for me.

Echo

1997-1998

. . .

45.

When you decide to stab your best friend in the back, you have to commit. I asked Belinda to go to New York with me for the weekend. Then I bought her a copy of the book. I called a rare bookstore downtown, and they had a leather-bound edition printed on archival paper with gilded edges. I knew she'd love it — and that she'd want to burn it after she found out what I'd done to her.

But I gave it to her anyway, despite all of it. I knew she'd think it was a special gift. She wouldn't know it was a parting gift. And why would she?

If she had just told me about it, I wouldn't have felt so threatened. But to see it casually under a book like that was an attack. A sacrilege. Winning the Oscar at such a young age made me paranoid.

But could I really blame the annals of fame? Could I blame my behavior on the attention from the press as my brain was hardwiring? Sure, but that didn't mean anyone should pity me or think of me as powerless. Child star or not, I chose to do this to Belinda.

When I handed it to her at a little Italian place in the West Village, her face lit up, and I said nothing at all. She hugged me and I let her, knowing this was the end of the friendship that had sustained me for years. Was that completely twisted of me? To give her the gift of a book

I stole from her? Yes. I could admit I wasn't a good person. I felt just like my dad, and as much as I didn't want to be anything like him, there I was, cruel and manipulative.

When the paparazzi came for us upon our exit, I decided to stop for the picture—we were dressed practically the same in jeans and those awful cowboy hats everyone used to wear, my arm in the crook of her arm and her other hand holding the book. I knew this would likely be our last photo together. I wanted the memory, the reminder of what I had sacrificed.

．　．　．

A week later, *Variety* printed that I would star in *Emma*. Belinda called me, and I wouldn't answer the phone. I was a coward, and I let it go right to the machine because that's what cowards do. I listened to all of her messages to torment myself. Cowards still feel guilt. I sat there all day replaying them. I deemed them "Belinda's stages of grief."

She started with disbelief: "I don't know why you couldn't tell me, Echo. Why couldn't you be honest with me?"

Then anger: "You had to give me the book? The leather-bound book to shove it in my face that you were going to get the part and not me? You wanted to see me excited so you could bring me down? What is it, Echo?"

Then the upward turn: "You're scared of me, aren't you? Because I'm a better actress than you. That's not what it is. I'm a better person than you."

She wasn't wrong. The meaner she got, the easier the messages were to listen to. I liked being torn apart by her. I deserved it. I deserved to listen to her explain how terrible I was. I *was* terrible. What kind of person would do this to her best friend? Only a monster.

I wasn't prepared for the stage of forgiveness: "I love you, Echo, and I forgive you. I know you have problems that you don't even understand yet. That you must have done this because you need it more than I do. And if you need this role *that* badly, then you should have it."

This made me feel worse. I felt surer when she was angry. Her voice, that calming voice that had gotten me through so many problems in my life, stopped me in my tracks. It shook me. I wanted to call her. I wanted to run to her house and talk her out of forgiving me. *You've made a huge mistake, Belinda. I want you to have the role*, I wanted to tell her. But I didn't do any of that because I was weak. I felt gross because I sabotaged my friendship with the only person who was ever there for me. This was what I desired. Now I got it, with her blessing.

I sat there, folded up, my back against the cold wall.

46.

I met Paul Reed on the set of *Emma*. We were shooting on an estate in the Cotswolds in England. I had just turned seventeen. All the rolling hills and the green valleys. Stone castles reaching up to the clouds and cottages surrounded by lush gardens. It looked like we had traveled back in time.

Paul had just been in the independent film *Anchor in the Sand* that was a huge hit at Sundance, but Hazel told me he was transitioning out of supporting actor roles. Paul was primed to be a lead. "He's got a *big cover story*, I heard," she said. "It's coming out after *Emma*. They want him to be the next young Marlon Brando. He's doing a movie out in Kansas soon. Something about a family whose farm is in jeopardy after generations of American living. I'm telling you — they're setting him up to be a heartthrob."

Hazel had worried that me playing opposite Hollywood's up-and-coming bad boy wouldn't work for Disney — she was still hoping I would do another film or two with them after this to solidify my legacy before I aged out — but I managed to convince her. He wasn't playing my romantic lead, I argued; they wanted him for Mr. Elton, a local vicar and a handsome but arrogant guy who needs to marry for money. Yes, we had a few too-close-for-comfort scenes together, and yes, I was seventeen and Paul was twenty-seven, but ten years older isn't a lot in Hollywood years, at least for casting purposes. Especially in the '90s. In *The Crush*, a sixteen-year-old Alicia Silverstone played a teen unhealthily fixated on Cary Elwes, who was thirty, and they had a full make out. And as far as I was concerned, Paul would be good for my transition from the teen genre to more serious films.

The first time I remember swooning over Paul was during a lunch break. It had been a full costume rehearsal. We sat across from each other under a chestnut tree, all of the flowers blooming and the pistils erect. He watched me as he took bites out of his BLT. We were almost two weeks into rehearsals at this point. (The entire cast had to learn "Regency" dancing and manners from the early 1800s and take archery lessons during a three-week pre-filming period.)

"I heard they offered you Knightley. Why didn't you take it?" I asked Paul. Knightley was the lead romantic role. He's the guy who gets Emma in the end.

"I want to be the scene stealer," Paul said. "I want to play a complex character. I thought it could be interesting to play a soft-spoken Elton. I'm trying to find that inherent sensitivity under his arrogance, you know?"

"Oh," I said, flush.

"Plus, I want to play the guy who gets inside Emma's head and makes her reconsider her entire life."

I had no words. He smirked at me. I couldn't finish my lunch. I made up an excuse, hurried back to my trailer, and locked the door behind me, out of breath. My petticoat rustling against my thighs. That night, I masturbated like I had never done before, Paul's voice, that soft voice, ringing in my head. I orgasmed with such force, gasping for breath, that I was embarrassed yet, at the same time, amazed by my body and its ability to feel that rush all over.

The next day at archery lessons, Paul helped me correct my positioning. "A square stance is easier," he said and bent down in front of me.

"Open your legs a little wider." I thought I was going to pass out. "Keep your arm as straight as you can and don't kink your wrist." He adjusted my arm slightly. His touch, so soft.

"You've done this before, I guess."

"I had to learn archery for a Canadian adventure movie I was in. I had much longer hair, though."

I could see Paul galloping on a horse, his long hair in the wind.

Paul wasn't my first crush. There was Jeff Stanwick, a PA I had met on *Holly and the Hound 2,* whom I kissed sometimes and who went up my shirt. There was Evan Roe, whom I met on a music video shoot. After a full day of making out for the video, he begged me to give him a blow job in his trailer, which I did. But I'd never actually dated someone. The people I met never seemed like they were looking for something serious. And I hadn't had sex either, which felt especially wrong, given that I was a legal adult in the state of California. It was time. I wanted to lose my virginity to Paul.

47.

The first night of shooting, after all of the training and rehearsing, we did the iconic carriage scene in which Emma refuses Mr. Elton's proposal. Mr. Elton was supposed to fall in love with Harriet, a new friend whom Emma considers her project.

My hair was swept up in a bun, curls around my face. The empire dress I wore pushed my breasts practically to my collarbone. Emma wasn't supposed to be sexy—she was supposed to be the girl next door—but wardrobe said I needed to look like a young woman. Luckily, I was well poised to play a girl who wanted to get fucked just then.

To calm down before the scene, I stepped out of my trailer to have a cigarette (one of the PAs kept them handy for me in her hoodie pocket—this was England, after all). With the lit cigarette in one hand, I hiked up my gown with the other, tucking it so it wouldn't drag against the ground.

"You're the coolest, sexiest Emma I've ever seen," Paul said, walking out from his own trailer next door.

I almost died.

In the stagecoach as Mr. Elton, he bent toward me and recited his line in a low voice: "I'm ready to die if you refuse me." His eyes locked on mine, and I leaned forward, wanting to kiss him. My hand on his knee.

Paul laughed out loud, and Daniel, our director, yelled, "Cut."

"Emma shouldn't be leaning in to kiss Elton. She wants to get away from him. She's repulsed by his advances. She sees Elton as a match for Harriet. Not for herself. You want to reject him," Daniel said to me.

But I wanted Paul all to myself. I wanted to kick everyone off the set and make out with him in the stagecoach. I wanted him to yank up my Regency-era dress and force me against the seat and lay the full weight of his body on top of me. Was there any way we could pivot the script so I could kiss him?

"I wonder if Emma has second thoughts about Elton because he is so handsome," I said.

"Wait, what?" Daniel said. "Uh, I don't think we have the authority to change Jane Austen."

"Forget I mentioned it," I said, embarrassed. "It's late. I'm not thinking clearly."

• • •

Later that night, back at the Rabbit's Foot Inn, one of the many places that the *Emma* cast and crew were inhabiting because there weren't any large hotels in the Cotswolds, I got the courage to seduce Paul.

His room was down the hall. I knocked on his door. My hair was wet from taking a shower. I was in a thin T-shirt and no bra. He had just gotten out of the shower too and was in a towel.

"Echo, you shouldn't be here," he said.

Who answers their door in a towel? He was waiting for me. *Don't lie to yourself*, I wanted to tell him.

"We've spent so much time together rehearsing these scenes for the last few days . . . and I know you'll be wrapping soon. I just thought it would be nice to hang out off set."

He let out a sigh, and I thought he would send me away, but he opened the door and invited me in. I sat on a chintz-covered daybed. He pushed his hair out of his face and looked down at me.

"How many movies have you made?"

"This is my sixth."

"Has anyone suggested you slow down? Sounds hectic."

"Paul Reed, are you saying you care about my welfare? Are you looking out for me?"

He scratched behind his ear and smirked. It was so easy to flirt with him. I wanted to lick him.

"So, what was it like winning the Oscar?"

"I don't usually talk about the Oscar."

"I'd love to hear if you want to tell me."

He was the first person I felt like talking to in a long time.

"It was one of the worst days of my life. Most people don't get that. But I was young. Too young, probably. Sometimes I want to toss it in the trash. But the paparazzi would rifle through my garbage and find it." I didn't mention anything about my father. I still felt protective over him.

"Yeah, they'd say you were ungrateful or something. A whole cover story about why you threw away your Oscar." He laughed and I laughed too. "Oscars are for people who like to follow the herd. I don't like to follow the herd. You don't seem like one of those people either."

I shook my head. I didn't know what to say next. He was still in his towel.

"You're a lot younger than me," he said, sitting on the bed at my side. His wet hair dripped down his naked chest. His cheekbones were sharp like the frigging Tetons. He wore a gold necklace with a pendant that I hadn't seen before. It was a phoenix. I was about to melt.

"I'm like a twenty-seven-year-old in a seventeen-year-old's body. I've been working since I was eleven. I own my own house. I make my own money. I take care of myself."

His eyes were a deep brown and so earnest looking I just wanted to touch his face. Kiss his eyelids and those long lashes.

"I saw you last month at a premiere," he said. "I don't think you noticed me. You had a buzz of people around you, but I couldn't take my eyes off you. No one in the room could take their eyes off you. What is it about you, huh? What do you do to people?"

My heart beat like mad, and I could feel the blood pulse through my ears. I placed my hands on his waist and touched the light line of hair under his belly button with my finger.

"Paul," I said and leaned in to kiss him. Our lips were so soft together, my hair around his face, and he growled at me, and it was everything that I wanted him to do. He tossed me over his shoulder, and I laughed so hard, and he slapped my ass and then flipped me down on the bed.

He slowly took off my T-shirt and my underwear and tossed them to the floor. I'd worn lace panties hoping that this would happen, but he didn't notice them anyway. He placed his fingers inside of me, and I never wanted them to leave.

"What if it was like this forever?" I said. "What if we walked around like this on set? What if Emma Woodhouse was the person who had Mr. Elton's fingers inside her for the rest of the movie? It would change *Emma*'s entire trajectory. People would be appalled."

"You're the softest girl I've ever touched," he said, and then I orgasmed all over his fingers.

It was the first time anyone touched me like that. Paul was my first everything.

48.

Word had gotten around set about me and Paul, so Hazel flew in for what she called an emergency discussion.

"I know you have a crush on Paul Reed. I've heard things," she said, perched uncomfortably on a flimsy chair in my trailer. I was going over my lines and barely paying attention to her. "And I also know you're openly smoking on set, Echo. You have to stop doing that. The paparazzi are going to slaughter you."

"First of all, that's just some bored people making up rumors," I said. "Anyway, so what if I did have a crush?"

"Listen to me, Echo. He's too old for you. He's already been engaged to two other women. I beg you to put down your script and hear me out."

I put it down to appease her.

"Darling, I'm going to give you some advice about life. Older men who like much younger women are usually very insecure and self-involved. They do it for an ego boost. Paul is a midlevel actor, and you're a household name. Do you understand what I'm saying to you?"

It didn't matter. She could have told me Paul had murdered someone, and I wouldn't have cared. Paul was deep in my brain, and my heart had taken over.

She rustled through her bag and handed me a packet of birth control pills. "For god's sake, at least take these. I have no idea what the abortion laws are in this country."

•   •   •

Paul and I spent the next four days in a fog. We got undressed in my trailer between takes and crawled into bed together. I didn't care that the crew had caught on.

"I don't want to hurt you, Echo. You're so soft. You can't let them corrupt you. Promise me you won't let them corrupt you." I loved this about him, that he wanted me to hold on to my innocence when it seemed to be slipping away. It made me breathless. I put my mouth on his and inhaled him. I kissed his ears, his cheeks, his neck, his fingers. Every night, he'd slip into my room at the inn. Mine was bigger than his and always had a fire going. It was an old inn with drafty windows, and I'd pretend we lived there together with the wind panting against the glass.

He'd tell me stories about how he grew up in the country, in a small town in Pennsylvania, and how his father would grow tomatoes in the backyard every summer, that his mother was a waitress at the café near where they lived. Everything about his life seemed so simple, and everything about me was complicated. I rested in his lap and stroked his chin. "Always look up in my eyes, Echo. I love looking into those delicate eyes." I liked that he saw me as vulnerable, because I saw myself as hardened.

Paul's role wrapped about four days later, and I sobbed when he left for the airport. He was going to be filming in New York next, then the Kansas film Hazel had mentioned.

I told Hazel that I needed a break after *Emma*, but Hazel wanted me to take a role with a prestigious director, do another big movie. I didn't care what she wanted. I couldn't stop thinking about Paul, and I needed to go be with him. I know this sounds ridiculous, but it hurt my bones being apart from him. For the remaining three weeks of the movie, I cried daily, and makeup would have to retouch me multiple times a day.

Each night, Paul and I would talk on the phone for hours and count down the days until we could see each other.

I noticed people around me starting to get irritated. They'd roll their eyes when I got emotional, call me a diva under their breath. I knew this was the type of thing that ruined my father, but I couldn't bring myself to care.

• • •

As soon as filming wrapped, I flew right out to New York. Paul was renting a small first-floor apartment on Barrow Street in Greenwich Village. The walls were all exposed brick complemented by worn-in leather couches. Huge floor-to-ceiling French doors led out to a little garden with black wicker furniture and string lights. It was the most charming place I had ever seen. I wanted to sew pillows for the wicker and bake him bread for breakfast every morning in the tiny kitchen.

When I arrived, I let myself in with a key under the mat. Paul was at a photo shoot with the magazine *Details*. Photo shoots bothered Paul. They made him feel like a product.

Truthfully, I had succumbed to being a product since I started working; it was part of being a Blue. I didn't picture it differently until Paul. He rejected the idea of being sold.

I rummaged through some drawers and found a pack of candles, then lit them all over the apartment so that when he got home, our reunion would feel romantic. I curled up in the bed with no clothes on.

But he came back angry. He barely gave me a kiss before launching into a tirade about how they kept asking him about the rumors about him and me and what it was like to work with me.

"I don't understand why this has to be about you when it's about me. They shouldn't be asking me about my personal life. Motherfuckers." Interviews and photo shoots were contractual. He couldn't get out of them because they were for a movie coming out in two months. He was also pissed the reporter asked him how he chose his clothes. "How do I choose my clothes? I wear whatever's on the floor."

243

"That's what you told them?"

I came to learn that nothing of Paul's was *ever* on the floor. He was meticulous about looking disheveled. The clothes in his closet looked like a retail store, everything folded.

"What was I gonna say? I have a stylist? It was a metaphor or whatever, Echo. Jesus."

I wanted Paul to be in love with me the way it was in the Cotswolds. I was used to volatile men, and I wanted to help him feel better.

Later, after hours of me placating him, he apologized for snapping at me and crawled into the bed. The two of us wrapped up in his soft white sheets.

"You're going to leave me because of my temper, aren't you?" he said.

"Are you crazy?" I said, caressing his face, stubble barely coming in on his jawline. "I've never felt like this before."

"I'm sorry about getting angry. You made it look pretty in here, baby. It's these vultures. They're trying to make me be someone I'm not. I can't be their poster boy and stare into the camera making googly eyes at girls."

"Girls love you, though."

"But what does this say about my mind?"

These were the kinds of lines I fell for as a seventeen-year-old. Paul wanted to be known as an artist, not as an actor. Was it possible to be true to yourself in this business? I loved him more for being true to that. The problem wasn't us or my age or Paul's temper. The problem was Hollywood's unrealistic expectations. I held on to that thought—us against the world—as I kneeled on the bed and unwrapped myself from the sheets.

49.

I promised Paul I would disguise myself when we were in New York. At least until my eighteenth birthday. I wore a baseball hat, and I tucked my shaggy hair underneath it as best as I could when I left the apartment. The paps got one picture of us at a little Greek restaurant together, but it was from far away and very blurry. No one ran with the photo except one small outlet. Hazel had threatened everyone else.

Paul bought two new red velvet couches because he wanted his place to look like a painter's apartment in Paris. Then he and I painted the floor black in our underwear. He didn't care that it was a rental. He said that he needed to feel like it was his space. He painted an X on my belly and told me I was his. I painted a Y on his chest and told him he was mine. We showered each other after, washing the black paint off our skin. "Don't wash it all off," I told him. "I want the shadow of your X forever."

I had turned into a bad poet.

When he worked, I paced his apartment with his pajamas on, smoking his cigarettes, filling up on old movies. There was a DVD shop on the corner, and no one noticed me there. If they did, they didn't care. *Citizen Kane*; *Suddenly, Last Summer*; *A Streetcar Named Desire*; *Double Indemnity*—actors' classics. Sometimes I'd take pictures of myself naked with my Polaroid, which is very tricky because you technically have to hold a Polaroid camera with two hands, but my skin crawled, waiting for him to come back and touch me again, for him to put his whole mouth, his tongue, over me. I'd slip the pictures in his jacket in the morning.

At first, it felt so amazing to be there, to wake up and go to sleep every night with Paul. I ignored Hazel's calls and checked in with my mother just enough to appease her. But as the days went on, most of which I spent on my own, I began to feel lonelier than I ever had in my life, which, ironically, was exactly what I'd come here to avoid.

I began spying on the neighbors across the courtyard with binoculars for a sense of company (I may or may not have been inspired by a recent viewing of *Rear Window*). He was a stay-at-home writer, and she came home from work at seven at night, at which point they ordered takeout and went to bed.

Another day, I sat by myself in the secret garden at St. Luke in the Fields Church. The berry trees reminded me of Belinda and Sandy's backyard, and I missed them so much it hurt.

But I didn't want to bring that negativity into my time with Paul. One morning he recited "The Sun Rising" by John Donne, a poet from the 1500s.

> *Shine here to us, and thou art everywhere;*
> *This bed thy center is, these walls, thy sphere.*

"That's us, baby," he whispered. "We're lovers who can't leave our beds. We can't leave the house. The sun shines on us. And our world is the bed, you see? The walls are the planets revolving around us."

His face was so sweet as he explained this to me. I didn't know how to tell him I was bored and claustrophobic, that "thy sphere" was closing in on me. That this apartment was my whole life, and as unsettling as it felt, I was incapable of doing anything else. I should have been studying for my GED or something. I should have taken an acting class. But I slept and watched old movies and took Klonopin and waited to turn eighteen.

This was what love was, I told myself. You were supposed to sacrifice yourself for the other person. This was what my parents were incapable of. My mother was in a relationship with her fear of the public eye and her depression. My dad was in a relationship with himself. Neither of them could focus on the other.

Paul focused on me—at least when he was around. At least when he was happy. That's all that mattered.

• • •

The days he'd recite me poems were the moments I knew things were going well for him on set. But on bad days, Paul was very different. One night, a few weeks into my stay, he got home from a demanding day of shooting and grabbed everything off our bed and threw it in the hallway. "When was the last time these sheets were washed?"

"What do I look like, a maid?" I retorted. I liked the idea of being a housewife in theory, but I'd actually never done laundry. Alma had always been around and even started coming to my new home when I moved. I gathered the sheets around my shoulders. "I want to smell like us. I'm never going to wash these sheets. How's that? 'This bed thy center is,' is it not?"

He paused, surprised that I'd have a response other than coddling. He took in my appearance, as if just noticing that I was still in pajamas and unshowered. "You don't seem okay," he said. "You seem depressed."

"Of course I'm depressed," I said, yelling at him. "I'm in love with you and I'm stuck in this apartment because of society's stupid rules. But I'll rot in this apartment until I can hold your hand in public if that's what you want." I wondered if I was telling the truth. If I were eighteen right then and there, would I really be acting differently?

"I want to get out of here. Please, Paul, let's go somewhere." He could see how desperate I was, so he agreed to go to a dive bar on Second Street and B, a place no one would look for us.

"I can order a Coke," I said.

"You're going to drink what I tell you to." He winked.

I wanted to be told what to do by a man as long as he loved me. No one knew who we were, and we drank vodka on the rocks and made out, sitting on the barstools. "You get more and more beautiful," he said and pushed my greasy hair off my face. The roots had come in on top so they were an inch thick, but he liked that. He said I looked like Debbie Harry in the '70s, and I drifted closer to him. I didn't tell him I brought photos of her to my stylist. I wanted him to think I came up with it on my own.

When Paul went to the bathroom, a woman with tattoos all over both arms stared at me like she knew me. I wanted to give her the finger, and why shouldn't I? I was a famous actress. I looked like Debbie Harry. I was a badass. And I didn't want her to watch me. I wasn't an experiment to observe. So I stopped holding back and flipped her off. No more Disney chick or Pollyanna. I finally felt free. It was the best night of my life.

We took another chance the next day when he had a break from shooting, but this time it was the middle of the afternoon. Paul was getting sick of the apartment too. Plus, as he said while getting ready, "We make our own rules, baby. You can't stop love." I wore big glasses and a baseball cap that read CBGB. I didn't want to seem out of place or paranoid, so I took half a Klonopin. Actually, a full one. Actually, two. My tolerance had grown considerably.

We walked down to the river where they had built the new pier.

"I want to marry you," he said to me. He stroked my cheek and kneeled down, the Hudson River whitecapping behind him. "I want to spend the rest of my life with you."

I wasn't sure if we could legally get married in New York State, but maybe when he did his next movie in Kansas, we could get married there. I was sure Kansas had easy laws, or breakable laws.

He pressed his face into my belly and I kissed his head, ruffled his hair. "I would marry you anywhere, any place, my love."

50.

My mother called me the next day and asked what I was doing with my life. She could only believe so many of my excuses.

"I'm doing a lot of staying in. I like it. It feels very interior. Floor-level apartments in Manhattan have exposed bricks. Did you know that, Mom? Maybe I'll write a screenplay about a woman who counts bricks."

"This isn't funny, Echo. This is exactly why I didn't want you to go into show business. You're becoming a recluse just like me."

I felt affronted. It had been a while since she'd given me anything but comfort. I was nothing like her. I wasn't a washed-up television actor past her prime. I was an Oscar winner. I had a future.

"I'm fine, Mom. This is a self-imposed break from life."

"Are you on something? Your voice sounds slurred."

"I was taking a nap," I said. "Look, I gotta go, Mom. Come visit me in New York if you want." But I knew she wouldn't.

"Same as me," she said, sounding sadder than I think I'd ever heard her. "You'll turn out the same as me."

A few nights later, Paul and I went for a walk through the Lower East Side. The more we went out and didn't get caught, the bolder we got.

There was so much construction going on in the area. Buildings for sale all over Avenue A. "I don't think I've seen one squatter since I've been in New York," Paul said. He stopped walking and pointed to the buildings on the opposite side of the street. "All those buildings used to be filled with squatters."

"I thought you grew up in Pennsylvania."

"Research for a role. My first movie. *Squat*," he said. "You were probably too young to see it."

"I saw *Squat*, Paul," I said defensively. I had never seen *Squat*. It was one of those pretentious slacker movies that did well at Sundance.

Paul seemed annoyed now, and we were out of cigarettes, so we went into the bodega on the corner. I asked for a pack of Marlboro Lights from the old guy behind the counter.

"Excuse me? Aren't you . . ." It was a man's voice from behind us.

He was in his early twenties, maybe younger, a college student in a navy blue windbreaker. He wasn't hard to size up. A frat boy probably just down here to buy weed. But my lawyer had already filed a restraining order against one guy who thought he was my boyfriend. A drawing of me dead on a balcony had shown up at Hazel's office. I was nervous when people approached me now.

"You're Echo Blue, aren't you?"

"No, she's not Echo Blue," Paul said, that anger in his voice. "Now get the fuck out of here."

"Paul—"

"It's two o'clock in the morning. This guy needs to start talking to you right here? Now?"

"I'm a huge fan," the guy said, and it was clear that he was drunk, tripping over himself toward us.

Paul let go of my hand, squeezed himself between me and Frat Boy, putting his palm on the guy's chest.

"Step back, asshole."

"I just want an autograph," Frat Boy whined.

"Well, you can't fucking have one."

Frat Boy continued to assert himself, coming toward me, as if Paul weren't even standing between us. The man behind the bodega counter was yelling in Spanish, and everything became a blur as I watched Paul, fully enraged now, shove the guy backward into a wall of cans. They came tumbling down on top of him, his body crumpling to the ground. Why couldn't they have been cereal boxes? It would have been so much softer.

Paul tugged on my arm, yelling, "Let's go, let's go," and we ran out of the bodega. The man behind the counter had one ear glued to his cordless phone as he rushed to check on the frat boy passed out on the floor.

Outside, I begged Paul to stand still and listen to me. I wasn't stupid. I had been in bad situations before. I grew up with chaos, and I knew we'd hear police sirens soon. A woman and her friend on the corner pointed at us. Our bubble had burst. We were out as a couple now. We were public property.

"Paul, we have to stay. That guy knew who we were. We're probably on camera in there."

"You know what's going to happen next, don't you? The paps are going to find out about this. We're going to be in the newspaper. We're going to be all over every single piece-of-shit gossip magazine."

"So what? I don't care. And I thought you didn't care about what people think either."

He looked at me funny, took my face in his hands, and lifted my chin up to his.

"I will protect you no matter what. I will throw a million guys into a wall of cans if I have to. I'll kill anyone who comes near you."

"What does that have to do with anything?" I asked.

Paul often played this part, the macho guy coming to my rescue. I had to admit I liked how he wanted to protect me. But the real problem here was that Paul didn't like me calling him out on his hypocrisy. He could say it was about protecting me, but I knew it was about protecting himself. Wasn't he the guy who hated capitulating to Hollywood's image of him? Then why was he so obsessed with hiding our relationship?

The two women kept pointing at us and whispering. I pushed his hands away from my chin.

"Paul, I've been doing this since I was a little kid. My dad has been doing this forever. My mother . . ."

"And they protected you?"

"Paul."

"Did they protect you?"

I shook my head. I could hear the sirens. Maybe he was right. Maybe we should have tried to leave. Now it was too late.

"We have to go back in there. We can't leave. They'll tell the police that I was there. You can get into this kind of trouble. I can't. Don't you see?"

I needed to calm him down, get a hold of the madness. Press the pause button. I wished I had a Klonopin, but I hadn't brought a purse. There was no keeping this under wraps. Paul would probably be charged with assault.

I took his hand and led him back to the bodega because it didn't matter that he was older than me. I was the bigger star. I was a household name. We'd have to stick to the story that this stranger, this "obsessed fan," was trying to attack me. No matter what the video cameras showed.

Goldie

. . .

51.

I was wrecked the next morning, like a hangover, that heavy anvil on your head, and I hadn't even had a drink. In the bathroom mirror, I hated myself. It should have been obvious that when I bleached and chopped my hair, I would end up looking like a cheap groupie, like Belinda called me.

The phone rang and it was Pench.

"Why aren't you in the office? Sick?"

Was I sick? I wanted to make a joke and say, *Yeah, sick in the head.* That's what Sam and I used to say to each other when we'd fake being sick so we didn't have to go to school.

But I did feel sick. It was hard to explain the disturbance of emotions that swept over me, the fullness of contradictions about Echo—about Belinda too. I didn't know what was real and what I had convinced myself of. If I really did know Echo. Why I was drawn to her.

I shuffled into the kitchen and stared into the fluorescent light on the ceiling. I could see Echo, her makeup washed down her face. Fake black eyelashes like ribbons on her cheekbones. I was opposite her. I was the one making her cry.

"I feel like I'm chasing Echo down like an animal. And I hate myself for it," I said. "I even bleached my hair out. Like hers. And I'm sure I look like some diabolical carbon copy, but I was really trying to embody her, you know? Be the *committed* journalist. Please tell me you know what I'm talking about."

Instead, he said, "Have you talked to anyone recently?"

"That didn't answer my question."

"But, Goldie, seriously. Have you?"

"Talked to anyone—like who?"

"Like a professional."

"I don't want to go to a therapist, Pench. I told you I've done the therapy route."

Going to a therapist would be an admission of defeat. It would be as if I had disappointed my father, because there I was, regressing to that place when I was a teenager, obsessed with a person I didn't know and throwing my whole life into her.

"Sorry to use this awful metaphor, but the therapy route doesn't have to have an off-ramp. Like, you can start and stop. This is a big story for you, Goldie. You've been consumed, as a journalist should be, but it might be good to work out some of the emotional stuff with someone."

"That was a really bad metaphor."

"I warned you." We tried to laugh. Nothing was funny. I was so tired.

I took a long pause. "I feel stuck," I said, realizing that I might be alluding to my life, and I didn't want to sound that way. So I clarified. "What do you do when you feel stuck in a story?"

"Are we not talking about therapists anymore?"

"We are not talking about therapists anymore, but thank you. And I will consider it."

"Okay," he said, sighing. "When I'm stuck, I write everything I know, and I try to think of the bigger picture. Sometimes we start with a vision for what the story is going to be, and it turns into something completely different. What has your story become, Goldie? You just need to reframe things."

WHERE ARE YOU, ECHO BLUE?

"Are you going to be the person in my life who gives me good advice now? Because I'm not sure I'm ready for this."

"If you want me to be."

It was quiet and weird for a minute, but we said goodbye and hung up. I ripped out a clean piece of paper. How would I reframe this? The story was about searching for Echo, and I clearly did my due diligence around that. I spoke to as many people as I could find and even got into her inner circle. There were only two key people I hadn't spoken to. Mathilde Portman was completely off the grid and impossible to reach. All I knew about her was that she had dropped out of the public eye, and Echo stopped living with her when she was about eleven. I also hadn't talked to Paul Reed, who Echo started dating when she was seventeen. Paul Reed wasn't a valuable lead, because they were clearly not together. He hadn't even been in the US for months.

What I did know was that if I connected the dots, it left Echo very much alone. This made me feel even more like a vulture. If that's not what I wanted, to be this kind of person, then why was I still doing it? My father had just died, and I probably should have been comforting my mother; instead, I was running around looking for Echo, and my quasi boyfriend was suggesting therapy. It was like every time I thought about Echo, I came back to myself.

"*It seems like you're looking for something else other than Echo,*" Belinda had said. And then it clicked. Echo wasn't the story. *I* was the story.

52.

The next morning, I went into work and rode the elevator, thinking about how I would pitch my idea to Dana. The numbers climbed up and up, a big striking bell at each floor. It was possible I might get fired. I basically botched my first big story. But if I could get her to give me one more chance, to trust me this one last time, it may not be over.

I made a beeline for Dana's office. She waved me in.

"Um, did something happen that I should be aware of?" she said, her eyes wide, staring at me, almost afraid.

"I know I look bizarre," I said, awkwardly tussling my hair. I was jumpy, out of breath. "But I have to talk to you." I relayed the conversation with Belinda about *Emma*, about the breakup, that Belinda didn't know where Echo was. "I have some good interviews, some excellent takes on how women are treated in Hollywood, but nothing concrete about Echo's whereabouts. I don't feel like I'm getting any closer. I don't know if it's possible to get closer. Not if I want to live with myself. I feel like I've hit a dead end. I know I've disappointed you. I've disappointed myself." I had to be careful with what I said next. "But I do have an idea about turning the story inside out. Making it more free-form. Something for the magazine that's a four- or five-part installment series. I think I'm onto something, Dana."

Dana looked skeptical. "Onto what?"

"You know, about me searching for Echo. And not finding her." Yes, I knew this sounded counterintuitive, but this felt like the only way to right my wrongs. I had lost myself in this process, but by writing an exposé of how my fandom (and, let's face it, ambition) had led me astray, maybe I could conjure up something poignant and not seem so unhinged. Maybe I could hold on to my career and myself.

There was a serious look on her face when she stood up and shut the door.

"Goldie," she said. "Goldie. Goldie." She leaned over and hugged me. It felt nice to be hugged. This is what happens when you're about to get fired by a nice person. They hug you.

"You're not the first journalist who didn't get the story, and you won't be the last. Fucking Geraldo Rivera had an entire camera crew with him to pry open Al Capone's vault underneath a hotel in Chicago and found nothing. It was a two-hour special! Live fucking television. Now that's a journalistic failure of epic proportions. And you've been going through a lot."

"Are you really comparing me to Geraldo Rivera?"

We both laughed. Me and Geraldo Rivera, the biggest tabloid journalist of them all. He invited skinheads on his show in 1988, and when someone threw a chair at his face and broke his nose, he seemed shocked. Was that *me*? Of course it was. That was what my life had turned into.

"Hello, Goldie? Are you here with me?" She snapped her fingers, and I came back to the present. "First, I need to check that you're actually okay," Dana said.

"Dana, I'm okay," I pleaded.

"All right." She sighed. "Look, I didn't want to tell you this, but I never thought you were going to find her. I did, on the other hand, have a hunch your search wouldn't be entirely fruitless."

This shocked me. "What are you talking about?"

"Come on, Goldie. Everyone knew this girl was either dead or she didn't want to be found. But you're a great journalist. You're tenacious. You're a killer, and you don't stop for anyone." I self-consciously stroked my newly blonde hair.

"And you like this idea?" I said.

"Yeah, I mean, the story's been saturated anyway. It's getting stale. People are starting to forget. Plus, I had a meeting with Stan Moranowski last week, and I swear he pushed me to find a multi-installment series about a celebrity that's not just your average profile. He wants something local. He's going to all departments about it to see who comes up with a fresh angle. I was racking my brain about what it should be. Now here you are in my office—and I can't believe I'm saying this—saving my ass. Echo Blue was last seen at MTV studios. I mean, that's *local*."

Dana and I mapped out what the entries should look like. I'd come completely clean. I'd detail my search for her and use it as a lens to dive into the dangers of celebrity obsession. It would come full circle to the conclusion that stars like Echo should be left alone. Yes, this was good. I'd redeem myself and write a story I could be proud of. A story of going off the deep end and coming back.

"So, eating a pot cookie at Jamie Blue's house? You want me to write about that?"

"I have to go over that with legal first, but Jesus Christ, Goldie—this whole thing is a gold mine. Every story I assigned to you before this was boring as fuck, and you made them exciting. That boxing story? You turned that into a soul-searching manifesto."

I didn't want to ever be this vulnerable in front of anyone, let alone my boss, but once she mentioned my father's favorite boxing story, I couldn't hold it back. I cried and I cried.

She cupped my chin and stared into my eyes. "Wipe those tears off your face and write."

53.

I spent days holed up in my apartment working on that first installment. I wished I had a dog to keep me company. "A normal person would go to a movie or at least go to a café, leave the house," Sam said.

But I needed to be tactile. I needed to pace, talk aloud. I couldn't do that at a café, and that's also why Dana gave me permission to do this out of the office. And let's face it—I was not normal. My own odyssey in searching for Echo, or whatever you want to call it, was not normal. And maybe for once that would be a good thing.

I bullet-pointed index cards and outlined my days tracking her. I broke that into sections, the people I spoke to, my recall still sharp. Then I lined up my own journey with what the tabloids covered for the pulse of how the culture responded to her disappearance. I checked out books on fan psychology and celebrity worship from the New York Public Library and sat for hours sometimes writing longhand because I couldn't stare at my laptop screen anymore or my eyes would fall out.

I printed page after page until my ink cartridge ran out. Writing had the power to make you hungry. So I ordered Thai food, and I cried over som tum. Why was som tum so spicy sometimes and not spicy at all the other times? I washed it down with Thai iced tea, that sweetness of condensed milk lingering on my tongue. No more crying. I had to write.

I listened to my interviews; I had already transcribed most of them, but I needed to hear the pitch of my voice. What did I sound like? What was my frame of mind? I had a photo album from sophomore year and flipped through the grainy pictures. There was one of me with an Echo T-shirt on, and I wore such a forced smile, a mouth full of braces. I got microwave popcorn and nutritional yeast from the bodega. Yellow flakes dropped all over my black shirt as I typed away. The more I wrote and processed, the more grateful I felt that I hadn't found her. I shuddered thinking about it. Would I have screamed her name in front of a crowd of people, exposing her, unable to stop myself after years of her skulking in my imagination? Would I have tackled her? I was more and more sure she'd disappeared to avoid people like me. How could I have lived with myself if I were the one to ruin that for her? I wrote and wrote, and wrote some more, unwavering, until finally it was all on the page. I felt exorcised. But I'd done it.

•   •   •

I filed the first installment a week later, and I waited cross-legged on the floor outside Dana's door, sipping coffee as she read it.

Three thousand devastating words. Now my life was in front of her.

"It's a masterpiece! It's a goddamn masterpiece!" she exclaimed after a painful twenty minutes and dragged me into her office. "This is going to be as big as when *Rolling Stone* published monthly installments of *Bonfire of the Vanities*. The rawness of it all. I don't want to edit a thing."

I wondered if Dana was my first female friend. Can you be friends with your boss?

From then on, it was full speed ahead. She wanted a flashy title, so we came up with this:

Where Are You, Echo Blue?
My Descent into Madness

It made me seem crazy—my madness—but wasn't I? Dana wanted me to take an author photo while my hair was still bleached and shaped like Echo's. They mocked up a cover image, a distorted picture of Echo with an overlay of me, like her second skin. It was creepy, as if I were Echo's ghost. I was conflicted about this approach: I was trying to erase the feeling that she was part of me. But it also did get at the essence of what I had written about. As uncomfortable as that might have been, it *was* the story. Nevertheless, the cover was striking. Beautiful. Now I just had to wait for the issue to come out.

The morning of February 23, 2000, the day the March issue was hitting newsstands, I could barely contain myself. All of the emotions I'd felt through this entire search were colliding, but most of all, I felt pride. I had done it. I wished my father could see. Now it was up for readers to decide whether it was any good—or if I would wind up with egg on my face by the end of the day.

• • •

While 2000 was the worst year ever for newsstand sales, *ME* single issues for March rose 55 percent, thanks to my story.

Pench bought me a cupcake to congratulate me. "It's from Magnolia. You know that cupcake place on the corner of Bleecker? I stood in a long line to get it. It better be good." He smiled at me so sweetly that I wanted to give him a blow job to thank him. I know that sounds crude, but I was still learning how to appreciate men. Pench was one of the only people who had known how deeply I cared about Echo when it was a dirty little secret, and he still wanted to be nice to me.

My editor-in-chief, Stan Moranowski, called me into his office to congratulate me. He wore a black suit and was partially balding. He looked like a businessman, nothing like a creative. Dana sat beside me with a broad maternal smile.

"No one reporter has made the marketing team happier since Dalton Kinsey wrote about JFK Jr.'s plane crash, god rest his soul," Stan said and lowered his head as if he were performing a silent prayer.

Newsstand sales for week two were even bigger than week one. I got booked on the *Today* show, *Larry King*, and MSNBC. But with big ad sales and media attention came a slew of disapproval. *New Yorker* critic Max Phillips wrote,

> *Instead of giving Klein a space to write,* ME *should have offered her therapy or, better yet, a restraining order.*

"When the journalists go after you," Pench told me, "that's how you know you've made it."

When the article launched online, commenters went ballistic, diagnosing me with a borderline personality disorder. They accused me of being a self-hating feminist because I promoted stalking (even though I swear I was doing the opposite). Some told me to kill myself. (*ME* didn't have moderators—our site was barely functioning—but they promised to delete threats.) I wanted to respond to each and every comment, tell them that the format gave me a chance to be true to myself and my search, but Dana told me not to respond to anyone. "You're a public figure now. You can't fight with people who disagree with you."

"Can't I defend myself?"

"Yeah," she said, happily chomping on her Nicorette. "Put it in the next article."

I should have been satisfied with the fame. I wanted this from the beginning, to be professionally successful. Twenty-three under twenty-three, right? But after the brief high I had felt from producing a story I was proud of, the name-calling and the criticisms got to me. *Inside Edi-*

tion did a salacious three-part series on celebrity-worship horror stories. Joanna with the nails put out a crude blog, writing about how I had ransacked their meetup.

> *Goldie Klein is a manipulator and a fraud. She should*
> *not be getting accolades for admitting that she's got a*
> *personality disorder.*

I had never hated myself more. Or felt more truly myself.

• • •

My mom came into the city to visit me. It was a big deal for her since she really hadn't gone anywhere since my father died. She seemed so small when she walked into *ME*. Her heavy foundation and her thick mascara, her eyes wide open, staring around the office. I always thought my mother looked so pretty, even if she did go heavy on the bronzer, but that day she just looked like a tired widow who worked at a makeup counter. Sam held her hand, thankfully, because he was better at reassuring her than I was. We went into an empty conference room to eat, and she gazed out at the view of downtown Manhattan.

I ordered the three of us Thai food for lunch. I craved the crunch of fresh peanuts and sprouted soybeans after eating it daily while working on the story.

"You seem miserable," Sam said in between sips of his Thai iced tea, while my mom was in the bathroom. "What's up with you?"

I went back to my cubicle to grab him the stack of letters I had hid in my desk. I dropped them on the large conference table when I returned.

"Hate mail," I said to my brother.

He read one from the pile. "'You're a dumb cunt and someone should teach you a lesson,'" he said. "Charming." Then he paused. "Hey, I have an idea."

Sam suggested I do a photo shoot of me reading my hate mail, and I pitched it to Dana. Three days later, I sprawled across my unmade bed with my hate mail covering my belly. I wore an old white T-shirt with a frayed collar, and my hair, still like Echo's, was greasy and unkempt. My cowlicks sprouted like waterfalls. The light was moody and the photos were oversize and dreamy.

The more the readers hated me, the more magazines they bought.

• • •

The third installment, for the May issue, was huge. I wrote about Jamie Blue, how he supplied me with a bathing suit and how we shared a hot tub. Legal insisted I omit the details about the mushrooms and pot cookie. Soaking in a hot tub with Jamie Blue was good gossip. It was expected gossip. Him supplying me illicit drugs was illegal, and he would sue.

And in the fourth issue, I revealed how Echo stole *Emma* from Belinda. *ME* had gotten calls from Hazel Cahn's lawyers threatening a lawsuit, but Belinda was on record. Belinda told the story without an ounce of guilt.

By the middle of June, I signed with a literary agency. *ME* moved me into an office. I got a raise. I could afford a hairdresser who dyed my overprocessed hair back to brown.

The view from my office window faced the west side, toward the Hudson River. Just a few blocks away from Lincoln Center. It should have been striking. The sky colored itself in between the buildings. But it was a buggy haze from up here. You really couldn't see for miles in the fog, not with all the pollution.

Over those months, all I could think about was Echo. I could hear her voice from old interviews when she was a kid, how innocent she was. Where was she now? Look at how strangers treated me on the street when they recognized me, with no slowdown on the hate mail, and I was a nobody. I couldn't imagine what she had gone through. I had given up on my search out of respect, but the fact still remained that she was out there on her own, with no redemption.

I thought I found what I was looking for. So why did I feel so empty?

Echo

1998–1999

· · ·

54.

Paul's lawyer got the frat boy from the bodega to drop charges once he wrote him a check, but it was too late. We were now an item in the papers. Our debut was a shot of us with Paul's arm draped around me, an ACE bandage on his left hand (seemed like overkill, but I didn't say anything) and a cigarette in the other. My hair was a mess; I was wearing one of his sweatshirts, but I looked happy. And I was happy. Despite the scandal, I had gotten what I had been wanting. We were out now. Hazel begged me to go back to L.A. and let the dust settle for another week before things proliferated. I agreed.

I spent my first night back in L.A. next to the window with a hammer, my calls to Paul going unanswered. I couldn't sleep alone after being so attached to him. And the paparazzi were back in droves immediately upon my return. Hazel was right that I could hide out in my house without feeling so exposed the way I was on the streets of Manhattan, but it didn't stop them from practically camping out on my block. Klonopin was no longer working after how much I'd been taking in Paul's apartment the previous month. Neither was anything else.

The next day, I went straight to Hazel's office. I needed something to do.

"Congratulations to Paul for planting his roots in the right place," Hazel said, tossing a tabloid my way with his face on it, looking like a Greek god. "He knew where the fertile garden was, didn't he? One big night with you, and he's Hollywood's newest rebel."

"I love Paul. And I don't want you trashing him."

She groaned, her head in her hands.

"I have nothing against Paul, Echo," she said, backing down, her voice softening. "He's a heartthrob—I get it. But he was a middle-rate star, and he attached himself to a forever A-list star, and now that's how he'll always be known. For the rest of his life, connected to you, even when he's married with three kids and living in Paris or wherever Paul Reed ends up."

"Do not dismiss my relationship, Hazel," I shouted, throwing my glass of water across the room. It hit the edge of her bookshelf and then shattered all over the carpet.

I couldn't believe I did it. It was the lack of sleep. The hounding press. The Klonopin not working.

Hazel's face was wide open. She steadied herself with one hand on her desk.

"I'm sorry," I said. "I'm sorry. I'm a mess. I—"

Her assistant, Daisy, came running into the room. "I heard a crash," she said, breathless.

"It's fine, Daisy. Just a spill," Hazel replied, sending her back out of the room.

Hazel came around to the chair where I was hunched over and didn't acknowledge the glass on the floor. "Let's let that be the first and last time you do something like that with me." She paused, as if recalibrating. "I've known you for so long, Echo. Sometimes I feel like I could be your mother. So it's important to me to help you save your career, which, let's face it, needs saving. I'm telling you, darling, you're going to have to turn on the charm for that *Emma* premiere."

Did I even want my career saved? I couldn't tell her the truth—that I didn't want to act anymore. That I wanted to be someone else. But what else could I be at this point? I'd have to keep going and going until I broke.

Next, Hazel gave me the news that I was already hoping for, which was that Disney officially dropped me after the bodega incident, and we decided that my next project should be an independent film. This seemed like the best way to ease back in. I was fine with it—in fact, I preferred it. I wanted to be in charge, and if the only option was to be in charge of my own destruction, so be it. Maybe doing something small would be meaningful. Maybe I would like what I was doing again. But there was one condition before Hazel could land me something good. I needed to follow my bad press with good press. Do an easy interview with someone compassionate and wise who could help me look more sympathetic.

Hazel handpicked Nickey Tanaka, a contributing editor at *Vanity Fair* who was known for interviewing outspoken, complicated women. "She's got a gentle take on everything I've read," Hazel said. "She'll be understanding if you talk about Paul. She'll make it look like a love story."

"It *is* a love story, Hazel."

"Of course it is, darling. That's what I meant."

I dressed in comfortable clothes for the interview, and we met at the Chateau, which Hazel said would be better than my messy little cottage. "Order a Shirley Temple or something," Hazel said. "It'll be a cute bit." I resisted taking a Klonopin beforehand so I wouldn't slur, which had happened a few times lately, given how many I now had to take. Instead, I got there over an hour early to order a martini to settle. No one was going to give me a hard time about drinking. They knew me at the Chateau; plus, they had an unofficial airtight privacy agreement with their guests. The martini warmed me up, but I was still shaking.

When Nickey approached the bar about fifty minutes early, her eyes shot directly to the empty martini glass in front of me, paused on it, then she looked up at my face. I lightly coasted the glass toward the bartender, whose back was to us. My stomach sank. This was an important interview so I could show the public that the emancipation (even though it had been three years now), losing the Disney contract, and the bodega incident were all blips. I was supposed to seem *in control*—that I, the good girl, was right on track.

Ordering the martini was a miscalculation of great proportions.

From the article "Echo's Blue Hotel," *Vanity Fair*, 1998, by Nickey Tanaka:

> *When I head to meet Echo Blue at the Chateau Marmont bar, I forget that she is seventeen years old. Blue seems to transcend age because she has been in our atmosphere since she was eleven. We watched her win the Oscar. She dominated the box office with hit after hit. She outranked her famous parents. Up-and-coming soulful bad boy Paul Reed is her new boyfriend. It's easy to forget that she is still underage.*

> *But when I see her familiar, ebullient face, the washed-out blonde hair, those rosy, full cheeks, I see a child. And in front of that child, an empty martini glass. We lock eyes, and she shoves the glass toward the other side of the bar, hoping, if I have to guess, that I won't notice.*

> *I notice.*

> *Blue shuts her eyes and sighs heavily, tossing her head back. Who can blame her? The tabloids and celebrity magazines have stalked her with a relentless, out-of-control-like vengeance with headlines that have read "Echo and Dad Break Up!" "Echo and the Bad Boy!" "Echo and the Bodega Fight!" "Echo Smoking on Set!" We haven't even started the interview, and I'm already witness to a delicate situation reminiscent of the tabloids she's fighting against. She's immediately defensive.*

"Yes. I drank a martini," Blue says, throwing her arms up in the air. "What high school teenager doesn't drink? There are kids pounding beers in their parents' garage every weekend and then getting in their cars. I had one drink in a bar, and I have a driver who is going to take me home."

"If you're the kid in the garage sneaking Bud Light, what does that make me?" I ask her. "The parent who caught you?"

Which leads me to my next question. Who is watching out for Echo Blue?

Hazel lost her mind. First at me, then at Nickey Tanaka. The Chateau Marmont released a statement: "Our guests' privacy is our utmost priority. We will not comment further on this situation."

We also released a statement: "Ms. Tanaka created a dramatic, false situation, and my words have been misused." Nothing about it was misused. Nickey Tanaka had the whole thing on tape. But that didn't matter. "Let her release the tapes to Larry King," Hazel said. "We'll say you were only joking."

I felt bad denying everything. Nickey was just as compassionate as Hazel said she would be. She seemed genuinely concerned about me. It left a burning in my heart, a distaste that I couldn't shake. I knew I'd get over this like I'd gotten over every other issue thrown my way. I could move past this with another box office hit, and people would forget. Wasn't that what Hazel always said?

And she was right—I could get over this. But I felt so tired, the desire to keep doing this—the song and dance, trotting out the good girl, that need to please people—waning.

55.

October, at the *Emma* premiere, if you look back at the pictures of Paul and me, you can see the damage in my face. He and I wore matching Regency-inspired garb, me in a ruffled black gown and him in a black velvet military coat. My eyes were swollen shut in some of the photos because of how tired I was, barely able to sleep when Paul was away in Kansas filming. "I've never been happier." That's what I told each person on the red carpet. Paul's protective arm swung around me; he never once let go.

Things got worse and worse with the paparazzi. It wasn't the wilds, it was Beverly Hills, but I felt like a prisoner. My lawyer had now filed restraining orders against three men. I worried that every guy with a camera was someone who might kidnap me or stick me in a hole in the ground. Paul was doing another movie in New York, and I was scared to be alone. I had the hardware store deliver me a long metal chain, and I wrapped it around the knobs of my French doors that opened up to the patio. I pushed one big club chair in front of the kitchen door and one against the door to the garage.

There weren't any curtains at the back of my house, because my decorator said the natural light was something I would want. I didn't want any light. Only darkness. I thumbtacked my long gray towels over the windows. I spent my days in bed. I don't remember what I ate. I didn't brush my teeth. I wore Paul's T-shirts and no underwear. I hated the smell of myself. My hair was in knots in the back of my head. Eyeliner from three days ago was smudged under my lashes. I was reading scripts, taking some meetings with producers, but I couldn't focus on what anyone was saying. Hazel was pushing me to commit, but I plunged into darkness, the couch, the bed, sometimes my floor, just to rest. I kept upping my Klonopin dose to sleep off the days. I waded in my pool at night. My hips hurt from so much lying down.

Finally, after three weeks of this, Paul got enough time off to visit. He called me at ten o'clock at night from the airport.

"There's like a zillion paps here."

"Oh my god, Paul. I'm so sorry."

"Those motherfuckers. They're not going to ruin us, baby. They're not gonna take us down," he was saying. Then I heard the phone rumble and him screaming something, but it was muffled.

"Paul? What happened?"

He was completely out of breath. "I picked something up from the ground and started swinging it at them," he said, then whispered: "I really made it, didn't I, babe? All those paps here just for me?"

I imagined photos of Paul on the cover of the *Post* the next day and the word games with the headlines: *Paul Reed Pap Run-In* or *Reed-prehensible Behavior* or *Reed Rumbles with Paps*.

He told me he was going to come straight from the airport, incognito. About a half hour later, Paul was pounding on the gate, shouting my name because he had forgotten his key.

I buzzed him in, standing at the doorstep with my hair in knots, a ratty T-shirt on. I shielded my eyes from the flashing lights as he came through. There was a horde of them, like ants swarming. Paul was wearing sunglasses and a yellow ski hat pulled over his eyes. It was not the incognito look I had in mind. He ran up the front walk and lifted me up in the air, holding me in one arm, cradling my ass. Me and no underwear.

He shut the front door behind us. It was all of five seconds, really, but they got it, their cameras intruding through the slightly open gate. They got it all. The rushing to the door. Me looking lovesick. My ass. The stained T-shirt. The whole thing. I didn't want to think this way, but it was clear to me Paul had wanted them to capture it.

"What's wrong with you, babe?" he said, putting me down. "You smell like shit."

He looked over at the chains on the patio doors. Then the towels over the windows and the chairs against the other doors.

"What the fuck is going on here?"

"It's to stop intruders," I said. "My lawyer had to file restraining orders for three stalkers. Not one. Not two. Three, Paul. Three. Didn't I tell you this? You should know these things."

"I know, baby, I know."

Then my legs gave out from under me. I curled up in a ball and rocked back and forth. Paul put a blanket over me, stroked my dirty hair, and hugged me from behind.

"What's going to happen to me?" I said. "What's going to happen to my life?"

"What are you talking about?" he said. "You're a huge star."

"I'm a child star, Paul. There's a big difference. People want to see me being happy and sweet. They're going to dump me unless I can do a new movie. You'll see. I'm going to be your problem. Then you'll dump me too."

Paul stared at me like he was searching for the girl he met on the set of *Emma*. The girl who had so much confidence and control. He didn't know me at all.

"We're going to have a life together. I'm going to protect you from those animals." He rocked me in his arms like a baby, and I whispered that I wanted to stay there forever. He waited ten more minutes and then stood up.

"Don't leave me," I said. "I think I'm going to be sick." Every part of my body felt numb. I was nauseous, and I couldn't even turn my head. I was tired. So tired. How had I gotten here?

I hated myself in that moment. I saw myself dead on the ground, with people crying around me. I saw my name in the papers. I saw people lining up for my funeral and paparazzi trying to get pictures of mourners from the bushes. I didn't see Paul saying anything at my funeral. I saw him crying with his agent, making sure the photographers got shots of him wiping his tears.

"Do you think my dad would come to my funeral?" I said.

"What? Echo, what are you talking about?"

"My dad!" I scratched at his legs. Pain crept through my skull. "Do you think he would come to my funeral?"

He kept saying my name over and over, telling me that I wasn't making any sense. Once you're crying that hard, it's very difficult to control it. I'd grinded away my entire life to smile for everyone, to be the perfect child or the perfect daughter or the perfect actor.

Part of me wanted to be the mess they cleaned up off the floor.

"I can't do it anymore," I heard myself saying. "I can't do it anymore."

"Who do I call?" Paul said, holding my face. "Who do I call, baby?"

56.

Hazel checked me in to Promises in Malibu and told me that it would be a temporary thing. Everything and everyone else were to blame. Her main concern was that the press knew I was getting help. She had no idea how many pills I was taking, how my mind had caved in on itself.

She talked quickly as she drove me down to Malibu. "We could plant a small story in *Hollywood Daily* about you. That you're exhausted. You need to get healthy. They'll fix you right up."

But nothing with me was ever small. Everything was gigantic and muddled and complicated.

The surfers bobbed on the water as we drove down the Pacific Coast Highway. The fog crept over the hills to the east. I squeezed my eyes shut and plunged into my hoodie.

• • •

I went to Promises addicted to Klonopin. When I first got there, they gave me more pills to sleep off the shakes from the withdrawal. I slept for four days. On the fourth day, I was terrified to leave my room. Agoraphobia, one of the more fun Klonopin withdrawal side effects.

They pushed cigarettes on me because they said smoking was the kind of good vice that I could use for a little while getting rid of the others. I was relieved to shamelessly smoke in public. Thank god group therapy was held outside, because otherwise we all would have choked.

Jessie Bell was in group with me. She had been on a TV show about a liberal New York–based family that moved to the Midwest, and she played the blonde-haired smart-ass kid. She was adorable when she was little. Fat cheeks, bangs, a little stomach. When she got older, she didn't age into her body well. The belly was still there along with acne on her cheeks from the many years of makeup. She was twenty, about two years older than me.

One day, we sat in chairs under a live oak tree overlooking the Pacific, splitting a cigarette. "What do I do with my life now?" Jessie asked me. "I tried auditioning for other roles, but everyone said stuff like, 'Oh, you were so cute when you were little.' So I guess they don't think I'm cute anymore. That's when I started cutting," she said, holding her arm protectively. "Cutting and Klonopin. Hard consonants saved me. And then they almost killed me. Now I'm here."

It was so awful to hear of her suffering. I felt worn. I didn't know what to say. We had both been drowning ourselves in the pain.

"We're in the same place," I said to her. "I don't know what's next for me."

"We are not in the same place at all," she said to me. "You're an Oscar winner. You're beautiful. You're always going to have a career."

But what if I didn't want one?

Hazel came for family day, and the two of us sat in the garden overlooking the beach.

"Well, this is nice," she said. Her sunglasses were so big that I couldn't even see her cheeks.

I wished it were my mother, not Hazel. But my mother told me on the phone that as much as she wanted to see me, she didn't want to have a setback.

"I can't come, honey. You know this, don't you? I'm not sure I could take it, seeing you there."

"What are you saying, Mom? That you're mad at me for getting myself into rehab?"

"Mad at *you*? No. I'm mad at myself, Echo. Your father and I—we did this. I'm mad at myself for not being able to stop it."

I could hear her blowing her nose, muffled sounds trying to conceal sobs, but they broke through. You know that kind of cry that creeps into your lungs, stabbing the back of your throat. It made me want to take a Klonopin. Rebound anxiety rocketed through my chest and brain. My legs shook. Sweat crept up the back of my neck. That part of my brain fired up like a plane crash, my heart speeding.

Now, in front of Hazel, my legs shook again, this new way my body was learning to cope, and she looked at me strangely. She gave me a box of handmade chocolates from a store in Beverly Hills.

"Edible gold drizzled on the outside. Two-hundred-dollar chocolates, Echo. Eat them slowly." It seemed perfectly normal that Hazel suggest I take up emotional eating in rehab.

I shoved three of the chocolates in my mouth, the bitter taste releasing its way over my tongue, and I started to accept that my mom wasn't coming. As much as I wanted her here, I didn't want the pressure of convincing her I was fine when I wasn't. With Hazel, I could be somewhat myself.

"Go ahead, darling. Eat them all. You deserve a pity party." She snatched one of the chocolates for herself.

"Did my dad even call? He had to have seen that I went to rehab in one of the papers."

"He called, but he wasn't sure if you wanted to see him."

"Bullshit," I said. "He didn't call."

"I'm not one to feel bad for a man in Hollywood, but he has his own problems, darling. He can't get a movie; he can't even get a television show. He's about to shoot a commercial in Japan and make an enormous amount of money. But that makes him feel like 'a whore'—his words," she snorted and continued. "I told him, 'Jamie, at least you're getting paid.'

So, no. The last thing you need is for your father to come here and start giving you his woe-is-me story. Pathetic."

My dad is most likely happy that I'm in this situation, I remember thinking. Now we had more in common. He couldn't relate to my rising star. But the *falling* star—that he understood. That was a person he'd come to know.

"Have you heard from Paul? Has he come to visit you?" Hazel said.

"No," I said. "He's been busy filming. Going very method this time, barely talking to anyone."

I didn't even know if that was true, but that's what he had told me when I last called him. He also told me he thought we should take a break. Not put the pressure of a relationship on my sobriety and my health. I didn't tell Hazel how dismissive he had sounded on the call. How uninterested.

"Maybe it's time to make a statement," she said.

"We haven't even broken up yet, Hazel. Don't make a statement." But I could see in her face that she knew what was next. He wasn't going to visit me here. And then eventually he'd let me go. What kind of person did you have to be to dump your girlfriend while she was in rehab? But of course he wouldn't do that. It was a bad PR look. Hence the "break."

Not far away, there was a man who looked about my dad's age. He was crying, and two young girls who must have been his daughters were sitting with him. I'm sure they wanted to slap him.

Hazel, who had been gazing at me, lifted her chin to the sky, tears running down her cheeks. I wanted to make a joke about her being human, but then she spoke.

"You are young, darling. You have a whole life ahead of you." Hazel had given me plenty of empty advice up to that point, but this time was something different. I wanted to tell her I had already lived a whole life.

"I want the Klonopin back. I'll tell you that much."

Hazel reached over and took my shaky hands in hers. I appreciated that she didn't act as if there was anything different.

"They wanted me to give up cigarettes when my mother died of lung cancer. Right before she died, when she was on morphine but was still somewhat lucid, she'd tell me that I'd better quit or I was going to end up just like her. And here I am to this day, unable to bring myself to do it. Smoking helps me remember her. Is that perverse enough for you? We can't get away from being our parents, can we?"

It was the first thing she had ever told me about her family. It hit me that I'd never even thought of Hazel as having parents. I didn't know anything about her. Yes, she wore a wedding ring, so she must have had a husband, but otherwise, I couldn't produce a single fact about her life.

"I'm really sorry, Hazel. I didn't know. I should have asked."

I knew Hazel wanted it that way. But it still didn't feel right. I briefly wondered if I had been wrong all this time about her. If maybe she did truly care. "Are you, like, having a maternal moment with me?" I said. And we both laughed at the absurdity of that.

Nothing more was said for at least ten minutes, both of us staring out at the ocean, until I finally asked, "How much longer do I need to stay here?"

"As long as it takes, darling. As long as it takes."

57.

Belinda was the first person I reached out to as part of my twelve-step program. I was supposed to make amends. I was supposed to forgive myself. I was supposed to forgive others. At Promises, they taught me that Echo the drug addict was a different person and that I could separate myself from that Echo, as long as I worked the program. And I wanted to, but I felt so much shame. I hated myself because I knew it wasn't just the drugs that made me stab my best friend in the back. No, that was more complicated.

Indigo Kaplan, my counselor, was a former child star herself who had been in the *Witch Mountain* series. In each of our sessions, she hammered in one message: "You don't want to see yourself as the cursed victim, which is the way the media portrays troubled child stars. You are not powerless. Your biggest failure is that you grew up and now you're dealing with very adult problems. Growing up is not a crime."

She was right. I was a grown-up now and was going to need a life after rehab. I needed to live with myself and take responsibility—it didn't guarantee that Belinda would accept my apologies, but I had to try.

I called Belinda relentlessly. Each time, her answering machine picked up. I was pleasant in my messages until I finally broke on the tenth call. I hollered her name, begging her for forgiveness, telling her that I needed her and that she couldn't just give up on me. Sandy answered in the middle of my diatribe.

"Please, Sandy. Please convince her. I've been doing so much work at Promises. I want to be clean. I want to figure myself out and get my life together." I hadn't been at Promises that long when I made that call, and I sounded dramatic, like I was doing a role. I could have told Sandy that it was the withdrawal making me sound manic, that the benzos actually rewired my brain. But I thought of how Indigo had told me to *"let people have their process."*

"Echo, you have to give her some time."

I wanted Belinda back, but I had no choice. I had to sit with the anguish of wounding her.

•   •   •

The other person Indigo urged me to make amends with was my dad.

"My dad is the last person I want to say sorry to," I told her on one of our walks.

"Amends aren't just about delivering an apology; they're also about forgiveness."

"Why should I forgive him? I was a child, and he was a narcissistic prick."

"Echo, I get that you feel resentment. I get that you have anger toward him. But to move on, you have to have compassion."

"Compassion for who? For *him*? Are you fucking kidding me?"

"No, sweetheart. Compassion for yourself. That's where it starts. With you."

I didn't understand what she meant. I felt sorry for myself, didn't I? Wasn't that why I was in rehab? Because I was a self-pitying actress with an Oscar, and I wanted to drown out my pain?

I thought of the time during *Stars Everywhere*. *"We are both stars of the movie, Dad,"* I had said to him. The constant ego affirmations I rewarded him with so he could continue believing he was a huge actor. And what was his response? "*I got upstaged by my own fucking daughter.*" His pout, his sour eyes. I remembered it all too well.

"I don't want to forgive him," I said. "I want to make him suffer. That would be nice."

"Nothing will change who your father is. Not a movie, not another award. But *you* can move forward. You can stop taking the blame for any of it. Forgiveness isn't forgetting what happened. It's about letting go of it."

I hated him. I hated him so much that it felt like I hated myself. I didn't want to live with that hate.

I didn't know how to let go either. Letting go was a different animal. You could argue that I let go during the emancipation, but I didn't. Not mentally. The emancipation was a spiteful move—I was mad and rightfully so. I'd always long for my dad; I couldn't erase that. But after working with Indigo, I no longer wanted to hurt him or publicly embarrass him. Rehab, it turned out, could be quite constructive.

58.

I had only been out of rehab for a few months when Hazel brought up the idea of me doing an MTV gig to tease my next movie, *I Hate Camp*, an indie picture that would start filming in January 2000. Sofia Chaplin, Charlie Chaplin's granddaughter, was directing. It was meant to be my big comeback. The irony was that Paul would have loved that project for me.

"It'll be good for people to see you. A quick hello. Sing that New Year's song, 'Auld Lang Syne.' Should old acquaintance be forgot, yada, yada," Hazel said. "You represent the teenagers of this generation. People want to see that you're doing well. You need to get your face out in public again, and not just doing community service, which, don't get me wrong, is wonderful. But you need a gig."

I had been spending my free time serving at a homeless shelter in Santa Monica because according to Indigo, whom I kept in touch with as part of Promises' outpatient program, the best way to feel good about yourself was to help other people. And she was right. It felt great to do something completely unselfish for a change.

When I told Indigo about MTV, she was worried. She said my first New Year's Eve sober shouldn't be spent at a party surrounded by all the forces that led to my decline. "The Hollywood structure doesn't allow for you to protect yourself. You need to be kind to yourself, Echo. *You* need to protect *you*." She made a good point. I had been feeling clean and healthy. Going to meetings. Hiking Runyon Canyon. The structured days were good, but the nights were excruciating. I couldn't sleep. My insomnia raged.

"I can't just ignore the publicity element of my job," I said to Indigo. "I want to stay on track. But I kind of need to do this for my career. And wouldn't it make me stronger? To know I could do it? That I could be in that kind of situation and not use?"

"Recovery is about choices, Echo. And recovery has its own risks of relapse. I can't stress that enough to you."

It didn't matter what she said at that point. I had already made my decision. It felt natural to let Hazel take control of my life again. Made me feel like me.

Sometimes, when I was having trouble sleeping, I'd get in my car and drive around because the paps didn't chase me at three in the morning. I'd often stop in at a big twenty-four-hour magazine stand and sift through their magazines, new and old, feeling like a tourist in my own life. Faces of stars stared out at me from the covers, the blown-up lips and the airbrushed skin. There were even silent-film fan mags with Clara Bow and Lillian Gish, their angelic cheeks and soft curls. Those covers made me feel nostalgic for a Hollywood that didn't exist. Then right between the tabloids and the vintage magazines, there I was, on the cover of *Rolling Stone* from over a year ago, right before *Emma* came out.

It read, "ECHO BLUE, THE LUCKIEST GIRL ALIVE."

I wanted it to be true so badly. I wanted to be her, this mythical Echo. And for the first time, I wondered if maybe it was possible. The worst had happened, and I was clean now. All I needed to do was try again, get back out there. Reclaim my place.

Goldie

. . .

59.

For months, I coasted on the stardom of the Echo Blue series. I was scared that I had written the story of my career, of my life, and that there was nowhere to go from here. I stared through the glass wall of my office, watching other reporters type away on their keyboards hungrily while I didn't write at all. The words didn't have any purpose anymore.

Writer's block wasn't a feeling; it was a canyon I couldn't climb out of. *"Writers who can't craft sentences don't read enough,"* my father used to say. I thought of him in his casket and realized, horrified, that I should have buried him with a red pen. I hoped he knew that *I knew* he would have loved that.

Pench sat with me a few times to brainstorm, his cheerful self trying to encourage me, but it ended up irritating me. Still, I think I was falling in love with him. I remembered my mother telling me that love was about how much you could tolerate. I used to think she only felt that way because she was stuck with my father, but I was finding it to be true. The longer I knew Pench, the higher my tolerance became. I thought about him during weird times of the day. When I was showering. Right before I was falling asleep. When I woke up in the morning. I liked that he was on my mind. It was good to have other people to think about other than

Echo. It was getting close to the end of the summer now, and after almost eight whole months, most of the news around Echo's disappearance had died down. It was only a matter of time until another young, white, blonde woman would go missing and take Echo's place in the news cycle. She didn't even have to be famous. When a girl like that disappears, it becomes immediate entertainment.

Dana got on my case about not having a new subject. She said I had to come up with more ideas at the Monday meetings or else other writers in the office were going to poison my coffee. "You deserve what you have, Goldie," she said, "but unfortunately, in this business, you have to continue to prove yourself. One-hit wonders don't get to keep their offices."

I thought about moving to L.A. The perfect weather was sickening, but I loved the canyons and how you could stare up and see palm trees everywhere. They had enough mudslides and floods to fill my need to complain about weather. I could afford an apartment there now. I could afford my own plane ticket. I could get a job at a movie studio doing PR work. They loved hiring journalists.

There was my mother, who moved into an apartment near Day's. I couldn't leave her. And fine, I would miss Pench.

One hot summer afternoon, I started playing with the idea of investigating Natalie Wood's death. I had always been fascinated by it, that the death of someone so famous was still shrouded in mystery. Movies brainwash us into thinking famous people are immortal. Wood's roles were like a stack of classic books: *Splendor in the Grass. Rebel without a Cause. Gypsy. West Side Story.* She was controlled by the studio and her demonstrative stage mother, who put her in movies at five. I called up the lead investigator on the case and requested a copy of the police report. Like I did with Echo, I could also analyze how the story was reported and delve into society's own complicity in what happened to her. Truthfully, I thought Dana might like it—it ticked a few boxes for *ME*: celebrity, mysterious death, tumultuous marriage. And I was surprised to feel that buzz of excitement again when I pondered the story. Plus, Natalie's daughter, Natasha Gregson Wagner, had been in a few independent films recently, so I had a place to start. As I went to write an email to Natasha's agent, I saw a new email from an address I didn't recognize.

> Goldie,
>
> Belinda was the first one to tell me your name. You remember her, right? The actress you desperately hounded to get to me? She told me that you were delusional. That I should be careful.
>
> So when your articles came out, I was hesitant to read them. I've seen enough poorly reported stories about me over the years to last a lifetime. But I'll admit it—I was intrigued. And, Goldie, you surprised me.
>
> You see, I think we might be able to help each other.
>
> Meet me at the Flower Café in Viola, NY, tomorrow if you're interested. Come alone or else you'll never hear from me again.
>
> Sincerely,
> Me

I sat for a full ten minutes in stunned silence. I had gotten a lot of fake emails and phony calls already. One guy said he had Echo trapped in his basement, and I had to come meet him alone if I wanted to see her. Dana called the police after that one. There were so many sick people out there. (I know, I know. The irony is I had been one of them. Except I changed!) But something about this one felt different. My instincts tended to be right about Echo.

I pulled Pench over to read the email.

"How do we know it's the real Echo? Aren't she and Belinda not even friends?" Pench said.

He made a good point. But looking back, Belinda's spontaneous confession was fishy. It came too easily, and I was so eager for answers I had missed it. Did she do it to get me off her scent? Or was I fooling myself again now? "I guess we don't know. But I have to go up there and at least see if it's her."

"Maybe I should go with you. What if this person is one of the many internet trolls who actually wants to kill you?" He ran his fingers through his hair. I liked seeing him worry about me.

"My father gave me pepper spray last year," I said. "I'll bring it with me, and look—the meeting spot is public, at a café, and it'll be daytime."

I didn't want to hear anything else from Pench because I didn't want him to convince me not to go. I wrote back to this person who could very well be Echo, thrilled at imagining her on the receiving end.

Nothing in the world could keep me from meeting you.
I'll be there.

I drove up the New York Thruway as fast as my old Honda Civic would go, speeding at eighty-five, then ninety, passing trucks and Winnebagos with bikes stacked up on the back. My mother was worried when I told her I needed it. I reassured her it was for a new story. "If it pans out, you'll be happy about it. I promise," I said. She handed the keys over and told me she loved me.

I crossed the bridge, over the Hudson, and drove until I passed the sign for River Valley College, the most relevant landmark near the meeting spot. It started to pour, so I pulled into a lot and sat in my car, watching students and professors scamper through the thunder and rain, trying to make out faces through the swishing of my windshield wipers.

Once the downpour let up, I drove over to Viola, where little one-hundred-year-old houses with dried-up blooms from wildflowers drooped messily on the side of the road. I passed a rare bookstore and yarn store, and then finally a motel that read VACANCIES on a wooden plaque outside. I went inside and booked a room for the night. The left side of the bed sunk in, and it made me queasy to think of all the people who had slept there before me. I thought I was past the obsessive-fan thing, but here I was, up in some creepy motel by myself, chilled to the bone. I had to remind myself I wasn't there to stalk Echo. *She* invited *me*. Okay, I had to accept that this might not be Echo. But what can I say? It *felt* like her. And going up there was a matter of doing something for myself that finally didn't feel self-destructive. It was closure.

• • •

I hardly slept and yet when I woke up that morning, my eyes were so clear. I went to the Flower Café, where she told me to meet her. I peeked inside. No Echo. I looked around outside and didn't see her either. I sat at a white, rusted metal table on the sidewalk and ordered a coffee—not that I needed one. I had already had two at the motel, and my hands were shaking. I felt like I was going to pass out. There was a heavy end-of-summer heat, even in Upstate New York. I only swiped deodorant under my arms when I left the motel, too riled up to take a shower. What if I smelled like a musty room?

This was a mistake. She wasn't coming. It was obviously someone playing a terrible trick on me, and I know, I know—I deserved it. It was one of my "fans" getting a good laugh. *Ha ha*. What a laugh.

That's when I saw her. She was thinner than I imagined. The blonde hair was long gone. It was dark, almost black, and cut in a pixie style, short to her head.

If she hadn't approached me, I would've missed her.

But it was undoubtedly her. I had memorized the angles of her face. The way her eyelashes seemed like they had been wisped by an angel. Her thick eyebrows and her wide jaw. She was a movie star, no matter what she did to disguise herself. Movie stars had bone structure that the

289

camera picked up. They didn't have round and soft faces like we did. The camera loved them for it.

"Hi, Goldie," she said in her raspy voice.

She hunched over the small café table and rubbed her index finger across her lip.

I had spent months looking for her. I had spent most of my teenage life studying her. I had written a series of articles, vulnerable and sometimes shameful, about my search for her for a major magazine. I was interviewed about my obsession. I had invested so much of my life scrutinizing her that I wasn't sure what to do now. I was stunned, really.

Everything existed. Nothing existed.

A bird cawed. Time stopped. A guitar played from a house nearby.

Echo Blue was here. She was right here in front of me.

60.

I wiped the sweat from my face and neck with my T-shirt as you lowered yourself into the chair across from me. My heart beat feverishly. I didn't know how to begin. *I love your work? I had a* Slugger Eight *poster on my wall when I was a teen?* If you read my articles, which you said you had in the email, you knew this about me.

"Thank you for meeting me here," you said. "This must feel weird to you."

"It's very weird. But I'm appreciative. I'm . . . I'm . . ." I said, stuttering over my words. "I'm very glad to meet you." I tried not to cry, but my voice broke.

All those years of pretending to be your friend, all those imaginary conversations ringing in my head. I didn't want to scare you off.

"I know you've met so many fans. I know you don't owe me anything," I said. "But how did you do it? Was it planned? Did you know you would walk out of MTV all along?"

"Let's slow down," you said, so full of confidence. "I'll tell you everything. But you have to be patient."

"I'm not good at patience."

"I can see that by your articles," you said and smiled.

You knew me. Echo Blue knew me.

"You changed my life," I said. "I couldn't have gotten through my teenage years without you. Those roles were instrumental to me." You must have heard this a hundred times. All those meet and greets, all those young girls clamoring around you. "I'm sorry; I sound like I'm fourteen years old again. I'm babbling."

I was so annoyed at myself for not being able to say the right thing to you. I felt like an idiot. I didn't know why I was there. Could that have been your plan? To get me to come meet you somewhere just to humiliate me, get me worked up so you could taunt me the way I taunted you?

"Those were great characters. I was moved by them too. And I wanted to be them just as much as everyone else did," you said. "I wish I had had my characters' confidence and stability. News flash: I didn't."

You were looking at me so closely, genuinely. Here you were. A person. Not a billboard or a commercial or on a screen. You were a person, just like I was. As fragile and confused as I was. I don't know why it was so hard for me to remember that.

"I liked how you portrayed me," you said and seemed to mean it. "You didn't make me seem crazy, which most people like to do. You know how they describe child stars. Unhinged. Drug addicts. Out of control. It's a favorite tabloid narrative."

"Right! Exactly," I said. "But in this case, you weren't the one who was crazy. It was me."

"That's true," you said, and we both laughed.

We were connected, weren't we? It felt like I had known you for a lifetime. And in a way I had. Except it wasn't reciprocal.

You leaned in, your wide eyes darting around, and I thought I was going to die. I could barely sit still. The waitress came over and brought you an iced tea lemonade without you even ordering it. So they knew you here. You had a pixie cut, yes, but you still looked like you. How did you get them to keep quiet? Did you pay them off? I had so many questions. You gulped your drink down all at once. Was it possible that you were as nervous as I was?

"How did you hide out? How did no one find you?" I said. "And why here? Why this little town?"

"I promise I'll tell you everything." I couldn't understand why you were being so coy, why you weren't forthcoming with your story after you'd invited me here. "But I need to be able to trust you, Goldie."

My heart squeezed; my chest tightened. I know you'll think I sound like a corny love song, but those were the words I longed to hear! Well, you didn't say, *I trust you.* You said, *I need to be able to trust you.* Semantics. I had imagined you saying those words for years, and now you were.

"You can trust me," I said.

• • •

You asked me to follow you to your house for more privacy. It was about a half hour walk, maybe a little more if we were going slow. *I don't care how long it takes,* I wanted to say, but controlled myself. I tried not to be eager and weird, but as we walked together toward the woods, it felt like the reenactment of all of my fantasies. You and I holding hands, telling each other all of our secrets.

"I wish I had met you under different circumstances. I think we'd be friends," I said and shuddered. I couldn't believe I let that out. "I'm sorry. I know that's too much."

"You don't even know me. Don't you understand that by now?" you said and held up a branch for me, letting me pass under it. "I doubt you'd actually want to be friends with someone like me. I've been through a lot." It was true. You weren't necessarily a good friend. I knew that from talking to Belinda.

You veered off on a graveled path. You said you loved the sound of the rushing brook and the rustling trees. I could see why you found solace here. You picked a fern and stroked it against your skin. You shut your eyes and threw your head back. You pointed to a cabin off the path. "That's my little place. Why don't you come inside?"

"My car's all the way back by the café."

"Leave it," you said. "We'll get it later."

As much as I still wished you just wanted to be my roommate, I was eager to find out the real reason I was here. But the fantasy still lingered, that you might want to get to know me too. It was magic. The fern against your face. The light through the leaves.

There I was. With you, Echo Blue. You were the biggest story of the year. The biggest story of my career, of my life, and you invited me into your house. Just like that, like we were old friends. (I know, I know.)

You felt safe, you must have, or else I would have been locked up in the back of a police car. What a dazzling revelation. All that mattered was that I was here in your company, and you wanted me here. Never in my life had I felt so important.

61.

Your cabin was even sweeter on the inside, and though it was muggy outside, it was surprisingly cool. There were wood-paneled walls and lacy curtains. There was a painting above the sofa that looked expensive, and it probably was. There was a photo of you and Belinda on the mantel of the massive flagstone fireplace. I was dying to ask you about her, about *Emma*. How you became friends again. Why you did it. I wanted to pull out my phone and take a picture of it, just to show Sam. Phones those days took fuzzy pictures, but it would have been a token. No. That wasn't good. I had to force myself out of that way of thinking. I wasn't a tourist in your life.

"I know you asked me to hold off on questions, but wasn't there a missing person report? Weren't the NYPD looking for you?"

"Yeah, there was a police search. I was able to tip them off," you said. "It's why it didn't turn into something bigger. They let me be."

I followed you into the kitchen, and you asked me if I was hungry for lunch. Lunch with you? Of course. You brought out a vegetable lasagna with vegan cheese. We sat down at your little table together, each with a slice on a plate.

"A caterer friend of mine who bought a big town house in Hudson opened a kitchen there. It's where all of the artists in Brooklyn are moving. Maybe you should do a story on that. How Hudson, the old whaling town, is being bought up by artists who've been kicked out of—"

"So why am I here?" I said. You stared back at me. I couldn't read your expression. My chest thrummed.

"Do you know what I like about this cabin, Goldie? It's so isolated. No one's around. A mile and a half from town. No one can hear what's happening." Your eyes glistened with anger, with revenge. You were an Oscar winner. How was I supposed to know if you were serious or if you were acting?

I pushed away from the table slightly.

"What's going on? You're not going to, like, do something to me?"

"You ate your lasagna," you said, smirking. "Was it tasty?"

I looked down at my half-empty plate. I glanced across at yours—you hadn't touched it. It became very quiet, like neither of us were breathing. Or maybe it was me holding my breath out of fear. Did you poison me? It wouldn't have been hard. Frat boys did it all the time. Girls across the country were getting roofied left and right. I started feeling dizzy. That's why you told me to meet you. Were you going to drug me and tie me up? Everything was fuzzy and off-balance. I told people where I was going. Hadn't I? Wait, had I?

"I don't understand . . ."

"What do you think is happening, Goldie?" You stared at me pointedly.

"Call nine-one-one," I screamed.

Suddenly, you snorted, the tension breaking in an instant. "I'm sorry; I couldn't help myself. You really need to calm down. What do you think I am? A total psycho?"

You handed me a napkin. I coughed in it, gagging.

"I feel like my throat is closing up," I said, but the feeling was already dissipating. It was just a panic attack.

"I promise you're fine," you said. "I had to torture you a little bit. I liked your articles, but you harassed the shit out of Belinda. You were going to feed me to the wolves if you had found me. You deserved it."

Still reeling, I lay down on the couch and you brought me a ginger tea. You were right. I did deserve that, and how could I blame you? In fact, it was this tough version of you that had always inspired me. That girl from *Slugger Eight* who told off her coach, the same fire in your eyes. That rage in your voice.

"Did you roofie this tea?" I asked, half joking. You laughed, and I knew I was safe.

"Okay, enough playing around. I have a proposition," you said. You were wearing a Joan Jett T-shirt with holes in the bottom and cut-off jean shorts. Your toenails were painted bright red. You looked so much younger than your age.

You walked over the creaky floor in your bare feet and sat next to me. You began talking. You began telling me your story.

Echo

December 31, 1999

. . .

62.

Backstage at MTV on Millennium Eve was a clusterfuck. I sat by myself in a corner, smoking cigarette after cigarette. It was unlike Hazel not to accompany me to a high-profile event like this, but it was also the millennium, and she had been invited to what she called "the biggest party of the century" in a producer's penthouse in the Sherry-Netherland. "You've been in New York for weeks, Echo," she said. "You've got to have a couple of people who could meet you." She sounded so dismissive, so sure I would be fine, so I lied and told her yes, sure, I had people. I would be fine. If Hazel was going to a party instead of sticking by my side, it meant that there were multiple stars there whom she wanted on her roster. That party was an insurance policy for Hazel. She had to make sure she had other irons in the fire in case my star faded out.

The bands had all gotten there before me, and the MTV VJs were already on air. I was the only person in the makeup room, and I felt lonely. My regular makeup artist felt awful about not being able to meet me, but she, like Hazel, was at someone else's party. I had been out of the loop since rehab, and she had been booked for months. So she put in a call to an old-school New York makeup artist, Michelle Rose, who was sweet. She reminded me of Sandy with her wild, frizzy brown hair. That very hippie look with a fringed scarf wrapped around her neck, rings on all of her fingers, and a deep Long Island accent. I bet she loved those hair-metal bands back in the '80s, like Poison and Ratt.

"Whaddya wanna listen to, honey? Now that all the rockers are out of here, we can blast some Stevie Nicks and be a little more laid-back. We can be mellow." Michelle put on "Gypsy," and we both sang along while she did a smoky eye on me.

"They could hold up a cardboard cutout of me, and no one would even know the difference," I said.

She lifted my chin up and dabbed my eyes with a cotton swab.

"Where's your people?" she said. "Everyone who comes here has an entourage. The girls, the guys. The actors, the bands. The divas. You can't possibly be here by yourself on New Year's Eve."

"My agent's on her way. She's stuck in traffic," I lied and looked away. I couldn't tell her the truth. That I had no friends. No family around. That my agent was at some penthouse schmoozing my potential replacements.

"How old are you, honey?"

"Nineteen."

She tsked like an old grandmother. Like she had seen things in her life but nothing worse than a nineteen-year-old girl with no friends and working on December 31, 1999.

How embarrassing. What kind of person was I that no one, not one person, wanted to hold my hand at this MTV New Year's party?

Michelle handed me off to Donna the hairdresser, who fluffed and sprayed my hair, lifted my roots up with gel. "I love it. Do you love it? I love it," she kept saying. She seemed hyper. I think she had been doing coke. Donna left the room, and I immediately brushed all the gel and hairspray out. The product gave my stringy hair a straw texture that I liked.

"Want champagne, honey?" Michelle said, reentering the room and holding out a glass.

I shook my head. Should I say I was sober? Indigo and I discussed this.

I didn't have to explain to anyone. I could just say, *No, thank you.* So that's what I did. I was dedicated to staying sober, but I missed the pills. I could have used a few Klonopin or Xanax that night to take the edge off. Limp Bizkit was out there on the stage doing Prince's "1999," and I had never heard anything in my life so muddled and ugly. I was edgy. I could feel myself sliding into a bad place. Was this what I wanted? This was Hazel getting me into the biggest gig. This was Hazel not thinking about what Echo *the person* needed. And I didn't need to be around hundreds of drunk people and ego-ridden rock stars, D-list celebrities and glamour queens.

I jostled my way through the greenroom tagalongs who were already stumbling over each other. I needed a quiet place to do a mantra that Indigo taught me. My phone buzzed in my pocket and I was sure it was Hazel wondering if I was prepared, if my makeup wasn't overdone. But when I looked at my phone, I froze.

It was Belinda's number. Was this a joke? "Hello?" I said, my chest heaving as I dipped into the coatroom. "Belinda? Is that really you?"

"It's me. I was feeling charitable," she said.

I sunk into a cluster of peacoats hearing her voice. I couldn't tell her how bad things were. That I was in a coat closet by myself.

"Oh, am I a charity case to you now?" I said. It came out more defensive than I wanted, but I was frightened of what she might say. Was she drinking? Would she lay into me? I wouldn't be able to recover from it— I really wouldn't. "Seriously, if I'm a charity case to you, that's fine," I said. "I'm just so glad to hear your voice."

"I was kidding. Of course I don't see you that way. I've actually just missed you. And it's New Year's Eve. We're not supposed to let old acquaintance be forgot or whatever, right?" She sounded sincere. "I thought maybe it was time I returned your calls."

I covered my mouth with my hand. I almost couldn't say anything at all; my mouth felt like it was full of cotton. It was as if she knew that's what I needed in that moment, that I felt so alone. I wanted her to know how sorry I was for the way I acted.

"I want to be someone else. Someone who doesn't try to destroy her best friend. Someone who doesn't burn all of the bridges in her life. I want to be a healthy person. I want to be a good person. I want to be a loyal person."

"You have the rest of your life to be a good person, Echo."

"I wasn't well when I hurt you. You know that, don't you?"

"Yes. I know," she said. "I meant it when I told you I forgave you right after it happened. I have. But moving on is something else. I don't know if I can ever trust you again."

I understood. I wouldn't trust me either. I couldn't promise her anything, though. In recovery, they tell you you're not supposed to. I could still end up being a narcissistic asshole once the dust settled, but I hoped that wouldn't be the case.

"Do you want to hear the craziest thing?" I looked around me to make sure no one was nearby. "I'm hiding in a coat closet at MTV, and I don't think anyone knows where I am."

She let out a grunt of a laugh. "Where are you supposed to be?"

"Talking to Carson Daly. Counting down the ball drop. You know, happy millennium!" I said. "Where are you?"

"I'm at a party," she said. I heard people singing along to a Tom Petty song in the background. It sounded so normal. "With non-industry people. At a friend's little house upstate. There's a fire. Someone made brownies."

"Wow, look at you. So conventional. I could not be more jealous. I am dying to get out of here. Out of everywhere."

"It's very average. Very nice," she said. "Actually, you *could* come here, you know. Not to the party, of course—a little too soon to have you stealing my thunder again"—she snickered—"but upstate. Escape for a little."

"How could I get there?"

"You're the one who said no one knows where you are right now. Sneak out. Take a cab up here; it's not that far. I assume you still carry a wad of cash on you? It might be hard on New Year's but not at the right price. I even have a place for you to stay."

She reminded me of the little cabin she inherited from her grandparents. "No one will find you there. I used to hate going as a kid because we'd see two other people a week. But the cabin's in the woods, just a thirty-minute walk into a town. You can live there. Hide away there until we have a better plan." The town was about two blocks long, she explained, where two artists from the city renovated this old hotel. I could get a cappuccino in the hotel lobby. There was a bookstore. A yarn shop.

I liked the idea of living in a little quirky town. It felt like a TV show or something. Maybe people would respect my need for solace. Didn't people who escaped to small towns want solace too? I wouldn't stay there forever, of course, but this time would give me a chance to figure out what I wanted for myself, without the background noise. The friend's house she was staying at was an hour away from the cabin, and she had an early-morning flight to catch. She could meet me for a couple of hours to get me settled in, but then she'd have to take off. Belinda said she'd be back to visit as soon as she had a chance. What if it was that simple to start a new life? It seemed so easy that I felt giddy from it.

"I really hurt you, Belinda. You might forgive me, but I'll never forgive myself for it," I said, my fingers pressing hard on the phone. Part of me felt like I didn't deserve her kindness in that moment. I didn't deserve her. "I have a lot of shit to figure out about who I want to be and what I want to do."

"All right, we'll have time for all of this later when I can get over there to see you," she said. We finalized the details and hung up. I felt alive— hopeful, for the first time in so long. I know I was being incredibly optimistic; my life wasn't going to suddenly be rainbows and lollipops because I stopped acting. But after eight years of being famous, I needed to see what it was like without the world revolving around me for a little while, without paparazzi rifling through my garbage cans, without the spotlight shining directly on me.

A synonym for the Latin word *claritudo* is *fame*.

Claritudo means brightness and clarity.

I grabbed someone's long black coat off a hanger, tucked my hair under a winter hat, wrapped a black scarf around my face, and crept out into the hallway. Everyone was still in the main studio watching Limp Bizkit butcher another song. I pressed down on the elevator and the doors opened almost immediately.

No one was in the elevator. No one was in the hallway. I was completely by myself. I pressed *L* for the lobby and the doors shut.

I got out to the street in the freezing cold, right next to the bright, huge stage set up under the ball. I asked a group of police officers where the exit was. They didn't recognize me.

"Right that way, miss. But if you leave, you leave for good," the cop said. "No coming back in."

"Yes," I said. "I want to go and not come back."

I knew I was telling the truth. I would not come back.

I strode through the barricades, the throngs of people crammed into Times Square. I stood there silent on the sidewalk, staring. All of that New Year's energy, the freezing people, the squeals, the glitter-covered top hats, the ball hovering over the street, the lights and the cameras—all of it was behind me.

My whole life was in front of me. Only an hour and a half away. If I were in L.A., and if I were in a movie, something huge would happen signaling this seismic shift in my life. Like the way when Harry realized he loved Sally, he had to run all the way downtown to tell her, "*Because when you realize you want to spend the rest of your life with somebody, you want the rest of your life to start as soon as possible.*" Or how when Thelma turned to Louise on the edge of the Grand Canyon and said, "*Let's not get caught. Let's keep going.*"

I'm here to inform you that when you walk away from your life *in real life* and it's New Year's Eve in New York City—the millennium!—it's nothing like a movie.

I strolled down Thirty-Eighth into the darkness of Manhattan, the wind whipping through my hair. Revelers ran, blowing horns in the middle of the road, and threw confetti from their fire escapes, but no one recognized me with the scarf around my face in the darkness. "Happy New Year!" I screamed behind the scarf, and then I felt it—a jag of excitement, a realization that no one was following me, not a single soul knew where I was.

I had five hundred in my pocket. No cabdriver would turn that down. Soon I found someone, and there we were, driving north on the West Side Highway. I called my mom because I didn't want her thinking I was dead. She understood. Of course she understood. The queen of the recluse actors. "You could stay with me, baby," she said, but I wanted to be somewhere new. Somewhere fresh. I couldn't go back to L.A., not the way I had been living.

On my way up to the cabin, I promised myself I'd never act again. Why not start the new year—a new millennium—with a bold proposition? This is what led me to this point. For the first time, I was deciding what I wanted. Not what was good for my dad, my mother, for Hazel, for anyone else. This was for me. Was it unprofessional to leave like that? Yes, it was, but that's what excited me about it. Maybe if I had more time, I would have planned it out differently, but I believe some of the best ideas come at the spur of the moment, an unrehearsed explosion.

When the driver pulled up at the cabin, snow crunching under the tires, Belinda was there waiting, standing in the front porch light, a big smile on her face, her breath a constant in the cold air.

· · ·

63.

I spent those first two weeks outside, walking the crunchy trails, looking up at the bare trees. I had always hated being by myself, but this was different. In the past, I felt abandoned, paranoid from my pills and the constant specter of the paparazzi right outside. But here, the solitude felt safe and peaceful, even therapeutic. There was an old, rusty Cherokee up at the cabin, so it wasn't a problem getting around. Plus, Belinda had a storage box of sweatpants, sweatshirts, and boots. I got a few basics at the general store in town—toothpaste, toothbrush, and a pack of big white underwear that I successfully shrunk in the dryer.

Belinda checked in every day at first; we had so much to catch up on. Sometimes at night during those early few months, I'd curl up in a creaky Adirondack chair on the deck outside, wrapped in my coat, the wind blowing against my cheeks. There were two blizzards that year, and I learned that I loved the snow. Movie sets could never make snow like this. It swirled outside the cabin windows. Afterward, icicles formed on the gables. Nothing was ever more beautiful.

When I finally felt comfortable enough to venture out, I created a routine. Coffee at the diner where I made a new friend, Kandy, who did recognize me but promised to keep it a secret. Kandy gave me one of those red-and-black-plaid hunter hats with the ear flaps, and I barely took it off until I had time to get my hair dyed and cut by a friend of hers at the local hair salon. Knitting sessions were at Bonnie's yarn store, filled with members too old to care about a washed-up nineteen-year-old star. And an evening sip-and-read book club at the little rare bookstore (I had tea), where, ironically, we read *Emma*. I promised them I'd give a dramatic performance of the script if they kept my presence quiet. This town was so small and intimate. People seemed to genuinely care about each other. I never wanted to go back to L.A.

·   ·   ·

It was during this time that you showed up at Belinda's acting class. She told me about how you confronted her at the bar, that you were relentless. She said you were obsessed with me in a way she hadn't seen before, and that was saying something. "She's going to figure out where you are, Echo," Belinda said. She told me she decided to admit it all to you—kudos on figuring out the *Emma* story, by the way. She thought our friendship breakup might be enough to sate you. And also that it would get you off her. Why would Echo Blue's best friend tell her dirtiest secret if she was in touch with her? And it worked.

Then *Manhattan Eye* started printing those articles about your search for me. (I'm sorry your father died, by the way. Sincerely.) Reading what you wrote, something opened in me. I don't know how you did it, but you captured the forces around me that pushed me to disappear. Someone finally recognized what I had gone through, what so many women in Hollywood have gone through. I'm not saying I wanted a pity party. I sound like it, I know—but it was the first time I read something about myself that was real.

You know what else? The way you searched for me? It tickled me. Surprisingly, I related to you. Our difficult dads, the sacrifices we made for our careers, how we both didn't seem to know exactly who we were.

Even after all the work Belinda had done to shun you, I wondered if maybe there was something you could do for me. As I said, I knew I couldn't stay here forever, and each cherry blossom that bloomed across this small town terrified me. Because the spring brought tourists. It brought new faces, people who would inevitably recognize me. They'd make their way here, and the jig would be up. I felt like my time was slowly coming to an end. You had devoted so much time to hunting me. But could you be the one to set me free?

Goldie

. . .

64.

You and I made a pact. I'd tell your story the right way. Why you left, how you felt about acting, your famous family, the truth behind it all. You said I could live in Belinda's family cabin and write about you as long as I didn't tell anyone where I was.

It was the best deal I ever made.

I stayed in the spare bedroom for three weeks, through mid-September, and you did most of the talking. And I wrote. I went to the library and printed out my work. You jotted down notes on my drafts. Sometimes I took walks in the woods by myself. I could see why you were here. The golden sunsets over the ridge of the forest. Kandy at the diner made good eggs. Your rose hips started to turn deep red.

My mom was worried when I told her I was taking a "self-retreat." Pench thought I was going into another dark place. Sam was convinced I had a secret lover. Dana was officially getting fed up—she wanted to know where I'd been. I told her I was working on a final surprise installment to the *Where Are You, Echo Blue?* series, but I was afraid to share more yet.

"You fucking found her, didn't you?" she said.

But I didn't confirm. I knew Dana meant well, but she'd tell me to put the story first. She was tenacious. She wouldn't understand that you were more than a story to me now. That your friendship and trust superseded it all. I owed that to you.

"I know this isn't the first time I've said this, but I need you to believe in me one more time," I said to Dana.

"Okay, Goldie. I'll be waiting."

*   *   *

One night, we were sitting at your kitchen table, drinking hot chocolate. I was lost in thought. In a year from now, in ten years, would we still share this bond? Or was this only a business arrangement to you? I didn't want to know. For now, I just looked across at you sipping hot cocoa and silently wished that you'd be in my life forever, that one day we would look back at this and laugh.

"So, Goldie, you got what you wanted," you said.

"What's that?"

"You got me. You got my story."

"I did," I said, and I sighed, but still, I wasn't totally satisfied. "There's more to this that I want to explore." I thought about what my father had said when I first told him I was going to try to find you. I remember his disgust. *"Where's the moral compass?"* he had said. That was the key. I wanted my next assignment to have a moral compass.

"It's weird," you said. "It's like we both needed an outlet."

Here I was, living with you. I felt so close to you. We'd built something under the most unexpected of circumstances. Didn't we? I know my thinking can be skewed, but I felt pretty sure of this.

All anyone needs to know is that it was a happy ending. Two women with very separate agendas ended up helping each other.

Could you root for us both?

stopped loving him, and he was a victim of this toxic system too. I had so much more growing to do, and I'd certainly keep my expectations low. I believed he missed me. I believed he carried regret. Maybe one day.

When people asked me later in my life about my career as a child star, I told them my best friend, Belinda Summers, forgave me. I told them about sobriety.

I told them that I met a journalist. Someone who gave me a gift.

In return, I gave that journalist a gift. I gave her myself.

Because I was the story all along.

Echo

. . .

65.

We both got what we wanted. Goldie got her feature, and I got freedom. Sure, people would always recognize me, always ask for my autograph. But I'd finally reclaimed my story. Doing that on my own terms saved me. And it only could have been Goldie. It had to be a fan. She had the platform. In the most complicated, roundabout way, she gained my trust.

I ended up enrolling in a few classes at River Valley—I wasn't ready to leave the area after all. Belinda came up to join me; she too had been dreaming of college. I didn't know what was next, but I knew I was no longer an actor, that I never would be again. I ended my contract with Hazel. After Goldie's exposé came out, the paps quickly grew bored of Viola, of my new drama-free life. I had eliminated all of the mystery when I told my story. They moved on to other pretty girls. I didn't have to be a recluse like my mother was. I didn't have to hide anymore. Now I got to live.

My mother came to visit me regularly; she too felt comfortable here. My dad didn't get back in touch. But I was starting to wonder if I could forgive him. We'd had moments. I remembered watching him bounce around his sets, everyone craving his attention. How he'd drape his arm around me, introducing me to the crew. *This is my baby girl.* I never

Goldie

· · ·

Epilogue

If I hadn't had proof that it had happened, I might not have believed it myself. But I had a few Polaroids that Belinda, when she came to visit once while I was there, took of Echo—wearing a hat so as to not reveal her new haircut—and me. She and I, bound together, standing by the kitchen window and the sun gleaming across my face.

"So, Goldie," Dana said. "Are you going to tell me? Where is she?"

I told her what I could but didn't reveal too much. This was one of the promises that I had made. I couldn't write about Viola, New York. Sure, they'd find her eventually. But we weren't going to make it easy.

I pitched my idea to Dana about publishing it as a blog post. We didn't need the magazine. I wanted to write stories that came out immediately.

"What do you mean a blog post?"

"This is too important to go out with yesterday's trash. *ME* needs to create something that exists outside of the print magazine, that can be a fresh start. And I want to write it. It should start with the last act to the Echo Blue story, but it should continue beyond that. We can cover celebrities and discuss them intelligently, but we'll hold ourselves accountable too. I want to create a place where people can write essays that aren't salacious but that get at the truth of this industry."

"So you want to create a gossip website? A cerebral Page Six?" she said, a confused look on her face.

"I want it to be the antithesis of Page Six," I said. I couldn't go back to stalking people, and I was tired of guessing about them too. I didn't want to prop anyone up, and I didn't want to bring anyone down. Was that even possible?

• • •

Within a month of its launch, *GOLDIE* the blog had almost nine million page views. One critic called me a "modern-day Hedda Hopper." But I was nothing like Hopper. I didn't want to ruin anyone's career. I wanted to engage readers in a public discussion. I wanted to understand who *we* were through celebrity.

I had to take more meetings with the higher-ups. *"How can we bounce off the page views? How can we use* GOLDIE *as a springboard?"* They needed the blog to inject *ME* with cash. Magazine editors were desperate. Bloggers were their saviors. Investors loved bloggers.

"How about we make it an übercelebrity blog that works in real time?" a marketing person offered. I didn't know his name. Blue Shirt. I'm sorry; it's an identifier.

He had a whole plan. "We can get readers to write in about exact locations of celebrity sightings," he said. "Then we'll send out an alert to subscribers, or even put pins on an interactive map, and our readers can chase down the celebrity of their dreams. These celebrities give up all privacy and a real life when they become famous, don't they? That's not our choice; it's theirs. That's the way it is and the way it's always been." He beamed over his new idea. Clearly he had not read my stories deeply, or he would know this was the opposite of what I wanted to do.

I thought about Echo and her new anonymous life. With Blue Shirt's concept, one person could've recognized her while she was food shopping, and her whole disappearing act would've been up in one minute.

I imagined our readers chasing Echo down the street with pitchforks and torches. Or worse, cameras and autograph books.

Before I found Echo, I would have signed up for that website in seconds. I wouldn't have even thought about it twice. That was not what I wanted now. I wouldn't allow them to turn my celebrity culture idea into their Frankenstein.

My editors and the marketing team stared at me, their faces aghast and thrilled all at once.

"Goldie, what do you think?" Dana said. I could see she was uncomfortable. Dana was a shark, but she wasn't evil.

"That's the worst idea I've ever heard," I said. "I think it would make us come across as unhinged. There would be lawsuits. You would ruin people's lives."

Blue Shirt looked at me with a defeated glare, and the celebrity-stalking platform was never brought up again.

• • •

That night, I stayed at Pench's apartment, a pre-war building on Ninety-Sixth Street with lofty windows that overlooked the Hudson. While he snored lightly next to me, I was restless thinking about all that had transpired. I would have to tell other stories now. With Echo, I made my obsession into a career. I dragged everyone around me into that obsession, but it was time to surround myself with new subjects. My father was right: there were other meaningful pursuits that I could sink myself into.

I missed my father. It wasn't fair that I wouldn't get the chance to have a relationship with him as an adult. I had finally accepted that he would be proud of me at this point. He might have been my biggest cheerleader. I'd never know. I'd set a goal and accomplished it, and now I was starting my own arm of *ME*. I regretted the time we had lost. But I wouldn't make the same mistake with my mother. I think he would have liked Pench too. Now that I thought of it, he probably would've liked him a little too much.

I got out of Pench's bed and traipsed through his apartment, admiring the bare white walls. White walls gave you the chance to think. I needed that at my place, to give myself fresh space—I still hadn't taken down my Echo collage; it had felt like it was too soon to do that, like I was putting her away. But it was time now. I crawled onto Pench's couch and glanced at the yellow moon outside, floating above the city. I curled myself into a fuzzy blanket, and though I hadn't thought about Echo that way anymore, with that compulsive fervor, I shivered, wondering if we were staring at the same moon. I wondered if I would ever stop thinking about her. I knew the answer.

GOLDIE

GOLDIE is a weblog written by Goldie Klein and published by
Manhattan Eye

Echo Blue's lips are a dusty rose, as if she smooths chunks of Vaseline onto them each night, then powders them in the morning.

No, not really. Echo Blue's lips are chapped and cracked. She picks at the left corner of her bottom lip, blaming their state on the dry heat.

That's not true either. There will be no mention of Echo's lips in this post, so if that's what you're looking for, you're in the wrong place.

You all know that I publicly searched for Echo Blue. Now I'm here to tell you that four weeks ago, she invited me to her hiding place to tell her story. I lived with her in the spot where she had been since the day she disappeared during the MTV Millennium Eve celebration, sending gossip magazines into a frenzy.

Echo and I spoke about her life. We spoke about her fans. She asked me to write about her.

Echo Blue is a person. She wants what you want. To live on her own terms.

So this time, we don't get to choose the stories we tell about her. She'll choose.

What's funny is that I didn't find her. Yet Echo found me.

"There's a saying I keep thinking about," Echo tells me. "'You can't run away from yourself.' But in my case"—she rubs her hand over her nondescript hair, picking at her BLT at a café—"I ran toward myself. And I found someone new."

Will Echo return to acting? She says no. What would be the glory in returning to an industry she hated, an industry that once dominated her? It's possible one day you might notice her in a small shop behind the counter, and you'll tell her that she looks familiar and ask where you know her from. Then you'll remember. It'll come swimming back to you, that giddy feeling when you first saw her movies. And that part of you will light up, and though you'll want to ask her about herself, and you'll want to take a photo, you'll hold back. You'll nod, with a slight smile, an acknowledgment of admiration. And once you leave the shop, you'll think, *She's not that same girl anymore*. And you'll be correct—she's not. Because Echo Blue is writing her own script.

Posted by Goldie on September 26, 2000 @ 10:04 a.m.

Acknowledgments

To Emily Sylvan Kim. You are my cheerleader. Your enthusiasm gets me through every book, you make every book better, and you've helped make my dreams come true. Sean Berard and Shivani Doraiswami at Grandview, thank you for looking out for me.

To Lexy Cassola, my heartfelt, tireless editor. This was an incredible experience for me because of your encouragement, your passion, and your faith in what you knew this book was able to become. To the entire publishing team at Dutton: Diamond Bridges, LeeAnn Pemberton, Lauren Morrow, Dora Mak, Alison Cnockaert, and Melissa Solis. To superstar Dominique Jones for working diligently to get this cover right. Thank you to the entire sales and marketing team for working so hard to get this book in the hands of readers.

I dove into research, and I am grateful to these books and their authors: *Can I Go Now?: The Life of Sue Mengers, Hollywood's First Superagent* by Brian Kellow; *The Cultural Significance of the Child Star* by Jane O'Connor; *Little Girl Lost* by Drew Barrymore; *A Paper Life* by Tatum O'Neal; *I'm Glad My Mom Died* by Jennette McCurdy; *Where Am I Now?* by Mara Wilson. The HBO documentary *Showbiz Kids* directed by Alex

Winter was an incredible resource. Also, thank you, Lygia Day Peñaflor, for answering my endless questions about on-set teachers.

To Tatum O'Neal for being a force of nature and an inspiration to me since I was a child. We didn't have many bad-ass girls in the 1970s when I was growing up, but your iconic roles (Addie Loggins in *Paper Moon*; Amanda Whurlitzer in *The Bad News Bears*; and Ferris in *Little Darlings*) gave girls everywhere permission to be strong yet vulnerable. To Lindsay Lohan, Miley Cyrus, Winona Ryder, Drew Barrymore, Britney Spears, and all of the other great child actors who felt that enormous pressure of growing up under the microscope of the public eye.

To my book group. Linda, Jodi, Marci, Becky, and Willie: Our monthly literary discussion fuels my brain. To my friends and family who read drafts, who brainstormed with me, who listened to me cry and rant, and who supported me throughout, especially Jodi Brooks, Sara Kaye, Miriam Rosenberg, Beth Block, Liz Adams, Melissa Adler, and Debbie Pavan.

To all the Krischers and the Adlers: I'm so lucky to have an expansive, funny, crazy, artistic family. Amy Krischer and Norman Krischer: Thank you for a lifetime of unconditional love and support. Jake and Elke: Thank you for putting up with me spreading my chapters across the tables and floors of our home. You are everything to me. Andy, I love you. After all these years, you're still my best reader and my best friend. I'm so lucky.

About the Author

Hayley Krischer is the author of two young adult novels, *Something Happened to Ali Greenleaf* and *The Falling Girls*. She is also an award-winning journalist who has written for *The New York Times*, *The New York Times Magazine*, *The Atlantic*, *Marie Claire*, *ELLE*, and more.